𝒟

Wings of Sorrow

For more information about Jessica Blair visit
www.jessicablair.co.uk

Wings of Sorrow

Jessica Blair

PIATKUS

PIATKUS

First published in Great Britain in 2008 by Piatkus Books

A CIP catalogue record for this book
is available from the British Library

ISBN 978-0-7499-0857-7

Typeset in Times by Action Publishing Technology Ltd, Gloucester
Printed and bound by Mackays Ltd, Chatham, Kent

Piatkus Books
An imprint of
Little, Brown Book Group
100 Victoria Embankment
London EC4Y 0DY

An Hachette Livre UK Company

www.piatkus.co.uk

Acknowledgements

This book would never have been finished but for the help of my twin daughters, Geraldine and Judith. Judith vetted the manuscript as it was written and Geraldine read the first complete draft in its entirety. Their advice and suggestions were invaluable. Throughout I have had the support and encouragement of my eldest daughter, Anne, and my son, Duncan. Though this is a work of fiction, I needed help with the factual backgrounds from a number of people. I am grateful to Mrs Irene Johnson and Miss D. Britten for allowing me to see their notes about their time in the Women's Land Army. I received help from Mr Arthur Credland, Hull Maritime Museum; Carol Tanner, Hull City Archives; Michele Wilkinson, Local Studies Library, Hull; Kerry Meal, Lowestoft Record Office; Toni Booth of the National Museum of Photography, Bradford; Mr C. T. Adamson (Scarborough Cricket Club); Pauline Judge and Jim Howson. To all of them, my thanks. The books and internet sites consulted are too many to list but I must mention three I found invaluable: *The Driftermen* by David Butcher (Tops'l Books, Reading, 1979); *Lilliput Fleet* by A. Cecil Hampshire (William Kimber, 1957);

The Women's Land Army by V. Sackville-West (Michael
Joseph, 1944).
I also thank Gillian Green, editor at Piatkus,
and
Lynn Curtis who has so expertly edited all my Jessica
Blair books.

THANK YOU
for making my life so interesting.

For

JILL

with my thanks for being there when my life needed a
new perspective.

Bill

Chapter One

Nineteen-year-old Jane Harvey's mind was on the sea as she left the house of her uncle and aunt in Scholes Park Road, Scarborough, Yorkshire's premier coastal resort. Since coming to live with them from Middlesbrough's growing industrial complex along the banks of the River Tees in February 1938, she had found her troubles soothed by the sight of it. No matter what its mood – tranquil, stormy, heaving with the rising tide or tranquil after the ebb – its vastness presented a distant horizon beyond which dreams promised to come true.

'Enjoy your walk, love,' her aunt called when she reached the gate.

Jane turned and smiled. 'Thanks, Aunty Mavis.'

'Will you end up at the cricket?'

'Yes. It could be an interesting last day. Expect me when you see me.'

'You've got your ticket?'

'Yes. 'Bye.' Determined to enjoy this bright, warm day, Jane closed the gate and waved.

Mavis came to the gate and watched her niece until she turned the corner into a side road from which she could make her way to the promenade on Scarborough's North Bay. Mavis felt great satisfaction that she and her husband David had been united in their desire to give Jane a new home after the cruel and unbending attitude of her father.

Jane filled the void in their lives which had appeared when it became evident Mavis could not have children of her own. They doted on Jane and her brother Tim, four years younger, joyfully welcoming the visits that were only allowed under sufferance by their strict father, after continuous pleading by their downtrodden mother.

Mavis thought there was brisker movement in the girl's steps today and hoped it was a sign of her coming to terms with her new life. She also took heart from seeing that her niece had taken more trouble to look smart. Jane used to take pride in her appearance, but after the trouble with her father had shown little interest in herself. However, with Mavis's encouragement, signs of the Jane she had formerly known were re-emerging. Today she was dressed in a white blouse and navy blazer with a cream linen skirt reaching just below her knees. She had let her coppery brown hair grow and wore it flicked under on her shoulders, a style Mavis knew she had picked up from the American film stars she studied on the screen and in the film magazines she read avidly.

When her niece had disappeared from sight, Mavis turned back to the house with a sigh, wondering where it all would end. Would Jane and her father ever be reconciled?

Jane breathed in deeply when she reached the promenade and felt invigorated by the sea air. She sensed today was going to be good, and was determined not to let it be spoiled by memories of the past or thoughts of whether she should return to Middlesbrough. Too much had happened for that ever to be possible. Whether her uncle and aunt sent 'progress reports' to her mother and father she did not know. She doubted it, for she was aware that the brothers' relationship, dominated by her own father, had finally soured twelve years ago when they'd left their North Riding country village to find more lucrative work elsewhere. Her uncle had taken the opportunity to break away from his brother's influence and, with Aunt Mavis's

2

backing, had moved to Scarborough where his interest in photography had developed into a thriving business on the back of the holiday trade which boomed there throughout the thirties. At the time they'd left the country, Jane had heard her father mocking his brother, calling his ideas 'namby-pamby' and saying he should get men's work as he himself had done, maintaining tracks for the Great Northern line. Being only seven at the time she could not voice an opinion – children being very much seen and not heard in her family – but in her mind she was sympathetic towards Uncle David.

She was grateful to him and her aunt for giving her a home; for never once suggesting that she return to Middlesbrough, and leaving any further decisions about her life to her. When she first came to Scarborough she knew she should think seriously about getting a job and contributing to the household expenses, but that had been shelved while she settled in to her new home. She couldn't put it off forever, though. She had considered journalism, for she loved expressing her thoughts and making observations. Before the trouble with her father she had kept a reasonably comprehensive diary; as the situation had worsened her notes became more detailed, especially when expressing her own emotions. It dawned on her that one day they might be useful as background to a novel, or perhaps her ability to elaborate her observations would lead to a career in journalism. Maybe now was the time to start, to purchase a typewriter and sound out the local newspaper. It was just a question of finding the right subject ... But wasn't it said that: 'Subjects are everywhere, it's a matter of training your mind and eyes to see them'? Maybe today, at the cricket ...

Reaching the promenade, she slowed her walk. After a few minutes she stopped to lean on the rail and stare out to sea. Mesmerised by the constant motion of the waves, she became lost in her thoughts, skirting the past and speculating about the future.

3

Jane sighed, brought her mind back to the present then straightened up, telling herself, determinedly, that mooning about was no way to start the day. She walked on at an unhurried pace, noting the scene around her – late-season holidaymakers making the most of the fine weather by enjoying themselves on the beach; children building sand castles or racing towards the sea; families settling into their temporary encampments, meeting up with friends, being happy together. Jane felt a pang of jealousy. Why hadn't her own childhood followed a similar pattern? Why had her parents never taken her and Tim to the seaside?

She threw such regrets from her mind as she walked past the row of small holiday chalets stretching as far as the curved Art Deco frontage of the Corner Café from which there were clear views across the North Bay to the ruined Norman castle high on the promontory that split Scarborough into its North and South sides. Beneath, the Royal Albert Drive and Marine Drive pursued their spectacular seaside route, a link to the South Bay and the bustling harbour. Jane had grown to love this walk, which she did most days when the weather permitted. Today it was perfect.

She found herself wondering what it was like inside the cliff-top hotels above her. She was passing the foothills now where twisting paths had been laid and flat areas dug out to accommodate tennis courts and putting greens, some of which were already in use. The cliff face steepened as it reached the promontory. Jane was always awed by its majestic height, and the screeching of the thousands of seabirds nesting on its ledges.

Reaching the South Bay, she was met by the noise of amusement arcades and funfairs housed between the shops, cafés and ice-cream parlours lining the foreshore on one side. The other gave access to a beach where further holidaymakers were making the most of their last few days of freedom. Jane always liked to drink in the vitality of this

4

part of town before climbing the steep cliffside gardens to what was regarded as Scarborough's elegant side. But today she was going to forgo that part of her walk for in the harbour yesterday she'd noticed three drifters, the *Sea Queen*, *Lively Lady*, and *Silver King*, that she knew from their markings came from Lowestoft. Together with the local fishing vessels and craft plying the holiday trade, they added colour and activity to the harbour and brought much-needed trade to the fishing port whose returns were diminishing after the heyday of the herring industry before the Great War.

She wandered along the harbourside, pausing to watch men busy in their boats. She admired two pristine yachts that must have berthed after she had left yesterday. But her eyes were mainly intent upon the drifters. Yesterday she had been disappointed that there was no sign of anyone on board. Today it was a different story. Five young men, one of whom was holding a soccer ball, were in the midst of laughing exchanges with a fair-haired young woman on the quay. Jane observed her more closely as she drew nearer. She judged the girl to be about her own age, and her lively manner and attractive personality were obvious from the way she bantered with the young sailors. They seemed to be a happy group and, though the sailors must be here to work, they generated a light-hearted atmosphere around them. Jane listened, attracted by the soft flowing speech with its drawn-out vowels.

'Hey, Nell, have you time to suffer another defeat?' called out a dark-haired, well-built young man whose sparkling blue eyes and fine-cut features gave him a striking appearance.

'No, Ewan, no time for that,' she replied promptly. The twinkle in her eyes showed her desire to accept the challenge. 'But I've time to beat you cheats!'

This retaliation brought a roar of laughter from the group on the boat. 'Cheats?' called Ewan. 'Don't be such a bad sport. Here, take the ball and try again. We'll be with you in a few minutes.' He threw the ball to her but aimed it to the left so that she failed to hold it.

Gasps of warning came from the men as the ball bounced towards the edge of the quay. Nell looked alarmed. She couldn't be the one to lose the crew's precious ball in the harbour. Jane's eyes focused on the ball. She judged its next bounce, stepped lightly forward and flicked it away from the edge of the quay. As she bent down to pick it up then she could sense the relief sweeping over the spectators.

With cheers ringing out from the deck of the drifter, Nell came running up to her. She reached out for the ball and gasped, 'Oh, thanks. You saved my life.'

Jane grinned. 'Would it have been that bad?'

'Worse.' Nell raised her eyes heavenwards. 'Especially from Ewan Steel and Simon Evans. They'd never have let me forget it.' She glanced back at the drifter. 'Ten minutes,' she shouted.

'Aye, before you taste defeat again,' came the reply, this time from a brown-haired man of similar build to Ewan but with more rugged features.

'That's what you think, Simon,' retorted Nell. She turned back to Jane 'Like to join us? We're going to have a game on the beach before we go to the cricket.' Her tone was friendly and there was warmth in her dark blue eyes. She held the ball tightly to her with her right arm. With the other hand she ran her fingers through her wavy hair. She was a neat and attractive figure in her light brown skirt and pale blue blouse, white ankle socks and sandals.

'Well, I'm on my way to the cricket too,' replied Jane.

'Then we can all go together. Come on.' Nell started off along the quay.

'Won't the men be sailing?' asked Jane, falling into step beside her.

'No, won't be doing until tomorrow evening. We've all come from Lowestoft to see this match against the Aussies, you see.'

'And the fishing takes a back seat?'

'We always pick one match in the Scarborough Cricket Festival to attend together. We actually come for ten days' holiday, but apart from the day of the match the men operate out of Scarborough while the rest of the families enjoy themselves.'

'Very convenient! Then the drifters will work their way back to Lowestoft?'

'Yes.'

'Is the fishing good?'

'Yes. Not as good as it used to be but we still manage to make a living, though how long for I don't know. The markets have been gradually diminishing. The men talk about turning to trawling, but the situation in Europe is casting a doubt over the fishing industry, as it is over everything else.' Realising her tone had become sombre, Nell gave a little laugh. 'Let's not think of that, we've more pleasant things to look forward to today.' They had reached the end of the quay and she led the way down on to the sand. 'Oh, by the way, I'm Nell Franklin. My father owns one of those drifters.'

'Jane Harvey.'

'On holiday?' asked Nell when Jane said no more.

'Oh, sorry, no. I live with my uncle and aunt in Scarborough. I've been with them since February.'

'Here we are, Jane.' Curious though she was, Nell curtailed her questions as they neared a group of people settled in a circle of deckchairs around two rugs on which stood three baskets laden with picnic supplies. Three older couples occupied pride of place in the chairs. They turned to face Nell and Jane with welcome smiles.

'I want you to meet Jane Harvey,' Nell announced. 'Jane, this is Mum, and next to her is Mrs Steel.' Jane saw immediately that Ewan had inherited his looks from this handsome woman. 'And this is Mrs Evans.' They all smiled and nodded at Jane as if approving of Nell's newfound friend. 'Then you've got the three musketeers

7

over there, my dad George Franklin, Mr Steel and Mr Evans.' She indicated the three men, casually dressed in short-sleeved shirts, their dark blue serge trousers held up by braces. There was the same air of determination and self-assurance in Mr Steel that Jane had noted in Ewan. 'Time you got your feet wet, gentlemen,' teased Nell, motioning towards their heavy black shoes. She turned to Jane, explaining, 'They don't like water, these chaps. Wouldn't think they owned those three drifters and talk of nothing else but fishing, would you?'

'Now, young lady,' intervened Jake Evans, 'don't be giving this nice girl the wrong impression. You know full well and I'll tell you what, I can talk cricket and football too.'

'And chat up the girls,' chuckled his wife Sarah. 'Beware, Jane.'

'Well, I chatted up the right one, didn't I, love?' came the quick reply to that.

'I can keep his mind on cricket and football, Mrs Evans, don't you worry,' put in Jane with a smile.

'You're a cricket fan, then?' Percy Steel asked her.

'Yes. I was at the match yesterday, and the day before.'

'Going today, love?' put in George Franklin.

'Yes. Wouldn't miss the outcome.'

'Then come with us. I'm sure Nell would enjoy some female company among us men,' he said, nodding in the direction of the five young crew members who were crossing the sand to join them.

'Maybe so,' called his wife, Flo, 'but not before we've shown you that you don't win a soccer match by cheating.' She started to push herself from her chair and her two women friends followed suit.

'You're playing,' Nell whispered close to Jane's ear.

'Aren't we going to be outnumbered?' she murmured.

'Two more are coming.' Jane pointed in the direction of two girls, both about fourteen or so, who were running over from the direction of the sea. 'They are Sylvia and

Amy Steel.' She went on to indicate the five boisterous young men. 'Simon and Neil Evans, Ewan and Walter Steel. The other one's Terry who works on my dad's drifter. You'll meet them all in the course of the game.'

'No doubt,' grinned Jane, delighted to have been welcomed so easily by this group of friends.

'You five,' Nell called, 'this is Jane. She's playing for us.'

'Only right,' shouted Ewan, 'after she saved your face. Come on, let's slaughter you women then we can get off for the start of the cricket.'

Four coats were soon installed to mark the goalmouths and, with everyone haphazardly lined up, the women kicked off. It became a game of push and shove with cries of 'Foul' ignored, shots that went laughably wide, and the ball getting stuck in the wet sand when it looked as if it had reached an undefended goal. Laughter abounded and Jane knew that, whatever the outcome, the game was being enjoyed by all. The ladies, though, seemed determined to win, no doubt to avenge yesterday's defeat and prove a point.

It had been agreed they'd play ten minutes each way, and when the first half was up no one had scored. It was the men's turn to kick off next. As soon as they put the ball down, Simon tapped it to Ewan who took a long shot towards goal and found the target. The ladies immediately made loud protests, saying they were not ready and that Sylvia had not had chance to take up her position in goal. The men would have none of it and the women were forced to accept that a goal had been scored legitimately. But now their determination had heightened.

Five minutes remained when Jane found herself free from anyone marking her and accepting a long kick from Amy. She brought the ball under control skilfully but after a few yards saw Jake Evans charging towards her. She judged his approach carefully and, when he started to do a sliding tackle in the sand, put her foot on the ball to stop it. He slid past without touching it. She was round him in an instant, saw Nell free and flighted the ball to her feet. Nell steadied herself and put her shot past Terry in goal. One each! Four minutes remaining.

The game became frenzied as everyone screamed for the ball, but no one made any real impression. Though the men tried more long shots, they were all saved by Sylvia who was determined not to be caught out again by male trickery as they tried to distract her in any way they could. With barely a minute to go, she saved a hard shot from Ewan and immediately kicked the ball hard and high. Jane, with her back to the opponents' goal, saw it coming. Simon was racing back but his feet were catching in the soft sand. The ball was dropping. Jane eyed it carefully. She must not let it lose momentum in the sand. With the ball inches from the ground, she swivelled and met it at just the right moment. It flew from her foot. As she fell back into the sand she heard a roar of female voices and knew she must have scored. She was pushing herself to her feet when she was swamped by all the members of her team, whooping and showering her with praise. She grinned and felt great satisfaction when she saw the men all glumly staring in her direction with expressions of disbelief.

'Cor blast!' gasped Simon.

Arm round Jane's shoulder, Nell's face bore a huge grin when she faced the other team and called triumphantly, 'What did you think to that?'

'Where did you learn?' asked Ewan in amazement.

'That would be telling,' Nell put in quickly. 'Say nothing.' She squeezed Jane's arm. 'Let's get a drink, then off to the cricket and let this lot brood on their defeat.'

Jane laughed and winked at Ewan whose astonishment was still clouding his features as they walked past him to the picnic baskets. 'Does everyone go to the cricket?' she asked Nell.

'No. The rest of the womenfolk are happy with their

knitting, books and nattering. The younger generation will amuse themselves on the beach, in the sea, and in the amusement arcades. Terry will go to visit some friends in Scarborough, but the rest of the men will go. We've got tickets. Have you?'

'Yes.'

'Good. Then we can spend the day together, if you like?'

'I'd like nothing better.'

It was a happy group that left the sands, and their cheerful exchanges made Jane feel even more at home. She had been accepted without question and was drawn by their natural easy-going attitude to life, though she guessed that when it came to the business of fishing they would be a lot more serious. It obviously brought them a good living.

'Your father been in fishing all his life?' Jane asked when they reached the promenade and set off around the foot of the cliff.

'Yes, and his father and grandfather before him.'

'And you are an only child?'

'Yes.'

'So there's no son to carry on and take over his drifter?'

Nell gave a sad shake of her head. 'No. I could manage the business side, Dad's seen to that, but it needs someone at the blunt end, too, and that means someone who can skipper the drifter at sea. I think when the time comes he'll sell out to Mr Evans or Mr Steel, both of whom, as you will have realised, have two sons.' Nell paused, hoping that would encourage Jane to reveal more about herself, but whether she was about to or not wasn't clear for at that point a voice from behind called: 'Hey, Jane, where did you learn to kick a ball like that?'

Both girls looked round and saw it was Ewan who had put the question. They slowed their step, allowing him and the other young men to catch them up.

'I said it was a fluke,' joked Simon. 'Ewan reckons it was skill.'

''Course it was skill,' Nell said indignantly.

11

'If it was,' said Simon, doubt in his voice, 'she's done a lot of practising.'

'I had a soccer-mad brother,' Jane informed them.

'Had?' Ewan frowned.

'He died of complications from scarlet fever,' Jane explained sadly. 'He was football mad. He played in a local mid-week junior team. When I was living at home he insisted I kick a ball with him on the local recreation ground, and he taught me a few things.'

'Seems he was a good teacher,' moaned Walter.

'He went to all Middlesbrough's first team home games.'

'Did you?'

Jane laughed. 'No. I got enough of football kicking a ball about with him.'

Ewan gave Simon a playful punch on the shoulder. 'There, I told you it was skill.'

He grimaced. 'How was I to know Jane had a brother who passed on to her everything he'd seen George Camsell do at Ayresome Park?'

'Come on, hand over that bob you owe me,' Ewan told him.

'You had a bet on me?' cried Jane.

'Yes, love, and I won,' replied Ewan with a grin, giving her a quick hug of appreciation.

Jane laughed. 'I reckon you owe me half of it then.'

'Maybe I do,' he chuckled.

As he released her and Jane spun away from his arms, she caught a momentary expression of disapproval on Nell's face. It was hardly there before it was gone, and then Nell's laughter and high spirits were mingling with those of the rest of the party again.

She linked arms with Jane and quickened their pace. 'We all have our own tickets. If we get separated in the ground, we'll meet on the beach later where we left the others.'

Jane nodded. 'What time?'

'After the match.'

'Could go on until six o'clock. I expect Mr Leveson-

Gower's XI will have declared overnight 57 ahead, so it will depend how well the Australians bat.'

'Or how well we bowl,' added Nell, lining herself up as a supporter of the English team.

'It could be interesting.'

'Very.'

They joined the throng of people converging on the main entrance to the cricket ground. Looking round, Nell saw they had become separated from the men. She caught Ewan's eye over the heads of the people between them and mouthed, 'See you around.' He nodded and raised a hand in acknowledgement.

When they got inside the ground they saw that it was rapidly filling up and the special atmosphere of Scarborough Festival cricket was already all-embracing.

'Where should we sit?' asked Jane.

'How about somewhere in that area below the press box?' Nell said, indicating the building that housed the sports writers.

'Good idea, we'll get a good view straight down the wicket there.'

They hurried towards the area, realising that because of the view it gave it would soon be full. As they passed the pavilion Nell gave Jane a nudge and with a slight inclination of her head indicated a tall, smartly dressed man in cricket clothes who had just passed them. 'Ken Farnes,' she whispered.

Jane nodded, for she too had recognised the good-looking Essex cricketer.

They found two seats and settled down, Jane wondering what it would be like to be sitting in the press box writing about the match.

'You've been in Scarborough with your aunt and uncle since early in the year?' said Nell.

Jane hesitated before replying. She realised that Nell wanted to know more about her, which was only natural. She could not deny the empathy between them. It was as if

13

they'd been friends for a while already. Nell deserved to know more about her, but Jane could not tell her the whole truth. Besides, if she did not reveal all, Nell would never know what had truly brought her to live with her uncle and aunt, and there was no need for her to hear about it. A half-truth would do.

'You must be wondering why I'm here with my uncle and aunt? There was some trouble at home with my father and it seemed better that I leave. He imposed a strict regime and we didn't see eye to eye over what I wanted to do, so I came here.'

'To live with your uncle?'

'Yes, he's my father's brother but they fell out years ago when we left our home village for better prospects. Uncle David and Aunt Mavis had no children of their own so Tim and I were always made welcome. It seemed natural I should turn to them when I left home. They have been very good to me about the whole thing. Now I'm over it, I really must think about finding a job.'

'Any ideas?'

'I haven't been trained for anything but I have an inclination to write. I might try freelance journalism, to see if I'm any good.'

'That could be more interesting than my job, working for my Dad, but I quite like it. I look after his accounts and correspondence, and it gives me quite a bit of freedom. I'm sorry about your family disagreement and I hope it all turns out well for you. We're here for another five days before returning to Lowestoft, so if you'd like to meet up again ...'

'Oh, I would, Nell, really. I feel I've found a new friend.'

'So do I! Let's make plans after the game. Here come Leveson-Gower's XI.'

The team, led by their captain R. E. S. Wyatt, was leaving the pavilion. Clapping broke out and was soon coming from every part of the ground, the white marquees and tubs of flowers on the opposite corner of the field adding to the festival atmosphere. Australia's batsmen soon followed and, having sportingly clapped them too, the crowd began to settle down in anticipation of a good contest.

The seats around Nell and Jane were all taken but people were still coming into the ground to find others elsewhere or else were prepared to stand, particularly outside the beer tents that had been erected along one side of the ground.

'Seen anything of our lot?' asked Nell.

Jane shook her head. 'No.'

'Most likely have glasses in their hands by now. They won't be able to do it tomorrow. They sail that night.'

'Skippers are strict about drinking before sailing, are they?' asked Jane.

'Not all skippers but Dad and the other two impose a twelve-hour ban before sailing. They say too much is at stake for anyone to be sailing while they're only partly on top of things.'

Their conversation drifted over all sorts of topics or into silence when certain parts of the play became all-engrossing. Jane felt more contented than she had done for a very long time when they left the ground later, euphoric at having seen the Australians beaten in England outside of a test match for the first time in seventeen years. In that buoyant mood it seemed natural that she should accept Nell's invitation to return with her to the beach.

There the women and children greeted her as if she had always been one of them, and in their general good mood instilled by enthralling cricket and beer, the men too were equally friendly.

Half an hour later, when everyone reluctantly realised that it was time to break up the party, Jane prepared to make her goodbyes.

'Join us tomorrow, Jane, if you would like to? I'm sure Nell would appreciate your company,' Flo Franklin suggested.

Delighted by the offer, Jane had no hesitation about accepting. 'I would like that very much.' She glanced at Nell, hoping that she too was pleased. The smile she received reassured her.

'Where do you live, Jane?' asked Ewan.

'Scholes Park Road, it's way over on the North Side.'

'You go round the Marine Drive?'

'Yes.'

Ewan turned to Nell. 'Should we walk with her?'

'Yes,' came the quick reply.

Jane, who was turning to say goodbye to Simon, caught a momentary glimpse of both disappointment and jealousy in his face. It made her wonder whose affections Nell really held. Her curiosity was halted when Ewan's mother spoke.

'What about your evening meal?'

'Probably won't want anything after what we had at the cricket, Ma, but if we do, we'll get something out.'

They set off in a light-hearted mood, exchanging snippets of information with each other, Jane's interest sharpened when Ewan suggested she should join Nell to watch them sail the following evening, about five.

'I'll be there. I love it round the harbour, it's always so colourful and busy.'

Ewan chuckled. 'And so grimy when we start stoking up.'

'I love it,' repeated Jane. 'It's so adventurous.'

Ewan roared with laughter. 'Adventurous? Hard work, more like! You must have romantic ideas of what it's like out there at sea.'

'There's always risk and danger,' put in Nell. 'The womenfolk have a worrying time when their men are at sea, but we accept it because that's our way of life and the sea is in our blood too.'

'How many crew members do you have?'

'Six. My dad, my brother, myself and three others. They come with us from Lowestoft and have three days off while we're at the cricket. They'll all be t'gither tomorrow,

16

getting ready to sail in the evening. There's the same number of men on the other drifters.'

Jane enjoyed their company until they reached the Corner Café where Nell and Ewan decided they would return to the digs where they stayed every year: three fishermen's cottages handy for the harbour in the old part of Scarborough.

'What about tomorrow?' asked Nell.

'You two meeting up?' queried Ewan.

'We thought about it,' replied Nell. 'You'll be busy preparing to sail.'

'Yes, I'm afraid so.'

'We could spend the day together and finish up by seeing them sail?' Nell suggested to Jane.

'Good. I'll meet you at the harbour at ten?'

'Couldn't be better.'

Mavis and David, who were enjoying a cup of tea when their niece walked in, were struck by her joyful mood.

'You seem to have had a good day, love,' commented Mavis.

'Oh, I have,' Jane replied. As she poured herself a cup of tea from the pot on the table, she told them all about it.

'I heard it was a good match,' said her uncle.

'I'm so pleased you met some nice people,' said Mavis.

'I'm meeting Nell tomorrow at the harbour at ten.'

'Why not bring her to lunch?'

'Can I?' asked Jane enthusiastically.

'Of course,' Mavis insisted, pleased that her niece had found a friend. It could be a real turning point in her life and Jane deserved a change in fortune.

'Thank you.' She came over to give her aunt a kiss. 'And I've decided I'm going to try and do something about getting a job, or at least earning myself some money.'

Both her uncle and aunt looked at her in surprise.

'Don't think you have to,' her uncle was quick to assure her.

'I know, Uncle, but it is time I started to do something. I can't depend on you all the time.'

Her aunt reached out and took her hand. 'Jane, we are delighted to have you with us, and whatever you decide, you know we will back your decision.'

There was love and gratitude in Jane's smile when she replied quietly, 'Thank you.'

'What are you thinking of?' asked her uncle.

'I'd like to try some freelance journalism. If I was reasonably successful, I might even consider journalism as a career.'

'Good for you,' Mavis encouraged.

'Show some determination and you'll succeed,' her uncle agreed. 'You'll need a typewriter. Go and get one, a good one. I'll sign a cheque and you can fill in the rest. It can go on my business account.'

Jane was speechless for a few moments, then with a cry of thanks she hugged her uncle.

There were tears of love and appreciation in her eyes as she straightened up. 'What have I done to deserve you two?' she said at length.

'You have brought us joy,' said Mavis, 'when we thought the chance of it had passed us by.'

'And we'd rather see some benefit from our money while we can,' added David.

Scarborough's foreshore was already a hive of activity around the amusement arcades, shops, ice-cream parlours and cafés when Jane reached the harbour the next morning. The quayside was busy too as pleasure-boat owners tried to entice holidaymakers to take a sea trip, and the men from the three Lowestoft drifters checked the gear and prepared for the evening sailing.

She turned on to the quay. As she passed the *Silver King*, she heard a shout: 'Hi, Jane!' She glanced across at the nearest ship and saw Simon in his shirt sleeves. He waved and gave her a broad grin.

18

She was flattered by such enthusiasm and returned it with equal fervour, then stopped to exchange a few words with him.

'You two spending the day together?' he asked, inclining his head in the direction of Nell who was talking to Ewan beside the *Lively Lady*.

'Yes. Don't know what we're going to do, but I have some shopping to get.'

'Nell will love that.'

She saw Nell look in their direction and wave.

She waved back and then said to Simon, 'Will she really?'

'She will. Doesn't get much opportunity to shop with someone of her own age, and you two seemed to get on so well yesterday.'

'We did, didn't we?'

'Nell's that type of person. Easy to get on with if she takes to someone. And by her comments when she and Ewan got back yesterday, it was obvious she liked you.'

'I'm so pleased. I liked her too from the moment I met her.'

'She's a fine girl.'

The tone of Simon's voice made Jane wonder if the relationship between them was more than merely friendship. But Nell was with Ewan at this moment, and it had been Ewan who had suggested he and Nell should accompany Jane home yesterday.

'I'd better go and see her. I'll be back here this evening to see you all sail.'

'You will?' The eagerness in his voice was not lost on Jane and again she felt a twinge of pleasure.

'I'd better go.'

'Good morning, Jane,' Nell and Ewan chorused.

'Hello,' she replied, and glanced at Ewan. 'Is the weather going to be good for you tonight?'

'I think so. The signs aren't bad. The wind is freshening a bit, but that won't bother us.'

'How far out do you go?'

'About forty miles. Depends where we find herring.'

'How do you know where they'll be?'

'They tend to be that distance away, give or take a few miles. Dad has a built-in instinct when he gets out there. Comes from spending years in the trade. Then when we get close to the area where he believes there will be herring, he'll have a look-out at the bow. He'll be waiting for the tell-tale phosphorescence that shines off them ... that's one of the reasons herring are known as the "silver darlings".' He glanced towards the wheelhouse. 'I'd better be going. Dad's looking a bit stern with me for wasting time talking to you. Enjoy yourselves.'

'I want a quick word with my dad,' said Nell, taking Jane's arm. They moved on to the *Sea Queen* where George Franklin was on deck overseeing the preparations. When the two girls appeared he came down the gangway on to the quay. 'What are you two planning on doing?'

'I have some shopping I need to do, Mr Franklin,' replied Jane.

'Oh, goodness me. My daughter's chief failing!' He looked heavenwards as if hoping to find divine help in curbing the enthusiasm he had seen coming over Nell's face.

'We'll have a smashing time,' she said eagerly.

'You do that, love. Here.' He fished in his pocket and handed her five one-pound notes.

Nell gave a loud whoop, hugged her father and gave him a big kiss on the cheek. Though he liked it and loved to indulge his only child, he tut-tutted with embarrassment. 'Off with you now. And have a good day.'

'We will, Dad, we will,' laughed Nell.

The two girls set off along the quay, calling goodbye to Ewan and Simon as they passed their vessels.

'My Aunty Mavis has invited you to lunch,' said Jane, 'so I suggest we have a leisurely walk home then after lunch we'll go shopping. I'm looking for a typewriter.' She went on to tell Nell how that had come about.

'That sounds splendid,' she approved. 'I know nothing about journalism or writing, but I'm sure you'll do well. You'll need good ideas for articles and stories, though.'

'I've just had my first,' replied Jane, excitement colouring her words.

'You have?'

'Yes, the drifters and the work they do.'

'But what do you know about that?'

'Very little at the moment, but I'll find out and then write about it. Having met you, I have a golden opportunity.'

'Speak to any of the three owners. I know they'll be only too willing to help you out, and so will Ewan and Simon. But you'd do well to tackle Simon first. He's never wanted to do anything but herring fishing, can see his whole life bound up in it; Ewan less so. He's restless. He'd leave tomorrow if he dare.'

'Why doesn't he?' Jane was curious.

'His father expects him to carry on in the business but Ewan doesn't really see a future there. The opportunity to leave without incurring his father's wrath could come when his brother's old and competent enough to take his place. Ewan figures his father wouldn't be so strongly opposed to losing him then. In the meantime, he puts up with the life. Don't get me wrong, he's a good fisherman but his heart and soul are not in it. Not like Simon's.'

These revelations made Jane wonder. Was Nell, too, bound up in the fishing industry? If so, would she lean towards Simon? If not, would she seek to escape with Ewan? Where did her heart truly lie? Then Jane wondered: What about me? Both the young men had flirted with her, and she liked it, but she had noted Nell's fleeting reactions. Jane knew she must tread warily; she did not want to lose this friendship which already meant a lot to her. It had given her more to think about, driving away the bad memories and showing her a glimpse of a richer, more stable future, if she could only grasp it.

Chapter Two

'I like her,' Mavis whispered to her niece when Jane brought the dirty pudding plates into the kitchen.

'I'm glad,' she mouthed with a smile.

Drawn by Nell's warm personality and friendly manner, Mavis had taken to her as soon as the two girls arrived. She liked Nell's openness about herself and her family and, knowing that she came from a good home, realised that this girl would be good for Jane. It was only a pity she did not live in Scarborough so that the friendship could develop further. However, she could make an invitation now so, when the two girls prepared to leave on their shopping expedition, she said, 'If you can manage to take a break from work some time, do come and visit us here. I know Jane would like that.'

'I will, Mrs Harvey. Thank you for the invitation, and for the lovely meal.'

'It was nice to have you,' replied Mavis, and gave Nell a hug to which she responded. Then she gave her niece a kiss and said, 'Mind you get the typewriter you like.'

'We'll expect great things from her, won't we, Mrs Harvey?' put in Nell.

'We certainly will.'

'I've had my first idea,' Jane revealed.

'And what might that be?' asked Mavis light-heartedly, so that Jane responded in like manner.

She laughed and called over her shoulder as she headed for the gate, 'That would be telling, Aunt.'

Mavis smiled and looked askance at Nell who merely raised her eyebrows and shrugged her shoulders as if denying any knowledge of Jane's idea, though Mavis suspected she knew very well what it was. Other aunts may have taken offence that their niece had chosen to confide in a comparative stranger rather than a close relation, but Mavis took delight in the fact that Jane had found herself a friend.

She paused at the gate and looked back. 'Don't forget, we're going to see the drifters sail.'

'I won't. I'll expect you when we see you. Enjoy yourselves.'

'She's nice,' commented Nell as they fell into step, heading for town.

Jane nodded. 'I was so lucky to have her to turn to after the trouble at home.' Nell hoped her friend was going to enlarge on that but Jane made no attempt to do so. Instead she said, 'Uncle David is just as nice. It was a pity he couldn't get home today. But we'll call on him when we're in town.'

'I thought he'd be out taking photographs?'

Jane laughed. 'Oh, no! I must have given you the wrong impression when I told you about my uncle and aunt. Taking photographs is only a part of Uncle David's business. He does studio work, offers a developing service, and has a shop that sells cameras and all the necessary equipment. You'll see it all after I've got my typewriter and you've spent some of that money your father gave you.'

Nell had stopped walking and was looking wide-eyed at Jane.

'Hey, maybe I'll buy a camera,' she laughed. 'What do they cost?'

'I don't know,' Jane chuckled, 'but my uncle will soon put you right.' She guided Nell to a shop in Westborough

24

where the owner was only too pleased to show these pleasant young ladies his stock of six portable models. After lauding the attributes of each in turn and making differing though slight criticisms of each, he suggested that Jane try them out.

'I'm no typist,' she explained.

'Ah.' He raised an eyebrow. 'Then I recommend you get some tuition. It'll be better if you learn to touch type rather than try to teach yourself, which inevitably leads to two-finger typing.'

Jane nodded. 'I'll think about that.'

'Come back if you decide to have lessons. I can recommend a young lady who is a very good teacher. She'll have you typing in no time if you're prepared to practise between lessons.'

'Thank you! But now . . . which typewriter?' Jane pursed her lips and ran her hand over them thoughtfully, bearing in mind what the shop keeper had told her. She eliminated two and the man nodded his approval. Then she said, 'That one.'

He smiled. 'Ah, the Good Companion.'

'Well, it's got to be that after reading that notice.' She indicated an attractive poster which read, 'Buy a Good Companion and you too can write novels and plays like Priestley'.

'You want to be a writer?'

Jane smiled and blushed. 'I'd like to be. Does Mr Priestley really use one?'

'Well, Imperial Typewriters, who manufacture them, got permission to use the name of his novel for their typewriter. The first to come off the production line in 1932 was presented to him. Whether he actually uses it or not I don't know, but I see no reason for him not to.'

'That was good publicity for them,' commented Nell.

'It was, and so was their coup in getting the "By Royal Appointment" insignia. So you've made an excellent choice. I was hoping you would choose that one, I think it will suit you admirably, but I wanted you to make the decision without my influencing you. And I hope it does well for you, and that you are as successful as Mr Priestley one day.'

'Oh, that I could be,' said Jane wistfully.

'Maybe you will, even if it is in a different field of writing.'

Within ten minutes Jane walked out of the shop, the proud owner of what she saw as her passport to a wide new world.

'I'm so pleased for you,' cried Nell enthusiastically. 'Now to meet your uncle and see those cameras ...'

'Are you seriously thinking of buying one?'

'Why not? If you can venture into a new field, why can't I?'

'Yes, why not? Maybe you can illustrate my articles.'

'Dreams, dreams, dreams,' laughed Nell.

Jane joined in the laughter as she said, 'How exciting, though, trying to make them come true.' She gave a little skip. She hadn't felt so joyous for many years, if ever.

They reached a shop window displaying twelve cameras in such a manner that they caught the eye individually. The two girls paused to study it. 'Your uncle really knows how to set a window out,' commented Nell.

'That'll be Miss Gibbs who serves in the shop. She's very good at window displays. She's engaged to be married and Uncle David dreads losing her. He's trying to persuade her to stay on, even if only part-time.' Jane started for the shop door and Nell followed.

'Hello, Miss Gibbs,' said Jane with a display of politeness.

The young lady inclined her head and replied with exaggerated courtesy, 'Good day, Miss Harvey.'

Then they both burst out laughing at this little ritual they always enacted when Jane visited the shop.

'Maureen, this is my new friend Nell. She's visiting from Lowestoft. Nell, this is Maureen Gibbs.'

26

Nell found herself exchanging greetings with a vivacious redhead, smartly dressed in a charcoal two-piece costume that showed off her figure to advantage. Nell could see why Mr Harvey did not want to lose her for such an attractive assistant could surely charm people, especially men, into parting with their money for a camera or whatever photographic material caught their interest. Mr Harvey would not want to be deprived of such an asset, one who could combine such charm with an eye for good display.

'Maureen, Nell wants to buy a camera,' explained Jane.

'I could sell her one, but I expect Mr Harvey would like to give you his personal attention.'

'Well, yes, I would like to introduce my uncle to Nell.'

Maureen pressed a button on the counter and a few moments later a door opened behind it and Jane's uncle came into the shop.

'Jane! How nice to see you here.'

'Uncle David, I've brought Nell to meet you.'

'Delighted!' he cried enthusiastically as he took Nell's proffered hand.

'I'm so pleased to meet you, Mr Harvey,' she replied.

'I'm sorry I was not able to get home to join you at midday but I had a big developing order to complete. I'm glad you called in. Now, are you two having a pleasant day?'

'I've got my typewriter!' Jane raised the parcel in its carrier bag.

'Oh, good,' said David. 'I look forward to seeing it when I get home.'

'I might not be home until late. We're going to see the drifters sail.'

'Right. But, look, you won't want to carry that all round the harbour. Leave it with me, I'll take it home.'

'Oh, would you?' cried Jane.

'Of course, love!'

She handed the carrier bag to him. 'No peeping!' she warned.

'Would I do that?' He grinned and placed the bag behind the counter.

'Uncle, Nell would like to buy a camera.'

'Ah.' He looked seriously at her. 'Have you done any photography before?'

'Well, no,' she replied. 'I had a boyfriend once who had a camera and I used it occasionally to take photographs of him, but that's all.'

'What sort of camera was it?'

'Oh, I don't know.'

'That's all right, we'll start from scratch. What do you want it for mainly?'

Before Nell had time to answer, Jane chipped in, 'To illustrate the articles I'm going to write on that typewriter.'

Her uncle smiled at her enthusiasm and said, 'Why not?' Then, turning to Nell, he asked, 'Is that what you would really like to do?'

She glanced at Jane and saw the almost indistinguishable nod of her head. 'Yes,' she replied firmly. 'I want to learn how to take good pictures for her.'

'How much do you want to spend?'

'I don't know, Mr Harvey. I've no idea what they cost.'

'Very well! Here's what I'm prepared to do.' David took a camera from a glass case and placed it on the counter. 'That is a very good camera. It's a Leica II, one of the up and coming breed of compact cameras that take smaller rolls of film, are easy to handle and to carry. It's simplicity itself to use. I will show you how. I'll put a roll of film in it now and you can take the camera out to see how you like it. It will take good quality pictures but you will have to compose those pictures, it can't do that for you. Use this roll of film and another I will give you, if you're so inclined, and come back tomorrow. I'll develop and print whatever you have taken and we'll see if you have a flair for photography. Then, if you show promise, we will talk some more about this camera and whether it will suit you.'

'Oh, Mr Harvey, I couldn't! I'd be frightened I damaged or lost it.'

David laughed. 'I don't think you'll do that. I'm only too pleased to try and help you both. Who knows? This might be the start of something big.'

'Oh, thank you so much, Uncle David.' Jane gave him a big hug.

He smiled, delighted to have pleased his niece and her friend. 'Now let me explain the camera and show you what to do . . .' He kept his instructions simple, telling them how to cope with the differing intensities of light, how to make the best use of focusing, and how to cope with movement. 'I know it may sound complicated but it isn't really. Once you have taken a few photographs, you'll find it easy.'

'Can I run through what you've told me again?' asked Nell.

'Of course.' When she had finished, he said, 'Good. You've grasped the basics. Tomorrow I'll see how you have put them into practice and whether you have an eye for a composition. What do you intend taking?'

'Like I said to Aunt Mavis, that would be telling! You'll see tomorrow,' put in Jane quickly, to prevent Nell spoiling the surprise.

David laughed. 'Well, I suppose I can be patient.'

When the two excited girls had left the shop, Nell said, 'Your uncle might have suggested something for us to take.'

'I have an idea,' replied Jane, and then hesitated with a teasing smile.

'Come on, tell?' urged Nell.

'Well, if I'm going to write about the drifters, you can photograph them. We can get to the harbour early, take some photographs of the boats and their crews, and then of them leaving later this evening.'

'Brilliant!' shouted Nell. 'Come on, let's get to the harbour and make a start.'

They hurried through the streets, weaving in and out of

the press of people: Scarborough folk going about their daily lives, holidaymakers wandering without a clue where to go next. Nell and Jane knew exactly where they wanted to be and Jane led the way unerringly by the shortest route. They came down the final slope only a short distance from the harbour. They ignored all the razzmatazz of the foreshore and ran across the roadway. Panting and flushed with excitement, they reached the quay and saw the drifters were a hive of activity as the crews prepared for the evening departure. Chains, ropes, nets, hauling gear, were all being checked; everything must be in tip-top condition, nothing left to chance. Men's lives could be at risk, especially on a heaving boat in an unrelenting swell. Everything must be directed at getting the best harvest from the sea. The men raised their heads when they saw the girls among a crowd of interested sightseers. They waved and then got on with their jobs, but Simon and Ewan gave them extra acknowledgement.

After walking past the three drifters, the two girls stopped and looked back.

'What should I photograph?' asked Nell.

'Anything and everything,' replied Jane.

'That's helpful,' returned Nell, a touch of sarcasm in her voice. 'I don't know what you intend writing about.'

'Nor do I,' she said.

Their eyes met and they both burst out laughing.

'We are a pair!' Nell grinned. 'I'll take pictures of the boats, the men and the gear, and then you can see if they fit in with what you're going to write.'

'OK. And save the second reel of film for when the ships return in the morning.'

'Good idea.' Nell stepped back and took a general view of the three drifters with smoke beginning to rise from their stacks. She moved in closer then and took pictures of the bows so that she had the names of the ships clearly visible. She started to take photographs of the gear and the men at work. When they reached the *Lively Lady*, Ewan looked up from the net he was examining and struck a silly pose.

'Cut it out, Ewan,' yelled an annoyed Nell. 'This is serious work. I don't want to waste film.'

He laughed. 'Serious work? I've never seen you with a camera before.'

'Well, you're seeing me now.' The tone of her voice warned him to tread carefully.

He held up his hands in surrender. 'All right, all right.'

'Carry on working but look at the camera with a nice smile.'

'Yes, miss,' he mocked, but did as he was told.

'That could be a good one,' commented Nell to Jane.

'Let's get one of Simon.'

'Hold on.' Nell swung round and clicked the shutter. She had seen Mr Steel looking out of the wheelhouse, cap at a jaunty angle and smoking his pipe. 'Must have the skipper with his cap on. Now, Simon.'

They moved on to the *Silver King*. Simon was at the bow, checking that the deck was clear for him to take in the bow rope when they cast off.

'Simon, fold your arms and lean on the bow,' called Nell.

He grinned. 'And strike a pose as if I'm looking into the distance so you can interpret my good looks?'

'The idea for the pose is a good one, but don't fool around.'

'Very good, miss.' He touched his forehead in mock salute then took up the pose. Nell altered her position three times before she found the angle she wanted. Crouching down, she made the shot so that Simon stood out against the background of the sky with just enough of the bow visible in the picture to show he was on board a ship.

'Thanks, Simon,' called Nell.

'A pleasure.' He gave a little bow. Nell moved away then to take some more pictures. 'What's this all about?' he asked Jane.

'She's illustrating some articles I'm going to write. I'll

want a lot of information and Nell told me you're a mine of it.'

'It will be a pleasure to tell you what I know. Talk when I get back.'

'I'll be here then.'

'What? It would lighten my lonely work to think of you waiting on the quay for me,' he replied with an edge to his words.

Jane smiled. 'Flirt! I expect you're like every other sailor.' He grinned but before he could say more she added, 'I'd better go. Have a safe voyage and a good catch. See you in the morning.' She felt his eyes on her as she walked away to join Nell.

'Now what?' asked Jane.

'I think I've got all I want at the present but we'll have some shots of the drifters leaving port, which I reckon should be in about three-quarters of an hour.'

'Let's go and get a cup of tea at that café over there.' Jane indicated a building across the roadway. 'We can keep our eyes on any developments from there.'

A couple were leaving a table in the window so Nell went straight to it while Jane purchased tea and a piece of cake each. They were enjoying their second cup when Nell said, 'I think we had better go.' Jane glanced across to the harbour and saw the activity around the three drifters had increased. They left the remaining tea in their cups and hurried from the café. Crossing the road, they saw members of the three families had come to see their menfolk sail. Greetings were shouted, messages given, without interrupting the work.

Mrs Franklin eyed the camera and shot a querying glance at her daughter. Nell offered a quick explanation and finished by saying, 'I must get shots of the drifters leaving. Come on, Jane.'

Before she could move away, Jane grabbed her arm. 'A moment! Get a couple of shots of the men casting off.'

Nell aimed her camera then they raced off and were in a

good position by the time the drifters were moving. The *Sea Queen* was first. George Franklin in the wheelhouse, issuing orders in a precise and commanding voice, his eyes everywhere, nevertheless found a moment to wave to his daughter and read her mouthed reply, 'Safe voyage, Dad.' Nell's camera clicked, capturing his action as he pointed to something and then she got the moment the *Sea Queen*'s bow cut the first wave to send a feathery white stream of water swishing along her sides.

As the *Lively Lady* approached, Nell got a perfect picture of Ewan in the bow as he waved to them, a broad grin on his face.

'He's full of life,' commented Jane as they responded to his gesture. 'He looks to be in love with his job. I can hardly believe what you told me about him wanting to give it up.'

Nell smiled. 'A lot of that's for the benefit of his father, but he does enjoy it for now. His attitude is: make the most of what you've got and where you are, but keep an open mind, ready to make and take decisions about what you want from life.'

'An attitude to be commended,' replied Jane. 'I believe he thinks a lot of you.'

'And I of him.'

Jane, wondering if there was a veiled 'Keep off' behind Nell's admission, said, 'I think Simon does too.'

'Well, we've all been friends since childhood,' she replied dismissively and changed the subject quickly as the *Silver King* neared them. Her camera clicked. The third drifter met the sea and set a course astern of her two companions. The girls watched the boats grow smaller and smaller against the wide expanse of sea.

Jane analysed her feelings and wondered if they equated with those of the families. But how could they? She had no one on board, heading into the vagaries of a sea that could turn killer at any time. What motivated men to tackle such a dangerous trade? She was beginning to see great potential in the subject of the drifters and the men who sailed them. If only her writing could match the power of the subject. At that moment a new determination overcame her. She would see that it did! This could be an important moment in her life, and it had started the instant she'd trapped a ball bouncing on the harbourside.

The two girls joined Nell's mother who had waited for them.

'Come and have a meal with us, Jane?' she offered.

'Thank you, Mrs Franklin. It is kind of you but my aunt and uncle will be expecting me.'

'She wants to see her new typewriter,' teased Nell.

Jane smiled. 'No, that's not the main reason but ...'

'No need to make excuses,' grinned Nell. 'I'd do the same. See you here in the morning.'

'You two getting up to see the drifters return?' asked Flo Franklin, a little surprised by her daughter's early rising.

'Pictures to take, Mum,' she replied. 'Tell you about it as we walk.' She told Jane, 'See you then. Don't be late.'

'I won't.'

The following morning Jane was up early and moved around the house quietly as she dressed, got a quick breakfast and left Scholes Park Road on her bicycle. She was thankful she had decided to put on a thicker jacket because when she reached the promenade she felt a bite in the freshening wind coming from the sea. She hoped it did not get any stronger otherwise the drifters would encounter a higher sea than was running at present. She saw no one as she pedalled along Royal Albert Drive and the Marine Drive below towering cliffs that in the dour early-morning light seemed more threatening than usual.

She focused her mind on the previous evening and the thrill of showing her typewriter to her uncle and aunt and then trying it out. The first words she put on the paper were 'THE DRIFTERMEN'. She had been longing to go further but had decided that for the moment it would be as well to write her thoughts in pencil until she had become a more proficient typist.

As she turned on to the quay she saw a lone figure standing close to a wall, seeking shelter from the wind. The figure straightened up when Jane neared.

'Hi!' Jane tried to put some enthusiasm in her voice as she jumped from her bicycle and propped it against the wall. She reckoned she had had the better of the bargain, for she was reasonably warm from her ride whereas Nell was shivering.

'It's a bit cold!' wailed her friend. 'I could still have been in bed.'

'You're here in a good cause.' The brightness Jane tried to generate was lost on her friend.

'I suppose so.' She looked skywards. 'Wish the wind would drive the clouds away and give us a better light.'

'Remember what my uncle told you about allowing for poor light.'

'How come you never took up photography?'

'Never showed any interest so I suppose my uncle never pushed it.'

'Your father was never interested?'

'No. His only interests were work and the pub.'

Nell waited but Jane offered no more. They lapsed into silence, drawing their jackets closer around them.

'Another half hour.' Nell broke the silence after a glance at her watch.

'How do you know that?' queried Jane.

'If they aren't in by then, they'll miss the best prices,' Nell pointed out, indicating the vans coming along the foreshore road. It was then Jane noticed activity around the buildings along the fish quay and realised the buyers were moving in ready to make their bids once they had seen the quality and size of the catches.

'Would you have come if you hadn't been taking photographs?' Jane asked.

Nell was silent a moment and then gave a reply that was

not altogether convincing. 'Maybe not, I'm on holiday.'

'That sounds as if you always meet them when they're fishing out of Lowestoft.'

'Part of my job.'

'And it's not here?'

'Dad lets me off when we are on holiday.' Nell paused and gave a little grin. 'Are you tucking away information for your writing?'

'Yes. I've a couple of angles I'd like to work on, but they might depend on your photographs and what I learn from Simon and the rest of the men. And I'd like to get a skipper's views on the herring industry.'

'You'd best talk to Dad about that because he's been in the trade all his life, but like I said talk to Simon first. You'll get a good solid foundation about the industry from him and then you can fill in with more details from my father.' Nell glanced at her watch. 'We'd better be making our way to the harbour entrance. I'd like some shots from the position we were in when they left.'

They moved away from the shelter of the wall and tried to snuggle further into their jackets when they felt the bite in the wind. It matched the cold light that was spreading from the east as clouds tried to smother any warmth the sun was willing to bestow upon sea and land.

Though the camera was held by a black strap around her neck, Nell also held it with her right hand as if fearing it would shake itself loose and be lost forever.

As soon as their vision reached beyond the harbour, she cried out in a tone that was a mixture of relief and excitement; relief that the men were safely home, excitement about what the catch would bring. 'There!'

Jane saw three sets of lights bobbing in the distance; three ships heading for port, fishermen coming home. She had not realised until that moment how much anxiety had built up in her. What must it have been like for Nell who had relatives and boy friends pitting themselves against the unforgiving sea? Jane had no one. Or had she been

36

concerned for Ewan and Simon?

'Can it be them?' she asked anxiously.

'Could be! Hope so, then they'll beat the Scottish boats, sell their catch first and get the best price.'

More lights appeared on the horizon. The girls were tense until Nell, recognising the vessels, yelled, 'It's them!'

The first suddenly seemed to be upon them; turning into the harbour, meeting the calmer water, relieved to be free from the heaving waves. Nell clicked several times. This was the *Sea Queen* and she wanted a good record of the first time she had photographed her arrival. She caught sight of her father gesticulating then.

'A reasonable catch,' she said to Jane.

She stored in her memory all the activity: the way Mr Franklin manoeuvred his boat until she came to rest alongside the quay; the orders he shouted and the crew's response, which gave the impression that they knew exactly what was coming and what to do.

They watched the *Lively Lady* and the *Silver King* find places at the quay, too, receiving only quick responses from Ewan and Simon when they saw the girls on the quay; successful docking required concentration. Unloading the boxes of fish from the *Sea Queen* was already underway and the catches from the other two soon followed. Nell noted every movement with her camera and was glad Mr Harvey had supplied her with a second film. She followed the fish into the huge shed where boxes were spread across the floor under the blazing roof lights, and finished off her film by taking pictures of the auction.

Above the clatter and chatter Jane tried to follow the words of the man who was auctioning the fish but it was a new and mysterious world to her, whereas to everyone else it was normal. They instantly knew what fish was being sold, what price it had made and who had bought it. But she recognised good material here for an article on another aspect of the herring industry. Coupled with what she already had in mind, she was beginning to envisage a series. She brought herself up short with a jolt as the burning question bit into her mind: Could she do justice to all this in words? In answer to her own question she said aloud, 'I can and I will!'

'Talking to yourself now – that's a bad sign. Maybe I should do something about it?'

Startled, she turned her head to see Ewan beside her. Jane blushed at being caught out but quickly gathered her composure and replied, 'And what do you think you can do about it?'

'Well, take you to the pictures.' His smile added a query to the statement.

'You'll want to be away to your bed after a night's fishing and be ready to sail again tonight.'

'I can set my alarm and fit in the afternoon matinee before we sail.'

She shook her head. 'Can't be done. I'll be busy the rest of the day.'

He put on a mock display of being crestfallen but quickly hid it when Nell came up behind them, something Jane noted with interest and, therefore, made no mention of his invitation.

'Did all go well?' Nell asked.

'Yes, but I'll tell you what, I've known better.'

'Prices are average. Dad will make a profit so he can't grumble. He'd like a better haul tonight.'

Simon joined them then. 'Are we going across the road, Ewan?'

'Can't miss Mrs Wesley's Yorkshire breakfast when we're in Scarborough,' he replied.

'You girls coming with us?' asked Simon.

'Love to,' Jane answered. 'I want something to put the warmth back.' She glanced at Nell who was nodding. 'Then we can go straight to my uncle's with the films.'

'Will he be there this early?'

'Oh, yes! He likes to get on with films brought in yesterday. He knows people like to see them as soon as possible.'

'Now there's a job,' said Ewan, a trace of envy in his voice. 'Feet on solid ground, better than tumbling around on a heaving ship.'

'Get on with you, Ewan, you know you'd miss it.'

'No, I wouldn't. Stormy waters, smelly fish. I should never have gone into it.'

'Couldn't escape, it was in your blood.'

'It was never in my blood, not like Dad and Walter, but I couldn't escape the family tradition and expectations. Never mind, one day I will.'

This line of conversation ceased when they reached Mrs Wesley's café and they all exchanged warm greetings with a stout lady in her late-fifties. She had opened this café in her twenties and her traditional breakfasts for returning seamen had become legendary.

They had just sat down when two of Mrs Wesley's young assistants put steaming mugs of tea in front of them. The girls moved away and Mrs Wesley was there beside them.

'Welcome home.' She gave the fishermen a broad smile. 'You've beaten the Scottish lads back.' She nodded in the direction of the harbour where the boats were now crowding in. 'How's Lowestoft these days, and how was the cricket?'

Ewan chuckled. 'Never forget a face, do you?'

'Never, and I've a good memory for facts. Saw your boats come in the other day and thought, My Lowestoft men are here for the cricket. And as that was over yesterday and I saw you sail yesterday evening, I was expecting you this morning.' She turned to Jane then. 'A new face. From what I heard when you came in you aren't from Lowestoft.'

Jane returned her smile. 'Middlesbrough, Mrs Wesley.'

'No formalities here, love. I'm Bet to my friends, and if you're with this lot from Lowestoft then you're a friend and just as welcome.' She winked. 'Now, is it the full one?'

'It is that,' said Ewan.

'The lot,' said Simon. 'The sea makes me hungry.'

39

'And you, young ladies?' Bet raised a questioning eyebrow.

Nell nodded.

Jane said, 'I've got to try it. I've been standing out there waiting for the boats coming in.'

'You'll love it,' beamed Bet, pleased that Jane was going to match the others.

As they waited, enjoying the warmth of the tea, the rest of the Lowestoft crews came in, chaffing each other with their banter. The three skippers took a table to themselves.

'That'll be fish talk,' commented Ewan quietly with a nod in their direction. 'With Dad it's fish, morning, noon and night. You'd think there was nothing else on earth.'

Jane detected a note of disgust in his voice. 'He must have an interest in cricket, he was at the match,' she said in Mr Steel's defence.

'Yes, well,' mumbled Ewan dismissively.

Jane's eyes widened when a plate was put in front of her: two fried eggs, three rashers of bacon, a sausage, a piece of fried bread, two fried tomatoes and a slice of black pudding were displayed on it. She thought she would never eat it all but matched the vigorous appetites of the two men, mindful that she'd snatched only a small early breakfast and that the sharp early-morning air had made her hungry. Finally she sank back in her chair feeling very satisfied. A few minutes later when all their plates were empty they were cleared away and a mountain of toast, butter and marmalade was placed on the table.

'Goodness me!' gasped Jane.

Simon laughed. 'You should see your face. We'll have to clear this lot or Bet will take offence.' He held the plate of toast towards Jane.

'Thanks. It does look delicious.'

'It will be. Bet knows how to get it just right.'

Ewan and Nell had fallen into conversation so Jane took the opportunity to ask Simon if he would help her with information about the fishing.

'I'd be delighted,' he replied. 'Think up what you want to know, but we'll only have tomorrow and Saturday. The ships will be heading for Grimsby on Sunday.'

'Oh, dear, I hadn't thought of that, and I want to see the photographs Nell has taken first.'

'When will you see them?'

'Later today, I hope. It depends how much work my uncle has on. Nell and I are going to see him when we leave here.'

'We can start tomorrow even if the photos aren't ready. Will you be here again in the morning?'

'Wouldn't miss it.'

'Even though it was so cold for you today?'

'I'll put up with anything for a breakfast like this.'

'Oh, not to see me return then?' Simon feigned disappointment.

'Maybe Ewan,' teased Jane. As soon as the words were out she wished he hadn't heard them; she had seen that momentary flash of jealousy flare in Simon's eyes again. Was that because she had posed Ewan as his rival for her or because Ewan was giving so much attention to Nell? To ease the tension she sensed in Simon, she said, 'And, of course, you.' Then she quickly added, 'Nell, I think we'd better be going. If we want to see the photos today we'd best be getting the film to my uncle.' She turned back to Simon. 'See you in the morning, no matter what the weather.'

'And bring your questions,' he replied, rising to his feet. 'But won't you see us sail this evening?'

'Of course she will,' put in Nell, seeing the possibilities here of a romance that might enable her to make a decision about where her own feelings truly lay. The three of them had been close companions all their lives and she had never been able to decide which man was dearest to her. One day it was Ewan, another Simon. She was torn between outgoing, restless Ewan who would seek new horizons if he could, and solid dependable Simon who loved the sea and the trade in

41

which he had been brought up. It was a trade she knew, and in which she respected family tradition, but was that what she wanted for her own future? Would a romance between Jane and Simon focus her mind on the man she wanted so that she could go for him, no matter what?

'I thought you might bring the films in soon after the drifters returned so I came in early to get some other work out of the way,' said David as he let them into his premises. 'How did you get on?'

'Well, I hope,' replied Nell, 'but the proof remains to be seen. I took both films. I hope that's not too many for you to deal with?'

David laughed. 'Not at all! That's simple compared to the numbers I have to deal with during the holiday period. August was very busy for me but business in developing and printing is tailing off now there are not so many holidaymakers about because the children are back at school. Right, let's have them.' He took the films from Nell. 'Come back at two o'clock this afternoon.'

It was with impatience that the girls watched the minutes tick by as they wandered about the town, window shopping, chatting aimlessly, pausing to have a morning coffee and then deciding to have something more substantial at midday, a meal which they purposely dragged out before returning to see if Jane's uncle had completed his task. It was with excitement and not a little trepidation that they pushed open the shop door.

Maureen flashed them a warm smile when she glanced up from the customer she was serving to see who had entered the shop. She indicated for them to go straight through to the room behind the shop. There they found Jane's uncle gathering up photographs from a large table in the centre of the room.

'Ah,' he smiled his greeting. 'I thought you'd be here dead on two so when I saw the quality of the negatives, I left everything else and pressed on with printing your films.' He paused.

'And?' prompted Jane, recognising a deliberate, teasing hesitation.

'Wait a moment. Let me clear the rest of these photographs from the table.' He smiled to himself as he did so; he could sense the girls' impatience though they were too polite to voice it. He put the pile to one side then said, 'I won't be a moment,' before disappearing into another room.

The two girls exchanged nervous glances but said nothing.

When David returned he was carrying a batch of prints, the top one covered by a sheet of tissue paper. He laid the pile on the table.

Nell stared at them in amazement. 'Did I take that many?'

'Two films each of thirty-six exposures makes seventy-two. Yes, young lady, you were extremely busy.'

'Not I, Mr Harvey, you. I'm sorry if I caused you so much work.'

David smiled. 'Ah, but I wasn't out in the open, in the chill, like you. I was tucked inside the darkroom. And I didn't do all these by myself. I had my two assistants working flat out so you could see them now. I knew how keen you would be to see your first efforts.' He removed the paper to reveal a picture of the *Sea Queen*.

No one spoke. David took away the next sheet of tissue paper. Nell's father, pipe in mouth, stared out of the wheelhouse. David worked through the pile one after the other, laying each print carefully aside without comment after it had been viewed. All he heard were the occasional gasps from one or other of the girls, little grunts of pleasure or a small moan of disappointment.

When he had shown the last one, Jane said, 'Well, Uncle David, what do you think?' She had formed her own opinion but wanted his; needed to hear the voice of an expert for she knew her uncle prided himself on the pictures he took and that he was highly regarded as a photographer in Scarborough.

'I think, for a first-timer, Nell has done exceedingly well. She will improve as she becomes used to the camera and takes more and more pictures.'

'You really think so, Mr Harvey?' said Nell, taking his words as praise indeed. She had never expected this.

'I know so, but you will only improve by working at it, and that will only happen if you want to.'

'I want to, Mr Harvey, I really do, especially if it will help Jane with her writing.'

'I think the photographs would help, as long as my writing is up to scratch,' said Jane.

'That too will only come with practice. Have you anything specific in mind?'

'Well, I was going to put something together about the herring industry. These photographs suggest a number of different angles. I've sounded out Simon Evans, one of the fishermen, for help.'

'He's the son of the owner of the *Silver King*,' explained Nell. 'Brought up in herring fishing.'

'These photos suggest articles about the men and their jobs, the boats, the methods and so on.' An eager excitement had come into Jane's voice.

'Hold on, you two,' laughed David. 'Don't get carried away. Mustn't run before you can walk. I think we should take a closer look at these photos. Most of them are good, one or two outstanding.' He paused then said, 'Jane, you didn't tell me Nell had an eye for a picture.'

'I didn't know she had,' replied Jane. 'How could I, we only met two days ago?'

'Of course.' David smiled at his own stupidity and eyed Nell. 'You have, young lady.'

'Maybe that's because I've always liked drawing,' she offered.

David raised an eyebrow. 'No doubt. Well, we'll see which of these photos you should use very soon, and then

44

decide which angle Jane should pursue. When do you return to Lowestoft, Nell?'

'Sunday.'

'Thursday today so we haven't very long,' mused David. 'What are you doing now?'

'We planned nothing, Uncle,' said Jane, 'except to see the drifters sail again this evening.'

'Right, supposing we look at these photos now?'

'But I expect you're busy, Mr Harvey,' said Nell.

'I have got a little time in hand so let's have a look.'

Within an hour the pictures had been sorted into those that David said could be used in the immediate future, those which he thought he could improve in the darkroom and those which he rejected but whose subjects could make a good picture if taken again from a different viewpoint. David explained his criticisms in such a way that Nell felt she was learning all the time.

'Now, we'll take the ones that could be used immediately and divide them into possible subjects.' Within a few minutes the particular aspect that was most photographed and therefore offered an immediate subject to Jane was 'Preparing to Leave'. Here were various activities that could form a story about the start of a fishing voyage.

They studied this in more detail and each made suggestions, finally deciding to take some more photographs of the fishermen coming on board and then of the drifters leaving harbour.

'Use my camera again,' David instructed, 'so that you keep to the same picture quality. And here are two more films. Though I think one will suffice, use both if you think it best. Then let me have them first thing in the morning after which we will meet up here again at two o'clock to make the final selection. It is up to you, Jane, to get all the relevant information to write your article on this subject.'

'I'll contact Simon and see what he says, Uncle,' she said. 'And thank you for all you've done today.'

45

'Yes, indeed, Mr Harvey.' Nell gave a little laugh. 'Isn't it all exciting?'

David chuckled. 'It's a pleasure to help two such charming and enthusiastic young ladies.'

Jane and Nell were in high spirits when they left the shop.

'I should see Simon as soon as possible,' said Jane.

'Then let's go and find him.'

'You know where he'll be?'

'More than likely at the cottage his parents rent for this visit. He'll be taking it easy before sailing.'

They found Simon sitting on the doorstep, enjoying the sun and reading the sports page of the *Yorkshire Post*. He jumped to his feet when he saw them and his face broke into a broad smile.

'This is a treat,' he enthused. 'Come in. Mum will put the kettle on.'

'Hold on, Simon,' laughed Nell, 'we're here for a purpose.'

He glanced askance from one to the other and then Jane quickly explained the reason for their visit. 'So can you help?' she finished.

'Of course! Look, the best idea is if we go to the boat. I'm about ready . . . just need my gansey and bag. Doesn't matter if I'm early, and I can explain things better there.'

'But we're taking your shore time,' Jane protested.

'It's my pleasure,' he replied. 'You coming too, Nell?'

'Yes.'

'Good.'

Jane noted the extra sparkle that had come into his eyes at Nell's agreement.

'I'm going to take some more pictures,' she said.

'Then I'd better look my handsome best.' He grinned and winked at her. 'Don't you think so, Jane?'

'Naturally.'

'Won't be long.' With that he disappeared into the house and the two girls sat down on the step to wait.

'He's in love with you,' whispered Jane.

Nell looked astonished. 'Get on. He can't be.'

'It's true. I saw it in his eyes when we arrived, and the way he spoke when you said you were coming to the harbour confirmed it.'

'It's just your imagination.'

Nell shook her head slowly but there was a certain lack of conviction behind it that made Jane think. Then the other girl said, 'No, we're just very good friends. Have been all our lives. We all grew up together, us and Ewan.'

Jane read a challenge to her in the way that Nell spoke Ewan's name.

'Oh, my,' she said lightly, 'the dreaded eternal triangle.'

Nell was about to contradict her but saw the teasing twinkle in Jane's eyes, even though her observation had been delivered with a serious undercurrent in her voice. Nell held her tongue and at that moment Simon appeared and the line of conversation was blocked, but it had given Nell something to think about.

From upstairs in the next-door cottage, in a state of undress as he prepared for the evening sailing, Ewan glanced out of the window. He stopped, shirt half on, eyes fixed on the three people walking away.

Nell! His eyes settled on her slim figure. Trim, he thought, a waist you could span and curves that enticed; a fine pair of legs, a smile that could set the pulses racing and lips that were a joy to taste. Next his eyes wandered to Jane. He wondered what her lips were like? She was not bad-looking, in fact, attractive, but in a different way from Nell . . . He recalled the sparkle he had noted in her eyes and wondered what would happen if he made a pass at her. Maybe he would find out. Or maybe Simon had his eye on her. They passed out of sight then and Ewan resumed dressing.

At the harbour, Nell went off to take the photographs she wanted.

'Before giving you details on preparations for sailing I'd better give you an overview of the industry,' Simon started to tell Jane. 'It's a tough trade, make no mistake about that. Unfortunately the great days of herring fishing are over. The best year was 1913, but the Great War altered things forever. Little fishing was done during the war years as most drifters were taken by the Admiralty for war duties.'

'With so little fishing, wasn't there plenty of herring after the war?' Jane queried.

'Yes, hopes were high, but the European markets that were there before the war disappeared in the subsequent economic upheaval. Decline set in, and with demand lessening many drifters left the trade.'

'But your father, Mr Steel and Mr Franklin still make a living. Or I presume they do, otherwise why continue?'

'The three of them were brought up as herring fishers. They've been determined to try and ride out the decline, believing they could take up the trade renounced by other owners, but things are looking less and less rosy. In fact, I know they've discussed selling their vessels and forming a partnership to buy a single big trawler.'

'Wouldn't that be the same?'

Simon smiled and shook his head. 'Not at all. They wouldn't fish for herring then but for other fish: cod, haddock, and so on. It would mean longer voyages to more distant waters. They haven't really got down to serious discussions yet. I think they still hope the herring, the "silver darlings", will pay off. And I think they are hesitating because of the political situation in Europe.'

'They think there could be another war?'

'Who knows?' Simon shrugged his shoulders. 'Now, we'd better get down to the material you need for your article.'

After hearing what she was trying to do he was considerate in his explanations, careful not to use too many technical terms. Jane listened intently, fascinated by his Suffolk accent, taking notes as he went along. They

48

approached the subject seriously but light-heartedly enough to enjoy what they were doing. A rapport soon flourished between them.

'How are you two getting on?' asked Nell when she rejoined them.

'Fine.' Jane smiled. 'I've plenty of material here to link with your pictures of the start of the voyage.'

'I look forward to seeing those,' said Simon.

'Then you shall.' Nell turned to Jane. 'What about the other angles you were thinking of?'

'I haven't broached those yet.' She glanced a little sheepishly at Simon.

'Come on, what's this?' he prompted.

'Well, I have other aspects of the herring fishing I'd like to write about but I'll need more help with background information.'

'Well, I'd be only too pleased to help, but on Sunday we head south. I'd have more time in Lowestoft and I tell you what, it would also be a pleasure if you were there . . .'

'Come to Lowestoft with us,' put in Nell quickly.

'Oh, I couldn't . . .' But Jane's mind was already considering the possibility so it was only a half-hearted protest.

'You could stay with us,' pressed Nell. 'We've a spare room. Then you'd be on hand to get all the information you want. I'll get Dad to buy me a camera and then I can take more photographs. We can work closely together, maybe on other projects if we get a chance – no, we'll *make* those chances ourselves by showing we are a good team.'

Chapter Three

Nell's suggestion sparked off all sorts of possibilities in Jane's mind. She realised this was the first time since leaving Middlesbrough that there had seemed to be a direction in her life. She had been happy enough with her uncle and aunt who could not have been kinder. Certainly without their help and love she dreaded to think what might have happened. But she had realised of late that she must do something with her life; she could not just let it drift. Was this the opportunity she needed? If so she must grasp it and turn it to her advantage.

Nell was offering her a chance, but what did Jane really know of her? Their association had been brief yet it seemed they had been friends forever, and Jane's uncle and aunt too had taken to Nell in the short time they had known her. But what would they say to Jane moving to Lowestoft? There was only one way to find out.

'Well, what do you think?' Nell prompted her.

Jane's eyes sparkled. 'It sounds exciting. Maybe an opportunity not to be missed.'

'Of course it is. If we don't try, we'll never know,' Nell enthused. 'Come on, say yes?'

'But ...'

'No buts,' cut in Nell.

'We don't know what your mother and father will say, for one thing.'

'They'll agree.'

'But what about your job with your father?'

'Oh, I can do that along with this.'

'You make it sound easy.'

'It is.'

'I've got to find out what my uncle and aunt think first.'

'Ask them then.'

'Do you really want to do this?' Jane was a little cautious.

'Definitely,' Nell said vehemently. She had been fired up by Mr Harvey's favourable comments about her photographs, especially when he had said she had an eye for a picture.

'All right, I'll ask them.'

'Good. This is exciting!'

Spontaneously the girls hugged each other, laughter on their lips, joy in their hearts. They were embarking on an adventure, and beneath it burned a desire to succeed in a new direction in their lives.

'You two look like cats who've had the cream!' Ewan's arrival startled them. 'What's the celebration?'

'We're going to work together,' replied Nell.

'Doing what?'

'Jane's going to write and I'm going to take photographs to illustrate her articles.'

'You think it's going to be that easy?'

'Don't be such a damp squib.' Nell's tone held a little hostility.

'We don't think it will be easy, but you get nowhere without trying,' put in Jane, her own tone sharp as well.

'Go on then, amuse yourselves. See you when I get back.' Ewan swung up the gangway on to the ship.

'What's got into him?' asked Jane.

Nell pulled a face. 'He gets like this sometimes when he's off on a fishing trip. Something else might have upset him.' She shrugged her shoulders. 'He'll get over it. Have you got the information you want?'

'I think I can make something out of it now. You are coming with me after you've got the pictures of the drifters leaving port? I might need your support when I broach the subject of leaving.'

'Oh, perhaps I shouldn't,' replied Nell hesitantly. 'It could look like a conspiracy if I did.'

Jane smiled. 'Well, isn't it?'

Nell picked up on the humour and chuckled. 'Come on, then, let's do it.' The girls linked arms and set off for Scholes Park Road.

When she heard the front door open, Mavis came out of the kitchen. 'Hello, you two, had a good day?'

'Yes, thanks,' replied Jane, and Nell confirmed it.

'You'll stay to a meal, Nell? It will be ready in a quarter of an hour.'

'Thank you, Mrs Harvey, that is kind.'

'Go into the front room. Your uncle's in there, Jane.'

When they went in after shedding their outdoor clothes, David laid down his newspaper and greeted them warmly.

'I've used those two films, Mr Harvey.' Nell handed them to him.

'Good. You're not losing any time, are you? I'll have them done as soon as I get into work in the morning.'

'I hope they'll be OK,' she said anxiously.

'I'm sure they will if they are up to those you have already done. What about you, Jane, have you gathered material for your article?'

'Yes, and I'm dying to start putting something down on paper.'

'A pity you haven't any typewriting skills, but they'll come, I suppose.'

'I'll practise, but in the meantime I'll use pencil and paper.'

'We must arrange some lessons for you ...'

Jane was saved from replying at what she saw as an awkward moment when her aunt appeared to inform them

52

that the meal was ready. As they rose from their chairs Jane and Nell exchanged relieved glances.

Throughout the delicious meal the conversation was light, but Nell casually gave out information about herself and her family, hoping it would ease the way when Jane put her query to her uncle and aunt. She did that when they were enjoying a cup of tea and chocolate biscuits after the pudding plates had been cleared away.

'Aunty Mavis, Uncle David, I have something to ask you.' Jane glanced apprehensively from one to the other. 'I . . .' She hesitated.

'Go on, lass, spit it out,' her uncle said with an encouraging smile.

She bit her lip and then said, 'Nell wants me to go to Lowestoft with her when her family leaves on Sunday.'

'That's very kind of her,' replied Mavis. 'Has her mother made the invitation?'

Nell looked embarrassed. 'No, Mrs Harvey, I invited Jane, but I'm sure Mother will agree.'

'Well, you would have to have her permission first, Jane.'

'I know, Aunt, but there is a little more to it than that . . .'

Mavis glanced at her niece with curiosity. 'Well, what is it?'

The next moment words came pouring out of Jane as she explained what she and Nell had in mind. There was no stopping her, and no one tried. Her uncle and aunt realised it was best for her to get everything out without interruption. The last words came with a sigh of relief: 'There, that's it.' She looked anxiously from one to the other and noticed Nell give her a smile. For a few moments a charged silence filled the room.

From the look that David gave her, Mavis knew he wanted her to reveal what she felt before he said anything.

'Well, this is a complete surprise. We didn't expect anything like this. I don't really know what to say. We thought you seemed to be settling down with us ...' She paused to calm the tremor that had come into her voice.

Jane felt a tug at her heart. Seeing her aunt's eyes dampening she quickly tried to allay any doubt that might have sprung into Mavis's mind. 'Aunt, please don't think I haven't been happy with you. I have, and I will always be grateful for what you have done for me. I can never repay all your kindness and love, and I don't want to lose those things in any way.'

Mavis nodded. 'I know. And we are very grateful to you for being the daughter we never had. You have filled a gap in our lives, and whatever you do in the future you will always be welcome here and part of our lives. I think both David and I knew that some day you would want to move on, but even though we expected it, it still comes as a shock. Lowestoft seems so far away.'

'Not all that far, Aunty. There's a good train service and I'll come to see you often. Maybe Nell will come too.'

'Of course I will, Mrs Harvey.'

Mavis gave a wan smile as if to say promises weren't always fulfilled. But then, realising that to give her niece her love and approval would draw her closer, she said, 'You have our permission. We won't stand in your way, if this is what you want to do.'

Jane jumped from her chair and hugged her aunt. 'Thank you for understanding.'

Mavis smiled and pursed her lips in a kiss.

As she returned to her chair, Jane glanced at her uncle and was relieved to see his approving smile.

'I agree with all your aunt has said. Now we haven't a lot of time, so first things first.' He looked at Nell. 'You must get your parents' permission. After all, it is going to affect their lives. Another person in the house can make a lot of difference. They may not want that.'

'I'm sure they will agree, Mr Harvey,' replied Nell.

'That may be so, but you must ask. Will your father be sailing Saturday evening, or is he one of those who won't

54

fish on a Sunday?'

Nell smiled. 'You're right, Mr Harvey, Father won't fish on a Sunday. There's strong superstition among some fisherfolk.' She glanced at Jane. 'Ewan's fallen out many a time with his father over this, but Simon wouldn't put a net down on a Sunday.'

'Right, if your father's going to be here on Saturday, I suggest he and your mother come to a meal with us. Say, six o'clock?' David saw the nod of agreement from his wife.

'That is extremely kind of you,' said Nell. 'I know they would be happy to meet you.'

'Very well! That's settled then. And provided they approve of your ideas, then of course we won't stand in Jane's way. We have been anxious to see her make a success of her life, after all. Jane, we will do all we can to help you. I think we could get down to some practicalities now, in advance of Nell's mother's and father's agreement to your going.'

'Thank you,' she said, going over to give him a quick kiss. 'I think you deserve that,' she laughed.

'And I think we all deserve another cup of tea,' said Mavis. She picked up the teapot and headed for the kitchen.

'When you talked about trying writing in one form or another and we got you a typewriter, I suggested you should take lessons and learn to touch type,' David told his niece. 'If you go to Lowestoft and stay with Nell's family, I suggest you still take lessons. Find someone to teach you and I will pay for whatever is necessary.'

'Oh, Uncle, you are too good to me!' There was a catch in Jane's voice.

'No, it is our pleasure. Who knows? We may be encouraging one of the great writers of the twentieth century!' Then he turned to Nell. 'Did you just concentrate on details of the pre-voyage aspects rather than general scenes?'

'Yes, I thought that best after our chat.'

'Quite right! If these are as good as the ones we have

already picked out then you will have an attractive spread to submit with Jane's first piece. And you both intend to work this article into a series, dealing with drifters and the herring fishing?'

'Yes.'

'That will mean more photographs then. I'll provide the film, processing and prints at no cost. It would be silly, you spending money on that in Lowestoft when I can easily do it for you.' He saw this as a means of seeing them more often, too.

The girls gasped in appreciation.

'I will only print those I think best suited to the angle Jane is taking. You will have to keep me informed, Jane.'

'I will.'

'Now what I suggest is that you work on this first article and then bring it, the photographs and yourselves to see the editor of the *Scarborough Evening News*. I know the gentleman in question, having done photographic work for him on occasion. I will get you an introduction when the article is ready. But,' David raised a warning finger here, 'it will only be an introduction. Don't expect any favours. Journalism and writing don't work that way. Anything you two show him will have to be of an acceptable standard. And, looking ahead, a word of warning: when your first piece is accepted, don't expect it to be easy to sell the second. That is often the hardest thing to do. You must maintain the standard of the first, if not improve upon it. The same applies to both writing and photography.' David leaned back in his chair then, pleased that the girls had been so attentive. 'Now, are there any questions?'

There was a moment's silence. Finally Nell spoke. 'This is so generous of you, Mr Harvey. We won't let you down.'

He smiled at her sincerity. 'I know my wife approves. It will give us great pleasure to see what you both make of this, especially if you are successful.'

'We will be, Mr Harvey, have no doubt about that.

Won't we, Jane?'

'Definitely. You'll be proud of us,' she added with conviction.

'Oh, there's one more thing.' David rose and went out of the room, to return a moment later with the camera he had loaned to Nell and which she had placed on the hall table when they arrived. 'Though you have not had a great deal of time with this, you will have grown used to certain features so I want you to have it.'

Nell gasped, 'Mr Harvey, I couldn't.'

'You can and you will,' he replied. 'This is the camera I have been using myself so I know it will be good for you.'

'But I can't take *your* camera.'

'Yes, you can. I have another on order, that will be mine when it arrives. And don't forget, I'm here if you want any more advice.'

Nell stared at him in astonishment, hardly able to believe what was happening to her. Then she leaped to her feet, tears of joy flowing down her cheeks, and hugged and kissed him. 'Oh, I'm sorry,' she said finally, blushing at her own daring.

David laughed at her embarrassment. 'Don't be, it was nice to be kissed by such a charming young lady.' He winked at her. 'Put it right. Give Mrs Harvey a kiss too.'

Nell laughed and did so. 'Thank you. I have found a wonderful friend in your niece, Mrs Harvey.' Her kiss lingered on Mavis's cheek.

She patted Nell's hand. 'This all sounds very exciting, but don't forget, see what your parents have to say first.'

'I'll ask Mother as soon as I get back. Father will be away to sea.'

'Let's go now,' put in Jane excitedly. 'I'll come with you.'

'But we ought to help with the washing up,' Nell pointed out.

'No,' laughed Mavis. 'Off you go! Mr Harvey and I will soon do that.'

The girls needed no second bidding and set off at a brisk pace. 'Are you sure about coming?' Nell asked as they reached the main road. 'It's a long walk.'

'It's shorter if we cut over the top of the cliff. I should be able to be back before it's too dark. I wouldn't sleep for wondering what your mother said.'

They reached a high point from which they had a good view over the North Bay. A little further on the harbour came into view. Drifters, their stacks smoking, were manoeuvring ready to leave harbour.

'There!' cried Nell.

They watched the Lowestoft drifters vie with the Scottish boats to leave the protection of the piers. White foam creamed from their bows when they met the waves, and smoke was whisked away from their stacks by the stiffening breeze.

'I hope this wind doesn't get any stronger,' commented Nell. 'If it does, it could get a bit rough out there.'

'But they'll be used to it,' said Jane. 'I don't think I'd like it, but isn't that a grand sight? So busy and lively with a real sense of challenge. Man against the sea.'

'I can tell you're going to be a writer.' Nell grinned. 'Come on.'

Mrs Franklin expressed pleasure at seeing them. 'Have you had a good day?' she asked.

'We have, Mum,' replied Nell.

'Have you eaten?'

'Yes. Jane's aunt invited me to stay.'

'I hope that wasn't any trouble?'

'It wasn't, Mrs Franklin,' Jane reassured her.

'Mum, I've something to ask you,' Nell began.

Flo Franklin eyed her daughter with a wry smile; she knew that tone of voice. 'This sounds serious.'

'It is, Mum. Well, maybe not serious ... but it's important.'

'Well, get on with it. You're usually more forthright than this.'

'Can Jane come and stay with us for a while?'

'If that's what you both want,' replied Flo. 'How long for?'

'That's just it, Mum, we aren't sure.'

Flo looked askance at her daughter. 'What's this all about?'

In a torrent of words Nell apprised her of the situation, after which Jane regaled her with the facts about her uncle and aunt's reaction.

Flo listened to it all without interrupting. Then, when the girls appeared to have finished, she said, 'If it's going to help you, I see no reason why Jane can't come and stay.'

'Oh, thanks, Mum.' Nell's face broke into a broad smile and there was glee in the look she gave Jane, who returned the smile with equal pleasure. 'What about Dad?'

Flo smiled. 'I'm sure he won't object to another young lady in the house. Besides, he won't dare counter my decision.'

Nell laughed. 'You mean, he spoils you, Mum?'

Flo's eyes twinkled at this.

'Mrs Franklin, my aunt and uncle told me to invite you and Mr Franklin to a meal on Saturday at six o'clock.'

'That would be nice. Please thank them.'

Jane finally walked back to Scholes Park Road feeling she had accomplished something today.

Her life had really taken a new turning with Mrs Franklin's agreement to her going to Lowestoft. She regretted she would be leaving her aunt and uncle but consoled herself with the thought that she could visit whenever she wished. And there would be films to send to her uncle, prints to be collected, and hopefully an editor to see.

The clock was striking the half-hour when the two girls walked into Mr Harvey's shop the next morning. Maureen looked up from a new display she was arranging, bade them 'Good morning' in the formal way she greeted customers, then smiled broadly as she added, 'Nice to see you again, Miss Harvey, and you, Miss Franklin. Mr Harvey said you're to go straight through.'

They found him in the next room with a pile of prints on the table.

'What are they like?' Jane asked eagerly.

'They're good. Judge for yourselves.' David showed them the prints individually and could tell from their little murmurs that they were pleased with them. 'You have done well,' he praised Nell when he'd turned the last one over.

'Now it needs some good writing. There is only one I wouldn't have taken.' He pointed to one of Ewan. 'That shows us nothing of the preparations, as do the others. It's a good portrait of a young man, but he is doing nothing and in this case we want action in the photographs. See, like this one which I think is the best of the lot.' He picked up a picture of Simon checking the nets. 'There is the light of enthusiasm in that young man's eyes. He loves his job, loves fishing. It shows, not just in his eyes but in his hands, too. We can supplement that impression by doing an enlarged print of his hands.'

'Interesting,' said Nell, who had thoughtfully taken in Mr Harvey's comments. She saw how such an arrangement would integrate with the text, each helping the other. It was something she would bear in mind for the future. 'Thank you so much for your help.'

'My pleasure,' he returned. 'Keep taking photographs. It's the only way to learn and improve. You have talent but it needs to be developed. Explore other themes. Don't wait for ideas from Jane.'

'Oh, it will be so exciting!' Nell hugged herself.

'I see I'm going to have to write fast to keep up with you,' laughed Jane.

'Nothing slapdash, Jane,' warned her uncle. 'The same applies to you. Practise. Write, write, write, and go on writing. It's the only way to learn and improve.'

'We'll keep each other on the right path, won't we, Nell?'

'We certainly will.'

The Friday to Saturday morning catch had not been so good, though overall the visit to Scarborough had produced a reasonable return. But it had made Percy Steel wonder if he should approach his friends George Franklin and Jake Evans again, about selling their drifters and going into partnership with a big trawler. Maybe he had better discuss it with Ewan first. After all, as the elder son he would inherit the business. But it would have to wait until they returned to Lowestoft, no point in bringing it up now. Besides, his son would want to make the most of his last night in Scarborough. No doubt he had plans, and Percy hoped that they involved Nell Franklin. He liked the lass and a marriage would amalgamate two fishing families, making it easier to entice Jake Evans into forming an even closer alliance. A vision of moving on to bigger boats, fishing further and further north, loomed large in Percy's mind.

He was right: his son did indeed have plans. Once the boat had docked and the catch had been unloaded, Ewan was away to the cottage to get a few hours' sleep before preparing for his night out in Scarborough. He heard someone running up behind him and turned to see Simon, hurrying to catch him up.

He fell into step beside Ewan. 'Dancing again tonight?'

'Of course.'

'Nell?'

'Who else?'

'Thought you might have had your eye on her friend?'

Ewan grinned, recalling the view from his bedroom window. 'Not a bad-looking girl, but not really my type.'

Simon raised his eyebrows in surprise. 'Is Nell, then?'

'You never know.' Ewan winked cheekily. 'Now, are you dancing tonight?'

'Yes.'

'The girl you picked up at the dance last week?'

'No.'

'Well, how about Nell's friend?'

'Jane?'

Ewan gave him a playful punch on the shoulder and laughed, 'Oh-oh, she must have made quite an impression. You remembered her name. You could do worse. As I said, she's not a bad-looking girl. In fact, I'd class her as good news. Get in there, boy.' And Ewan gave him another playful punch.

When they reached the three cottages rented by the families from Lowestoft, he said, 'Let's call on Nell and arrange tonight.'

Ewan tapped on the door, opened it and walked straight in.

'Hey, you just can't walk into people's homes like that,' Simon protested.

'I'm almost one of the family,' said Ewan over his shoulder. 'Hello, Mrs F,' he greeted her breezily when she appeared from the kitchen to see who had come into the house.

'Oh, it's you two back from the sea,' she remarked. 'That husband of mine not with you?'

'More interested in the price for the catch,' teased Ewan.

'Get on with you. I suppose it's Nell you want?'

'Not if you were younger, Mrs F.' And Ewan gave her a wink.

She glanced at Simon. 'What on earth do you make of him?'

He smiled. 'Not much, Mrs Franklin, but he's a good pal.'

'And always will be,' returned Ewan. 'Now, Mrs F, is Nell in?'

She had already moved to the bottom of the stairs. 'Nell,' she shouted, 'Ewan and Simon are here.'

'I heard them. Be down in a moment.'

Almost immediately there was a patter of footsteps and Nell appeared.

'Hello, gorgeous,' said Ewan, his eyes appraising her trim figure neatly displayed by a light blue flared skirt and tight-fitting white blouse, worn open at the throat.

'Hi,' she returned casually, as if brushing aside the compliment she saw in his eyes. 'Hello, Simon.'

His heart beat faster. It seemed to him that she turned a little more of her charm on him than she did on Ewan – but was she merely teasing Ewan by doing that? He nodded and smiled with undisguised admiration.

'Fishing over, dancing tonight!' Ewan, his voice full of laughter, grabbed Nell's waist and whirled her round the room.

'Not tonight, Ewan.'

He stopped abruptly and looked down at her in disbelief. 'You can't be serious?'

She nodded. 'I am.'

'No! You're having me on?'

'I'm not.'

'Yes, you are. I'm taking you, Simon's taking Jane.'

Nell shook her head. 'You aren't. Jane and I have another date.'

'What?' Ewan gave her a thunderous look. 'Who with? I'll settle them.' Nell's lips twitched in amusement at his reaction. He saw it and touched them with his finger. 'Now I know you're having me on.'

'I'm not. Jane and I truly do have another date. So have Mum and Dad.'

'What's going on?' he demanded. 'I thought we'd have a date for our last night here.'

'You shouldn't jump to conclusions. You never asked me to go dancing tonight.'

'I thought you'd know.'

'Well, you shouldn't take things for granted. As it happens, we've been invited to a meal with Jane's aunt and uncle so that's where we are going. Now off with you, I've things to do.'

Ewan's lips set in a line of disappointment. 'Cor blast!

You're a hard lass, Nell Franklin. Isn't she, Simon?'

'Maybe, but I'll tell you what, she's a pretty one. You slipped up, Ewan.'

'So what are you and I going to do?' he asked, eyeing his friend. 'Drown our sorrows?'

Simon grinned. 'You never know.'

'Whatever you do, behave yourselves. You'll have another chance to put things right with Jane and me in Lowestoft.'

'Lowestoft?' said Simon.

'Yes, Jane's coming to stay with us there.'

Nell went on to tell them briefly what was to happen and why.

'Good news,' enthused Ewan. 'Now we'll be a proper foursome.'

'We'll see you sail for home tomorrow,' said Nell, 'and the next time we meet we'll all be in Lowestoft.'

The evening at the Harveys' was a success. Both girls were pleased with the way the two families took to each other.

'I do appreciate the kindness you have shown to my niece in this short time,' said Mavis, as they settled in the lounge to have a pre-dinner glass of sherry, 'and the way that you are giving her a home in Lowestoft. It's very comforting to know she will be safe with you.'

'It will be a pleasure to have her. She and Nell have got on so well and both George and I appreciate that they're planning to work hard together on their new idea.'

'You have a talented daughter,' put in David.

'She's never done much in that line before,' George told him, a trifle dubiously.

'Ah, but she has an eye for a picture. I understand it stems from her liking for drawing. Let me show you some of the pictures she has taken.' He produced the prints, and George and Flo were surprised by the results. 'You can see Nell has a talent that should be nurtured. With your permission, I would like to help all I can?'

'That is very kind of you,' returned George, 'but you must let me pay for the camera?'

'No. My payment will come from seeing Nell develop her talent, and work well with Jane.'

'Nell tells me that you have offered to supply her with film, and will be doing the processing and printing?'

David nodded. 'Yes, I did.'

'Hold your hand, I insist I should at least pay for the films and materials you will use.' Before David could protest, George went on quickly, 'I won't take no for an answer. You must let me do that.'

David saw it would be hurtful if he refused. 'Very well, then, thank you.'

'And there is one other thing: we have a friend in Lowestoft, a widow named Mrs Easterby. She can teach Jane typing. She's a good woman who I know would do it for nothing and be horrified if I offered her money, but I'll see she doesn't lose out. She loves fish, so leave that to me.'

'That's very good of you.' David glanced at the girls. 'Now it's up to you to make the best of this chance.'

'We'll do that, Mr Harvey,' said Nell with enthusiasm. 'Won't we, Jane?'

'We surely will.'

'I expect the meal will be ready now. Take everyone into the dining room, David. Jane, come and give me a hand,' Mavis ordered then and they enjoyed the rest of the evening.

Sunday morning service over, the Lowestoft families prepared to leave for home. Ewan and Simon, nursing headaches, countered Nell's jibes with, 'Your fault. And Jane's. It wouldn't have happened if you two had come dancing.' Nell watched them sail then rejoined her mother who was awaiting a taxi to take them to the station. Ten minutes later three cars, one for each family, had arrived and within a matter of minutes they were all in the hustle and bustle of the station. Jane joined them there, together with her uncle and aunt who had come to say goodbye and wish them all well.

Leaning out of the window, seeing a tear trickle down Mavis's cheek as she waved goodbye to them, Jane sensed she was taking a major step. How odd to think it had started just a few days ago when she went to catch a ball on Scarborough harbour.

In Lowestoft the Franklins lived in a bay-windowed house situated south of the harbour, an area where shipowners and masters had built houses befitting their station. As Mrs Franklin and Nell showed her round, Jane felt the warmth and friendliness of the house. Mrs Franklin was the motherly sort, with the ability to make people feel at home, though she had a strong personality, too. Nell relished the prospect of having her friend under the same roof.

It was obvious to Jane from the pictures and artefacts displayed around the house that Mr Franklin's heart and soul lay at sea. Lined, weather-beaten faces stared out from sepia-tinted photographs. His ancestors? Models of two drifters, protected by glass cases, stood on the oak sideboard. A harpoon hung on one wall. Had an earlier Franklin hunted whales? So many questions raced through Jane's mind. She saw them all as possible subjects for articles.

'Oh, Mrs Franklin, this is wonderful,' she gasped when she was shown into a bedroom and Flo Franklin announced, 'This will be your room, Jane.'

A wardrobe and chest of drawers stood against walls that were papered with a rose pattern. A multi-coloured crocheted bedspread covered the single bed and Jane just knew that, when it was turned back from the bed head, there would be pristine white sheets and pillows beneath. On one side of the bed stood a small table with a bedside

66

light, and at the other side was a wooden chair with a cushion that matched the bedspread. The floor was carpeted in deep red, and matching curtains hung at a window over-looking a small, neatly kept garden.

'Thank you so much,' Jane went on. 'I know I'm going to be very happy here.'

'I hope so, my dear. Now, you get settled in, I'm going to put the kettle on, and find those cakes I bought in Scarborough.'

When the door had closed Jane and Nell flung their arms round each other.

'This is going to work!' cried Nell. 'Want to unpack now?' she asked.

'May as well,' replied Jane, opening the first of her two cases. 'Where should I put my typewriter?'

'I have two tables in my room, I don't need them both. I'll put one over there, next to the chest of drawers.'

'If you're sure that's all right?'

Nell was quickly out of the room and back again. She picked up the typewriter and set it on the table. 'There,' she said with a flourish. 'You can work quietly in here and produce masterpieces.'

'Sure I can,' chuckled Jane with exaggerated confidence.

'Read "The Death of a Drifterman" by the greatest of all crime novelists, Jane Harvey!'

They both burst out laughing at this and were laughing still when they answered Mrs Franklin's call of, 'Tea's ready.'

Enjoying a refreshing cup of tea in an atmosphere that made her feel at home, Jane asked, 'Will the menfolk be back this evening?'

'No, love,' replied Flo. 'What you probably hadn't realised and nobody will have told you is that the drifters work their way south only gradually.They were up off the Shetlands earlier in the year, and apart from a week at home for the regatta in August, they've been off the Yorkshire coast since then. Now they will follow the fish along the Lincolnshire coast, using Grimsby as their port. It'll take them to the end of the month to be here for the great autumn fishing off Lowestoft.'

During the next two weeks Jane settled in easily with the Franklins, and they with her. It seemed she had been one of the family for a long time. Nell introduced her to the little town, which she found fascinating with many of its narrow streets still cobbled near the harbour. It had all the trappings of a busy port, the hustle and bustle around her focusing her mind on lots of different stories. But first Jane had to complete the articles she had started in Scarborough. Mrs Franklin had introduced her to Mrs Easterby, who was pleased to have an enthusiastic pupil to whom she could pass on her typing skills. Jane quickly established a happy relationship with her tutor and worked hard, practising in her room whenever Nell was away tending her father's business.

At eight o'clock on Saturday the first of October, Jane was awakened by a loud bang on her door. This was then flung open by Nell who burst in, urging her to get up. 'Drifters have been sighted! Up! Up!' She flung the bedclothes off her friend.

Jane's initial groan was stifled as the words made their impact and brought her wide awake.

'Come on,' urged Nell. 'We're off to the harbour!'

Jane swung out of bed, ran to the bathroom and returned to fling on some clothes before running down to the kitchen where Flo was making her a bacon sandwich and Nell was pouring her a cup of tea.

'Wrap up well,' advised Flo. 'It's dull out there, and a mite chilly.'

Within a few minutes the two girls were hurrying down to the harbour, Jane with her pencil and notebook and Nell with her camera.

'Several Scottish drifters in already,' observed Nell when they reached the quayside and worked their way to a more advantageous position. They watched several more boats manoeuvre for berths before Nell shouted, 'There's Dad!' She waved and received one in answer, followed by a thumbs-up sign. 'It's been a good catch.'

'Good,' replied Jane. 'And there's the *Silver King*.'

'Simon's home. That'll please you,' said Nell with a twinkle in her eye.

Jane let the remark slip as she waved back to Simon who was obviously pleased to see them. But in fact it was Ewan she was looking for.

Five minutes later they were watching him throw out a rope from the *Lively Lady*. No sooner was the boat tied up than he was on the quay and sweeping Nell into his arms.

'It's good to feel you,' he whispered in her ear as he hugged her close.

She kissed him then pushed him gently away. 'Welcome home.'

He winked. 'Got to go. Get this lot unloaded then away to be ready for our Saturday night out.'

Jane kissed him on the cheek then. 'Welcome home,' she said in her turn.

Simon came running up to join them. 'Hi, you three. Plans for tonight?'

'Our house at five?' Nell suggested.

Ewan and Simon promptly agreed. Ewan went off but Simon waited a moment. 'How's the writing, Jane?'

'Good. Been working hard at my typing too, and should have the article finished in the next few days.'

'I'm pleased to hear it,' he replied. 'See you later.'

It was a light-hearted foursome who headed into town at five o'clock that evening.

'Which cinema?' queried Ewan.

'Odeon,' replied Nell.

'Fine by me.'

'And me,' said Ewan. 'Away we go and hope we can find seats in the back row!'

'We're going to see the film,' said Nell, without making

69

it sound too convincing.

'You said you'd nearly finished the article, Jane?' queried Simon.

'Should do next week, then off to Scarborough with it a week on Monday,' she replied. 'If Nell agrees and can get the time off.'

'Don't be away next Saturday night or there'll be two lonely sailors out looking for new talent,' quipped Ewan.

'I said, a week on Monday,' Jane reminded him.

'They're going to make us both famous, Ewan,' said Simon with a touch of admiration for what the girls were attempting.

'Famous? That'll be the day,' mocked Ewan. 'I tell you what, only person who'll be famous here will be me,' he added boastfully.

'What, through fishing?' said Simon doubtfully.

'Of course not! Whoever heard of a famous fisherman? There *are* other opportunities in the world.'

'Here we go again!'

'He's right, you know,' put in Nell, a little more seriously.

'There you are,' cried Ewan, delighted he had support. 'That's my girl!' He grabbed Nell by her waist and swung her round, narrowly missing two elderly passers-by who took no offence but laughed instead at the antics of the younger generation, remembering their own youth as Ewan called out, 'She's a grand mawther.'

'Maybe,' said Simon. 'But what else do you know but fishing? Better the devil you know than the devil you don't.'

'You need to have vision, Simon, and seize your chance.'

Detecting where this was leading, Jane broke in. 'Hey, quit it! We're having a Saturday night out, not a serious discussion of what we want from life.'

'Right you are, m'silver darlin',' cried Ewan, and gave her a kiss on the cheek. 'Sorry to get on to my hobby-horse! No more of that.' He held up his arms in surrender.

Jane smiled and savoured his term of endearment.

As they neared the centre of the town where people were drawn by the bright lights of the shops, open until ten on a Saturday night, they found themselves separated into two pairs as they jostled and weaved their way through the crowds, though they were still in sight of each other.

Jane felt Simon's hand press against the middle of her back as he guided her past four people standing in the middle of the pavement, deep in conversation, seemingly oblivious to the fact that they were obstructing others. As they passed by Simon's hand slipped into hers. Jane did not take it away for she sensed the gesture was one of helpfulness and friendship rather than anything deeper. That suited her; she knew she was not ready for a serious relationship. She still suspected Simon's heart really lay with Nell, and wondered why he did not press his case with her. Was he letting things take their own course, believing that relationships would sort themselves out if ever Ewan fulfilled his threat and left the boat? But Jane privately considered that a dangerous attitude to take. It gave Nell no clear choice to make and allowed the larger-than-life Ewan to win her merely because he made more of a show of his affections.

Her thoughts were halted when they reached the cinema. No back row seats were available. 'I'll have to behave myself then!' quipped Ewan, who received a light punch on the shoulder from Nell for his frivolity.

'Best fish and chips in Lowestoft now?' asked Simon when they eventually emerged from the cinema.

'And then the Palais to dance the rest of the night away.'

At the end of the last waltz, close on midnight, they left the dance hall thoroughly elated by their wonderful Saturday night. They were pleased that the wind had dropped and had left a clear sky from which a magical moon cast its silvery light across the roofs of Lowestoft. Though they set off home together at a leisurely pace, they soon drifted apart. Jane felt Simon's hand in hers again and wondered if she should respond differently. She held back, wary of doing anything that might signify that she was committing herself to anything deeper. It was the same when they stopped near the Franklins' home, knowing that Nell and Ewan were making their own good nights further along the road. Simon let his hands slide round her waist. As he looked into her eyes, Jane saw the confusion in his of someone who wondered whether he was doing the right thing. He kissed her on the lips. 'Thank you for a pleasant evening,' he said. Still he held her and she did not pull away.

'I enjoyed it too, Simon.' Jane raised herself on tiptoe and kissed him back. She sensed a little bewilderment in him, as if he wasn't sure what he should do next. 'And I enjoyed that too, but please don't read anything very much into it. I don't know where my heart lies yet. Let's keep this a friendship we can cherish and enjoy.'

He nodded, his mind awhirl. Her lips had been tender and warm but their touch had brought only confusion. In his heart of hearts it was Nell he loved and always had, ever since they were at school. But was that because he had never looked elsewhere? He knew she had feelings for him, but was that only friendship, almost a brother and sister relationship, because of Ewan? Now Jane had come into his life. He liked her but did his feelings run any deeper? He watched her walk up the path to the front door. There she turned and raised her hand. He acknowledged it then walked the few yards along the street to his own home, wondering why she did not want to go beyond friendship. Had something in her past made her cautious? He wished he could read her mind.

Chapter Four

When the three drifter owners had seen the sale of their catch at the fish market, Percy contacted George and Jake as they were leaving. 'I'd like a word before you set off home. Over a pint in the Mariner's Arms. On me,' he added as an enticement.

'All right by me if you're digging into your pocket,' teased Jake with a wink at George.

Seated at a round table in the snug, with their pints on the table and their pipes charged and drawing to their satisfaction, George and Jake looked enquiringly at their host.

'Now, Percy, it's obvious you have something on your mind so spit it out,' prompted George.

Percy hesitated and took a sip of his beer, using the pause to gather his thoughts. 'Yes, I have. We've managed only small profits recently, nothing like the pre-war years when there was a stronger market. We all thought that would return after the war but it never happened. You know the reasons why. The big question is, what are we going to do about it?'

'That hobby-horse again,' said Jake, picking up his tankard.

'Call it what you like, but you know I have a point. Deep down, you have to agree it makes sense for us to sell our drifters, pool the takings and buy a big trawler. If we need more cash we'll go on the lug with the bank.'

'That's as may be,' said George, 'but at the moment we're all independent. How are we going to get on as just the one concern?'

'Oh, come on, George. We've been friends since school-days, and our families were all close before we were born. We couldn't fall out if we tried.'

'*Shouldn't* fall out, granted, but who knows what would happen if we didn't see eye to eye? As it is we share infor-mation and some equipment but we go our own way in business and everything's all right,' grumbled George.

'But surely we're big enough to deal with any differences of opinion in a single business?' said Jake.

'Does that mean you agree with Percy?' asked George.

'He has a point, the herring trade is in decline.'

'Maybe, but here's something else for you two to think about that doesn't affect me. You both have two sons, how's it going to be for them?'

'We'll write it all into the agreement. Maybe make them shareholders.'

'As things stand they'd inherit the drifters one day. Maybe that's how they would still like it to be,' argued George.

'We'll have to ask them,' replied Percy. 'Hold hard, I'm not asking for a decision now. Think it over, talk to them, and we can consider it again when the herring season's over.'

'All right,' agreed George. 'But what about the situation in Europe?'

'You mean this Hitler fellow? The politicians are dealing with *him*.'

'I'm not too sure. Chamberlain has been running back and forth, but I don't know if he's getting anywhere.'

'Aw, come on now,' protested Percy. 'You've seen the pictures this morning of him arriving back in England with a signed piece of paper. "Peace in our time," he says.'

'That's as may be,' countered George. 'Look how Hitler reacted after they met at Berchtesgaden in September. That

74

meeting achieved nothing even though all the main European powers were there. Judging from his past, he's just as likely to break this latest agreement, and that could mean trouble.'

'You mean, war?' queried Jake.

'Aye, it could come to that. I hope not, but I'm not too happy about the situation.'

'We've got to trust our PM. He knows more about the situation than we do,' said Percy.

Jake gave a little nod but George sensed doubt in it.

'All I'm saying,' he continued, 'is that we need to be cautious. I reckon we should wait and see how the situation in Europe develops. If everything blows over, then I will seriously consider what you are proposing, Percy.'

'What about you, Jake?' he asked.

'It's difficult. I'd be all for pooling our resources and buying a trawler, but the European situation is tricky. We don't want to commit ourselves then find we are faced with something that could ruin the enterprise. I think maybe George is right. We should hold back for a while.'

Percy gave a little shrug. 'If that's what you both want, so be it. We aren't going to fall out over this. All I ask is that you keep it in mind.'

As George and Jake were giving him this assurance he rose from his seat and went to the bar. A few minutes later the barman arrived at the table with three more foaming tankards.

Percy raised his. 'To us! May we never fall out.'

Jake and George raised their fresh tankards and repeated his toast.

'And may the autumn fishing be successful,' added Percy.

'I think that's first class,' said Nell after she had read Jane's final version of the article entitled *The Hunt for the Silver Darlings*. 'You're going to take it to your uncle?'

'Yes. Today's Friday. I won't be able to do anything

with it until after the weekend. We can have our Saturday night with Ewan and Simon, as arranged.'

'We daren't alter that,' laughed Nell. 'Don't want them in a sour mood. When will you go?'

'If you can come with me, we'll go when you can manage it.'

'I'd love to. You could take the photographs with you, but I really don't want to miss this. I'm sure Dad will say yes, especially if I have Mum on my side. I'm on top of the work at the office.'

'Good. We'll try and make it Monday then. Maybe stay the week.'

Mrs Franklin was in agreement when they put the plan to her. 'You are sure your work is up-to-date?' she checked with Nell.

'Certain. Dad can see to selling the catch, and I'll make the entries and total up when we come back from Scarborough.'

'I'm sure your father will say yes, but if he's not keen, leave him to me.'

But they had no problem with George Franklin. Knowing how hard Jane had worked and that his daughter would like to be there when the photographs were presented, he readily gave his agreement.

A telegram from their niece asking if she and Nell could visit for a week had provoked an immediate reply of 'Delighted' from Mavis and David. Mavis had then buzzed around the house getting beds ready and preparing food, in particular the meal they would have on the evening of the girls' arrival. Now she and David, anxious not to be late, hurried on to the station concourse.

'Just made it,' he panted when they saw the train slowing at the platform. They stopped at the barrier near the ticket collector and eagerly searched the approaching passengers for the two girls. Then they were there, tickets surrendered and offering hugs all round.

'We've a taxi waiting,' said Mavis, linking arms with her niece while David called a porter to take charge of the two cases then walked with Nell, enquiring about her family.

The taxi was soon pulling up outside the house in Scholes Park Road. Twenty minutes later, having tidied themselves after their journey, they were sitting down to a sumptuous meal that started with Yorkshire puddings and onion gravy. With everyone satisfied, heaping praise on Mavis's accomplishment, and the washing up quickly done, they went into the lounge.

'Now, down to business,' said David as they settled into comfortable chairs.

'Can't it wait?' his wife suggested. 'The girls have only just arrived.'

He gave a little smile. 'I think they're anxious to know if I have anything to tell them.' He turned to Nell. 'You brought the photographs we chose before you went to Lowestoft?'

'Yes, and the films I've taken since we went home.'

'Good. Let me have them, I'll do them tomorrow.' He glanced at Jane then. 'And you've completed your piece to go with the photographs?'

'Yes. Do you want to read it?' She started to rise from the chair but was halted by her uncle.

'No. You'll want me to comment, and I'm not prepared to do that because I think you need an independent opinion, someone better qualified to judge writing than I am. I've arranged for you to see the editor of the *Scarborough Evening News* tomorrow morning at eleven. He'll look at Nell's pictures as well.' The two girls exchanged excited glances at this.

'Wonderful, Uncle! Marvellous,' cried Jane.

'How can we ever thank you, Mr Harvey?' said Nell, her face wreathed in broad smiles.

'Don't try. It's a pleasure to help you both. Just do well. And don't be late because the editor will be on a tight schedule.'

'We'll be there,' said Nell.

'What's his name?' asked Jane. 'We'd better know who we are talking to.'

David laughed. 'Of course. Mr Wheater ... Dan Wheater.'

At quarter to eleven the next morning Jane and Nell introduced themselves to the editor's secretary who sat at a desk in the outer office to guard the inner sanctum of the chief. They were directed to take a seat and sat there in nervous silence, watching every movement of the second hand on the large clock that hung in a prominent position on one wall. The secretary's typewriter beat out a regular rhythm that seemed to issue a staccato warning. As she listened to its mesmerising tempo, Jane longed to be as proficient.

'Wish I could type like that,' she whispered to Nell.

The hands on the clock moved forward.

They came to eleven o'clock. A buzzer startled the two friends.

The secretary smiled. 'You can go in now.' She rose from her chair and went to the door. 'Miss Harvey and Miss Franklin, sir,' she announced. Holding it open, she stepped to one side to allow Jane and Nell to enter the room.

Jane sensed a no-nonsense atmosphere here even though there seemed to be piles of paper everywhere. They did not strike her as being chaotic but rather the opposite, neat and arranged so that the editor and his secretary knew exactly what was there. A man of medium build came out from behind his desk to greet them with a smile. He held out his hand.

'Jane Harvey,' she said, feeling his firm grip. 'And this is my friend, Nell Franklin.'

Nell shook hands too and said with a friendly smile, 'We are pleased to meet you, Mr Wheater, and appreciate your seeing us.'

'I have a little time to spare. Please sit down.' He

indicated two chairs that had been placed opposite his.

The girls sat, knowing that they had already been sharply scrutinised. Mr Wheater leaned back in his chair, rested his elbows on its arms and steepled his fingers in front of him.

'I'm going to be blunt with you, I don't think you would want me to be any other way. My judgements will be made sincerely and are meant to help you.'

'We appreciate that,' replied Jane. 'We would not want it any other way. If you think that we have no hope of success then it's best we know now.'

'I'm glad to hear you take that view. There's no room for favours in this trade. Talent is all. Now, I understand from your uncle that you work together, as a team?'

'That's right,' replied Jane.

'What is the subject of your piece? In just a few words, please.'

Jane hadn't prepared for this. 'Th-the departure on a fishing trip of the drifters that visited Scarborough.'

He nodded brusquely. 'Now I know what to look for in the photographs. We'll have them first, please. Spread them out on that table.' He indicated an empty surface by the right-hand wall and rose from his chair.

Nervously Nell approached the table. The moment of truth was close. Mr Wheater stood by while she spread out the prints. Satisfied, she stood back and half turned to him. He stood closer to the table, not speaking as he cast his eyes quickly over the photographs.

Nell glanced across at Jane who was still in her chair. She cast a glance heavenwards then winked back at her friend. Nell's tension heightened when she noticed Mr Wheater examining each picture more closely.

Finally he straightened up with a grunt. Whether of satisfaction or disappointment, Nell could not tell. Her heart beat a little faster.

'Miss Franklin, I can't believe that Mr Harvey told me you had done little previous photography of any consequence. These are good. It is obvious you have an eye for a picture.

'Now for your piece, Miss Harvey.' He took it from her and resumed his place behind the desk. He read the first page then flicked straight to the last one.

Jane's heart sank. It couldn't be any good if Mr Wheater had not bothered to read it all. Then she noticed he was studying the first page again, followed by a glance at each succeeding page though only sufficient for him to take in a few words or sentences. He reached the last page again and then placed the typescript on the desk in front of him. He sat looking at the two girls for a moment then nodded and said, 'I can use the article with three pictures.'

The girls stared at him, hardly believing what they were hearing. The sensation deepened when he went on to say, 'I'll pay you three pounds for the article and a pound for each photograph, then you can't fall out about who gets most.' He smiled to see the way the girls' mouths had dropped open. 'Is that agreeable to you?'

'Agreeable?' stuttered Jane. 'I'd say it is! Wouldn't you, Nell?'

'Definitely.'

'Good,' replied Mr Wheater, still smiling at their reaction. 'I'll get my secretary to draw up a notice for our accounts department. They'll open an account for each of you and then any future work can be dealt with through them and cheques sent to whatever address you specify. Leave your details with my secretary when you leave.'

'Oh, thank you, Mr Wheater, this is wonderful,' said Jane, starting to rise.

The editor glanced at his watch. 'I've a few minutes more so I'll give you some general pointers now.' He looked at Jane. 'That article is good. There are one or two faults, but you have nice observation and much of it comes to life. I will personally edit this for publication. Look out for that version and then compare it with your typescript. You should be able to learn from it. Try and replicate that style, which is necessary for the *Scarborough Evening News*, but stamp your own mark on it too. You will see what I mean. Now, I think we can get two more articles out of this subject. For example, a drifterman's life, and what happens when the men return with their catch.'

'You want me to do those too, Mr Wheater?' asked a wide-eyed Jane.

'Of course! It's your subject. It would be unfair to put one of the staff writers on it. Besides, your writing will bring a breath of fresh air to the features pages. Keep your eyes open for other subjects too. I'm sure you will eventually progress beyond local newspapers but don't forget us when you do.'

'How could I ever do that, Mr Wheater?'

He smiled and turned to Nell then. 'Now you know the angles of the next two articles, do you think you can illustrate them?'

'Yes, sir!' she replied with alacrity.

'Good. Supply me with the same number of shots as you brought in today so I can make my own selection. I'll use three for each article. Oh, and by the way, I'll pay you the same rate.'

They both enthusiastically expressed their thanks.

'Now, Nell, I think I can see a real future for you in photography if you can go on producing work like this.' He opened a drawer in his desk, drew out a small card and passed it to her. She glanced at it and saw the name 'Glen Aveburn'. 'He is a freelance photographer who as you will see from his address lives in Yarmouth, not far from you in Lowestoft. He has relations in Hull and has done quite a substantial amount of work from there. I have been able to use his Yorkshire subjects from time to time. I know his freelance base is expanding because he's good, so sometimes he has to hand work on to someone else. I think he might be interested, if you are?'

'I am without a doubt, Mr Wheater.'

'I'll get my secretary to write to him tomorrow. You can

contact him yourself when you return to Lowestoft.' The editor stood up then. 'As much as I would like to stay chatting to such two charming and enthusiastic young ladies I have work to do now. There's a paper to put to bed. Well, it only needs tucking in, but I have to see to it. Let me have that new material as soon as possible.'

He shook hands warmly, wished them well, and said he looked forward to seeing them again.

The girls could hardly contain their excitement as they walked from the building. Eager to impart their news to Jane's uncle and aunt, they set off at a quick pace. First they called on David, knowing he would be at work.

He was delighted with their news, and told them that he had already dealt with Nell's next films, congratulating her on the results. 'We'll discuss them at home this evening. I'm not going to hold you up now since I know Mavis will be anxious to hear how you got on.'

Her delight set the tone for the rest of the week Jane and Nell spent in Scarborough. Apart from enjoying themselves, they used the time there to explore fresh topics they could develop for other features, but foremost in their minds were the two drifter articles Mr Wheater had commissioned. By the time they returned to Lowestoft, they knew exactly how they would tackle them.

The day after their return they took the bus to Yarmouth and introduced themselves to Glen Aveburn, surprised to find he was a man in his early-twenties when they'd thought they would be meeting someone much older. First impressions when they walked into his office, at the top of a rickety flight of stairs in a building that had seen better days, were not good. The only furnishings were one wooden chair and two large tables, littered with paper, unopened envelopes, and photographs of all sizes. The largest prints were pinned haphazardly to the walls. Nell's eyes swept over them in a professional way. She saw they covered all manner of topics: landscapes, portraits, local events, and a few more experimental shots.

Glen himself was only a little neater in appearance than his office. He wore chemical-stained grey trousers and a dark blue pullover rubbed thin at the elbows. A brown shirt drained any note of colour from his face, and his shoes needed a good brush. But the two girls realised the appearance did not reflect the man, for his eyes were bright, filled with interest and curiosity. Though he could not be described as handsome, there was something attractive about his features.

'Ah, Miss Franklin and Miss Harvey.' His voice was smooth and velvety. 'Mr Wheater contacted me and said you would be calling. He asked me to look at some photographs but made no further comment about your work, nor who exactly took the photographs?' He gave only the slightest pause before glancing quickly from one to the other of them. 'Or do you both serve as photographer?'

'I don't.'

'I do.'

They both spoke at once which made the three of them grin. The ice was broken.

'Right, Nell.' He paused, looking embarrassed. 'Sorry, I mean ... Miss Franklin.'

She gave him a smile. 'Nell, please.'

He returned the smile. 'Let me see your pictures. Here.' He moved to one of the tables and with a sweep of his hand pushed the papers towards one end; several fell to the floor but Glen ignored them. The photographs he treated differently, almost reverently, as he placed them out of the way.

Nell spread her own pictures out on the table. He did not look at them as she did so but entered into a quiet conversation with Jane, enquiring about her writing and the projects she was pursuing for Mr Wheater.

Nell straightened up after the pictures had been displayed to her liking. She was not able to accommodate them all and left what she considered the less good in a small pile. Then she looked round at Glen.

'Ready?' He raised an eyebrow.

She nodded.

He came to the table. He made no comment as he scrutinised the photographs, and as the minutes ticked away Nell's nervousness grew more and more intense. This wasn't helped when he turned from the table and said, 'Let's all sit down.' Then, in an embarrassed voice, 'Oh, there's only one,' he added as if he had just realised it. 'There's a stool in my darkroom.' He hurried over to it and reappeared with a stool. The girls sat down and Glen perched on the edge of the table.

'All Mr Wheater told me in his letter was that you were new to serious photojournalism . . . so, tell me, how serious are you? Are you really interested in making a career out of it?'

'As far as any woman is allowed,' replied Nell.

Jane nodded her agreement.

Glen smiled. 'You have a point. It isn't a female pursuit in general, but together you are better than good. People will really take notice. So how prepared are you to be better than good?'

Both Nell and Jane looked a little puzzled. He did not seem to be considering the photographs.

'More than determined,' replied Jane with a firmness that left him in no doubt. He surmised that she desired to break away from something in her past and saw writing as an escape route.

'Yes indeed,' said Nell, equally firmly.

Glen nodded. 'Then I'll tell you something about myself. I work from here.' He gave a little smile. 'I know it looks rough but I haven't the time to keep it tidy. Besides, I know where things are and it's not as if it's my home. Which may make you wonder where I do live. In Norwich, as it happens, with my mother and father.'

Both girls hid their surprise.

'Well, the name Aveburn may mean nothing . . .'

'Aveburn? Norwich?' broke in Nell. 'Not the factory owners . . . boots and shoes?'

'Precisely. That's my father's line of business. Now you are wondering even more why I am here. Well, I have always been interested in photography and wanted to make it my profession. My father could easily have set me up but I didn't want that, I wanted to make my own way. He understood because he set out in exactly the same way, except that he had absolutely nothing to begin with whereas he did buy me my cameras and the equipment for the dark-room. I refused his offer to build me a studio in the grounds at home, and I refused any other help he offered by way of introductions except for one similar to the one you just experienced.'

This is all very interesting, thought Jane, but where is it getting us?

'From then on I was on my own,' Glen continued. 'And though I say it myself, I am doing all right. It hasn't been easy but I persisted. Now I am at a stage where I need someone to help me expand the ideas I have. So, tell me a little about yourselves?'

The girls looked at each other. Who was going to go first?

'You, Nell,' prompted Jane.

She gave him a quick rundown of her background and how she turned from drawing to photography.

'I can see from these that you have a good camera so what . . .'

'Jane's uncle gave it to me.'

Glen looked quizzically at Jane and she explained how that had come about, through her uncle's photographic business in Scarborough, then went on to tell him of her own ambitions.

'Have either of you sold anything?'

They explained about the recent sale to Mr Wheater.

Glen raised an eyebrow. 'He did not mention that in his letter. He must have been impressed, which explains why he put you in touch with me though left me to make up my own mind. Well, I have.'

The girls held their breath. They had not even had a hint so far as to what he thought of the pictures.

'The photographs are good, Nell . . . some of them very good. You have a flair for composition. Your technique will improve the more work you do on learning the different properties of the supplementary lenses. Jane, if Mr Wheater has taken your piece then you must have talent too.' He left a moment's pause to let his words sink in. 'This is what I propose, tell me if you are interested. My work has expanded and I now need someone to whom I can delegate assignments.

'I cannot fix specific rates. I would pay based on the nature of the assignment, the quality of the work and the time involved. It would also be an advantage for you to be able to tackle darkroom work, Nell. If that interests you and you want to learn, I can teach you. How does that sound?' She was about to speak when he stopped her. 'It's unfair to ask you to decide now. You need time to consider my proposal.'

Nell smiled and gave a little shake of her head. 'An offer like that takes no consideration, but there is one thing I must ask. I do a certain amount of clerical work for my father. I would want to continue with that but see no real difficulty in fitting it in because it does not entail working regular hours.'

'That would be perfectly all right. The only thing that might get in the way would be if we had a deadline to meet. So long as you could be flexible?'

'That's all very nice for me, but what about Jane? We had hoped we would be working together, with me illustrating her articles.'

'I am coming to Jane. I would like all three of us to work closely together. If we can establish a reputation for producing good work, the commissioning editors will eventually approach us with features ideas they want developing. That's where Jane's contribution would come in: she'd provide the copy. We pool our ideas and the sky's the limit! What do you think, Jane?'

She stared at him for a few moments without speaking. Glen smiled. 'Well?'

'This is unbelievable. You haven't even read my work.'

'As I said, I set store by Mr Wheater's judgement.'

'Then the answer is definitely yes.' She glanced at Nell whose broad smile registered relief and approval.

'We are extremely grateful for what you propose,' she said. 'When we came here we did not expect to leave with our future mapped out.'

'Nor did I expect what I have been considering for some time to fall into my lap. Now, I don't want to make our association too rigid. I think we should have something in writing so that copyright in our individual work is established. Is that agreeable to you both?' They nodded their approval and he continued, 'What I suggest now is that you finish those two assignments for Mr Wheater and then we three are in business.'

Over the next fortnight, while keeping in touch with Glen, they concentrated on the work for the *Scarborough Evening News*. Whenever the opportunity arose Jane quizzed Simon and Ewan about life on board ship, and with their help interviewed other crew members of the three drifters.

When she and Nell discussed this article, Jane brought up the subject of the photographs, indicating what she would like to see.

'I'll have to persuade Father to allow us on board,' her friend pointed out.

'Is that a difficulty?' asked Jane.

Nell gave a little grimace. 'Well, sailors are a superstitious bunch. There are those who think it a bad omen for a woman to step on board a fishing vessel.'

'Not your father, surely?' said a surprised Jane.

'Well, not really, though he is superstitious in other

ways. But there are a couple of crew members who are dead set against a woman on board.'

'And what do they think will happen?'

'Bad catch.'

'Can we sneak on?'

'I wouldn't dare! But I'll have a word with Dad.'

At first Nell's father was reluctant to comply with the request, but when he knew how much was riding on the two articles, he relented and allowed them on board when he knew the two crew members would be at Sunday morning church service with their families.

The next day they went back to Scarborough where Jane's uncle developed and printed the photographs to illustrate the final two articles. When they delivered them and the copy to Mr Wheater he was highly satisfied, and delighted to hear that they were to work with Glen Aveburn.

Three days later they returned to Lowestoft, determined to learn and profit from this new association.

Chapter Five

The sun glimmered on a gently undulating sea when Nell and Jane, determined not to waste time and opportunity, took the bus to Yarmouth. Their constant chatter hid the anxiety that gnawed at them.

'Good to see you both,' Glen greeted them breezily.

'You've got another two chairs, I see,' commented Jane with a smile.

'I reckoned we'd better be reasonably comfortable when we discussed work.'

'Sounds as though you haven't had second thoughts?' commented Nell.

'I haven't. In fact, I can see our collaboration developing into something really big.'

'It won't be for want of trying on our part,' said Jane.

'Good. How was your visit to Scarborough?'

'Really well. Mr Wheater plans to run them as a series three nights running. He was kind enough to say he would send us the tear-sheets when they appear.'

'Good for Wheater! I look forward to seeing them. Now, I'm glad you've got his assignment out of the way because something exciting has cropped up.' Glen paused. The girls held their breath. 'Father decided his firm should publish a brochure extolling the virtues of shoes. Before you say this is a clear case of favouritism, let me tell you there was an open pitch for ideas, which had to be submitted anonymously in sealed envelopes. A completely independent panel of four in London opened them and judged the submissions. I was working on mine when you first came to me but didn't mention it in case nothing came of it. The final decision was made while you were in Scarborough ... 'I ... no ... WE got it!'

There was a moment's silence then the girls let out whoops of joy. Glen jumped to his feet and went into the darkroom to reappear with three glasses and a bottle of champagne. 'I was hoping you'd come in today so we could christen our first project together in the right manner. Then we can get down to work, discussing what needs to be done.'

Glasses were filled, toasts drunk, and all three of them expressed their certainty that this would be the best brochure ever produced.

Glen gave them a rough outline of what was expected by his father's firm but reassured them that it was very much up to them the way they approached the subject.

After a while Jane frowned. 'This is great, but it isn't what I expected I would be writing.'

'I thought you might take that view. Mr Wheater believes you have talent so you should be able to find a way to breathe life into what at first sight may seem a mundane subject. Remember what we are trying to do – persuade people to buy shoes.'

She nodded. 'I think you flatter me, but I'll work on some ideas. I would like to see the shoes as soon as possible.'

'Naturally. I've arranged to visit the factory on Monday, if that's all right for both of you?'

Jane and Nell left Yarmouth excited at the prospect of working together, though once on the bus for Lowestoft Jane lapsed into a thoughtful silence. Recognising her friend's change of mood and expecting some words of wisdom, Nell remained silent until she could bear it no longer.

'Out with it,' she said finally, giving Jane a dig with her elbow.

She started. 'Oh ... sorry.'

'What's wrong? We've just got a commission, remember?'

Irritated with herself, Jane tightened her lips and gave a little shake of her head. 'I know, I'm sorry. It's just that this project isn't what I'd expected to be doing.'

'Maybe, but it will be good practice. I was a bit disappointed at first but it is a start. It's a firm commission, not speculation on our part. We'll develop some ideas to put to Glen. We've been lucky so let's build on it.'

Jane nodded and had brightened up by the time they left the bus. As they walked up the garden path Nell made a suggestion. 'Fancy getting up early to see the drifters return?'

'You mean, you can't wait to see Ewan!' teased Jane.

Nell gave her a friendly cuff. 'It'll give you the opportunity to see Simon too.'

'Why not? It will get them in the mood for our night out.'

'I don't think that will take much doing. It will be a relief not to be off again soon after landing their catch. Thank goodness for superstition – no Sunday fishing.'

The next morning Mrs Franklin satisfied their eager appetites before Jane and Nell hurried off to the Hamilton Dock, constructed close to the older Waveney Dock when the facilities there proved inadequate for dealing with the increasing number of Scottish boats coming south for the autumn fishing.

Knowing her father and his two friends continued to use the Waveney Dock, out of habit and because the Scottish drifters jostled for position in the newer one, Nell chose an advantageous point from which they could watch the arrival of the boats. The girls cast their eyes over the drifters already unloading their catches; none were the boats they wanted to see. Four more vessels entered the harbour.

'Here they come!' called Nell, drawing Jane's attention to three of the boats, line astern, closing in on the harbour

91

entrance. 'Thank goodness they're coming in on the flood, it makes it easier. If conditions aren't right, a southerly wind and a swell can be tricky. I've known boats hit the dump heads.' Seeing the mystified expression on Jane's face she added, 'The ends of the piers at the entrance to the dock.'

Jane nodded. More information. She locked it away in her mind. That term had never arisen when she was writing the articles for the *Scarborough Evening News*, but who knew what the future might bring?

The three drifters were manoeuvred quickly and without mishap to their berths, and even before they were tied up preparations were in hand to deal with the catch. The hawseman was soon ashore, taking a sample to the sale ring. His swift return signalled a satisfactory deal and landing the catch continued apace.

'May as well go,' said Nell. 'They'll be too busy to give us any attention.' They had exchanged the customary signals with Ewan and Simon when the drifters had docked and knew from that they would see the men later.

The catch dealt with and eager to have some sleep before meeting Nell and Jane, Ewan and Simon hurried home.

When Simon reached the Franklins' house late in the afternoon, Ewan was already there so the four friends lost no time in heading for the Odeon for the first house.

'You two seem to be in good spirits,' commented Simon after the initial exchanges.

'Because they're with us,' quipped Ewan.

'It's more than that. I reckon they have something to tell us.'

Nell and Jane exchanged glances that said, Let's keep them dangling.

'Is that so, girls?' pressed Ewan. 'Out with it.'

'Who knows?' said Jane smoothly.

'I believe I do,' countered Simon. 'You've been up to something while we toiled to make a penny.'

'That's as may be,' said Nell. 'You'll have to wait until after the film.'

'Aw, come on,' pleaded Ewan, with a flirtatious glance at Jane.

She shook her head. 'No.'

'We wouldn't have finished telling you by the time we got to the Odeon and an interruption would spoil it. You'll have to wait,' Nell repeated.

They resisted all further cajoling and pleading to be given a hint.

Emerging from the cinema, the two girls kept up a flow of comments about the picture until they were all seated in a late-night café awaiting their order.

Jane winked at Nell. 'Do you think we should tell them now?'

'I think so. They've been very good, not trying to pester us since we came out of the cinema.'

'Not interested now, are we, Simon?' said Ewan dismissively.

Nell gave a derisory laugh. 'Tell that to the Marines.' Knowing that their curiosity needed to be assuaged, she said, 'We've got a commission.'

Ewan and Simon expressed delight and the evening proceeded in a celebratory mood that was carried over into their visit to the Grand Palais de Danse. They danced every dance, exchanging partners, but Ewan made sure that Nell was his partner for the last waltz, leaving Simon to take Jane into his arms and glide away to 'Who's Taking You Home Tonight?'

She felt comfortable in his arms, something she had only felt before with her aunt and uncle. But that was different, they were family, whereas what she was experiencing now was with a comparative stranger who knew nothing of her past. An alarming thought flashed across her mind. If he knew of her life in Middlesbrough, would these moments be different? *To kiss you good night at your doorway ...* The crooner's words jolted her into the present, banishing thoughts of the past. Her future looked so much brighter.

As they walked home the couples gradually drifted apart.

Jane felt Simon's arm come round her waist. She did not tense nor pull away, but moulded herself closer to him as their steps fell into rhythm.

'Simon, it's been a wonderful evening.'

'It still is,' he replied.

Their steps slowed as if neither of them wanted to reach home. He stopped at a darkened shop doorway and turned her into it. He pulled her tight and his lips met hers, gently but with meaning.

'Simon,' she said huskily, 'I am enjoying being with you, but please remember what I said about friendship. I still want it to be that way.'

The silence lengthened. Jane feared the worst, that she had spoilt a relationship which she enjoyed. Relief spread through her when he finally nodded. She reached up and kissed him then. His arms clasped her as he returned the kiss. Both of them knew they had reached an understanding. The future ... who cared, so long as they could enjoy what they had now?

In spite of the grey clouds that hung over Lowestoft Nell and Jane were full of enthusiasm on Monday as they hurried to the station, Nell armed with her camera and Jane with notebook and pencil.

They had watched the drifters sail on Sunday evening. Such a hustle and bustle around the docks as boat after boat belched smoke from its stack and jostled to get out of the harbour. Timber creaked and groaned, leather and rope chafed, engines screeched, orders rang out, men and boats were cursed. But despite it all the drifters left Lowestoft on a favourable sea and a kindly wind.

'Good morning both,' Glen greeted them as he joined them on the platform, his tone bright in anticipation of an interesting day.

Their train departed on time and Jane, once comfortably seated, raised the question of her approach to the subject.

'I hope your father isn't going to be too narrow in his requirements?'

'That sounds as though you have been giving it some thought already?' said Glen.

'I have a couple of ideas, but it will depend on the shoes I see. Do we have to bring in the actual manufacturing process?'

'You will find that the presentation is entirely up to us, though Father and his associates will of course have final approval. Let's wait and see what you think.'

Reaching Norwich, Glen escorted them to the outskirts of the town where large gold letters on a four-storey brick building announced Aveburn Shoes. They entered the building by the main entrance, both girls admiring the ornate keystone surround and double oak-panelled doors. On one side of the large hall stood an office with floor-length windows which allowed the two men inside to see who entered the building. One of them jumped to his feet on spotting them and came out to greet them.

'Mr Glen,' he said with a broad smile. 'It is good to see you.'

'And you, Jenkins,' Glen returned the greeting and then added, 'Miss Harvey and Miss Franklin.'

'Pleased to meet you,' returned Jenkins with a pleasant smile.

'Jenkins is part of the furniture, he's been with the firm twenty-five years,' explained Glen.

'And happy years they've been. Seen Mr Glen grow up into a fine young man.' Jenkins turned to him. 'Your father told me you'd be coming, said you're to go straight up.'

'Thanks,' said Glen, and glanced at the girls. 'Follow me.' He started for the wide staircase with its elaborate wrought-iron banister. 'Top floor,' he said as they reached the bottom step and then followed the red carpet all the way to the top and along the corridor. Reaching an oak door, Glen knocked once then held it open for the girls to enter. A middle-aged woman in a smart two-piece looked up from her typewriter.

'Mr Aveburn,' she said warmly. 'Please go straight in.'

Glen smiled his thanks and led the way into a large office. A man immediately rose from behind a large desk on which stood three small piles of paper, neatly arranged. A telephone stood conveniently to hand, and a tray held several pens and pencils close to a notepad. The layout reflected the neatness of the man himself. The way he held himself erect emphasised his imposing six foot two. Jane and Nell found themselves admiring his rugged features from which sparkled deep blue eyes.

'Nell Franklin,' Glen said for introduction. 'Nell, meet my father.'

'Very pleased to meet you, Miss Franklin.' He gave a slight bow as he took her hand.

'Nell, please, Mr Aveburn. It is an honour to meet you.'

'And Jane Harvey,' put in Glen.

'Welcome, Jane! You have no camera so you must be the writer?'

Jane smiled. 'I am, and pleased to meet you.' She knew that her copy would have to be spot-on; nothing would escape this man's attention.

'Please, sit down.' Mr Aveburn indicated the three chairs that had been arranged for his visitors and returned to his chair behind the desk. 'Though I am leaving the way you approach this entirely to you, I thought I had better point out one or two things.

'In case you aren't aware of it, there are many boot and shoe factories in Norwich which is the centre of the trade in Britain. We at Aveburn's have many rivals, and that is one reason for commissioning this brochure. It has to be aimed at retail outlets to persuade them they should stock our shoes, and also at their customers. In other words, everyone is to be persuaded to buy Aveburn shoes! You will notice that I said shoes – that is all we manufacture. No boots, no slippers, just shoes.' He paused then added, 'Any questions so far?'

'How big is the brochure to be?' asked Jane.

96

'I have no preconceived ideas about that. It will be decided when we see what you produce.'

'And that applies to the picture content as well?' queried Nell.

'Yes. I expect plenty to choose from, but I accept that you will have made a choice as you relate pictures and text to each other. You have *carte blanche*. I have faith in my son's work. He won this commission on merit. I don't know your abilities, but I trust his judgement.' He gave the arms of his chair a gentle slap as he stood up, saying, 'Now I'll take you to our General Manager who will look after you. He knows all about the project and our aims. Ask him about anything you need to know and for whatever facilities you require. All I ask is that you specify visiting times with him so that disruption is kept to a minimum. It's a competitive world out there.'

'We'll make sure we keep any upset as small as possible,' Glen reassured him. 'I can't guarantee how many visits we will have to make but we ...'

'Make as many as you want – you know the time scale. All I ask is that you produce a brochure that will increase sales.' As he was speaking Mr Aveburn led the way to an adjoining room.

This office was about half the size of his. A man of a similar age to Mr Aveburn rose from his own paper-strewn desk, but there the similarity ended. He wore a grey suit but looked as though he would never give the appearance of being smartly dressed. His shirt collar was crumpled and the knot in his tie not nearly as neat as it could have been. His face was thin, giving his nose a sharp appearance; his grey eyes were dull, yet Jane observed an alertness there that spoke of a deep knowledge of what went on in this factory. She felt that this was a man who could be of great help to her, if only she could strike the right note with him.

'Ladies, meet my General Manager, Charles Parry,' said Mr Aveburn. 'Charles, this is Miss Franklin and Miss Harvey.'

Charles smiled, shook hands and welcomed them to Aveburn Shoes, then he exchanged a greeting with Glen. Jane was taken with his smile, which expressed not only a welcome but an interest in them, and she was pleased that his handshake was firm. She couldn't abide limp handshakes.

'I am pleased to meet you, Mr Parry,' she said. 'No doubt we'll meet on several more occasions during the coming weeks, so please call me Jane. It will make for an easier relationship between us as I rely on you for information. I'm sure Nell agrees?'

'Of course.'

'I will leave them in your hands, Charles,' said Mr Aveburn, turning for the door. 'All three of you call on me again before you leave.'

Even as the door was closing, Charles was ushering them into seats. As he sat down himself he waved a hand across his desk and said, 'This may look chaotic but I know where everything is; it's the way I work. Don't be put off. Everything you want to know is in here.' He tapped his head.

'I can verify that,' put in Glen. 'Charles has been here almost as long as my father. What he doesn't know about Aveburn Shoes and shoe-making isn't worth knowing.'

'You flatter me, Mr Glen,' he replied, relishing but embarrassed by the praise.

'I think not,' countered Glen.

'Where would you like to begin?'

'I think for this visit a general tour with some outline information so that Nell and Jane can get the atmosphere and feel of the subject. Then we can make a specific date for more detailed study.'

'Very good.' Charles rose from his chair and led the way from his office. He directed his first words to the girls. 'As you have probably been told, we only make shoes so we are always looking forward, trying to anticipate fashion trends and keep ahead of our rivals while also catering for present-day needs.'

He took them through the designing rooms and on to the main factory floor where rows of women, ten to a row, were working at special sewing machines. There must have been five hundred in this room, concentrating with a willingness that indicated they were happy to be working for Aveburn Shoes. Most were simply dressed in plain or patterned frocks, some with lace collars, some buttoned to the neck. A few of the women wore overalls, others pinafores.

The room was high-roofed with many long windows, producing an effect of light and space. Clearly, thought had gone into the working conditions.

Charles confirmed Jane's opinion when he said, 'This is our latest machine room, built three years ago.'

'Was the previous one on this site or is it still in use?'

'We modernised the old one, but because we wanted more storage space we reduced the working space. There'll be only a hundred machines there now. It's adjacent to this building, to the right. You can wander in there when you want, but for now I'll take you to the building on the left.'

This was occupied entirely by men, they saw, some working at machines and others at lasts.

Jane was curious. 'Mr Parry, I thought I'd angle my story to one person making an individual shoe, but from what I have seen so far that does not seem to be the case?'

Parry smiled. 'You are an observant young lady. The women you saw are all skilled workers doing different specialised finishing jobs, which you will notice when you walk the full length of the machine room. The men here are doing what we call "clicking" . . . that is, cutting the necessary shapes out of the leather. Others stretch the leather over lasts to shape the cut pieces. Some of the women we saw in the last room were sewing these shapes together to form the uppers. The uppers then go back to the men to have the soles sewn on. The men who do that have stronger sewing machines because it is tough work. The product is then examined by another group of women for blemishes, and yet another packs the finished product into boxes.'

'Very interesting,' said Jane, who realised she should not have come here with a preconceived idea about how she would tackle her work.

'That is only a broad outline,' said Charles. 'No doubt you'll want more detail later, Jane?'

'I certainly will. Is it all right if I talk to some of the workers?'

'Of course! There is a supervisor to every ten rows so just have a word with them first.'

'I will. And thank you for introducing me to shoe manufacturing.' Jane gave him a broad smile.

'Have you got any ideas, Nell?' he asked.

'Oh, yes.'

'And you, Mr Glen?'

'Most certainly, Charles! And no doubt we'll have more when we discuss our observations together.'

'I'll leave you to look round on your own then. When you go to the design room ask for Mr Fred Durham, the head designer. He knows about you and what you are doing.'

'Thanks,' said Glen. 'We'll see you before we leave.' He watched Charles's retreating figure for a moment before turning back to the girls. 'What do you think?'

'There are so many ways to approach this. I suggest we should think things over on our own and meet up again later to discuss what we have come up with,' said Nell.

'What about you, Jane?' he asked. 'Are you happier with the project now?'

'Yes. I agree with Nell's suggestion. We have got a good general idea of what goes on here but I'll certainly need more detail. I would like to have a closer look at what goes on in the design room.'

'Let's do that now,' said Glen.

When they entered the room they saw twelve men seated in pairs at small oblong wooden tables. They were all working with various pieces of leather, paper, drawing materials and pliable framework that could be twisted into any desired shape.

A rotund man with a red face that beamed a warm welcome left his table and came to greet them. 'Ah, Mr Glen, how nice to see you.' His affability was all-embracing. 'Young ladies, welcome to my domain.' He gesticulated with his arms wide.

'Nell Franklin and Jane Harvey, Fred,' Glen introduced them. 'Girls, the one and only Mr Durham, life and soul of Aveburn. Without him there would be no shoes to make.'

Fred laughed. 'You get no better, Mr Glen. Girls, take no notice of him. I'm just a humble servant who tries to do his best. I know about your brief so come and go as you please. Ask and you will be informed. We design everything here. As you see, we work in pairs on the designs after we have all discussed what we think future trends will be. Our ideas come from our study of fashion and our own imagination, but we do subtly sound out wives, sisters, aunts, sweethearts, friends and acquaintances. We pool our ideas and work on them at least two years ahead. Next year's shoes are already being manufactured. We have just about finished our designs for the following year, and are already discussing ideas for the year after.'

'So far ahead?' Nell showed her surprise.

'Have to try and keep ahead of our rivals. Hopefully our ideas for the future will prove to be right.'

'Can we see next year's shoes now?' Glen asked.

'Of course! You'll need to think about what you have to present and how you can best do that.'

Ten different shoes, from a walking shoe to a superior model for evening wear, were brought out for them to see.

'I thought the two-fabric shoe had been phased out,' commented Jane, indicating an elegant court shoe of leather and cloth.

'In general it has, but there are those who took to it and

101

still choose it for certain occasions. The two-fabric shoe came in on the back of the Depression when economies had to be made in the materials we used. There are still people who like them so we cater for that, even though it is a shrinking market. You will notice in most of the other shoes a touch of Hollywood. Films attract people. They take the viewers out of a mundane world, in uncertain times; they absorb the Hollywood glamour and then want to imitate their favourite stars. One way they can do this is through their choice of shoes. Our designers study films, try to anticipate trends, and apply ideas generated that way to their designs.'

'We'll take some quick photographs of these now so we can work out how to angle our presentation.'

Glen and Nell set about taking the photographs while Jane made some entries in her notebook. Glen made no suggestions to Nell except to say, 'You may as well shoot the complete film.'

When they left Mr Durham they paid a brief visit to Mr Parry and arranged to return in three days' time.

'We're going to need a room where we can photograph individual shoes and arrange displays,' Glen told him. 'And it has to be suitable for Jane to use as her office.'

'It will all be ready, Mr Glen, you can be sure of that.'

After a brief visit to his father to reassure him that the visit had been productive and they would be returning in three days to begin work proper, they left Norwich.

'Should we meet the day after tomorrow to discuss our thoughts and ideas?' Glen suggested when they were seated in the carriage for their return journey to Lowestoft. 'It will give us all day to sort out our individual approach to the project, and enable me to develop and print the two films we have taken.'

The girls readily agreed and settled on going to Yarmouth so Glen could finish the printing rather than come to them.

They were euphoric as they walked home from the bus

stop. Their mood soared yet higher when Mrs Franklin pointed to a package waiting on the table.

'That came by post for you two.'

They saw the Scarborough postmark and ripped the package open. Inside were three copies of the *Scarborough Evening News* with a note from Mr Wheater saying he had decided to use the three articles immediately and they had appeared the previous Thursday, Friday and Saturday.

Flo Franklin was as excited as they were when she saw *Photographs by Nell Franklin* alongside *Text by Jane Harvey*. 'This calls for something special to follow the roast chicken I'm preparing. How about peaches and cream?'

'Such luxury, Mum?' objected Nell half-heartedly.

'Why not? This is a special occasion.' Flo slipped on her coat and left the girls absorbed in the newspapers. When she returned with the peaches and cream she also smuggled in two large boxes of chocolates along with two delicate necklaces adorned with crosses which she planned to present to the girls after the meal as a memento of their first appearance in print.

This surprise prolonged the air of excitement. When they had thanked her Nell added, 'I wish Dad had been here.'

'He'll be just as excited and proud when he gets back to port,' her mother comforted her.

The euphoria continued the next morning when the post arrived for there were more copies of the papers from Jane's uncle and aunt together with a note of congratulation that also expressed their pride. 'We'll take these for Glen to see tomorrow,' said Jane.

'Thought of any more subjects for Mr Wheater?' asked Nell when they were on the bus to Yarmouth. 'There's one,' she added quickly, pointing to a pile of logs, tree cuttings and flammable rubbish.

'Bit late! It's Bonfire Night tomorrow. We'll have to think well ahead if ideas are fixed to dates,' Jane pointed out.

'And we should be concentrating on the shoe project,' added Nell. 'But we can do several things at once when we get used to working with Glen. Aren't you going to tell me what you have in mind for the shoes?' Since breakfast she had been trying to get Jane to tell her.

Jane gave a small smile. 'No. I want to put it to you and Glen at the same time.'

Nell shrugged her shoulders as if she didn't mind and said teasingly, 'Be like that then.'

'You'll soon find out,' said Jane, hurrying away as they got off the bus.

Nell took a few quick steps to catch up with her friend and a few minutes later Glen was congratulating them on the articles about the drifters.

'*Now* tell me,' Nell pressed Jane. Glancing at Glen she added, 'She won't tell me what she has in mind.'

'Photographs first,' replied Jane. 'I've been working from memory. When I see them, I'll know if my idea can work.'

'Right, through here,' said Glen, leading the way to the next room. 'I have them laid out for you.'

The girls shrugged themselves out of their coats as they followed him.

Black-and-white prints were spread out for them to study.

'Interestingly, Nell and I have taken different angles, though there's some overlap. That's good because it helps widen our ideas on presentation and how we should photograph individual styles. We'll discuss that in a few minutes. Now let's hear how your approach fits in with our photographs, or vice versa.'

'I am not bothered about the angles you use, what I want to see now is just one picture of each shoe. It doesn't matter which. You will be making the final choice of photographs for the brochure.'

Glen quickly chose one picture of each of the ten styles, some taken by him and some by Nell.

Jane arranged the ten in a line across the table, studied them and then moved them around until she was satisfied that she had them in the right order: outdoor style followed morning wear, afternoon wear, evening wear, ending with what she considered the most glamorous shoe.

'To link with the copy I have in mind, I'd like a photograph of the ten shoes in that order. Then we have a photograph of the first shoe about which I write on its own. That is taken away and you then photograph the remaining nine. Then you photograph the second shoe and take it away, and so on. Except for this one.' She indicated the fifth shoe and pushed it out of the way. 'Eventually that is the only one left and is the last to appear on its own. To accompany it I will write a sentimental piece that hopefully will make it the best-seller of them all.' She paused, looked at them, hoping to read their reactions but they told her nothing. Glen and Nell were still absorbed in the pictures, obviously considering her request seriously.

Glen looked up and glanced at Nell as if seeking her opinion, not wanting to influence her by voicing his thoughts. She raised her head with the same query in her eyes. She gave a little nod then and he read it as approval. He felt relieved because he wanted harmony throughout this project and this was a good test. He knew there would be difference of opinion at other times, but this was a major step and to be able to move forward from it without any differences augured well for the future. He looked at Jane.

'I think that is a brilliant idea. It will focus people's attention on all the shoes, but when number five is not taken out in sequence they will wonder why and so be more focused on it when it does appear. Immediately the picture of that shoe comes up they will want to read about it and find out why it has received particular attention. Good thinking, Jane. Get working on it right away.'

'Wonderful idea,' said Nell, giving her friend a hug. 'I knew you'd come up with something brilliant.'

'Now you know why I wouldn't disclose my idea before.

I needed the photographs to explain it.'

Glen turned to Nell. 'You and I can get working on the actual photography tomorrow. For now we can be thinking of backgrounds, angles, etc. But first I should tell you – we will be working in colour.'

'Colour?' Both girls were astounded. This was something they had not anticipated.

'Yes. It's been around for some time but wasn't really commercially viable until fairly recently. Kodachrome appeared in 1935 and Agfacolor a year later. We'll use Agfa. Because it's fairly new and more expensive than black-and-white, we have to be extra-careful and make sure we don't have to make any repeats. I'll get their professional laboratories to develop and print the film.'

Nell quaked at this, 'I hope I can live up to your expectations.'

Glen grinned. 'Nervy? Don't be. You'll handle it all right. We begin in earnest tomorrow so relax for the rest of the day. Come on, lunch is on me.'

He took them to a small hotel where he was friendly with the owner and rated the food highly. Glen kept off the subject of the project and the girls followed suit, enjoying getting to know him better.

At the end of the main course, Jane could contain herself no longer. 'I know we are keeping off the topic of work but I need to put something to you. If you don't think it is a good idea then I can forget all about it.'

Glen and Nell fixed their eyes on her and waited for her to go on. When she didn't, Nell prompted, 'Well?'

Jane looked quickly from one to the other. 'I was wondering if it was a good idea to expand the articles we did for the *Scarborough Evening News* into an illustrated book – maybe call it *Driftermen*? You could take a lot more photographs in Lowestoft and Yarmouth, Nell, and Glen would have greater opportunities than you to get on board some of the vessels.' Realising her tongue was running away with her, she stopped suddenly and looked anxiously at them. Their faces were solemn. Her heart sank. A few moments that seemed like an eternity passed, then she saw Glen wink at Nell and realised he must have signalled to her previously to adopt this teasing silence.

'I think it's a great idea,' he said.

'So do I,' added Nell, pleased that ideas for future work were already being generated.

Jane's face broadened into a delighted smile. 'I hoped you would agree. I can see a lot of potential in the subject and we are so near it all.'

'We can be thinking about it while we are doing the shoe brochure,' approved Glen.

The rest of the day passed quickly and by the time Glen saw them to their bus, arrangements had been made for him to meet them at Lowestoft station the following morning.

During the next fortnight they visited the Aveburn factory every day with the exception of Saturday and Sunday. Everyone there knew what they were working on and took an interest. The promotion was aimed at increasing sales and therefore guaranteeing their jobs. Glen and Nell went about taking photographs of people at work to record the various aspects of shoe-making, and Jane put questions to which the workforce responded. At the end of the two weeks they had all the material they wanted.

As they rode to Lowestoft in the train that Friday, Glen suggested they should try to have the mock-up of the brochure ready by the end of next week. 'Think you can complete your copy by then, Jane?'

'Yes. I've been playing about with it at home. I'll have it all finished on Tuesday.'

'Good. As you know I took the colour film to be processed last week so I should have it back by Monday. Would you like to come to Yarmouth on Monday and Tuesday, Nell? We can print the black-and-whites then we could all meet at my place on Wednesday to work on the mock-up?'

'I've not done any printing yet,' Nell pointed out.

'I know, but if we are to continue working together it would be advantageous for you to learn right away. It's easy enough.'

'OK. I'll be there.'

Jane was surprised by the readiness with which Nell agreed to share a darkroom with Glen, but quickly dismissed the thought as being unworthy of her. After all, working in a darkroom was the natural progression of photography.

'That's terrific, I knew you would.'

Glen's exclamation came quickly and in a manner that made Jane wonder if he was perhaps growing interested in her friend as more than a colleague. Again she admonished herself. In any case, was it so wrong, if he had such feelings? It had nothing to do with her, Nell could look after herself. And no doubt if Glen did make any advances, she would tell him about Ewan.

When Nell informed her mother that she was going to Yarmouth to work with Glen on Monday and Tuesday, Flo Franklin sought an opportunity to have a quiet word with Jane.

'I'm pleased for you both the way this association seems to be turning out work-wise, but I haven't met this young man and don't know what he is like ...'

Jane realised Flo was seeking her opinion.

'He's a respectable young man from a good family, very keen on his work. This is a working relationship, I'm sure there is nothing more to it than that. I think it presents a good opportunity for Nell to develop her skills. I don't think you need worry, Mrs Franklin.'

She gave a little smile. 'It's a mother's prerogative to worry. I suppose it's only natural for me to want her to move in her own circle. I wouldn't want her to get hurt.'

'There's nothing snobbish about Glen or his father. You needn't worry on that score, Mrs Franklin. And I'm sure Nell knows where her heart truly lies.' She paused for just a moment and continued, 'We are seeing Ewan and Simon tomorrow as usual.'

'Thanks, Jane. And please don't say anything to Nell?'

'Of course I won't.'

As they walked home after dancing until the late hours of Saturday night, Jane slipped her arm through Simon's. She felt thoroughly at ease with him now, saw him as dependable, solid, someone who treated her with deference and care. She sensed he was holding back any other feelings because he respected her, but also because he did not want to mar their friendship. Whenever Jane wondered about her own attitude she always came to the same conclusion: she was not ready for a settled relationship.

Simon's thoughts about Jane were becoming confused. It had always been Nell for him, but lately he'd started to wonder if Ewan could ever be driven from her mind. Since Jane had stepped in to save the situation on Scarborough quayside, his old certainties had been challenged. Maybe *she* was the girl for him? If ever she agreed to be more than a friend . . .

'Simon, this project we have been working on for Aveburn Shoes is nearing an end. We hope to get more paid work but beyond that I would like to do an illustrated book that Nell and Glen would be involved in.'

'Sounds a good idea. Have you a subject?'

'I thought I might develop the three articles into a full-length book.'

'You mean, tell the story of the driftermen's life and trade?'

'Yes.'

He paused a moment before replying enthusiastically, 'That's a splendid idea, Jane.'

'I'll need a lot more information.'

'You can depend on me.'

She could tell from his tone that he was genuinely excited about the project.

'I'll need a lot of photographs to choose from, some of them taken on board, possibly some at sea.' She gave a little laugh. 'I haven't suggested it to Glen yet because I don't know whether that would be possible?'

'I don't see why not as long as he does not get in the way and realises it can be tough and dangerous out there. It isn't happening immediately, is it?'

'No. It's something to think about while we pursue other projects. Though he has said little about them, I think Glen is working on a couple of other ideas to submit to the news magazine *World Scene* as well.'

'Then let me think about which boat he should sail on. I'll have a word with my dad.'

'Thanks, Simon, you're an angel.'

'I'll have a decision for you by the time I get back.'

'Where are you going?' Jane could not disguise the concern in her voice.

'Dad's talking about having a couple of weeks' fishing off Plymouth before Christmas. We'll sail on the second of December and be back about ten days before the festivities, ready to start again in the second week of the New Year. Will you be in Lowestoft for Christmas?'

'I think I should spend it with my uncle and aunt in Scarborough.'

'Not going home to Middlesbrough then?'

'Don't ask me that, Simon.'

He knew it was no good saying any more. Jane was tight-lipped as always about her early life there.

'Do your aunt and uncle make a lot of Christmas?'

'Yes, to a certain degree, but they do make more of New Year. That's the case the further north you go.'

'Christmas is our big time,' he explained. 'We don't make a lot of New Year – to my mind, it's just another year gone by.'

'Why don't you come to my aunt's for New Year then?' The query was out almost before Jane realised it.

'Is that an invitation?' he asked.

110

'I wouldn't have said it if it wasn't, but don't take it too seriously.' Jane felt she owed him something for all his help and hoped she would not regret it.

Simon stopped walking and turned her to him. 'Thanks,' he said. 'I accept and I will be looking forward to it.' He kissed her then and they lingered a few moments. 'Are you sure it will be all right with your aunt and uncle?' he asked as they walked on.

'I'm sure of it, judging by the tone of their letters asking me about the friends I have made. They'll be pleased to meet you. I'll write to them tomorrow.'

Chapter Six

Nell's thoughts were all of Ewan as she rode in the bus to Yarmouth. Knowing he could be jealous, she had not told him that she would be spending most of the day in a dark-room with Glen. She found that streak in Ewan both attractive and infuriating, and had seen no reason to account to him for her movements. After all, he was away to sea, having left last night. Because he would be in and out of port as quickly as possible during the next week, they had made no arrangements to meet until next Saturday.

Now she had to admit that beyond her eagerness to learn about developing films, she wanted to learn more about Glen, too. She knew something of his background: a well-to-do family, a good education, understanding parents who knew he wanted to find his own way in a creative job of his choosing. During their photographic sessions at the factory she had found him easy and pleasant to work with; someone who was willing to listen to suggestions even if he didn't always agree with them. She found herself admitting that he was not bad-looking either and had an attractive air about him ...

'Hello, Nell,' he greeted her brightly. He took her outdoor coat, put it carefully on a coat hanger behind the door and dropped her woollen hat, scarf and gloves on a small table. 'Glad you're keeping well wrapped up,' he commented. 'There's a distinct chill in the air this morning.

Have you left Jane writing?'

'I heard her tapping away when I was getting up. Keen to get something down before breakfast. She is determined to become a writer.'

'I realise that, and I've no doubt she'll succeed. I'm not sure what really motivates her, though. I reckon it's something from her past that makes her want to prove herself.'

'You could be right. I know nothing of her life in Middlesbrough, she's very tight-lipped about it. I never press her for information. I think she'll tell me when the time is right.'

Glen nodded. 'I've got the chemicals ready mixed so we can go straight into printing. I'll show you the mixing sometime, but over the next few weeks we'll concentrate on how to print photographs to the standard required by magazines and newspapers.'

When he shut the door of the darkroom Nell was aware of a dull red light, otherwise it was in total darkness. She was also aware of his closeness. 'Your eyes will become accustomed to this in a few moments,' he said. 'If we used anything stronger than that light we'd ruin the sensitive paper on which we print the photographs. Seeing any better yet?'

'It's coming,' she replied, beginning to make out shapes that in a few moments took on more solidity.

'This is the enlarger.' He indicated a piece of equipment standing on a waist-high bench that ran the length of one wall. He pointed to two dishes holding some sort of liquid. 'The first contains developer, the second fixer, and then we have a big bowl of water.' He went on to inform her how the enlarger worked and show her how the negative film was inserted into it. She gasped when he switched the enlarger on and she saw the negative's picture projected on to the white base of the enlarger. Glen went on to explain about exposure and how it was calculated for each individual negative, after which he went through the whole process while she watched and followed each step until a positive result was deposited in the water to be washed.

'Glen, that's magic,' she said, awed.

He laughed. 'It's easy. After you have done a few straightforward prints I'll show you ... not today, but some time in the future ... how to manipulate pictures to get them to your liking or fulfil a brief. Now, I'll do one more. You follow carefully and then I'll guide you while you do one.'

Nell let out a whoop of joy when she saw her own picture appearing, and in her excitement flung her arms round Glen.

He laughed, enjoying not only her exuberance but also her closeness.

'That's good,' he praised her when she finally decided the photograph was as she wanted it. 'We'll do some more now, and we may as well use the negatives we took at the factory. We'll need them for our meeting with Jane here on Wednesday.'

They worked steadily until Glen called halt at midday. 'That was very successful. I'll take you to lunch now and then we'll come back and do a few more, but only a few. I want you to get home in daylight.'

'Oh, I'll be all right if there's more work to be done.'

'No, I insist you reach home in daylight. You will be back to do more tomorrow.'

As Nell rode home she reflected on how much she had enjoyed her day, not only for what she had learned and achieved but also for Glen's consideration and his attentiveness over lunch at his friend's hotel. She found him so easy to get on with. Someone who, while serious about his photography, also got a lot of fun out of it. She liked that. And she was aware that he had made no objection when she had flung her arms round him in her excitement. In fact, she had felt a definite response. She looked forward to tomorrow.

Jane was eager to hear about her day but disappointed that Nell had not brought one of the pictures for her to see.

'You'll see them all on Wednesday. Hopefully I'll produce some better ones tomorrow.'

In the warmth of the darkroom, bent over dishes, charged with shared excitement, Nell and Glen became aware of a new quality in their closeness. Their arms touched, and Nell felt as if an electric charge had gone through her. She half turned. He did the same. As if it was the most natural thing in the world their arms slid round each other and their lips met. Neither of them wanted the moment to stop and the kiss lingered. When their lips parted embarrassed apologies flowed from both of them, in such a manner that they both stopped talking at the same time and burst out laughing.

Then Glen's voice took on a serious note of apology. 'Sorry, Nell, I shouldn't ...'

'Why not?'

'Well ...' He stopped talking, as if searching for words, then added quickly, 'I shouldn't have assumed ...'

Nell's thoughts had also been racing. She had enjoyed his kiss. She did not want to show disapproval or hurt Glen by outright rejection, but if their association was to go on and meant more time together in the darkroom, she had to get matters in perspective. There was Ewan to consider.

She reached for his hand. 'I liked it, Glen. I think you're a wonderful person even though I have known you only a short time, but I should tell you there is someone else ... someone I have known all my life.'

'I understand.' She could hear the disappointment in his voice. 'A fisherman?'

'Yes. Ewan Steel. He sails on his father's drifter ... he'll inherit it one day.'

'And he has your heart?'

'Yes.' Her reply was so quiet that Glen wondered if some of her heart was still free? And he wondered even more as Nell went on, 'I don't want this to spoil our friendship or to mar our working relationship.'

115

'I'll see it does neither. I like you, and I like working with you. I think we can achieve something worthwhile with our photography.'

'Thank you, Glen, you are such a nice person.' She kissed him on the cheek and did not pull away when his hand rested for a moment on her hip. Then she got back to the matter in hand. 'I told Jane I'd have better pictures to show her tomorrow. Do you think these are good enough?'

'They are an improvement on yesterday's, and will go on improving as you learn more tricks of the trade.'

Jane was enthralled when she saw the prints that Nell had produced. The colour work had been returned from the professional printing lab, too, and immediately the two girls could see the impact it would make.

'The colour shots are bound to overshadow the black-and-whites,' said Nell, disappointed that her pictures would not stand out.

'No,' countered Glen. 'Arranged correctly colour can enhance black-and-white, imbue it with fresh impact. You'll see. Now, Jane, let's see what you have written.'

She passed over the typescript to Glen and a copy to Nell. 'That is the order I envisaged, I hope the photographs fit in with it.'

Glen and Nell sat down to study the copy. Jane watched them closely, trying to gauge their reactions as they read, but their expressions betrayed nothing. She had written about the history of Aveburn, and in the same vein about the making of shoes. Neither was done in great detail, because the main object of the brochure was to promote the sales of the ten new designs, but there was sufficient information to hold people's interest.

Glen finished first and when he looked up she thought she detected a twinkle of approval in his eyes.

Nell finished and looked at Jane with open admiration. 'I love the way you've woven a story with each shoe playing

116

a part. Keeping that particular court shoe, saddened by rejection, until right at the end when it weaves its magic for the young woman, is brilliant!'

'It certainly is,' Glen praised her. 'People will want to follow that story right through and their attention will be drawn to each shoe as they go along. Now we'll make a dummy, placing pictures and text together, and tomorrow we'll take it to Father.'

By the end of the afternoon, after careful deliberation, they had pictures and text arranged to their liking.

'I'll paste it all up this evening and meet you at Lowestoft station tomorrow,' Glen announced with a satisfied sigh.

As they rode in the train to Norwich the next day, he showed them his final paste-up. Turning the pages, both girls realised what an eye-catching presentation it was, and Nell saw that Glen had been right in saying that in the final presentation the colour photographs would complement the black-and-whites.

Satisfied as they were, they approached Mr Aveburn's office with some trepidation. He sat behind his desk, turning the pages of the dummy slowly, without speaking. When he reached the end he stood up and left the office. The girls glanced anxiously at Glen who, making nothing of his father's reaction, grimaced and shrugged his shoulders. A few minutes later Mr Aveburn returned with Mr Parry and Mr Durham. He indicated the dummy on his desk and they both perused it. When they looked up there was a look of surprise and approval on their faces. Glen's father ordered, 'Get Wilf Bentmore down here right away.'

'I'll see to it myself, sir,' said Durham and hurried from the room.

'Biggest printers in Yarmouth,' Glen explained to Nell and Jane. 'You like it then, Dad?'

'Like it? I think it's a work of genius. I love the way the story draws attention to each individual shoe, and the twist at the end really focuses the attention. The photographs could not be better, in my opinion.'

Exulted by such praise, the three friends grinned their delight and hugged each other.

'Charles, away with you and work out how many brochures you think we might need. Have a figure we can work on by the time Wilf gets here.'

'What now?' Nell put the question as they returned to Lowestoft. Immediate euphoria gone, they felt themselves to be in a vacuum. No work. Where could they turn?

'We must plan new ideas,' said Glen. 'Not stagnate. We can't afford to wait until things happen for us, we've got to make them happen.'

'We can work on my idea of a book about the drifter-men, but that will take time.'

'It's a good idea but not the sort of thing we can easily do while working on more immediate projects. As there is nothing in the offing, we could be working on the photographs for the book, I suppose. How about getting me on one of the drifters?'

'Do you actually want to sail on one?'

'Why not? It will make good material.'

'Are you a good sailor?'

'Don't know, but I'll soon find out.'

Nell raised her eyes heavenwards. 'It's a rough, hard life.'

'That's something else I'll find out by the time I return, isn't it?'

'On your head be it. They'll be coming in this evening, laying up tomorrow, Saturday, and sailing Sunday evening to start fishing after midnight. I'd better see if I can get you a berth on that sailing because Dad may decide to go fishing off Plymouth with Mr Evans and Mr Steel.'

'To sail on Sunday,' confirmed Glen.

'I'll do my best. Here's my address. Can you come to Lowestoft on Saturday morning?'

'I'll be there.'

118

Seeing the uninviting gun-metal sea under a glowering sky, Glen wondered about the wisdom of his decision to sail with the drifters. Never having been to sea before, a certain foreboding had overcome his enthusiasm of the previous day. He tightened his lips and firmed his resolve to see this through. After all, if he wanted to make his living as a photographer, he would have to take on all manner of assignments. Primarily he had Jane's book in mind, but he may be able to make use of the photographs in other ways.

Nell's directions had been clear. Soon after alighting from the bus he found the house he was looking for.

When Nell opened the front door, not only was he welcomed by her friendly smile but by the smell of baking bread.

'Mum and Dad are in the kitchen, do you mind?' she asked over her shoulder as she led the way along the hall.

'Of course not,' Glen replied brightly. 'That smell is very tempting.'

She gave a little laugh. 'You've hit Mum's baking day.' They reached the kitchen. 'Mum, Dad, this is Glen whom I've told you about.'

Her mother looked up from the pastry she was rolling on a wooden table set at right angles to one wall. A highly polished black range occupied the opposite wall. The fire in the grate was also directed to heat the side oven. Mr Franklin, looking contented with his pipe and paper, was sitting in a Windsor chair to one side of the fire.

He removed his pipe. 'Good morning, young man.'

'Hello, Glen.' Wanting to make Nell's friend feel truly welcome, Flo used his Christian name.

'Good morning, Mrs Franklin, Mr Franklin.'

'Just about to make a cup of tea,' she said. 'You'll have one?'

'That would be lovely,' he replied.

'And I'm sure he'd like a slice of your new-baked bread, Mum,' put in Nell, pulling out a chair from under the table.

'Sit down, Glen.'

He took the seat and she went over to a cupboard and brought out five cups, saucers and plates.

'So you want to sail on a drifter, young man?' said Mr Franklin.

'If that is possible, sir.'

'Oh, I can make it possible, but have you been to sea before?'

'No, sir.'

George Franklin grimaced. 'Ah, well, there's always a first time. We've all had to make that first voyage. It won't be pleasant. You may feel seasick, and I tell you what, that isn't a pleasant experience. You'll feel as if you want to die. On the other hand, it's possible you might take easily to it. Once we clear the harbour, the drifter will never be stable until we reach Lowestoft the next morning. Conditions will be cramped ...'

'I'll cope, sir.'

'Nell tells me you want to take pictures of life on board and the men at work?'

'Yes, sir.'

'I don't mind that but you must not get in the way when the men are working. It's heavy and dangerous work, especially when we're casting and hauling, and much of it will be in darkness or poor light.'

'That doesn't bother me, sir. I'll use a fast film and flash.'

'I don't pretend to understand that but I bow to your judgement.'

Nell took the kettle from the reckon, filled the teapot and brought it to the table. Mrs Franklin took one of the white loaves from a cooling tray and started to slice it. Nell left the kitchen and Glen heard her shout, 'Jane, tea up!' She returned and a few minutes later Jane appeared.

'Hello, Glen,' she greeted him breezily. 'Got your berth?'

'He has,' said Mr Franklin. 'If he still wants it after what I told him.'

120

'I do, Mr Franklin.' Glen nodded his thanks to Nell as she placed a cup of tea in front of him then handed him a plate on which there was a slice of bread. 'Butter, treacle ... help yourself.'

Jane and Nell sat down at the table and Flo joined them.

'We sail tomorrow, six in the evening, then we'll be on the home grounds ready to fish at midnight. I aim to be back in Lowestoft by first light.'

'You aren't staying out longer?' asked Glen.

'No. The fishing here has been tailing off. If I make a good catch, I want to be back in port as soon as possible. If it's not good, I want to return and decide whether to move on. One voyage will probably suit you better, too. See how it goes. If you find you want more photographs, contact me again. Be on board by five.'

'Thanks, that is very kind of you, Mr Franklin.'

'You are helping Nell.'

'She will make a good photographer. There's still a lot for her to learn, but there always is, no matter how good you are.'

'She tells us the shoe project went well,' said Flo.

'It did. The final result was highly approved of by my father and his two right-hand men. This is wonderful bread, Mrs Franklin.'

She smiled her thanks and said, 'You're on your own in Yarmouth, I believe. You shall have a loaf to take back with you.'

'Very kind of you.'

Nell saw this as a sign that her mother approved of Glen.

Their conversation was interrupted when there was a knock on the front door and they heard it open straight away.

Ewan breezed into the kitchen. 'Good morning, all.' The laughter in his eyes dimmed momentarily when he saw a stranger, a young man, sitting at the table like one of the family.

'Ewan, this is Glen. Glen – Ewan.'

121

Glen, his mouth full of bread and treacle, could only nod in greeting. So this was Nell's boy friend? He was handsome and carried a devil-may-care aura. Glen felt an immediate pang of jealousy.

'Ah, the photographer Nell told me about,' said Ewan, a little too dismissively for her liking.

'He's sailing with Dad tomorrow,' she said, feeling she had to counter Ewan's offhand attitude to anyone he felt earned their living too easily.

Ewan raised his eyebrows. 'Is he now? That'll be interesting.'

Glen would not be drawn by the inference in these words. 'Looking forward to it, and to getting some good pictures.'

'If you aren't heaving your guts up too much to take them. It can be mighty rough out there.'

'Job's comforter,' snapped Nell. 'Take no notice of him, Glen.'

Ewan glanced at Jane as if to say, Is there something between them?

Mrs Franklin, sensing the tension, quickly intervened. 'Cup of tea, Ewan?'

'No, thanks, Mrs F. Must be off. Things to do. Just popped in to confirm tonight with Nell and Jane.' He glanced at them both. 'Six o'clock, Odeon?' He did not wait for an answer but said, 'So long, all,' and breezed out as he had breezed in.

Flo noted a flash of annoyance cross her daughter's face.

At five o'clock on Sunday afternoon Nell and Jane walked on to the quay where the *Sea Queen*, *Lively Lady* and *Silver King* were tied up. All around the harbour preparations were being made to sail: fishermen hurrying to their respective boats, men checking nets, machinery and tackle, others seeing the decks were clear to facilitate easy movement and avoid any hazards.

'Come to see me off or your greenhorn?' called Ewan, a

122

derisory note in his final word.

'Cut it out, Ewan. He's only a greenhorn so far as fishing is concerned. You'd be one if you were trying to take photographs the way Glen does,' countered Nell.

'That ain't a job,' mocked Ewan.

'Hold you hard. It's as much a job as yours is.'

He gave a derisory snort. 'Well, we'll see how he gets on. Here he comes. And here's a kiss to remember me by.' He swept Nell into his arms and hugged her so tight she could not escape until he relaxed his hold when Glen reached them. Ewan was not going to let any newcomer ignore the fact that Nell was his girl.

Jane turned away, wishing she was in his arms, instead of Nell.

Embarrassed, Nell glared at Ewan. His smile had a touch of triumph in it.

'See you when I get back,' he said huskily. 'Hi, Glen. Have a good trip.'

'Thanks, Ewan.'

'Don't be too seasick.' He had to put in a parting shot. Then he turned away swiftly and swung himself on to the *Lively Lady*, in one easy athletic motion.

'You're on the next vessel, Glen,' said Nell, starting along the quay.

'Have a good voyage,' Jane told him. 'I'll go and see Simon.'

'I'll join you in a few minutes,' called Nell as Jane headed for the *Silver King*.

Simon saw her coming and left the drifter for the quay. 'Thanks for coming,' he said. 'Having you see me off gives me a sweet memory to carry every minute I'm at sea.'

Jane gave a small smile. 'I'm flattered, Simon.' He glanced round. There was no one near. He licked his lips. 'This may not be the place or the time but I've got to say it ... I've got to let you know I love you, Jane.'

Her heart skipped a beat. What should she do? She hadn't expected this to happen but it had. 'I'm honoured

123

you feel that way about me but I'm not ready for a serious relationship yet, Simon. I enjoy your company, you are a good person, but please don't get romantic ideas about me.'

'The way I feel, you can't *stop* me having them. I love you, but I will not allow that love or my feelings for you to intrude on your life until you allow them to.'

She realised that without either of them being conscious of the gesture, their hands had clasped together. Jane pressed his as she said, 'Please keep friendship foremost in your mind for the time being.'

'That sounds as if there's still hope? It also tells me there is something you are holding back.'

Jane's eyes clouded. 'Please, Simon, ask no more.' She kissed him on the cheek. 'Friendship, for the moment?' she whispered.

'It's yours,' he replied quietly, 'and with it my love.'

'Safe voyage,' she whispered with an intensity that set his heart racing.

He smiled, swung back on board, and blew her a kiss which she returned. Jane's thoughts were whirling as she watched Simon walk away along the deck. When he looked back before disappearing below, she held her hand high then walked slowly back along the quay.

'Those look to be serious thoughts,' commented Nell.

Jane, startled by the words, looked up to see her friend coming towards her and gave a wry smile.

'Simon?' quizzed Nell.

Jane gave a little nod. 'But I don't want to talk about it.'

Nell had hoped her query might lead Jane to reveal more about her feelings and her past history, but she was disappointed once again. 'I think he's in love with you,' she said.

'When I first met you, I thought he was in love with *you*. Remember, I said so?'

'I do,' replied Nell. 'But I told you then and it's still the same now ... Ewan, even though he has some irritating faults, is for the most part charming, kind, and ...' she hesitated.

'And you love him?' added Jane.

'Yes.'

Jane wondered if the speed of Nell's reply was more to convince herself than Jane.

'Let's find a vantage point to watch them sail,' she suggested.

When they finally set off for home Jane put the question, 'Are we getting up to see them return?'

'I think we should welcome Glen home after his first voyage. It may be his only one on drifters,' replied Nell, the quickness of her decision and the reference to Glen making Jane wonder if there was more behind it.

Knowing the girls' plans, Flo was up before them. When they crept quietly downstairs and into the kitchen, much to their surprise they found her there, wrapped in her new dressing-gown, enjoying a cup of tea.

'Mum, what are you doing up?' asked Nell.

'There's a pan of porridge on the reckon. I thought you should have something warming. It will be cold on the harbour and you don't know how long you'll be hanging about.'

Both girls relished their surprise and were profuse in their thanks when they left.

'There's one in already,' said Nell, somewhat surprised to see a boat. As they neared the quay a note of alarm came into her voice. 'It's the *Sea Queen* ... Something's wrong, that's an ambulance!' They started to run.

When they neared the boat there were still people milling around on the quay as the ambulance drove away. They anxiously scanned the group of fishermen on the drifter's deck. 'Father's there,' said Nell, some relief in her voice. The crew's attention now seemed to be directed towards one man but they could not see who. Mr Franklin, noticing the two girls, came quickly on to the quay.

125

'What's happened, Dad?' asked Nell anxiously.

'It's Terry ... broke his leg.'

'Is he going to be all right?' asked Jane.

'As far as I could tell it's a straightforward fracture, but the doctors will see to him. He's lucky to be alive.' Alarm gripped the girls as they waited for him to go on. 'The fishing had been reasonable. I decided we'd make one more cast – a good one would have really given us a more than break-even return. Somehow Terry got tangled in the net. He would have been dragged overboard with disastrous result if it hadn't been for Glen's quick thinking.'

'Glen?' both girls gasped.

'If he hadn't been taking photographs, he wouldn't have been where he was. In fact, no one would have been there under normal circumstances. He saw what was happening and was quick-thinking enough to use the axe jammed against the nearby hoist. He grabbed it, and with one blow severed the line holding the net. That saved Terry's life.'

'And the net?' said Nell.

'We had to let it go, but what's a net where a life is concerned? All I can say is, thank goodness Glen chose this voyage to take his photographs. He's a hero. Well, you can see that by the way the crew are fussing round him.'

'How did he do otherwise?' asked Nell.

'Just fine! Had his sea-legs right away. I tell you what, you'd have thought he'd been born to the sea. I've seen regular sailors succumb, but not Glen. Now, with all the fuss over, I'd better get back and see to the catch. I'll send him over to you.'

Carrying his photographic equipment, Glen jumped on to the quay in front of the two girls. 'Hi,' he said. 'Thanks for being here.'

'Had to welcome our partner home,' replied Jane.

'A hero,' put in Nell admiringly.

'Anyone would have done it,' he replied dismissively.

'Not necessarily,' said Nell. 'You saved Terry's life. And Dad said you have sea-legs.'

126

Glen laughed. 'That'll disappoint Mr Ewan.'

'Not what he'll be expecting when he returns,' grinned Nell, imagining his face when he heard.

'I've taken a lot of pictures, and I've had a chance to think about using them apart from in your book, Jane. We have a news story now and I'd like to get these to London as soon as possible,' Glen told them.

'London?' Both the girls looked puzzled.

'Yes. What I have in mind needs these films developing right away. I'm going straight back to Yarmouth now to develop and print them. Would you like to come and help, Nell?'

'Of course,' she replied, caught by the excitement in his voice.

'Jane, what I have in mind needs some background colour about life on board during a fishing trip. You did something like it for the *Scarborough Evening News*, but this will need a bit more drama to it.'

'If I come with you, you can tell me what you observed?'

'Yes, I can, but it will only be an outsider's view.'

'The *Silver King* is coming in now. If I wait until she's docked, I'll see if Simon can come too. You two go on now and get started on the developing, Simon and I will follow. On the way we can decide what's wanted.'

'Good idea,' Glen enthused. 'Bring your typewriter. Come on, Nell. See you later, Jane.'

She was thankful to see a few berths still vacant. It meant the *Silver King* would not be queuing up for a place to unload her catch. Excited and wondering what Glen had in mind, she hurried along the quay, dodging the baskets of herring being slung ashore and skipping round the men handling them. Intent on their work, eager to be through it as quickly as possible, they took little notice of her, relying on her to look out for her own safety.

Simon saw her coming, waved and then concentrated on handling the baskets that were being hoisted out of the hold. When Jane reached the drifter she caught his

127

attention again and signalled she would like to speak to him as soon as possible. A few minutes later she saw him have a quick word with another member of the crew.

'This is a nice surprise. Thanks for coming,' he said as he jumped ashore.

'Good to see you, too,' she replied, then quickly acquainted him with what she wanted.

'Sounds exciting. The unloading is going well, but I'll have to have a word with Dad.'

'OK, I'll wait.'

She watched Simon disappear into the wheelhouse where she knew Mr Evans would be keeping a careful eye on the unloading. When Simon reappeared he informed her he would be free in ten minutes.

'I'll go and get my typewriter. See you at the bus stop.'

'Tell me more about Glen's idea,' said Simon once the bus was underway.

She told him the little she knew, and went on to describe how Glen had saved Terry.

'That'll push Ewan's nose out of joint! He thought Glen would succumb to seasickness and the trip would be a waste of time.'

They fell to discussing what Jane could put in her article. When they left the bus to walk to Glen's studio, she said, 'I'm grateful for what you are doing, Simon. It means a lot to me ... well, to the three of us ... to get this right. I want to build up a story of life on board related to Glen's photographs.'

After greeting them and thanking Simon for coming, Glen told them, 'I think we should get some good prints from these negatives, but we shall see.'

'What exactly have you in mind, Glen? And why London?' Jane asked.

'You know about *World Scene*?'

'Yes. The best photojournalism.'

'I think the subject of a drifter's voyage should suit

them. After all, most people like herring but how many of them know what it's like for the men who bring them to their plates?'

'Good idea,' enthused Jane.

'And I understand you had some drama on your voyage?' said Simon. 'That could work in very well.'

'I really should know the style of writing they use to support their pictures,' Jane pointed out.

'There are several copies of the magazine in the pile over there. Study them while Nell and I print the photographs. I'm sorry to make this such a rush job, but it's a subject that needs handling quickly. That's why I want to take the photos and copy to London myself, today if possible.'

'I'll do my best,' said Jane, and she and Simon went off to study the magazines.

Nell went to the drying cabinet and found the first reel of film ready to print. She and Glen went into the darkroom to start the printing. Jane and Simon saw, from the looks on their faces when they reappeared, that they were satisfied with the results. With the prints laid carefully on a table, Jane and Simon perused them while Glen and Nell started on the rest of the negatives.

The morning went well. By midday all the prints were completed and Jane had formed an idea of how she would like to tackle the story.

'I'm desperate to get to London. Can we work through without a break?' Glen suggested.

They all agreed and began to choose the sequence that would have the most impact and still be faithful to the life and drama of sailing with the drifters.

'I don't know how you managed to get those pictures of the danger Terry was in, then the immediacy of the moment after you had saved him,' commented Simon admiringly.

'With a camera always ready, instinct and swift reactions,' replied Glen, playing the incident down.

With the final selection made, Glen and Nell returned to the darkroom to try to improve a couple of the selected

129

pictures while Jane and Simon worked on the text.

When the final copy linked to the sequence was passed to Glen, the other three waited anxiously. He read it carefully and, when he looked up, said, 'This is terrific. You've captured *World Scene*'s style perfectly. You're brilliant, Jane. What a gift you have.'

She blushed at the praise. 'Just seems to be instinct.'

'I think it's more than that,' said Simon. 'Working with you today has opened my eyes. I am really looking forward to making my own humble contribution to your book.'

Their eyes met but neither of them was sure what to read into the exchange.

Soon afterwards, Nell, Jane and Simon accompanied Glen to the station and wished him good luck, knowing that success for him today could mean a great deal to them all.

Chapter Seven

It was midday when the *Lively Lady* finally limped into Lowestoft and found a berth. Tempers were not at their best but Percy Steel soothed his crew somewhat when he announced that he would not rush repairs to the engine that had caused them such trouble. They would have three nights at home and sail again on the evening of December the third. He also promised to recompense them for loss of pay.

With the catch landed and sold, albeit at an unrewarding price, Ewan picked up the news that was still circulating around the harbour of Glen's heroism in saving Terry. Wanting to know more, he hurried to the Franklins' home.

He made his customary breezy entrance and faced the usual domestic scene of Mrs Franklin preparing a meal and Mr Franklin enjoying his pipe, having had his sleep since coming ashore.

'You're late back,' said Flo, noting that Ewan was still in his sailing clothes.

'Engine trouble! Just got in,' he replied. 'There's a rumour running around the docks about your voyage, Mr Franklin.'

'No rumour, lad,' replied George.

'Glen Aveburn really saved Terry's life?'

'Aye. Quick reactions he had.'

'He wasn't seasick at all?'

George smiled. He knew that Ewan had been getting at Glen about sailing with the drifters. 'It was as if he'd been at sea all his life.'

Ewan was at a loss for words so veered away from the subject. 'Is Nell at home?'

'No. She went to see the drifters return with Jane. Jane's been back for her typewriter since. Said she was going straight to Glen's studio in Yarmouth and Nell had already gone ahead. Some story they're working on.'

'Did she say when she would be back?'

'No.'

'I see. When she does, tell her I'm not sailing until the third. I'll call for her at five.'

With her mind still on Glen and his trip to London, Nell's reaction to Ewan's message was muted. Nevertheless, anticipating where he might be taking her, she changed and primped herself for an evening out.

Guessing why there was some tension in him, she slipped her arm under his as they left the house. Believing in clearing the air, she came straight to the point.

'You heard about Glen?'

'Aye,' he grunted.

'And you don't like being proved wrong?'

Ewan stopped and swung her towards him. Face to face, she saw the annoyance burning in his eyes. 'I didn't like you gallivanting off with him!'

'I was working.'

'Working?' Derision touched his voice.

'Yes, working.'

'In a darkroom?'

'Yes.'

'And what else happens in that darkroom?'

She stared at him for a moment then gave a little laugh. 'You really *are* jealous.'

'I'm not!' he snapped, annoyed to have been caught out.

'Yes, you are.' Her laughter rang out as, her arm still

132

linked with his, Nell walked on. 'Do you know, Ewan Steel, I think you're more attractive when you are?'

He stopped, pulled her to him and kissed her passionately then. 'I love you, Nell Franklin.'

She responded to his kiss but made no response in words.

Later, recalling the moment, she wondered why?

Smog added to the early-evening gloom when Glen arrived in London. He went straight to the Strand Palace Hotel, the place he knew his father used on his regular business trips to London. There he made himself known and acquired the use of his father's usual suite. After a meal, tired from the journey, the concentrated work in the darkroom and making the final presentation, he went to bed earlier than usual.

He awoke with a start and for a moment wondered where he was. With realisation driving the haze from his mind, he glanced at his watch. 7.30! He had meant to be up before now. He swung out of bed and twenty minutes later was walking into the dining room. A word with the waiter ensured there was no delay with his breakfast.

He felt a buzz when he walked into the offices of *World Scene* later that morning. He was in the magazine that featured the work of some of the best photographers in the country. He felt humble, and fearful for a moment that his work and that of Nell would not measure up to the standards of this widely read publication. For one moment he wondered how he had dared to entertain the idea of trying to sell work to such a prestigious magazine.

His doubt fell away when he approached the vivacious young receptionist and was welcomed with a friendly smile. 'Good morning, sir.'

'Good morning,' returned Glen, annoyed that there was still a touch of hesitation in his voice. He took a grip on himself and asked with rather more firmness. 'I'd like to see someone.' He indicated his briefcase. 'I have an interesting project to show them.'

'Yes, sir! Have you an appointment?'

'No, my partner and I took the photographs just two days ago. I arrived in London from Yarmouth last night.'

'And you thought *World Scene* would be interested?'

'I hope so,' he replied with a smile.

'May I ask your name and the nature of your submission: hot news, feature with some immediacy, or feature that could be used any time? If I know that, it will help in directing you to the correct person.'

'Glen Aveburn. I would say, feature with some immediacy.'

'Thank you, sir, I'll see what I can do.' She consulted a directory and dialled a number.

A few moments later she spoke. 'Elaine, I have a young gentleman here, Mr Glen Aveburn, with a feature I think might be of interest to Frank.' There was a pause. 'Right. Thanks, Elaine.' The receptionist looked at Glen. 'If you'd like to take a seat, sir, Elaine will be with you in about ten minutes. She will take you to Frank Horton who deals with news features.'

'Thank you.' He went to a seat, one of several placed around a low oblong table on which were copies of the day's newspapers and recent copies of *World Scene*. He picked up a magazine and casually flicked through it, but with his mind fixed nervously on the forthcoming interview nothing really registered with him.

'Good morning, sir.'

Startled, Glen looked up to see a pretty, raven-haired girl smiling at him. He hadn't heard her approach, the carpet dulling the sound of her footsteps. Nor had he realised how much time had slipped by. He dropped his magazine back on the table and sprang to his feet, spluttering, 'Good morning.'

'I am Elaine. Will you come with me?'

'Thank you.'

She closed the doors and pressed the button for the third

floor before she said, 'You haven't met Mr Horton before?'

'No. It's the first time I've dared to approach *World Scene*.'

Elaine smiled. 'We're always on the lookout for suitable features, and welcome contributions from outside sources. Mr Horton is easy to get on with but, I warn you, does not suffer fools gladly. If your work does not make an immediate impact, you'll be shown the door.' She saw Glen's face drop and gave a chuckle. 'Don't be alarmed, he's not an ogre.'

The lift came to a stop, the doors opened, and Glen found himself following her across a narrow hall to a small office.

'That's my desk,' she whispered, hoping to calm some of the nervousness she sensed in this young man whose whole future probably rested on the contents of that briefcase. She knocked on the inner door, hesitated and then opened it. 'Mr Glen Aveburn,' she announced, and stood to one side to allow him to enter the room.

The office was imposing. A tall thin man rose from behind a large oak desk on which papers and photographs were strewn. It was placed at an angle so that light from three tall windows fell across it from the left. To the right of the windows was a medium-sized empty table. Two large tables, obviously being used to sort photographs into sequences, occupied the other walls.

'Glen Aveburn, I'm told?' The tall man held out his hand. 'Frank Horton.'

'Pleased to meet you, sir,' replied Glen.

'You have something to show me? Let's get down to it straight away.' He indicated the table beside the windows.

Glen flicked open the cover of a folder in which he had arranged photographs and text in the way he visualised they could appear in *World Scene*, then took a step aside.

Frank Horton read this as an indication that the young man wanted him to take over and was not going to intervene with comments on the pictures, copy, or what he was

135

aiming to present; his submission would speak for itself. Horton liked that. He turned the pages, pausing to take in the pictures and read some of the accompanying copy.

Nervousness began to overwhelm Glen. His mouth felt dry. He kept glancing at Frank Horton but could read nothing from his expression. Finally he let the last page and outer cover drop.

'Sit down.' He indicated a chair in front of his desk, resumed his own and placed the folder in front of him. Glen felt uncomfortable under Horton's gaze as the man studied him for a few moments. 'Tell me something about yourself?' He sat back in his chair and kept his eyes fixed on Glen the whole time he was talking.

'I live in Yarmouth but my family come from Norwich where my father owns and runs Aveburn Shoes. I could have gone into the business but I wanted to be a photographer so I moved to Yarmouth where I set up a studio. I have done work for several newspapers throughout Suffolk, Norfolk, and parts of Yorkshire. Locally I have done commercial work for a variety of firms to promote their businesses. I do all my own processing and printing. Well, that's not strictly true on this project and the previous one.

'For those I recruited a young woman who was brought to my notice. She has a natural talent I could not ignore so we came to an agreement to work together. Along with her came a friend who has ambitions to be a writer. They had just broken into the market with a series of three articles, and their collaboration impressed me. I realised I could use the writer to expand my own work so she and I also came to an arrangement. It is through them and their contacts that we worked on the project you have just seen.' Thinking he had said enough, Glen stopped talking.

Frank nodded and straightened in his chair. 'What was the project before this one?' He tapped the folder in front of him.

'It was a brochure for shoes which my father will produce.' He quickly went on to explain that they had not

136

won the contract because of his family connections.

'So you have not done any photojournalism before?'

'No.'

Frank pursed his lips thoughtfully. 'Then I must say, the three of you have done exceedingly well. The photographs alone tell a story, which is what we like to see, but coupled with the writing they really make an impact. I can tell the young lady who wrote this has studied our magazine. Oh, I'm not saying the whole production is perfect, but with one or two adjustments in the writing and cropping one or two of the photographs, we can definitely use it.'

Glen could hardly believe his ears. 'You'll take it?'

'I most certainly will, but it has got to be an exclusive. You will have to sign an agreement to that effect. Not only does this submission show the hard and dangerous work of the driftermen, it also shows what goes on ashore to get the herring to market and highlights some of the problems the industry is facing.'

Glen swallowed hard. 'I'm overwhelmed, sir. I am exceedingly grateful, and I know Nell and Jane will be overjoyed.'

'Which is which?' asked Frank, smiling at Glen's exuberance.

'Nell is the photographer, Jane the writer.'

'Now, we will pay you our usual rates. They are set out here.' He passed a printed sheet of paper to Glen whose eyes widened when he saw the figures. 'You're happy with that?' said Frank, seeing his expression.

'I certainly am.'

'You have come to a top magazine. If we see talent we like to reward it, then we know we'll see more good work in the future.'

'Well, thank you again, sir.' Glen started to rise from his chair, not wanting to take up any more of this busy man's time, but Frank Horton stopped him. 'Wait a moment. I want to run through this material with you and show you what I intend to do. Come back to the table.'

Ten minutes later Glen had learned a lesson on how certain aspects of his photographs could be improved and how a few alterations to the text gave it more impact.

'Satisfied with what I've done?' Horton asked.

'Without a doubt,' replied Glen.

'Good. I'm going to rush this through. It has a news aspect because of the man's injury. It will appear in next week's issue. You've caught us right at the start of production. I'll call the printing manager.' He picked up the phone and within a few minutes a man in his forties bustled in. No time was wasted. 'Next week's issue, Max,' said Horton, handing over the folder. 'I've marked the crop lines and alterations in the text. Kill the hat article, it can be used in any issue.'

'Just in time,' said Max, and bustled out again.

'Man of few words,' commented Horton as the door closed, 'but a wonder at his job.' He leaned back in his chair and eyed Glen. 'Now, young man, I'm impressed with your work and that of your two friends so, while all this has been going on, I've been thinking. I have a proposition to put to you ...'

Glen, wondering what was coming next, was all attention.

'Would you be interested in working as a stringer for us?'

'I'll say we would,' replied Glen, his eyes brightening at the prospect. But a thought clouded his enthusiasm. 'Would that exclude us from doing other work?'

'Not at all, but we would expect anything we take from you to be exclusive to us. We'd expect you to look out for suitable subjects, and be prepared to pursue any idea we put to you because we think you are the person to do it.'

'That seems a very generous proposition.'

'We would pay each of you a retainer of £3 a week, and for that would expect to receive an idea a fortnight. If we take up the offer we would expect you to work on the idea straight away. Any idea coming from us would

138

take precedence. For the finished project we would pay you at the rates on the sheet I have given you.'

'That sounds even more generous.' Glen smiled.

'Good. I'll get my secretary to send contracts to each of you. Leave her your address. Can you be contacted by telephone?'

'Yes.'

'Leave her your number too. I think that is all. Have you any other questions?'

Glen hesitated then shook his head. 'I don't think so. But I must say thank you on behalf of the three of us. This day has turned out even better than we expected.' He rose from his chair as Horton did so.

'Next assignment, bring the two girls to meet me,' said Horton, still subconsciously admiring the talent he had seen in those photographs.

'I will indeed, sir. They'll be thrilled.'

Glen left the building in a haze of euphoria that propelled him to check out of the hotel and head straight for the station.

Reaching Lowestoft in late-afternoon, he hurried to the Franklins' house.

'Glen!' Nell gasped when she opened the door and saw him. 'Come in, come in,' she urged. 'What happened?'

'Jane here?' he asked.

'Through there.' She indicated the door on the right and moved to open it. 'Glen's back,' she announced.

Jane dropped the book she was reading and jumped to her feet, excitement in her eyes. 'How did it go?'

Mr Franklin looked up from the paper he was reading. 'I'm glad to see you, young man,' he said amiably. 'Now these two might finally settle down.'

'Good news or bad?' pressed Nell. 'Wait! Mum must hear.' She poked her head round the door and shouted, 'Mum!'

A few moments later Flo hurried into the room, querying the urgency of the call and acknowledging Glen.

Everyone listened intently as he told them about his reception at *World Scene*. Nell and Jane couldn't contain their excitement when he told them about the retainer and the new door that had opened for them.

'Unbelievable!'

'Never expected ...'

Mr and Mrs Franklin, too, expressed their delight and congratulations.

'So the *Sea Queen* and her crew are going to appear in *World Scene*? What do you think to that, Flo?' said Mr Franklin proudly.

'Aye, and some of the photos taken by our girl!' she replied with equal enthusiasm.

'Mum, they may not be mine,' warned Nell. 'Glen took some too.'

'About half and half,' he intervened quickly. 'And there was a little alteration to Jane's copy to fit in with the magazine's lay-out and style. But Mr Horton was delighted with the way you'd written it. I'll tell you all about that later, Jane. Now, we must celebrate, so on my way here I rang my friend in Yarmouth and booked us a table at the hotel. A taxi will be here at quarter to six for you all. Simon too if you can let him know?'

Jane's face fell. 'He'll be sailing.'

'And so will I,' said George Franklin. 'But you all enjoy yourselves.'

Nell screwed up her face. 'I've a date with Ewan. He's not sailing until the third – trouble with the *Lively Lady*.'

'If you've nothing particular planned, bring him along.'

Nell thought she detected a note of disappointment in Glen's voice, and a trace of reluctance at having to invite Ewan. 'Can I?'

'Of course.'

'Glen, this is most kind of you,' said Flo, 'but count me out. You young people don't want your style cramped by me.'

Her statement brought protests from him but she was

140

adamant. 'I'll be happier this way. You all have a good time.'

'I'll go and let Ewan know,' said Nell, heading for the door.

'I'll leave as well,' said Glen. 'See you all in Yarmouth.' They left together.

'Glen, you've done a wonderful job getting this acceptance and retainer,' said Nell. 'I am *so* grateful. You have given me a whole new perspective.'

'Your photographs played their part,' he replied with admiration. 'I think the three of us will do very well. I'm sure Mr Horton saw our contributions as being in equal measure.'

'Have you any ideas what we should do next or if there's anything Horton might be looking for?'

'He did tell me something, and we'll pass this on to Jane. He wants to highlight life as it is in all its aspects, down-to-earth to glamorous, disreputable to highly respected. Obviously people will play a central role in the pictures but he doesn't want a mere assembly of portraits. He could do that from a variety of sources. He wants the camera to really tell the story. If it does, then coupled with Jane's tight, to-the-point writing, the whole thing will make double the impact.'

'Did he give any ideas for possible subjects?'

'Nothing in particular. He leaves us to look out for them, he'd like one worked-out idea a fortnight, but at the same time, if he's interested in something that suits our style, he'll contact us. So it could be anything. Success lies in observing the principles I've just mentioned. We achieved them in *The Driftermen*.'

Nell chuckled. 'Little did Jane know what her idea would lead to.'

'She certainly didn't,' agreed Glen with a smile. 'Now we've got to grab our chance. Keep your mind open for ideas and, remember, involve people.'

'I will.' They had reached the crossroads. 'This is where I leave you.'

'Sorry about that,' he said with a touch of disappointment. 'See you later.'

'I look forward to it.' As she hurried away her thoughts dwelt on Glen and the exciting times that beckoned, but she pushed them to the back of her mind as she knocked on the door of Ewan's home.

It was opened by his mother. 'Hello, Nell,' she greeted her with a smile. 'Come on in, I'll give Ewan a shout.' She added with a twinkle in her eye, 'I expect it's him you've come to see, not me.'

Nell stepped into the hall from which a staircase led directly to the next floor. 'Thanks, Mrs Steel, but it's always a pleasure to see you.'

Mrs Steel laughed. 'Get on with you, there's no need to get round me. Come on through.' She shouted to Ewan and led the way to the kitchen. 'I'm just peeling some potatoes. Will you stay and eat with us?'

'That's kind, but I can't. Maybe Ewan won't either when I give him my message.'

Mrs Steel looked at her askance but it did not elicit any more information. She wasn't bothered; she heard her son rushing downstairs and knew in a matter of moments she would be put in the picture.

'Hi, love,' Ewan called as he burst into the kitchen. 'I thought we were meeting later, but the sooner the better.'

'We're partying. Well, a get-together anyway, to celebrate. I thought I'd better let you know.'

'Celebrating what?'

'You know Glen sailed with Father?'

'How could I forget? Something of a hero and never seasick!' Ewan raised his eyes upward as if chiding the gods for letting him down.

'His pictures were marvellous, so he took them and mine and Jane's copy to London – and sold them to *World Scene*!'

'What?' Ewan looked doubtful. 'You're having me on.'

'No, it's true. Not only that, we've been put on a

retainer by the magazine. I'll tell you all about it this evening. We're all going to Yarmouth. Glen has booked a table at his friend's hotel. Be at our house by quarter to six. Glen has ordered a taxi to take us to Yarmouth.'

'This sounds exciting, Nell,' said Mrs Steel, turning from the potatoes she was peeling. In that moment she saw her son scowl and discreetly left the kitchen. She believed they were old enough to deal with their own problems, and it was best for parents not to intervene unless asked for advice.

'What's up with you?' asked Nell as the door closed. 'You'd think I'd handed you a damp squib.'

Ewan's lips tightened. 'Glen, Glen,' he muttered. 'Is that all I'm going to get from now on? It's all right for some, born with a silver spoon in their mouth!'

'Hey, hold on,' Nell responded sharply. 'Glen makes his own way.'

'That's what he tells you.'

'It's true. He chose work for himself rather than go into his father's factory. He never asked for help and his father respected that decision. So, Ewan Steel, you can just get yourself into a proper mood for this evening. I don't want you showing any jealousy or hostility that will spoil it for everyone else. Note, I said jealousy because that's exactly what it is.'

'Stop talking squit,' snapped Ewan.

'I'm not. Just look at you now. Come here, you great galoot.' Nell grabbed him by the arms, pulled him to her and kissed him full on the lips. As she expected from the mood he was in, he resisted momentarily then returned her kiss. She broke away before it became too passionate. 'Now, get yourself ready and in the right mood.' She swung open the door and was gone before he could say anything more.

When Ewan arrived at her house later Nell could tell that he still resented her upbraiding but he was expert enough not to let it show to anyone else. By the time the taxi arrived he had absorbed some of the excitement that gripped the girls.

Glen greeted their arrival warmly and dismissed Ewan's congratulations on his heroic first trip with the drifters as something anyone would have done. His ability to make everyone feel at home and draw all of them into the conversation, allowing little to be said about the results of his visit to London so that Ewan would not feel like an outsider, created a real impression on Nell.

Inevitably, conversation turned to the crisis in Europe.

'Chamberlain's peace initiative seems to be holding,' commented Ewan when the topic was raised.

'On the surface, yes,' agreed Glen. 'But I don't trust Hitler after the way he has torn up previous treaties. Look at the way he just walked into Sudetenland, and we let him.'

'So you think we should have gone to war?' asked Ewan.

'I'm not saying that, but I think we should have shown our teeth then to avoid what I think is now inevitable.'

'You mean, war?' said Jane.

'I sincerely hope not, but I think the government are afraid the situation is worsening. Today it's been announced there is to be a national registry for war service, though only on a voluntary basis. I think that's a sign that they have the worst scenario in mind.'

'Hey,' cut in Nell, 'we're supposed to be celebrating, not having a wake.'

The topic of war was dropped and the party soon resumed its easy atmosphere.

She was in high spirits when they started for home and appreciated Jane leaving her with Ewan when they reached Lowestoft.

'Well, that wasn't so bad for you, was it?' she said as she took his hand and they strolled a few yards away from the Franklins' house.

'No,' he agreed reluctantly. 'But Glen's a bit of a show-off.'

'He's not. That's only your preconceived idea of him. Glen's a decent type. I know he's from a different station in life, but that doesn't stop him being one of us.'

'One of us?' snorted Ewan. 'How can he ever be that?'

'You mean, because of his moneyed background? That doesn't come into it. I told you, he's making his own way in the world. All right, maybe his father makes him a living allowance, I don't know, but if he does that's all it will be.'

'But it makes things easier for him.'

'Not in his work, he's out on his own there, and you've got to give him credit for what he's achieved. I tell you what, Ewan Steel, Jane and I are lucky to have met Glen, so you'd better get used to me working with him. I've got a chance there that I'm going to take.'

'And maybe get too big for your boots!'

Nell's eyes blazed. 'Is that all you think of me after all these years? We've been together since we were kids. Surely you know me better than that?' She started to walk away, trying to hide the tears that had risen to her eyes.

Ewan reached out and, grabbing her arm, pulled her back. His arms came round her and held her tight so there was no escape. 'I'm sorry, Nell. It's just that you'll be spending so much time with him ...'

'Jealousy gets you nowhere,' she replied. 'It's a working relationship, that's all. Be happy. I'm achieving something. Haven't you always said you wanted more than to be a drifterman all your life?'

'Aye, but ...'

'And you may get your chance, if war comes.'

'I thought you banned the mention of war back there?' Ewan smiled.

Nell grimaced and shrugged her shoulders as if agreeing that war was inevitable. 'You may have to go, love.'

'Like our fathers in the last one. Taken over with their ships by the Admiralty to work as minesweepers, escort vessels and the like.'

The thought made Nell cling to him more tightly.

'Don't think about it, love, just think about now.' Ewan kissed her and she returned his kiss to drive uncertainty from both their minds.

Chapter Eight

Dear Aunt Mavis and Uncle David,

In my last letter I told you my exciting news about our success with the brochure for Aveburn Shoes. Now I have some more exciting news: we have sold an article and photographs to *World Scene*! It is another piece about the drifters but different from those Nell and I did for the *Scarborough Evening News*. It should appear in next week's issue. Not only that, the Features Editor liked our work so much that he has put us on a retainer. But I'll tell you all about that when I see you.

That is the purpose of this letter. May I be with you over Christmas, probably coming on Wednesday the twenty-third, and be with you into the New Year?

And there is one other request. I think in an earlier letter I mentioned Simon Evans, who works on his father's drifter and is one of our group? Well, he has been most helpful in giving me lots of information about the drifters and their crews. His family make more of Christmas than New Year, so I wondered if I could ask him to spend New Year with us as a way of saying thank you for helping me? I hope you will say yes.

Longing to see you. All news then.

Love,

Jane

*

She re-read the letter and, satisfied, sealed it in an envelope and stamped it ready for posting.

A reply came by return.

Dear Jane,

Delighted you are coming for Christmas and New Year. Of course you must invite Simon. Looking forward to meeting him.

Oh, and congratulations on your success with *World Scene*. Longing to see the article. Will write no more now. We'll have lots to talk about when you are here.

Take care.

Love,

Aunty Mavis

P.S. Your uncle sends his love. He is so excited you will be here. He says to bring some of Nell's photographs for him to see.

Jane experienced a sense of contentment as she folded the letter and replaced it in its envelope. Whether that was because she would spend Christmas and New Year with her uncle and aunt or because Simon would be joining them, she could not decide. Maybe it was both.

Ewan's father decided to work off Plymouth the rest of the year to take advantage of the fine herring that attracted buyers from the London market. 'We'll be back in Lowestoft no later than the eighteenth when we'll lay the *Lively Lady* up for cleaning and repairs until the tenth of January,' he informed his family. His wife and daughters were used to this but it did not go down too well with Ewan, who regretted the time he would be away from Nell.

She, too, lamented his coming absence and said so when she came to the dock to see him sail. 'And don't be eyeing those Devonshire lasses,' she added.

'Would I ever?' he protested.

'I know you, Ewan Steel.'

'Well, remember this, Nell Franklin.' He pulled her sharply to him then and kissed her so passionately it brought cat-calls from members of his crew. Nell was left gasping for breath when he released her and, without a word, jumped on deck.

She smiled to herself and decided not to wait to see the *Lively Lady* sail.

During the next fortnight she took the opportunity to learn more about processing and printing in the darkroom in Yarmouth. After her third visit she found sharing the close space with Glen beginning to disturb her and was forced to make herself recall Ewan's kiss on the quay. Hadn't she issued a veiled warning to him about the Devonshire girls? And wasn't she letting her own feelings be influenced by circumstances now? She was pleased whenever Jane decided to accompany her so that all three of them could discuss ideas for future work, and yet on those days did she not experience a tinge of annoyance too that her friend was there, cramping her style?

Their discussions were lively and resulted in three ideas being submitted to Mr Horton. The replies that came back by return were sharp and to the point: 'Not suitable'; 'Needs a human touch'; 'Think again'.

'Well, what now?' asked Jane, despondent at the continued rejection.

'Don't look so glum, Jane.' Glen tried to raise her spirits, though he too was disappointed and knew Nell felt the same. 'We can't win them all.'

'What about *Winter at the Seaside*?' suggested Nell. 'We can aim at the bleakness, the absence of holidaymakers and so on.'

'Not a bad idea,' said Glen. 'The photographs would need to be atmospheric. Doing them in black-and-white will help that. Let's start to put something together. I think in future we should submit some photographs with our ideas rather than just a suggestion on paper.'

'You're right, Glen,' said Nell. 'We took Mr Horton's

words about wanting ideas too literally.'

'Even an idea should have impact,' added Jane. 'I think up to now we've had things too easy. Well, Nell and I have. We've become complacent, thought everything we did would be accepted. This is a jolt, which could be good for us. We must turn it to our advantage.'

'You're right,' agreed Nell. 'What about doing a photographic piece entitled, *Preparations for War?*'

'Bit of a sombre subject,' objected Jane. 'What do you think, Glen?'

'Very topical, with the situation as it is.'

'Do you really think there'll be a war?'

'Who knows what Hitler will do? He wants his own way under the guise of its being good for Germany. He makes out he doesn't want war, but I don't trust him.'

'But Mr Chamberlain says we have peace in our time?'

Glen gave a snort. 'Oh, Hitler can easily ignore that. I reckon Chamberlain's merely bought us a bit of time, and it wouldn't surprise me if he knows it himself. Preparations for war are going on, and it's right for us to do so under the circumstances. So we have a subject involving civilians – gas masks, Air Raid Precautions, possible evacuation, volunteers, and so on.'

'But what if war doesn't come?' said Nell.

'Then we re-title it, *Preparations for the War That Never Was*,' he chuckled. 'So there we have two subjects to put to Mr Horton, that one and *Winter at the Seaside*. I suggest we concentrate on the latter and keep our eyes open for pictures to illustrate the former. Apart from concentrating on the subject in hand, I suggest we build up our own picture library too. Hopefully we'll sell to markets other than *World Scene*. For example, though it is too late to submit Christmas material now, we could build up a portfolio on that topic for the future.'

'Now we *are* getting organised,' said Nell. 'These rejections are already doing us some good.'

Over the next five days they scoured Yarmouth,

Lowestoft and the neighbouring coast for suitable ways of depicting *Winter at the Seaside*. Glen and Nell developed and printed the pictures while Jane wrote a succinct piece that got to the heart of the cold desolate scenes that had supplanted their lively, magical summer. With the four best photographs telling part of the story, Glen felt they would whet Mr Horton's desire to see more and despatched them to London.

Mid-morning the following day, just after Nell and Jane had arrived at his studio, the telephone rang. On hearing the first words he cast a sharp glance at the two girls. It drew their attention which heightened when he said, 'You've received them, Mr Horton?' A pause. 'That is good news, sir.' His face broadened into a smile of satisfaction and the girls guessed their work had been accepted, which was further confirmed when he gave them the thumbs up sign. 'Yes, we have ten more.' A pause. 'That should give you a good choice. I'll get them off to you right away.' Another pause then, 'Yes, sir, that is most acceptable. While you are on the phone, may I ask if the title *Preparations for War* interests you?' There was a longer pause that was followed by a brief discussion as to what the article should cover.

Jane and Nell got the gist from the one side of the conversation they could hear, but excited congratulations on the acceptance of the winter piece flowed before they learned more.

'Mr Horton is already entertaining the war idea. He said almost everyone at *World Scene* believes it is inevitable and that is the attitude being taken by the magazine. It will influence the main features of each issue until the direction in which Europe moves is decided. They do not want their articles and photographs to be alarmist but feel they need to depict what is going on in the lives of ordinary citizens. They have a number of photographers and journalists working on this theme and are gathering all the material together to use when they think the time is right. He

151

suggests we concentrate on aspects of Lowestoft and the East Anglian coast, particularly as we are so close to Europe and could be singled out for early bombing attacks should hostilities come. We must not forget the human aspect, and should be careful not to breach security. So we'll build up the subject at a reasonable rate, but must not lag behind.' He paused then asked, 'Any questions?'

The girls took a moment to consider and said with a shake of their heads, 'No.'

'Right. Nell, you and I had better get the rest of the prints for *Winter at the Seaside* ready.' Glen rose from his chair and Nell followed him to the darkroom, leaving Jane to consider which aspects of *Preparations for War* they should tackle. By the time Nell and Glen emerged from the darkroom, satisfied with the prints they had produced, she had several items listed.

Over the next ten days they accompanied an ARP warden who was urging members of the public, in the wake of Hitler's threat to Czechoslovakia, to take Air Raid Precautions seriously and join the service. They also photographed the preparation of sandbags, people being fitted for their gas masks, and one lady who, certain that war would come, was buying up yards and yards of material to black out the thirty windows in her house. Without disclosing secrets, they photographed preparations against invasion along the coast and how one farmer, on the premise that there would be measures to evacuate children to his area of Suffolk, was converting two of his brick barns into reasonable accommodation and fitting them out with bunk beds. 'Too old to fight,' he told them, 'it's my contribution to the war effort if Hitler's foolish enough to take us on.'

At the same time Jane gathered material for two articles on aspects of country life but was disappointed when a local paper and a magazine rejected them. She drew consolation from the fact that the war material was building up nicely. As the fortnight since the drifters had left for Plymouth drew to a close, Nell and Jane pushed their work to the back of their minds without ignoring it altogether. Ewan and Simon would soon be home and Christmas and New Year were near.

'I've an invitation for you two,' Glen greeted them when Nell and Jane walked into his studio. He handed each of them an envelope.

Mystified, they glanced at it but did not recognise the writing. Because the quality of the paper seemed to demand careful handling they were cautious when they slit the envelope and extracted a sheet of paper. The brief message inside made them look at Glen with pleasure and excitement.

'Your father and mother have invited us to a meal on Wednesday evening,' Nell gasped.

He smiled. 'I know, and I hope you are going to accept. It's to celebrate the publication of the brochure. Because of the situation in Europe, Father got the printers to do a rush job without lowering their usual standards. He wants to present you both with a copy, and Mother thought it would be nice to do so over a meal.'

'It is most kind of them,' said Jane. 'Of course we accept, don't we, Nell?'

'Certainly.'

'We must write an acceptance right away,' said Jane.

'I can tell them,' Glen offered.

'Oh, no, we must write,' Jane insisted. She went to the table she used while at Glen's studio and produced two sheets of paper. 'Here you are, Nell.'

She copied her friend's words. When the acceptances were sealed into envelopes, they handed them to Glen.

'We'll have to find out the best way to get to Norwich,' said Nell.

'No need. Father said to tell you he will send a car for you and return you home.'

The girls were almost overwhelmed by such generosity and looked forward to Wednesday with mounting excite-

153

ment. They spent hours trying to decide what to wear.

'Well, have you decided?' asked Flo when they came down for breakfast the day before they were to go to the Aveburns'.

'No, Mum,' replied Nell, pulling a face.

'A case of, "I haven't a thing to wear",' commented her mother.

'Exactly,' replied Nell.

'What about your nice yellow...?'

'Oh, Mum, that's out-of-date,' Nell interrupted.

'The blue one you got last year?'

'It has a mark on the sleeve,' she protested.

'Hardly noticeable.'

'I couldn't ...'

'I suppose you're in the same boat, Jane?' said Flo, ignoring her daughter's cry.

Jane tightened her lips and nodded.

Flo looked heavenwards. 'What a pair!' She went to her handbag, standing on a small table beside the door. When she turned back she handed each of them some money. 'Here you are, go and get yourselves something new.'

'Oh, Mum, thanks!' Nell flung her arms around her neck and kissed her on the cheek. 'You're a brick!'

'Oh, I couldn't, Mrs Franklin,' said Jane, embarrassed by such generosity.

Flo smiled. 'Of course you can. We can't have one of you in a new dress and not the other. Now, say no more.'

'But I must say thank you.' Jane kissed her on the cheek.

'Get your breakfast and off with you.'

Breakfast was eaten quickly and the girls prepared to leave.

'Choose wisely,' called Flo when they reached the door. 'Remember, you won't have time to change them. You'll be showing them off tomorrow.'

'You girls eaten?' were the first words Flo greeted them with on their return in the early-afternoon.

154

'Yes, Mum, we grabbed something,' replied Nell, brushing aside her mother's concern.

'We've had a wonderful time,' laughed Jane.

'Tried on every dress in Lowestoft, I expect?'

'Just about.' Jane grinned.

'Come on, Jane, let's put them on for Mum.' Nell headed for the stairs, Jane at her heels.

Flo smiled. 'Oh, what it is to be young,' she whispered to herself. 'I only hope Hitler doesn't mess up their lives.'

That thought was driven from her mind when a few minutes later the girls reappeared.

Nell's wine-coloured jersey dress, draped across the breasts, came into a tight waist around which there was a broad band of the same material. The dress fell in soft pleats down the front to just below the knees. The shoulders were only slightly padded with the sleeves becomingly fitted at the elbows and wrists. Her hair, which she had had waved earlier in the week, was worn long, down, and flicked under at the shoulders. She wore her simple necklace with the small cross.

In contrast Jane had her hair swept up on top of her head and pinned into curls. Her dark green dress had slightly wider shoulders to emphasise her slim waist. The upper half was cut plain, tight across the breasts, and buttoned down the front to just above the waist. Her sleeves were a little fuller than Nell's but still came tight at the wrists.

'You both look beautiful,' gasped Flo admiringly. 'You have indeed chosen wisely. Turn around.'

Delighted with her praise, they both did a slow turn so that she had a chance to give her added approval. 'Lovely,' she said finally. 'Now off with them, you don't want them marring for tomorrow evening.'

She had hardly finished speaking when they heard a knock on the front door and it opened and closed. They exchanged glances of surprise.

155

'There's only one person opens and closes a door like that,' commented Flo.

Almost at the same moment Nell was gasping, 'Ewan!'

With that the kitchen door was flung open. 'Surprise!' The word almost died on his lips when he saw such unexpected elegance before him, but being Ewan he reacted to the situation quickly. 'Ravishingly beautiful.' He stepped towards Nell.

Reading his intention, she raised her hands and backed away. 'No, Ewan! Don't mess my dress.'

He stopped in his tracks. He read the warning in her eyes but still indicated his intention. 'What, not kiss my girl? You don't mind, Mrs F, do you?'

'No, Ewan, don't touch me,' Nell answered for her mother. 'I've just bought this dress. It's special.'

With twinkling eyes he turned to Jane then. 'You wouldn't deny a sailor home from the sea a kiss, would you, Jane?'

She hesitated. 'Well ... '

Ewan threw up his arms in despair at her indecision. 'What's going on?' His frivolity turned to seriousness.

'We've just got new dresses because we're going to Mr and Mrs Aveburn's tomorrow evening.'

'Hey, I'm home!' said Ewan in a tone that showed his clear disapproval.

'So I see,' retorted Nell.

Flo, sensing an atmosphere developing and trusting her daughter to handle it, slipped quietly from the room followed by Jane who was thankful that she was standing close to the door. A confrontation between Nell and Ewan was one in which she did not want to be involved.

'Well, I thought you'd be welcoming me back with open arms and we'd be going out,' Ewan was saying.

'So we would, but you've come home earlier than expected.'

'Aye, and look what I've found – my girl all dolled up and gallivanting!'

'Hold on, Ewan Steel, I'm *not* gallivanting. This is an

156

invitation from Mr and Mrs Aveburn to celebrate the brochure we did.'

'It may be from Mr and Mrs Aveburn, but I'll bet our clever Mr Glen's behind it. He's showing off, trying to entice you with a show of affluence.'

'He isn't,' snapped Nell indignantly.

'That's what you think. But I tell you what, he'd better not think he's going to get his hands on *my* girl.'

'Jumping to conclusions, aren't you? That I'm your girl?'

Ewan's lips tightened; his eyes narrowed. He stepped forward and new dress or no new dress, grabbed Nell and pulled her roughly to him. His arms encircled her waist in a tight grip and his lips met hers with fierce passion. Then he released his hold and swung away. As he reached the door he called out, 'I love you, Nell Franklin!' then slammed the door behind him, leaving her speechless and staring. Tears came to her eyes then. She stamped her feet in exasperation and ran her hands over her dress, trying to return it to its pristine condition.

The door opened slowly. Her mother peeped in, then stepped into the room followed by Jane.

'You all right?' Flo asked tentatively.

'Yes,' replied Nell irritably. 'But Ewan is so blinkin' exasperating.'

'He seemed to make his intentions clear as he went out, even though he was in a huff.'

'Maybe,' Nell grumbled. 'Then why does he rile me with snide remarks about Glen all the time? He thinks he's behind this invitation and is just showing off, using his family's money to entice me.'

'Heat of the moment, love, and disappointment that the homecoming he was expecting didn't materialise. Ewan will get over that.'

'Maybe.' She glanced down at herself. 'And he crushed my dress!'

'Can't see a thing,' put in Jane reassuringly. 'You

157

expected it to be crushed so you think it is. Come on, let's get changed and put them aside to wear tomorrow as new.' She held out her hand to Nell who took it gratefully, finding a measure of comfort in her friend's reassurance.

'Everything will be all right, love,' said her mother as they walked from the room. 'Don't let it spoil tomorrow.'

When the two girls had gone upstairs Flo grabbed her coat and hurried out to turn in the direction of the Steels' house. She breathed a sigh of relief when she saw Ewan coming out. She would rather have a word with him alone than in front of his parents.

'Ewan, just the person I wanted to see. I want to ask you a favour.'

'What's that, Mrs F?'

'I'm taking no sides in what went on a few minutes ago between you and Nell. You can sort your own troubles out. All I ask is that you keep out of her way tomorrow. Please don't spoil an evening she has been looking forward to.'

He did not reply immediately. Although only a few moments passed it seemed an eternity to Flo. For one moment she thought he was going to refuse her request. Then he smiled and said, 'Anything for you, Mrs F.' He gave her a quick kiss on the cheek and, whistling, walked briskly away.

Chapter Nine

The highly polished black Humber Hawk that drew up outside the Franklins' house brought some surprised looks from those who saw it. Such motor cars were not usually seen in this area. Those that were were of much more modest design and proportions; skippers saw no good reason to spend money on a car when they spent more time at sea than on land.

Nell and Jane, knowing the time of its arrival, had already donned their outdoor clothes and had been watching for it from the front window. They gave each other a meaningful look. This was grander even than they had expected.

'Mum!' Nell shouted.

Her mother, on tenterhooks, bustled into the room behind them and peered out of the window. 'My goodness,' she gasped. And added, 'Oh, my,' when a dark-suited man emerged from the car, placed a peaked cap on his head and started for the door. 'Best behaviour, girls,' Flo whispered, just loud enough for them to hear the comment she felt obliged to make, though she knew there really was no need for it. 'Have a nice time,' she added in a firmer tone and accepted their goodbye kisses, but held back when they answered the knock on the front door.

'Good day, young ladies. I'm Gordon, here to escort you to Mr and Mrs Aveburn.' The chauffeur led them to the car, saw them comfortably seated in the back and then drove smoothly away. Feeling like queens, Jane and Nell winked at each other and exchanged reassuring smiles that also betrayed their excitement at moving in a world of affluence such as they had never experienced before.

The smooth ride was not hurried but no time was wasted. On the outskirts of Norwich, Gordon turned through a gateway where the wrought-iron gates had been left open for his return. The drive ran alongside a garden, neat under its winter dressing, before turning in front of a large brick house. A multi-coloured glass fanlight surmounted the oak front door, and on each side were long narrow windows in similar style. The double-fronted house had a two-storey bay window on either side of the door. There was an air of solid permanence about it and as Gordon helped the girls from the car they felt it was a friendly house, too, a sensation they realised could only have been created by its occupants when Mr and Mrs Aveburn hurried into the large hall to greet them warmly, Mr Aveburn introducing them to his wife as two maids took their coats.

They were immediately enveloped in the warmth of a lady who exuded unforced charm. She was of average height and slim, her pretty floral print dress flaring slightly from her tiny waist to the top of her calves. The high neckline was cut by a V that dipped to her breasts and was adorned by a simple circular diamond brooch. Her dark hair, swept back from her ears, curled under at the nape of her neck. Her pale blue eyes sparkled with life, and the girls knew that those eyes were taking in everything about them without being critical.

As Mr and Mrs Aveburn escorted them to a room on the right they wondered where Glen could be. Then they heard a pounding sound and he appeared on the stairs, adjusting the collar of his shirt as he did so.

'Never ready on time,' commented Mrs Aveburn with a touch of despair, but both girls read love in her tone, too.

160

'Hello!' Glen called as he crossed the hall to join them.

Once they were seated in a drawing room that had all the trappings of affluence, Jane and Nell were put completely at their ease by a host and hostess who did not stand on ceremony and respected their guests' comfort. Glen persuaded them to have a sherry and they both relaxed in its warming glow.

'This is a little thank you for all the work you did on that excellent brochure,' announced Mr Aveburn. 'I arranged it for tonight because I knew we were taking delivery from the printers today.' Rising from his chair, he went to a side table from which he picked up four brochures and handed one to each of them.

Mrs Aveburn took a quick look through her copy and then remarked, 'This is the first time I've seen it – it looks wonderful.' She examined it more carefully. 'I love the layout, and I'm looking forward to reading your story more carefully, Jane. It seems a brilliant idea.'

'I'm sure it will increase our sales,' said Mr Aveburn. 'I got the distribution brought forward because of the situation in Europe. I fear it could worsen so we've got to make our sales earlier this year.'

'You think there will be trouble, Mr Aveburn?' queried Jane.

'I hope not, but everything points to it.'

The conversation was interrupted when a maid came to announce, 'Dinner is served, ma'am.'

As they rose to go to the dining room, Nell and Jane exchanged a glance in which they both expressed the hope that they wouldn't put a foot wrong during the meal. They need not have worried; Mr and Mrs Aveburn kept the mood informal and enabled their guests to talk about themselves, the life of the driftermen, Lowestoft and Scarborough.

The conversation came back to the present situation when Glen asked, 'Do you really think there will be war, Dad?'

His father shrugged. 'I know Mr Chamberlain is doing

all he can to avoid it but I think he knows it's inevitable and has merely bought us some time to further our preparations.'

'Your father has formulated contingency plans for the factory, should the worst happen,' said Mrs Aveburn.

'How would it affect you?' asked Nell. 'People will still want shoes.'

'Yes, they will, my dear, but less so. If war comes, men will be drafted into the Services and there is a distinct possibility that many women will serve as well, particularly if hostilities are prolonged. The Services will all want shoes to issue to their forces so much of our production will be switched to supplying them. Plans for doing so are all in hand and we are ready to manufacture as soon as the government gives us word. Of course, civilians will still want shoes, and we will continue to make them, but it will be at reduced capacity.'

'Let's hope it doesn't happen,' put in Mrs Aveburn, 'but I agree with my husband, it is highly likely. We can't ignore the signs. Hitler's calmer attitude at the moment doesn't disguise his ambitions. I'd say it was the calm before the storm.'

'I've seen sandbags being filled,' put in Glen.

'There, and that might seem nothing but we're vulnerable along this coast to sea bombardments.'

'I heard of one store that had run out of heavy curtain material already,' put in Jane.

'People anticipating a blackout.'

'My uncle and aunt said they believed the rumours about evacuation they had heard circulating in Scarborough were true,' Jane added.

'Which all points to a country preparing for war,' said Mr Aveburn, 'but it may never happen, and this evening was not meant to be gloomy, so let's change the subject.'

The rest of the time passed by pleasantly and Nell and Jane were profuse with their thanks. They were dignified when they left the car after being brought home, but as

162

soon as it disappeared they raced excitedly into the house and were soon pouring out the story of their evening to Mrs Franklin.

The next day Ewan asked no questions about their evening with the Aveburns and showed little interest when the subject was touched upon in the course of conversation over the days leading up to Christmas. The Lowestoft drifters returned one by one in time for the festive season and Jane welcomed Simon back enthusiastically.

He came to the station on the twenty-third to see her leave for Scarborough. She had made her goodbyes to the Franklin family, leaving behind Christmas presents she had enjoyed wrapping up.

'Keep warm,' said Simon with concern as they waited on the platform along which a bitter wind was blowing. 'I'll see you a week today. You know the time I'm supposed to reach Scarborough.'

'I'll be at the station to meet you,' she replied. 'Oh, they aren't giving us long,' she added when she heard the approaching train.

'They aren't,' he said regretfully. He took her hands in his and looked intently into her eyes. 'Take care of yourself. I'll miss you over Christmas.' He kissed her and held her tight as the train clattered to a halt, belching smoke and steam.

'I'll be thinking of you, Simon.'

He gave her a quick kiss, stepped past her and opened a carriage door. As she got in, she felt his hand go into the pocket of her coat and looked askance at him.

'A little present.'

'You shouldn't have,' she said, 'but thank you.'

He opened the window for her, closed the door and Jane leaned out.

'See you soon,' she said.

'I look forward to that,' he replied sincerely.

In the silent moments that followed when it seemed as if they could never find the words to say, they were aware of

163

doors slamming and a whistle blowing. With a hiss the train started to move out.

'Merry Christmas, Jane.'

'Merry Christmas, Simon.'

Their fingers touched then he was lost in a cloud of steam, to reappear with his arm raised in farewell. She waved back and stayed watching until he was out of sight then closed the window and sat down. She let her mind wander into thoughts of the man she had just left and tried to analyse her feelings for him. How he would react if he ever learned her full story . . .

Jane received a royal welcome from her aunt and uncle. Though they knew much about her life in Lowestoft from her letters, they were eager to hear about it from her own lips, especially about 'the young man who is coming to stay with us at New Year'. She was careful not to enthuse too much about Simon for fear of giving the impression that their relationship was serious.

Her uncle and aunt were delighted to see the shoe brochure, enthused over her writing, and told her to inform Glen and Nell how much they admired the photographic work and layout.

Though her writing was never far from her mind, Jane found that being in Scarborough again relaxed her. She was sure that would benefit her when she returned to Lowestoft, and hopefully gained more assignments.

After attending Midnight Mass on Christmas Eve, family presents were exchanged when they arrived home. Because of late rising on Christmas Day they were to have their Christmas dinner at five o'clock. Mavis had made early preparations so after the chicken had been placed in the oven they went for a brisk walk on the seafront, enjoying the sharp air and watching the grey sea heaving towards the sea wall in a motion that seemed to express anger at being able to go no further.

The whole day passed off well even though there were

164

moments when Jane wished her brother was still alive and sharing the festivities with them. She was thankful that her uncle and aunt did not mention him or her parents. Knowing she had not sent them a Christmas card pricked her conscience especially when the priest at Midnight Mass had spoken, 'a season of goodwill when the Infant should lead us towards a love for each other, especially members of our own family, at a time when rifts can be healed'.

Relaxing on Boxing Day afternoon Jane wondered how the big party planned by the three Lowestoft families was developing. She had no doubt they would all be having a good time.

She was right in that assumption. The fact that each family followed the Christian faith of their choice was no barrier to their friendship. Each respected the other's beliefs and their right to attend whatever religious service they chose. Food was plentiful, a spread to which each family had contributed; conversation was light and frivolous; traditional games were played, and in the small space that was available the younger ones danced to records played on the latest wind-up gramophone, recently purchased by Simon.

The party tailed off in the afternoon when the young ones made their own amusements, mums and dads settled into two groups, and everyone else did their own thing, knowing that the frivolities would begin again later when plates of sandwiches, sausage rolls, cakes of every description, trifles and a Christmas cake would be made available.

Nell and Ewan slipped away to walk by the sea. She slid her hand into his. 'Thanks for this beautiful bangle,' she said, tugging the end of her sleeve back so that she could see the long snake-like shape clinging tightly to her right wrist.

'Think of me whenever you wear it.'

'I will, but I'll think of you at other times too!'

He stopped and kissed her. 'I love you, Nell.' His voice

was dreamy, sensual, and she felt it flow over her.

'And I love you too,' she responded, returning his kiss.

In the quiet of her bedroom, still wide awake in the early hours of the following morning, those moments on the beach clashed with her thoughts of Glen and the string of pearls that she had hidden in a drawer along with a note saying, 'A Happy Christmas, Nell. Thanks for your company, it has made this year special for me, and thank you for your talent. I hope we can go forward together. Love, Glen.' She had found them both in her bag when she had returned home from his studio on the last working day before Christmas. Knowing what others might read into the gift and what Ewan's reaction would be, she had kept them a secret. Now, as she recalled the thrill she had experienced when she found them, she knew she faced a dilemma over the two men. One was a dashing, handsome extrovert who had been her lifelong beau. He had an eye for the girls and enjoyed flirting with them. The other was steady, thoughtful, considerate, good-looking if not eye-catchingly handsome. He was talented in something that had captured her interest, a man from whom she could learn and with whom she could work closely.

Nell tried to dismiss her dilemma by thinking of Jane, wondering how her Christmas had been and considering her relationship with Simon who she knew was going to Scarborough. Nell found herself wondering if he knew any more about Jane's past than Nell herself did.

Wrapped up well against the cold, Jane waited in pleasurable impatience at Scarborough station. How many times she looked at the station clock she did not know but it never seemed to move. There were only two other people on the platform who also appeared to be waiting anxiously. A porter emerged from the office and stood looking in the direction from which the train should come. Did he know something? He unfastened a button on his overcoat, reached into his waistcoat pocket and pulled out a watch. He looked at it and slipped it back into his pocket. Desperate for some information, Jane started towards him but she had only taken three strides when a distant noise stopped her. The train! A few minutes later she saw it and became aware of her heart racing faster.

Then the train was there. It was stopping. She glanced at it eagerly as doors started to open and people emerged on to the platform. Jane craned her neck. There he was, striding along with the crowd. She stepped in his direction. Passengers passed by her. She waved. He saw her. His face broke into a broad delighted smile. She responded. Then they were standing in front of each other.

'Hello, Jane.'

'Hello, Simon.'

For a moment they both drank in the sight of each other, then they burst out laughing and with their momentary embarrassment gone flung their arms round each other and kissed, oblivious to the stragglers who smiled and passed them on the platform.

'It's good to see you, Jane.'

'And you.'

As they turned to head for the exit, she linked arms with him. 'Have a good journey?'

'Yes.'

'I've a taxi waiting. How's everyone in Lowestoft?'

'Fine. I'll tell you all the news, little as there is, as we go.'

By the time they reached Scholes Park Road he had brought her up-to-date.

Anxious not to fuss the first young man Jane had brought home, Mavis still could not help it once introductions were over. Reading more into their relationship than friendship, she was pleased with Jane's choice. Simon's rugged features, bearing the tan of a life spent at sea, were undeniably attractive. As he slipped out of his overcoat she saw his broad fingers and felt the strength in them as he shook hands.

167

'I am pleased to meet you, Mrs Harvey, and you too, sir.'

'Welcome to our home, Mr Evans,' she responded.

'Oh, please ... Simon.' He said it with such a sincere wish to be on the friendliest of terms that the ice was instantly broken.

The fourth of January, when they had to return to Lowestoft, came all too quickly. They had enjoyed being together and sharing some of their time with Jane's uncle and aunt. They had attended a New Year's Eve party where, on the stroke of midnight, they had held each other in the joy of sharing this moment heralding in 1939. Their kiss had lingered throughout the twelve chimes and afterwards they joyously exchanged good wishes with other revellers. When they reached home they found Mavis and David had waited up for them, to toast the New Year and the future.

The day before they left, Mavis got her niece to herself while David took Simon to see his shop and studio.

'We like him, Jane. Simon's such a thoughtful, friendly young man.'

'I'm glad, Aunt, but don't read too much into our relationship. We are just good friends.'

'A little more than that, I think.' The twinkle in Mavis's eyes was unmistakable.

'No, honestly.'

Mavis gave a shrug of her shoulders. 'Well, if that's what you say. But ... who knows?'

Jane let the matter drop but thanked her aunt for her kindness to Simon.

When David and Simon returned, her uncle handed Jane a carrier bag. 'Give that to Nell.'

She peeped into the bag and saw a pile of films. 'Uncle, she'll be delighted with these. But so many?'

'I've been laying in some stock in case war comes. Film will be in short supply then, my allowance will be small.'

168

'But . . .' Jane started to protest again at his generosity.

'Just give them to her from me. Tell her and that other young photographer to get in as much film as possible. It will never go wrong, and you can never tell what opportunities for work may arise if war does come. It would be a pity to be without film then.'

'Yes, I'll tell them.'

'You think there'll be a war then, Mr Harvey?' Simon asked.

'If Hitler wants it we can't avoid it, and I don't trust him.'

'If it comes, what will happen to you, Simon?' Mavis asked.

'Well, certain drifters and trawlers are already earmarked for service in case of war. My father's is one of them so it will be one of the first to be converted to wartime specifications and become an active member of the Royal Naval Patrol Service, minesweeping, hunting U-boats, or on escort work.'

'Well, whatever happens, God be with you and keep you safe, young man.'

'Thanks, Mrs Harvey.'

'And any time you'd like to visit us, you're welcome,' added David.

As they sat back in the railway carriage the following day, Jane smiled at thoughts she didn't reveal when she said to Simon, 'You seemed to be a hit with my aunt and uncle.'

'I'm glad,' he replied. 'I liked them, and I enjoyed being with you without having to snatch meetings between sailings. Now our partings will be longer. We'll be sailing to fish off Plymouth again, then back to Lowestoft for a while before making for the Shetlands in late-February. After that, it's down the Yorkshire coast where you met us last year, and on to Lowestoft in October.'

'Won't you get back before then?' asked Jane.

Simon read a touch of disappointment in her voice and quickly reassured her that they would come into their home

169

port occasionally, depending on how the fishing was going and if the drifter needed any attention that couldn't be seen to in a nearby port.

'We'll just have to take life as it comes,' she observed. 'Really, life is always like that, no matter how we try to plan it.'

Simon sensed she was reflecting for a moment here on something in her past, but did not press her to disclose her thoughts.

They were welcomed enthusiastically by the Franklins and Nell was more than excited to receive the bag of films. As soon as he got the news they were back, Ewan called in with plans to celebrate their reunion the following night.

As Nell and Jane were preparing for that evening, Nell called her friend into her bedroom. 'Shut the door,' she said. 'I've something to show you.'

Curious, and detecting a serious note in Nell's voice, Jane crossed the room. Nell opened a drawer, took something from it and placed it on top of the chest.

Jane gasped when she saw the string of pearls.

'Read that,' said Nell, pushing the note in front of Jane who, after reading it, looked at her with surprise and a touch of alarm. Before she could speak Nell said, 'No one else knows about it. You are the first and probably the last.'

'What are you going to do?'

'I can't wear them unless I'm ever going to be completely alone with Glen. Mum would ask too many questions, and just imagine what Ewan's attitude would be! You remember he said Glen was using his background to entice me? You don't think he is, do you?'

'Nell! Glen wouldn't ... he's not that sort of person. He'd want you to accept him because you love him, not for what he can give you materially.'

'Then I'll have to give the pearls back and hope he understands. I don't want to offend him, and I certainly don't want to hurt him. I like him too much for that.'

'I think he's in love with you.'

'That's what I'm afraid of ...'

'Afraid?'

'Afraid of being forced into a choice. I don't want to hurt either of them.'

'You might have to, one day.'

'Ewan and I have been together since childhood. Glen has come into my life with so much to offer – professional opportunities I don't want to lose.'

'You shouldn't decide who you love for either of those reasons. Because you've known Ewan all your life, other people's expectations are maybe influencing both of you. A new person in your life can change your whole outlook.'

'Oh, Jane, I truly don't know what to do.'

'Then maybe life will decide for you.'

Six days later, while there was still daylight, the two girls watched the drifters sail. As she did so, Nell felt it was no coincidence that she had received by yesterday morning's post a letter from Glen, asking her and Jane to meet him at his studio the day after next.

Before they reached the studio, Jane made the excuse that she wanted to buy some chocolate and would be with them in just a few moments. 'It'll leave you free to have a few words with Glen in private.'

'Thanks,' said Nell with an appreciative smile, knowing Jane would take her time over choosing what she wanted.

'Jane not with you?' asked Glen when he greeted Nell at the door.

'She's gone to buy some chocolate, she'll be with us in a few minutes,' Nell explained as she led the way into the studio. When they were in the room she said, 'Glen, however can I thank you for the beautiful necklace?'

'Don't try,' he replied. 'I don't want thanks, just the reassurance that you know I think a lot of you. You have become an important part of my life, and not just because of our work.'

171

Nell raised her hand to stop him. 'Please, Glen, don't say anything that will make this situation more awkward for me. I like you a lot but I don't know whether I can go beyond that. Only time will tell.'

'I know there's Ewan, and I respect your feelings for him, but you aren't married or even engaged so I hope there might still be a chance for me?'

Nell bit her lip. 'I can't make you any promises at the moment, Glen. Besides, work has drawn us together.'

'It's developed into far more as far as I'm concerned.'

'Please, say no more for now. Accept the situation as it is. And will you take the pearls back? I couldn't accept them as a sign of love.' She took them from her pocket but he did not take them.

'Please keep them, Nell, as a sign of deep friendship.'

She could not deny this plea. The last thing she wanted was to cause Glen anguish. 'In friendship then,' she said, making her acceptance with quiet sincerity.

He kissed her on the cheek and at that moment they heard a knock on the door.

Once Jane was with them and they had sat down with some coffee, Glen said, 'Now we are almost a fortnight into the New Year, I think we'd better think seriously about future work and what we might aim at.'

'Before we get down to that, I must tell you Jane's uncle sent me twenty-five films!' Nell put in then.

'Wonderful.'

'He's been stocking up in case there's a war. Says film will be in very short supply if there is,' Jane explained. 'He told me to tell you to do the same.'

'I certainly will, and I'll write and thank him for the advice. But won't these leave him short?'

'He says our need may well be greater than his because of the different role in which we are working.'

'That's extremely kind and thoughtful of him. Now, have you got any more pictures for *Winter at the Seaside*?'

'Yes, I've two reels here,' said Nell, taking them from her handbag.

'Good. We'll develop them in a few minutes. What about *Preparations for War*?'

'I've taken two reels, but I think we will need to go further afield to cover other aspects.'

'We'll see how they fit with mine. What about the writing, Jane?'

'I've been working on different angles. I'll discuss them some more when we see the pictures.'

'Right, Nell, should we get cracking on the developing and printing?'

Jane watched the door close behind them. She had been in the darkroom and, though she had not experienced it in the same way as Nell, had no illusions about the intimate atmosphere there would be in that small dimly lit space where two people of the opposite sex would be pressed into close proximity. She pushed away those thoughts and turned to the typescript she had brought with her.

When Nell and Glen emerged from the darkroom Jane sensed they were delighted with the new prints.

'There are only five that are rubbish,' commented Glen as he spread them on the table to be examined. 'These are all *Winter at the Seaside*, the others are in the drier.'

As they sorted the pictures and married Jane's copy to them, they became more and more satisfied with their work.

'I knew what Nell was attempting. Now I've seen them linked with yours, Glen, I'll brush up my copy while you two finish off the additional prints for *Preparations for War*.'

They were pleased with these too and put them with those they had previously studied.

'*Winter at the Seaside* is finished, in my opinion. It ought to go to Mr Horton straight away,' Glen said.

'Are you going to take it?' asked Nell.

'Yes, but Horton said that next time I had to take you two to meet him as well. Would that be possible if we went tomorrow?'

Nell looked dubious. 'Mum is away at Aunty Josie's. She won't be back for four days and Jane and I promised to look after the house. Mum never likes to leave it empty.'

'We'll be back the day after tomorrow,' Glen pointed out.

Nell still looked doubtful.

'I'll look after the house,' Jane offered. 'You two will manage without me. The pictures are the most important part of the project. Take my copy, of course, Mr Horton can edit it as necessary. Apologise for my absence and tell him I'll be glad to accept his invitation next time.'

'Is that all right with you, Nell? No chaperone,' asked Glen.

'Of course,' she replied, moved by his concern.

'I'll ring Mr Horton now then. We'll stay overnight at the Strand Palace, the hotel my father uses. I'll ring there after I've verified our appointment with Horton. Separate rooms, of course.'

Nell smiled. 'Of course. Otherwise I wouldn't come.'

'You'll be all right on your own?' Nell asked her friend as she was leaving the house the next morning.

'Of course,' Jane reassured her, and added teasingly, 'Now, off with you. And ... behave yourself.'

'As if I wouldn't!'

Nell was meeting Glen at the station to catch an early train for London. Jane settled down to do some writing but at eleven, because the day had brightened, decided she needed some fresh air. She walked to the harbour and then along the stone pier towards the lighthouse. She delighted in the sight of the waves being whipped into whitecaps by the wind. Reaching the end, she stopped to breathe in deeply, enjoying the sensation of the cold sea air streaming into her lungs. About to turn away, she stopped and stiffened. A drifter. As far as she knew from the talk before the men sailed for Plymouth, they shouldn't be back yet. Wondering, she watched it heading for port. It seemed to be making slow headway. She was curious, and in spite of the nip in the air she waited.

Ten minutes later she recognised the *Lively Lady*. Jane remembered her returning early before with engine trouble. What had gone wrong this time? The question had only just entered her head when she was struck by a thunderclap. Ewan was back ... and Nell was in London with Glen! She racked her brain, trying to find some feasible excuse why Nell was not at home but could think of none that would stand further enquiry, and deceit might only make the situation look worse. As the *Lively Lady* entered the harbour she decided the truth was her best course of action. Let Ewan make of that what he would.

He was visible in the bow, ready to throw a rope ashore. He saw her, grinned and waved. Jane walked along the harbour wall and watched the boat tie up.

Ewan leaped straight ashore. 'Hi, my lovely!' He swept her up in his arms and whirled her around. 'Kind of you to greet a sailor home from the sea. Where's Nell?'

The dreaded question but Jane answered it head on. 'In London with Glen, on business with the features editor at *World Scene.*'

For the briefest of moments Ewan's face darkened, then he grinned and said with apparent enthusiasm, 'Then that leaves you and me free to have a night out together. I'll call for you at six! Thank God for engine trouble again.' With that he leaped back on board, turned away and called, 'See you soon.'

Jane smiled to herself, gave a shake of her head and started to walk towards the town. Ewan was incredible. Had Glen's performance when he had sailed on the *Sea Queen* brought a measure of respect for his rival for Nell?

If so then Ewan had gone up in Jane's estimation, not that she had ever held him in low esteem. No, there was much to admire in Ewan Steel and she was not the first girl to note it, nor the first to succumb to his flirtatious charm. As she quickened her step Jane realised she was really excited at the prospect of a night out with him.

Chapter Ten

As she settled down in the carriage with Glen, who had been solicitous for her comfort, Nell had a feeling of kicking over the traces. Many girls of her age yearned to break away from their parents' restrictions and expectations, and lead lives of their own. She wondered what her mother would think, and how would Ewan react, if they knew she was heading for London like this? Oh, well, she thought silently, neither of them need ever know. She was determined to enjoy this outing and her newfound sense of freedom.

On reaching London, Glen escorted her with aplomb through the sea of people hurrying for trains, hastening to leave the station or killing time until their train was due. He led her to the taxi rank and in a few minutes was giving the driver their destination.

He smiled reassuringly at her when he sank back on the seat beside her. 'All right?'

'Whew! So many people! I've never experienced anything like this. All the rush and bustle ... where's everyone going?'

'That's London.' Glen grinned. 'The hotel we're going to is rather more sedate, don't worry.'

As they pulled up outside the hotel the taxi door was whisked open for them by a liveried commissionaire who greeted them pleasantly, saw them out of the taxi and, while Glen was paying the fare, snapped his fingers to bring two pageboys running. Smart young men in wine-coloured uniform trousers and fitted waist-length jackets, buttoned to the neck, pillbox hats of the same colour perched cheekily on their heads, took charge of the two suitcases.

They led the way towards an entrance that overwhelmed Nell. Glen saw her eyes widen with wonder and knew she had never seen anything like this before. 'The hotel was built in 1907 but much of it, particularly the entrance and foyer, was redesigned in 1930 in Art Deco style,' he explained. Broad marble stairs led up to revolving metal-finished doors, which gave on to a sumptuous foyer where innovative use had been made of mirrors and marble and exceptional lighting.

'Good day, Mr Aveburn. It is good to see you again, sir.'

Even Glen was impressed by that. 'Do you ever forget a face, Giles?' he asked of the head receptionist, neat in his pristine white shirt, grey tie and black suit, a handkerchief placed just so in his top pocket.

'You haven't forgotten mine, sir.'

'But you see so many people across this desk.'

Giles gave him a little knowing smile. 'I make it a point to remember our best customers and their families. Your father is one of those.' He turned to Nell who had removed her gloves as she entered the hotel. His gaze flickered across her fingers and enabled him to make his next greeting. 'And welcome to you too, miss.'

Nell returned his smile. 'Thank you.' She tried to play her part even though she was overwhelmed by all the opulence, dazzled by the pale pink marble walls with door cases of translucent moulded glass and chromed steel.

'Giles, I booked two single rooms for tonight. Alas, we shall have to return home after our business is concluded tomorrow.'

He examined a ledger on the desk. 'That is correct, sir.

178

I'm only sorry it couldn't be your father's usual suite which is being redecorated.' He signalled to the two pageboys who had been standing by with the luggage, and handed each of them a key. In a few minutes they were opening the door to the first room.

'Miss,' said one of the boys as he stood back to let Nell enter and then waited for Glen to follow.

He glanced round the room quickly. 'Will this be right for you?' he asked.

Keeping a tight rein on her true feelings in front of the boys, Nell said, 'Splendid.'

The boy placed her suitcase beside the dressing table. The second addressed Glen. 'You are next door, sir.' Glen followed him from the room after whispering to Nell, 'I'll see you in a few minutes.'

Dazed by what was happening to her, she stood in the centre of the room, taking in the opulence of the maple and walnut bedroom suite with the dressing table mirror shaped like a flower, and the comfortable-looking bed with its arched bedhead and colourful bedspread in a geometric design. She shook herself as if that would return her to the world she knew and leave this magic carpet ride behind. She saw her case standing where the pageboy had left it, confirmation that what she was experiencing was reality. She picked it up, placed it on a stool and was unpacking the few things she had brought with her when there was a gentle knock on the door. She opened it to find Glen standing there.

'May I come in?' he asked quietly.

'Oh. Yes. Do,' Nell spluttered, and then took a grip on her emotions to hide them from him.

He stepped inside and closed the door. 'Is everything all right for you?'

'More than that,' she replied. 'Thank you.'

'If there is anything you want, just ring that bell there.' He pointed to a bell-push on the wall beside the bed. 'Or ask me and I will see to it. Is there anything you would like to do now?'

179

'I ...' Nell hesitated. 'I have never been to London before,' she added, hating to admit it. 'Can we take a short walk?'

'Of course. You freshen up and then we'll go out. Bring your camera.' Glen glanced at his watch. 'We'll just be in time for some tea at Lyons Corner House. We'll take it easy, come back here for our evening meal, and then relax ready for our appointment tomorrow morning. How does that sound?'

'Wonderful!' she replied.

On reaching the door, he paused. 'Ten minutes enough?'

She nodded.

He smiled. 'Enjoy it all.'

As the door closed Nell thought, I certainly will, and pirouetted in the direction of the bathroom. 'My own bathroom! What would Mum think?'

On the way out of the hotel Glen booked a table for dinner at eight. He took Nell down the Strand as far as Trafalgar Square, and then along Whitehall, pointing out Downing Street and the Prime Minister's dwelling.

'That's where it all happens, Nell. The fate of the country is decided there. It looks like some of the people here are expecting the worst.' He indicated sandbags piled around the front of one of the government buildings, paused and quickly took a photograph of them. Several more to illustrate *Preparations for War* were taken as they made their way east along the Embankment and circled St Paul's before heading back to the hotel.

When they paused outside the doors to their rooms, he said, 'I'll call for you in an hour. Enjoy the luxury.'

Nell smiled. 'I will! I intend to soak in my lovely big bath.' He started to turn away but she stopped him. 'Glen, you must let me contribute something towards all this ...'

'Of course not,' he said with a shake of his head. 'This will all come out of the business. I know we haven't officially set it up yet but that is something we must do when we get back home. It will be the fairest thing to do for the three of us.'

'You mean, you are satisfied with my and Jane's contribution?'

'Perfectly happy. In fact, I bless the day you two walked into my life. It widened my horizons. I think we can create a thriving business between us.'

'Thank you, Mr Wheater, for that letter of introduction! It certainly changed my life, and I know Jane feels the same.' Impulsively Nell kissed Glen on the cheek. Automatically their hands met. They stood looking into each other's eyes then and his other hand came to rest on her waist.

'No, Glen. Don't spoil my first visit to London,' Nell sighed at length.

He held her gaze for a moment then let his hands drop. 'I'll respect your wishes, Nell.' He turned towards his own door then swung back and said, 'I think I'm in love with you, though. No, I *know* I am.' With that he went into his room, leaving her staring at the closed door.

She stood there, unable to move as his words sank in. It was only when she heard voices and realised that someone was coming up the stairs nearby that she started and fled into her own room. There she leaned back against the door, her mind awhirl. Glen! Did she really mind what he had said? Who wouldn't feel flattered by it? She recalled the sincerity in his eyes and knew he had no intention of placing her in a compromising position. He respected her, and that meant a great deal to Nell. She pushed herself away from the door and, as she moved slowly across the room, experienced a return of her earlier euphoria. Laughter trilled on her lips as she slipped out of her coat and flung it on the bed. She was still smiling as she ran the water for her bath.

As she lay soaking in luxurious style, she wondered momentarily what Jane would think if she could see her now.

*

181

In Lowestoft Jane had similar thoughts when, in the darkness of the cinema, Ewan chose the back row and slipped his arm around her shoulders. Jane did not protest.

When they came out of the cinema the wind was sharp, cutting its way down the narrow street towards them. They paused outside and turned up their coat collars.

'It's only nine,' Ewan pointed out. 'There's a nice cosy bar attached to the Prince's Hotel. I know the barmaid there, she'll rustle us up some sandwiches. How about it? It will be quiet there on a Tuesday night in winter.'

Jane's hesitation was only slight. There would be no one at home, and if she invited him to take some refreshment there, he might misconstrue the invitation. 'Why not?' she replied. It seemed the safer option.

'Good girl.'

They started off against a wind determined to chill them to the bone. Ewan put his arm round Jane again and pulled her closer. She did not object, she was thankful for the protective warmth it brought, but she also felt a shiver run down her spine and knew it was not from the cold. They fell comfortably into step. Their conversation was light-hearted and Ewan's comments about some aspects of the film made Jane laugh aloud. They burst into the bar, thankful for its light and warmth.

'Hello, Ewan. I'm surprised you aren't with the drifters,' a slim, dark-haired barmaid greeted him warmly.

'Returned with engine trouble,' he replied, flashing her his roguish smile. 'Peggy, can you rustle us up some sandwiches?'

'For Ewan Steel, anything,' she replied lightly.

These exchanges made Jane wonder how far 'anything' went?

Ewan saw Peggy's curiosity in her glance towards Jane. 'Peg, this is a friend of mine – Jane.'

They smiled at each other as Peggy acknowledged her with, 'Welcome to the Prince's. Now, what will it be?' she added, half turning to Ewan.

'A pint of best for me, please.' He looked at Jane questioningly.

'An orange squash, please.'

'Nothing stronger?' he queried.

'No, thanks.' She didn't miss the momentary look of surprise Peggy cast Ewan. It made Jane wonder if he had brought other girls here. Did the charmer who courted the girl he had known all his life also like to exercise his attractions elsewhere?

They found a corner table away from the other occupants of the bar. Jane felt comfortable with Ewan. He was so attentive; conversation flowed, banter was exchanged tit-for-tat, and laughter was never far away. She enjoyed being alone with this handsome man who had the ability to make her feel special, though she did wonder if this was a ploy on his part . . . or was that merely wishful thinking on hers?

They were into their second drink when Ewan allowed the smile to slip from his lips and his eyes to take on a more serious light. 'What are Nell and Glen doing in London?' He leaned forward, elbows on the table, creating an air of confidentiality as he lowered his voice.

Jane responded likewise. 'They have an appointment with Mr Horton at *World Scene*. They've taken him the latest photographs and my article that he commissioned. It was important for both of them to be there to discuss them.'

He gave a little nod. 'Shouldn't you have gone too?'

'Yes, but Mrs Franklin is away and she doesn't like the house being left empty, so I volunteered to stay.'

'How convenient for them both,' he muttered.

'Hey, what's this? Ewan Steel, jealous?'

'Well, they're spending more and more time together.'

'Inevitable when they're both photographers.'

'Yes, but . . .'

Jane placed a reassuring hand on his arm. 'Nell got interested in photography when you were in Scarborough, remember, before she met Glen. He's provided the means for her to pursue it further – something she dearly wanted to do after she and I had our success with the *Scarborough Evening News*. It's a working relationship, Ewan, nothing more.'

'How do you know what goes on in that darkroom?'

Jane too had sometimes wondered, and she knew Glen had strong feelings for Nell though that was not for Ewan to find out from her lips. She moved her hand from his arm to press his hand in a comforting gesture. 'Don't think like that, Ewan.'

'I know I shouldn't.' He smiled wanly and met her gaze, sensing empathy in it. He started suddenly and said, 'You're a good friend, Jane. I'm glad you're here. Let's make the most our time together.'

Lost in each other, they had not noticed the other customers leave, nor were they aware of the glances that Peg constantly cast in their direction. What she wouldn't give to be sitting there with Ewan Steel!

Eventually, reluctantly realising they would have to face the cold again, Ewan and Jane put on their coats. Or, rather, he helped her into hers, squeezing her shoulders momentarily as he did so.

'Goodnight, you two. Keep warm,' called Peggy. 'It's a poor winter we're having.'

The chill blast when they opened the door confirmed her remark. They automatically linked arms and, matching strides, leaned into the wind.

Reaching the Franklins' house, they sought shelter in the doorway.

'Thanks for a lovely evening,' said Jane.

'It was my pleasure,' returned Ewan. 'I enjoyed it.'

'So did I, very much.'

'With Mrs Franklin away tonight, don't you mind being on your own?' Ewan enquired then. 'Or would you maybe prefer some company?' With each word his charm became more alluring. He was so close Jane couldn't help but respond. She teetered on the edge of betrayal. Ewan sensed it and the kiss he gave her sent such a thrill through her then that she held his lips with her own. Suddenly, she broke the almost overpowering contact. Her hands came down from around his neck and pressed against his chest.

'No, Ewan. Don't.'

'Tempting, isn't it?' he teased with just a touch of seriousness in his tone, the light from a streetlamp catching the gleam in his eyes.

'Don't!' she repeated with greater emphasis, though her heart was racing. But rather than loyalty to her two friends, it was memories of Middlesbrough that really held her back ... 'Nell. Simon,' she said to try and quell his persistence. She felt Ewan's hold on her relax.

Jane eased herself further away. 'Respect my wishes, Ewan, please. Don't go any further. Don't ruin the friendship we four have, or the lovely evening we have had tonight.'

Even in the dim light she could see the answering smile come over his face. 'Your wish is my command.' He kissed her quickly on the cheek then strode off down the street. She watched his handsome figure pass through a pool of light and vanish into the darkness. Each knew this evening would never be mentioned again by either of them.

Nell was awake early and took the opportunity to luxuriate again in a hot bath. She was making a final appraisal of herself in the full-length mirror when she heard a tap on the door. She unlocked it to be met by Glen's smile and a cheerful, 'Good morning.'

She returned his smile and greeting, and added, 'Come in.'

He followed her into the room and pushed the door to behind him. 'You are looking smart this morning,' he said, admiring her mustard-coloured wraparound skirt and white blouse. Its sleeves were loose-fitting and buttoned at the wrist. With it she wore a simple necklace of coloured beads and a plain thin celluloid bangle on her left wrist.

185

'Thank you,' she said, smiling shyly. 'I thought I'd better try to make an impression on Mr Horton.'

'You'd do that anyway,' Glen said. He saw her blush and added quickly, 'I hope I didn't upset you last night? That's the last thing I'd want to do.'

She heard concern in his voice. 'Glen, there is absolutely no need to apologise. I was flattered, still am, but please, try and understand.'

'I do. Come on then,' he went on brightly, as if he was enjoying the song playing in his heart. 'A good breakfast and then off to our appointment.'

'Nervous?' he whispered as they were escorted into Mr Horton's office, an hour or two later.

She gave a little nod, thinking, Here I am, Nell Franklin of Lowestoft, fisherman's daughter, walking into the office of one of the most influential men in the magazine world.

A few moments later she was shaking hands with him as Glen made the introductions. They exchanged the usual niceties during which she knew Horton was making an immediate assessment of her. She was smart enough to realise he was building on this during the hour they spent with him while he examined their submissions.

Finally he turned away from the table on which the prints were spread. '*Winter at the Seaside* is very good. I like that sense of desolation in many of the photographs, especially those that reflect the life and gaiety now absent. I'll keep them all to make my final choice and return those I cannot use or want to put on file. Tell Jane the copy fits perfectly. I'll only have to make one or two minor alterations.'

'She'll be delighted,' said Nell.

'I'm only sorry she couldn't be with you.'

'I'll tell her so, Mr Horton, never fear.'

'Now ... *Preparations for War*! This collection is coming on nicely. What I want you to do is really keep on top of the subject, build up an extensive portfolio, because I intend to combine it with work by top photographers all

186

around the country. That feature will run over a number of weeks when war becomes a certainty.

'Whatever happens, grasp new opportunities, keep in touch, and remember you are on retainers to *World Scene*. Forget the fortnightly submission of ideas. There'll be plenty coming up. Let me have them as they occur.'

Though a little subdued by Mr Horton's assumption of war in Europe, their young minds shrugged aside this dismal forecast and replaced it with euphoria at the acceptance of *Winter at the Seaside*, and Horton's comments on their other pictures and ideas. They looked forward to relating their success to Jane.

Lacking the protection of London's buildings, they noticed the keen bite in the coastal wind as they hurried from Lowestoft station to the Franklins' house. With greetings exchanged, Jane soon served them a warming cup of tea and a piece of Flo's special treacle tart each.

'You've just missed Ewan,' she informed them, believing it was better Nell should hear it from her than anyone else. It should not appear that she had some reason for withholding the information.

'Ewan?'

'Yes. The *Lively Lady* developed engine trouble again. Mr Steel decided it was better to limp to his home port rather than seek repairs somewhere on the south coast. They arrived on Tuesday, not long after you'd gone to London. The engineers worked on it the rest of the day and into the night. They finished off this morning and the *Lively Lady* sailed a short while ago.'

Nell pulled a face. 'Did Ewan say when he expects to be back?'

'Not exactly. His father's decided to rejoin the other drifters off Plymouth. He thinks they'll all be back here some time in February to lay up and clean up ready for Shetland. Now tell me what Mr Horton thought?'

'He was delighted with our work and said there would

187

be only minor alterations to your copy,' enthused Nell.

'And he hopes you'll be able to visit him next time,' added Glen. 'Nell will tell you all about it, I must be off. Should we meet again on Monday?'

With that agreed he left. Once the door was closed behind him, Jane wanted to know everything about the visit to London.

Nell waxed enthusiastic about the hotel, emphasising the luxury such as she had never seen before.

'And how did you get on with Glen?'

'Nothing happened,' she replied demurely. 'I had a most pleasant time, and Glen was very attentive.'

'And?' prompted Jane, wanting more.

Nell hesitated, then said, 'I had to tell him to consider Ewan.'

At that statement by her friend, Jane felt a twinge of conscience.

'He understood, and agreed with me that nothing should spoil the friendship between the four of us. Now, did you see Ewan while he was here?'

'Briefly.' Jane startled herself by how easily the answer came. Immediately she started convincing herself that it was true; it all depended what was meant by briefly, after all. Four hours in twenty-four could be termed brief. But had what happened in those four hours made them rather more significant than she had implied?

On Monday the three colleagues met in a more gloomy frame of mind. Jane reported that three articles meant for the *Scarborough Evening News* had been rejected on the grounds of insufficient space, though Mr Wheater had been kind enough to suggest that one of them about seaside piers might be of interest to *Country Life*, if it were accompanied by excellent architectural photography. Glen informed her that he had some shots that might be of use. He would make fresh prints in the next two days. That softened his own news that some photographic work he had hoped to obtain for Nell and himself had fallen through. The firm concerned had decided not to proceed because of the threat of war.

'But everything is quiet on the political front,' protested Nell. 'I think some people read too much into Hitler's past threats.'

Glen looked doubtful at her observation. 'Remember Mr Horton's view, and he's much closer to things than we are. Mind you, I do agree that things are quieter. I only hope it isn't the calm before the storm . . .'

The calm continued, though, and the possible storm was forgotten with the return of the drifters to Lowestoft, particularly when the three captains announced that they would not sail for Shetland until February the twenty-second, giving their crews three weeks ashore. It was a welcome break though they all knew it would not be an idle time as the three skippers expected their vessels to be put into tip-top shape: equipment overhauled, engines serviced, nets repaired, everything in the crew's quarters spotless by the time they sailed again.

On their second night ashore the three skippers met for a drink and the subject of a partnership was raised again, but this time George Franklin was even more adamant that it was not the right course.

The topic was debated through three pints of beer and finally George's caution prevailed.

On the second Saturday night after their return to Lowestoft, Ewan and Simon called for Nell and Jane.

'Where to tonight?' asked George, seated comfortably in front of a roaring fire, puffing contentedly on his pipe in the company of his wife whose needles were moving quickly in her determination to get these socks finished for her husband before he left for Shetland.

'Bite to eat and then the dance,' replied Ewan with marked anticipation of an enjoyable evening ahead.

'You wouldn't drag me away from this fire on a cold night like this,' commented George.

'Come on, Mr Franklin, you were young once. Didn't need a fire to keep him warm then, did he, Mrs F?'

Flo smiled at the memories that conjured up. 'Your ears would blush, Ewan.'

'I knew it,' he laughed. The two girls, ready to enjoy their night out, appeared then. 'Oh, dash,' added Ewan in mock disappointment. 'Simon and I were just about to hear stories of your dad's courting days.'

'Off with you, young fellow,' ordered George playfully.

Ewan scuttled for the door as if about to be chastised. He opened it and ushered the other three out. He was about to follow them when Mr Franklin called after him, 'And I could *still* show you a thing or two.'

'Is that a promise?' asked Ewan with a challenging grin, and ducked out of the door as a cushion came hurtling across the room.

These exchanges set a light-hearted mood for the evening. The two couples linked arms. Ewan and Nell took the lead, but easy banter passed between all four of them. Nell did not think once of the pearls hidden in her drawer nor did she dwell on Mr Horton's pessimistic words. Jane did not give Middlesbrough a thought. Though Ewan's attractions were visible tonight, as always, she dismissed them; she had Simon beside her, and in many ways he had more to commend him than Ewan did. The only thing that disturbed Ewan's and Simon's thoughts was the fact that in sixteen days' time they would be leaving these two attractive girls behind for life on the rolling sea with a bunch of scruffy sailors.

'Fish and chips?' Simon enquired generally.

'Of course,' replied Ewan over his shoulder.

Reaching the fish restaurant, they were fortunate to find that a table for four had just been vacated. Even in the winter it did a brisk trade on a Saturday night, as the younger set would brave any weather to have their night out. With most people in the restaurant knowing each other, the atmosphere there was cheery. That carried on

190

when they entered the dance hall where the music was already in full flow. Simon guided Jane on to the dance floor and they glided into the foxtrot. Neither of them spoke. They enjoyed being close and moving as one. Then the music stopped. The couples on the floor clapped and waited while the leader of the band announced that the next dance would be a quickstep. Immediately the band struck the first note, Jane and Simon were in step. The tempo was fast; Simon never missed a beat, and under his guidance Jane matched him. The music stopped suddenly on a high note, almost catching everyone out in mid-step, but Simon knew what was coming and made a last swirl, coming to a halt at just the right moment. Jane laughed and he matched the merriment in her eyes.

'Oh, I enjoyed that,' she gasped, out of breath.

'So did I.' He grinned at her as they strolled to the side of the dance floor.

'Where did you learn to dance?' she asked. 'I've always appreciated how good you are.'

'I don't know that I'm all that good,' he replied modestly. 'But I enjoy it, and especially so now that I have you as a partner. You follow so well.'

'You make it easy for me. But you've not told me where you learned?'

'Only by coming here, though my sister Marcia and I used to dance to records at home. She was keen and I picked up a lot from her even though she's two years younger. Then we started coming here. For a couple of summers she attended classes, and whenever I was home from the fishing she taught me what she'd learned.'

'Very useful.'

The band struck up with 'Always' then. They turned to each other and immediately moved into the waltz.

'Remember this?' he whispered, close to her ear. 'The first tune we danced together. How many times have I hummed it since, thinking of you?'

She looked up at him and saw the feeling in his eyes. 'It's

191

special to me too, Simon. Yes, I remember that night with deep gratitude. You came into my life at a time when I was faced with big decisions and you helped me make them.'

'You never said.'

'I didn't want to burden you with my troubles. Besides, at that time I wanted nothing more than companionship from you.'

'And now?'

She hesitated then said, 'For now, I'm not yet ready to go further. Life can lead us in unforeseen directions, you know.'

He wanted to ask what she meant by that but was reluctant to do so for fear it would raise an obstacle to their closeness. 'As you wish. Please, remember I am always here for you.'

She embraced him lightly. 'You are so good, Simon.'

'Nothing more?'

'Maybe. Just wait a while.'

'Always. Like the words of this song.'

He started to sing quietly as he held her close:

'Not for just an hour
Not for just a day
Not for just a year
But always.'

Jane slipped willingly into a dreamland that was theirs alone.

The music stopped, clapping broke out and there were cries of 'More'.

And more there was, with couples whirling by to the quickstep, gliding through the foxtrot, and moving smoothly through the waltz.

Nell let herself dream in Ewan's arms. She knew she was the envy of many in the room, for when he danced Ewan had the sort of body that could set any girl's imagination on fire – especially when he performed the tango. Having grown up with him, and danced with him from an early age, she could match him. Their dancing together was generally much admired.

Ewan was guiding her skilfully around the floor which was crowded for a quickstep when someone offered him a greeting in passing: 'Hello, Ewan.'

He acknowledged the greeting while Nell looked sharply at the couple who had passed on.

'Who's that?' she asked.

'Peggy. Barmaid at the Prince's.'

'I didn't know you went there. A bit posh, isn't it?'

'Only occasionally, if I happen to be passing,' he said lightly.

The movement on the dance floor brought the two couples close again.

'Holding someone else's hand tonight, Ewan?' said Peggy, and then was gone again.

Nell glared after her and turned back to Ewan without missing a step. 'What did she mean by that?'

He shrugged his shoulders. 'I don't know. What could she mean? Nothing, I suppose.' He moved into a series of complicated steps so that Nell had to concentrate on those rather than Peggy's remark. But she did not forget it and kept an eye on the other girl. Half an hour later, when they stood talking to Jane and Simon, she noticed Peggy heading for the ladies' cloakroom. Nell excused herself and headed that way too.

She found the barmaid renewing her make-up. As she came to stand beside her, Nell eyed her in the mirror.

'Excuse me,' she said, 'what did you mean by that remark you made to Ewan just now?'

'Nothing,' replied Peggy, running her finger over her eyebrows.

'Oh, but I think you did. You don't just make a remark about holding hands for nothing. What exactly did you see?'

Peggy smiled to herself; the mischief-maker in her was prompting her to reply.

193

'He was in the Prince's where I work ...'

'Holding someone's hand?'

'Yes.'

'When was this?'

'About three weeks ago.'

Nell did a quick calculation. Three weeks! She was in London with Glen then. Ewan had had one night in Lowestoft ... 'Have you seen the person he was with here tonight?'

Peggy eyed her. 'I don't know that I should say ...'

'Sounds to me as if you have.'

Peggy tightened her lips. She was really enjoying herself now. 'Well, maybe. But what's it to you?'

'That's none of your business but it *is* important to me. Now come on, tell me?'

Peggy could see a bust-up looming right in the middle of the dance floor. She would enjoy that.

'Yes, as a matter of fact, she is here.'

'Well, who is it?'

'She appears to be with Simon Evans.'

'Jane?'

'Yeah, that's the name he used the night they were in the Prince's,' Peggy announced triumphantly.

'Thanks.' Nell spun round and strode from the ladies'.

Peggy grinned and muttered, 'That'll teach you to spurn my advances, Ewan Steel!' She gathered her make-up together and quickly followed Nell, expecting a scene, but there she was disappointed. She saw Nell gathered into Ewan's arms and the pair of them moving into a sensuous waltz. Maybe later? But no! Peggy left the dance hall after the last waltz, disappointed.

Chapter Eleven

When they left the dance floor Nell bit back the snide remark she was about to make to Jane. It would only have drawn Ewan into the situation, and even Simon wouldn't have escaped. Better to have it out with her face-to-face in the privacy of Jane's room. Nell had subdued her feelings and made her departure from Ewan as normal as possible. Now she sat on the edge of her bed, waiting.

Her lips tightened impatiently. She was not looking forward to the confrontation ahead. She really liked Jane; was pleased that the other girl had come into her life. They got on well and worked together in harmony. Maybe she should say nothing, let sleeping dogs ... but that would be no good. What she had heard, and the questions it raised, would constantly worry her. Better get it all out in the open and find out if there was any substance to the story. She wanted to get this over.

Five more long minutes passed then Nell heard the front door close. Jane was back. She tensed and strained to listen for her coming up the stairs. Footsteps? A creaking stair? She wasn't sure. Then she heard the faint click of Jane's bedroom door closing. She pushed herself from her bed and went quietly to Jane's door. Her knock was light. She did not wait for an answer but opened the door slowly, saying, 'May I come in?'

'Of course,' came the soft reply. 'Thought you might be in bed.'

'A word,' said Nell.

'Oh? A serious one by the look on your face,' Jane said teasingly.

'It is. What have you been up to?' The note in her voice struck Jane then.

'What do you mean?' Her question was accompanied by a puzzled frown.

'Holding hands with Ewan!' The words were blurted out, in not at all the way Nell had rehearsed them.

'What are you talking about?' Jane did not like the implication behind those words.

'What else went on when I was in London and you were here on your own? Oh, yes, I heard you were seen at the Prince's with him. Heads close together, tête-à-tête, holding hands. Must mean something, especially with him taking you to a posh place.'

Jane was shocked by the implication. How did Nell know where they had been? Then it struck her: Peggy. She had been at the dance and must have said something.

'Hold on, Nell, you're jumping to conclusions here,' Jane protested.

'Am I? You deny being there then?'

Jane knew it was no use doing that. 'No, I don't, but . . .'

'Ewan's mine. Keep your hands off him!'

'Nell, he returned unexpectedly. I was alone. Wasn't it natural for two friends to spend an evening together?'

'Holding hands! And what else?'

'Nothing else! And the hand-holding was a gesture of reassurance about you being in London with Glen, just the two of you.'

'That's what you say now,' rapped Nell testily.

'Believe what you will,' hissed Jane, annoyed to find herself doubted.

Nell glared at her. 'I've seen the way you've eyed him.'

'Rubbish! You've a vivid imagination, that's all.'

196

She poked a finger at Jane. 'What are you playing at anyway . . . eyeing Ewan, out alone with him *and* stringing Simon along? You *stay away* from Ewan. He's mine and always has been, so don't you go getting any ideas. And don't play with Simon's affections either.'

'Oh, what now? Concern for Simon?' mocked Jane. 'While you've got Glen dangling on a string. It's *you* who should make up your mind! You go and do that. And I'll be out of your life in the morning, and back to Scarborough where I'm wanted.'

The threat jolted Nell. She felt a cold shiver run down her spine. 'You don't mean that?'

'I do, and I will go if you think I'm trying to steal Ewan,' replied Jane with a firmness that left no room for doubt.

Nell bit her lip. This had got out of hand. She had never expected it to lead to such a threat. She had imagined issuing a warning, that was all. Had she been hasty in her judgement? Had Peggy just been fanning the flames? But Jane had not denied that she and Ewan had held hands . . . couldn't that have gone further? Still, without proof or an admission, were her doubts worth the chasm that was yawning at Nell's feet?

'All right, I accept your explanation,' she said. 'I don't want you to leave. We've developed a good friendship and we work well together. If you go now all that will be lost. We can't break up a team that is already establishing a good business.'

Jane hesitated. But would their relationship ever be the same? No, it wouldn't. Nell's veiled accusations had left their mark, but Jane figured she was big enough to cope with that and push it to the back of her mind. She swore then that she would be careful not to arouse those suspicions again.

'All right, I'll stay, but we can't just pretend this conversation never happened . . .'

'I regret what I said, Jane. I won't repeat it.'

'Very well.'

There was only a moment's hesitation then, 'Good night.' Nell was out of the room quickly, leaving Jane whispering, 'Good night' to the closed door. A tear trickled down her cheek, then another. Finally she sank on to the bed and sobbed silently.

During the next fortnight it was an uneasy peace that held between Nell and Jane, though they were skilful enough to keep it hidden from others. They were thankful that Flo was so absorbed in getting things ready for her husband's sailing day that she did not notice the strained atmosphere. Ewan and Simon were equally too occupied for thoughts of any possible rift to occur to them.

Sailing day was suddenly upon them. With the Lowestoft fleet bound for Shetland, there were many families down on the harbourside to wave goodbye.

When Nell and Jane arrived, Ewan and Simon were quickly ashore. They made their private goodbyes then, as Ewan swung on board the *Lively Lady*, Nell could not help herself from saying, really for Jane's benefit, 'No returning early, mind, Ewan.'

To which he replied, not realising the deeper implication, 'If she goes to London, Jane, go with her.'

'I will,' she laughed, and turned immediately to Nell. 'We'll have a good time there, won't we?' With that lighthearted query the thin layer of ice that remained between them was almost dissolved.

'Be sure you do,' said Simon. 'And don't mope in our absence.'

'Would we ever?' replied Jane.

'Remember us.' He pulled her to him and kissed her on the lips then. 'And remember that.'

'I will,' she whispered as he went aboard.

As Nell walked away, Jane glanced at Ewan. He winked at her and she felt a thrill run through her. Nell looked back and noticed the exchange. She said nothing but locked it away in her mind.

A week later the two girls took the bus to Yarmouth. They knew Glen would be processing some films he had taken for a small local building firm who had been given a prestigious job in the town.

They let themselves into the studio to find it empty but the red light by the door of the darkroom indicated he was in there and busy.

Nell went close to the door and called, 'It's Jane and me.'

'Be with you in five minutes,' Glen replied, pleasure in his voice.

The girls spent the time looking at the photographs spread around the studio, passing no comment between them.

'Hi,' Glen greeted them when he emerged.

'We thought we'd better come and have a talk about the projects we might tackle next.'

'You've heard?'

'Heard what?'

'Hitler has denounced the Naval Treaty we had with him.'

'Denounced?' said Jane. 'That means he's saying it's wrong, it doesn't mean he'll go any further.'

'True,' agreed Glen, 'but it's a step nearer to tearing it up. He's also denounced the Non-Aggression Pact with Poland.'

'I don't like that,' commented Nell.

'Nor do I,' agreed Glen. 'I think we'll see a lot more preparations for war in case it comes, so I think we should look out for further suitable subjects and photograph everything we can. Jane, you ought to be keeping a comprehensive diary of the major events and what is happening in everyday life.'

'I'll do that immediately.'

'And I think we ought to pay Mr Horton another visit. We have more photographs to show him, and *Preparations for War* could be expanded, maybe broken down into themes. He's probably thought of doing that already but it's worth mentioning, showing him we have independent ideas. Have you any others?'

Jane offered a suggestion. 'From what I've seen of *World Scene* and what you told me after your visit, Mr Horton likes people to be centre-stage, so why not pictures of them in one of their natural environments – the pub? Link the pictures with their views of Hitler and the possibility of war. You'll have to do it, though, Glen. Us two venturing into pubs wouldn't go down too well.'

'Unless it was a posh one,' Nell muttered, just loud enough for Jane to catch her words.

She hid her surprise. So the incident was still not fully eradicated from Nell's mind? 'If you gather the material, I'll do the necessary writing. Nell can do the donkey work in the darkroom.'

'Thank you very much for volunteering for me,' she retorted.

'That's a good idea, Jane,' Glen approved. 'We'll put it to Mr Horton.'

'Most of our food supplies come from abroad,' cut in Nell. 'If war comes, our farmers are going to have to produce more. Maybe there's a project in that?'

'We'll mention that too. When should we all go to London?'

'I'm always free,' said Jane.

'With the drifters away, there's nothing much for me to do for Dad so I too can go whenever. What about two days' time?'

'March the second.' Glen picked up his diary. 'That will suit me. I don't have another appointment until the eighth – that's in connection with the photos I was working on when you arrived.'

'The building project in Yarmouth?' asked Nell.

'Yes. They look good, especially those you took.' He rose from his chair. 'I'll ring Mr Horton's secretary now.'

A few minutes later, after making his request, he said, 'Ten-thirty? That will be fine.' There was a brief pause. 'I see.' Another pause. Nell and Jane wondered what was happening but could read no answer in his expression. 'Yes, I'm sure that will be all right. I'll ring you back in a few minutes.'

The girls were looking at him with anxious curiosity as he turned from the phone.

'What about that then?' he said, appearing still to be considering what he had just been told.

'What?' they both demanded, irritable at being kept in the dark.

'Mr Horton wants us to spend two more days in London after our appointment with him.'

'What?'

'Why?'

'His secretary didn't say. It's his request we should do so, if at all possible. He must have something in mind for us.' Glen looked anxiously at the girls who, apart from surprise, had shown no reaction as yet. 'Well?'

'It means being away for four nights,' said Nell.

'That's all right by me,' replied Jane.

'You haven't a mother to convince,' Nell pointed out.

'This could be an opportunity not to be missed,' said Glen, 'otherwise why invite us to stay?'

'Well, this visit will include a chaperone,' said Jane, turning that fact into a slight dig at Nell. 'I'm sure we can convince your mother,' she added, in order to dilute her previous remark.

'OK, I'll sweetheart Mum,' said Nell, rising to the veiled challenge.

'Good.' Glen returned to the phone, confirmed their appointment and booked their accommodation.

Two days later they were sitting in the train bound for London. Mrs Franklin had made some precautionary remarks but had raised no objection when told there would

201

be the three of them. She was pleased that her daughter's venture was turning out well for her and, being a woman who constantly looked to the future and not back at the past, she realised there were exciting opportunities open to Nell, even if this was still a male-dominated world.

Jane was excited and overawed when she walked into the Strand Palace Hotel but kept her reactions carefully subdued, acting as if this was an everyday experience for her. Once in the privacy of their shared room, though, she let them show and allowed Nell to act like the experienced guest, even though she had made only one visit here.

As they were going to be in London for the next three days they decided to savour the hotel after a short walk down the Strand and Fleet Street, viewing the newspaper buildings in which they hoped their future work would be used, as well as in *World Scene*. Then Glen, smartly dressed in a suit for once, proudly escorted two pretty young ladies, dressed in the latest eye-catching fashions, to the dining room where they relished the attention paid to them and enjoyed an excellent meal.

The following morning they met over breakfast and were at the *World Scene* offices promptly for the meeting with Mr Horton. He welcomed them and said how pleased he was to meet Jane. 'I like your style, you have a natural gift for words,' he told her.

'It is kind of you to say so.'

'I mean it. I never say what I don't mean. And before I go any further, I must say I'm pleased with the speculative work you have been sending in and the way you are developing *Preparations for War*. That theme could easily expand further with the new developments taking place in Europe. But now, you will be wondering why I asked you to stay on longer in London. Well, more of that later. First, have you any new ideas?'

Glen elaborated on what they had discussed in Yarmouth.

'Two useful ideas with distinct possibilities. In fact, the

pub one could benefit from your stay in London. I see you have brought your cameras ... good.' He leaned back in his chair and for a moment surveyed the three young people on the opposite side of his desk. 'I don't want to sound alarmist but you, Nell, and you, Glen, have both heard my opinion on the likelihood of war. No doubt they told you, Jane?' She nodded. 'Well, I think we have moved a step nearer with Hitler's latest denunciations. Before long we will see actions speaking louder than words, and our work will be coloured by that.'

'Might you have to close down?' asked Glen, alarmed by the prospect.

'No, I don't think so. Our reputation is high and we have a loyal readership. If war comes, people are going to want to know what is happening wherever there is conflict, and what the situation is for non-combatants also. War will influence lives all over the world. So I'm building up a team of photographers. I'm not suggesting we'd send you off willy-nilly anywhere in the world, but I would like to know what you each intend to do should war come. I know you probably can't answer that now, you may not even have considered it, but I would like you to give it some thought. We'll meet again tomorrow, and the following day, at the same time as this. Today I suggest you explore London with your cameras. You, Jane, with your note-book.' He opened a drawer, took out three small cards, wrote on them and handed them one each. 'Take these. They'll identify you as bona fide employees of *World Scene*. Drop your films in at reception before five. They'll be processed and printed overnight for you. I'll see what you've got in the morning. Think over what I said about the future, and we'll talk again.'

The three friends left the offices of *World Scene* feeling mystified.

'What do you think he was getting at?' asked Jane.

'Don't know,' replied Glen.

'Why does he want us to take photographs of London

today? He'll have his own batch of photographers working out of that office,' put in Nell.

'All I can think is that it's some sort of test of our ability and imagination.'

'But why now, if he thinks war is coming? And how can he expect us to say what we might do then?' protested Jane.

They had reached a Lyons Corner House.

'Let's get some coffee or something and make a plan,' suggested Glen, ushering the girls through the door. A waitress, known in Lyons terminology as a Nippy, escorted them to a vacant table and returned a few minutes later to take their order. Having seen the sumptuous cream slices being consumed at a nearby table, they ordered one each to be served with their coffee. Jane then produced her writing pad and started taking notes on the lavish décor and the general atmosphere of the place. The customers sat deep in serious conversation or idle gossip or merely 'watched the world go by'. To it all she added a comment on the mood created by the pianist flowing effortlessly from one tune to another. As she wrote she joined in her companions' conversation.

'Have you a plan for taking photographs when we leave here?' she asked.

'Not really,' replied Glen. 'I think we'll just wander, see what happens.'

'Why not start here then?' Jane suggested, looking around her. 'This is normality, isn't it? People here don't seem to be giving a thought to war. Or if they are, they're not showing it. We could do a feature on that.'

'A very good idea, Jane. I can do it without being obtrusive, and I won't take a photograph without asking the subject's permission, though I want the pictures to look natural . . .' Glen glanced around him. 'I'll clear it with the management first,' he added, rising from his chair. He was back in a few minutes, telling them with a smile, 'It's OK. In fact, the manager was delighted that his Corner House might feature in *World Scene*.'

'While you were away, Jane and I discussed what we should do next,' Nell informed him. 'We think we ought to concentrate on people rather than views unless the latter are directly relevant to what might lie ahead.'

'You mean, war?'

'Well, there are signs of buildings being protected everywhere. I assume that is because the government believes the situation is worsening.'

'OK,' agreed Glen. 'We might take in Downing Street, and hopefully get some pictures of the comings and goings at Number Ten. Quite often there are sightseers there. We might get some photographs of them and their views on Hitler and the coming of war.'

At fifteen minutes to five they were handing in their films at *World Scene*'s offices. As they stepped back into the street afterwards they breathed a collective sigh of relief.

'That was more tiring than I expected,' said Jane, running her fingers across her forehead.

'London pavements are hard,' commented Nell.

'You've certainly seen a lot of London on your first visit, Jane,' said Glen, and then made them an offer. 'Don't suppose you two would like to go to a show this evening?'

Both girls groaned and shook their heads. 'Thanks, but it's a long soak and a nice meal for us.' Nell spoke for them both, and Jane agreed.

When they were shown into Mr Horton's office the following morning they found him studying their photographs. He greeted them pleasantly and, pointing to the pictures, said, 'You've done well. I like the Lyons Corner House, I'll run that in three weeks'. People outside Number Ten I'll hold on to for the time being. It could link in nicely if the position in Europe worsens. I like your interpretation of the Embankment, but the attempt at capturing Trafalgar Square lacks impact, as does your depiction of street art.

'Now what I have arranged for today is that each of you

should spend some time with a staff member. Nell and Glen are to go to a photographer each, and Jane to one of our writers. I want you to do the same tomorrow. When you finish that session at four o'clock, see me before you leave.'

They had no questions so Mr Horton summoned the people he had chosen to show them the ropes and made the introductions.

As they left the building, the young woman who had been assigned to Jane, who seemed to be in her mid-thirties, commented, 'Mr Horton must think highly of you three. It is very rare for him to arrange this sort of training.'

This observation made the three friends feel very privileged and heightened their determination to make the most of this opportunity.

Mr Horton kept them waiting a few minutes at the end of their second day with *World Scene*. It was obvious he had been gathering reports on them.

'Have you enjoyed these last two days?' he asked when he finally sat down behind his desk.

'Very much,' replied Glen.

'I learned so much about angles that will enable me to put more meaning into my photographs, tell a story through them,' Nell enthused.

'Excellent. My experiment paid off.' He looked at Jane then. 'What about you, Jane? It would be different for you.'

'It was an eye-opener,' she said. 'I learned how to see, rather than look. My observation in the future will be much sharper and, hopefully, have more depth.'

'Good. That is exactly what I hoped would happen.'

'May I thank you on behalf of all of us for the trouble you have taken?' said Glen. The girls agreed with him.

'You can thank me by the work you put in for *World Scene*. I saw talent in the first article you brought me, and I'm glad I nurtured it. Now, remember I asked you what

206

you might do if war comes? Have you thought of your answers yet?'

'It's difficult to say,' replied Glen.

Mr Horton nodded and pursed his lips thoughtfully. 'I know, maybe I shouldn't have asked you, so I'll give you a piece of advice, for what it's worth. Whatever you do, as far as is possible I would like you to carry your cameras and your notebook. I know film will all but dry up, but I hope the magazine will be allowed some in order to keep a record of the country's participation in the war. I have been stock-piling, so in all probability I will be able to supply you with some from time to time.'

'I, too, have been buying in as much as I can, and I'll continue to do so. I'm sure my father will help also,' said Glen.

'Good.'

'My uncle will have been adding to his stock, and I know he will take whatever allowance he gets because it's his livelihood. He has said he'll pass on what he can to Glen,' added Jane.

'This is all excellent news. So if war does come you'll be able to carry on. As I say, have your cameras with you constantly. Record, but be sparing. Let each picture really tell so that you aren't wasting precious film. Wherever you are, if you have difficulty with processing, send the film to me. We can deal with it here. Jane, will you keep sending reports and observations also? We'll use what we can, and what we can't we'll keep on file so that your work will be here for you, whenever you want it. I am making the same arrangement with all staff members. Now, that piece of advice! If war comes you will in all probability be conscripted, which will probably mean you'll be slotted in wherever the authorities see fit. If you want any say in the capacity in which you serve, then volunteer. The same applies to you two girls as Glen here.'

'You think they will be called up too?' said Glen doubtfully.

207

'I'm sure of it. Look, as men are drafted, many essential jobs will need filling, especially those that contribute to the war effort. Think about it. I'm not saying, act immediately. See which way the situation is going, but don't leave your decision too late.' Horton glanced at the wall clock and stood up then. 'I'm afraid I must get on, I have an editorial meeting in five minutes. I wish you all the best of luck. Keep the work coming in, and I will always be pleased to hear where life is taking you.'

Embarrassed but not ungrateful, he brushed aside their thanks for all he had done for them, saying it was his pleasure to know them. As the door closed on them he sat down with a deep sigh, thinking of the son and daughter he had lost in a tragic boating accident last year while on holiday in Scotland. They would have been the same age as the young people who had just left his office, deep in excited speculation about their fortunes in the conflict ahead.

As they walked back to their hotel, Jane said wistfully, 'A nice man and a busy one. I wonder why he made time for us?'

Chapter Twelve

As Nell, Jane and Glen cooperated and developed their work, surmounting the disappointment of rejections with the triumph of acceptances, the drifters slowly made their way south from Shetland, and the world slipped nearer and nearer to war. There were many who drew optimism from Prime Minister Chamberlain's statement, 'The outlook in international affairs is tranquil,' and the Foreign Secretary's, 'It is a mistake to see crisis in everything.' They were prepared to close their eyes to the real reason for Britain's booming economy and falling unemployment: rearmament. An atmosphere of uneasy normality settled over the country. It was sensed more in towns, but touched outlying areas along the coast and in the countryside too. The expectation of war and the desire for peace made for strange bedfellows.

But when daily newspapers dropped through letterboxes on the sixteenth of March, the way ahead seemed clearer.

Mrs Franklin collected hers, stared at the headline and walked slowly into the kitchen.

'What's up, Mum?' asked Nell, concerned by her mother's ashen face.

Flo dropped the paper on the table, diverting her daughter's and Jane's attention from their breakfast.

They all saw the news: the previous night German troops had marched into Prague, and the Munich Agreement, on which Chamberlain had pinned his hopes for peace, was negated.

'But it still says nothing about war,' pointed out Nell.

'Can we stand by and see this happen?' countered her mother.

Yet in the succeeding days this seemed to be the case.

Nevertheless, the news from land had alarmed the driftermen, some of whom had had personal experience of the Great War and knew what conflict meant for sailors. George Franklin contacted his friends by radio and after an exchange of ideas the three skippers decided to continue fishing but be prepared to head back to Lowestoft if the situation worsened. They were off Eyemouth, close to the Scottish border in early-August, when they heard that the Reserve Fleet was fully manned. Without question they immediately left the fishing grounds, landed their catches at Eyemouth and headed for home.

About the same time, Nell and Jane were called to a meeting with Glen.

'The situation has been worsening all year, but more so since April when Hitler tore up the naval agreement with Britain,' he pointed out. 'He's still ranting and raving about Danzig and Poland. Mr Chamberlain has warned him that an attack on Danzig could mean war and has reaffirmed we will stand by our commitment to Poland. Now we have the Reserve Fleet fully manned . . . things look grim. Have you thought any more about Mr Horton's advice?'

'Not really,' said Nell.

'Nor I, but maybe we should.'

The *Sea Queen*, *Lively Lady* and *Silver King* were among the first Lowestoft drifters to reach home port. It had been expected that the ships would return early and so families were not surprised when word flashed through Lowestoft that some had been sighted. When the news reached the Franklin household, Flo, Nell and Jane lost no time in reaching the harbourside, as did the Steel and Evans fami-

210

lies. There was no disguising the anxiety that replaced their usual joy at having the crews home, for they all knew that their menfolk would face greater danger before long.

Nell and Jane stood side by side to wait.

'Another early return for Ewan,' Nell muttered meaningfully.

Jane's lips tightened. 'I thought that was all water under the bridge?' she countered.

'Just a warning! Water has a habit of seeping in where it's not wanted.'

'Nell, stop these snide remarks. I thought the incident had been forgotten? I told you, there was nothing in it.'

Nell could see that she had offended her friend. 'I'm sorry,' she apologised. 'I suppose it's having Ewan near again, and my anxiety over what will happen to him next.'

'I'm anxious for Simon, for Ewan too, for all the crews. So please, let's support each other.'

Ewan leaped on to the harbourside, grabbed Nell and swung her round off her feet. 'Home again!' he cried cheerily, enjoying the feel of her arms clinging round his neck. Jane slipped away to the *Silver King*.

'Good to see you, Simon,' she said. 'Welcome home.'

He kissed her and said, 'Good to have you here.' Then he turned to greet his mother who was busy hugging his father. 'Hello, Ma.'

Sarah Evans returned his greeting and turned her attention to her younger son Neil while Simon winked at their younger sister. 'You been behaving yourself?'

'Of course.'

When Simon turned back to Jane she saw the love in his eyes. 'No fish to land so we'll soon be free.' He glanced round. 'Ma, can Jane eat with us?'

'Of course, Simon.'

'You will, won't you?' he asked belatedly.

'Thank you, Mrs Evans.'

'Good,' he replied. 'Then we'll team up with the other

two and go to the dance.'

'I'd like nothing better. It will help us to forget the real reason why you're home early.'

He gave a little nod. 'Ewan!' he shouted. 'Dance? Jane's eating with us. We'll call for you.'

'Right, Ma's asked Nell. See you later.'

That evening the four friends never mentioned the possibility of war. Their very exuberance spoke of a single-minded determination to enjoy themselves, for who knew what tomorrow might bring?

The following morning at ten-thirty there was a knock on the Franklins' door.

'Glen!' Nell gasped on seeing him. 'This is unexpected.'

'Hello, Nell, is your father in?'

'Yes,' she replied, wondering at this request.

'May I see him?'

'Oh, yes, of course, come in,' she spluttered. 'He's in the kitchen, talking to Mum.' She led the way. 'Dad, Glen's here, he wants to see you.'

'Good morning, Mr Franklin. I'm sorry for troubling you at home.'

'Come in, lad.' George liked Glen; there was no snootiness about him even though his parents were so affluent. George knew they had not let success go to their heads. He knew Nell liked this young man and was happy about that because it made for a good working relationship. 'Sit down.'

'Like a piece of apple pie?' Flo asked.

'Would I, Mrs Franklin!' Glen said brightly, recalling the first time he had visited this house. 'There's none to beat your baking.'

'Get on with you.' She smiled as she slid a piece on to a plate and put it in front of him.

'No matter how good that is, lad, don't let it distract you from the reason you're here. You looked serious when you came in. What is it?' asked George.

Glen paused with his spoon poised, about to cut into the pie. 'You're back early because of the likelihood of war?'

'Aye. I thought it best to be getting home.'

'What will happen to your drifter now?'

'She'll serve as part of the RN Patrol Service. Certain vessels are already marked for it and their crews have done training in some aspects of the work throughout the year. The *Sea Queen* is among those.'

'Will you still be skipper?'

'Oh, yes! I'll be Captain RNR and the crew will all be given ranks appropriate to their length of service and status. All my crew have done the necessary training so once the *Sea Queen* has her war-dress and paint, we can go into action straight away.'

'Will you need any more crew members?'

'More than likely because of the duties we'll be called on to do.'

'But you are likely to keep your existing crew?'

'Yes, they know the boat so it makes sense to keep them. Extra men may come from anywhere. They'll be assembled at Lowestoft and allocated as required. What are you getting at, lad?'

'Will you sign me on, sir?'

'What? You want to serve on the *Sea Queen*?'

'Yes, sir! If I wait to be called up, I could be sent into the Army or RAF and I don't want that. I want to go where I choose so I thought if I volunteered for service with you, I'd get what I want – the sea.'

George could not hide his surprise. 'But you've seen no service there.'

'Well, I managed that voyage with you.'

'Sure enough, but that was ...'

'I know what you are going to say, sir, but I swear I will not let you down.'

'But the different jobs ...'

'I'm a quick learner, sir, and I can do a lot of that learning while the *Sea Queen* is in port.'

213

'There are rules and regulations regarding men serving in the Patrol Service.'

'I believe if you sign me on as a fisherman and pull a few strings, I can stay with you if war comes and be part of your Patrol Service crew.'

George said nothing. He concentrated his thoughts and no one interrupted them. He felt flattered by this young man's faith in him. 'Aye, maybe I could, but . . .'

'Give Glen the chance, Dad,' pleaded Nell.

George glanced at his wife and saw her give an almost imperceptible nod.

'All right, young man. I'll sign you on as one of my present crew. Leave the rest to me. Those strings may be hard to pull but I'll make sure they don't get knotted or tangled. You'll have to start out as a deckhand, the rest is up to you.'

'Mr Franklin, thank you. I'll not let you down.' Glen's face lit up with excitement. 'What happens now, sir?'

'I think you'd better eat that apple pie,' said a smiling Flo.

They all burst out laughing as Glen tucked into his pie with gusto. He said he would write to Mr Horton and let him know what course he had chosen.

Two days later Glen became a fully fledged crew member of the *Sea Queen*. Mr Franklin put him under the tutelage of Terry who, fully fit again, was now ready for anything and eager to teach the young man who had saved his life.

As August slipped towards September, the clouds of war gathered overhead. On the twenty-second, Britain and France reaffirmed their commitment to support Poland in the face of an aggressor.

The Franklins' house was not the only one in Lowestoft, or indeed in the country, affected by gloom. George left the house early on the morning of the twenty-third and when he returned he told everyone that they were to join the Steel and Evans families at the concert hall in Sparrow's Nest, to

214

attend the second house of the revue *Road Show*, starring the popular comediennes Elsie and Doris Waters, otherwise known as 'Gert and Daisy'.

'We all need brightening up,' was George's comment when he put the tickets on the kitchen table.

It was a night they would remember for a long time to come. After rollicking laughter generated by all the performers, the three families adjourned to the Steels' home where they enjoyed a feast. George had acted not a day too soon because that same week the Admiralty moved in to take over all of Sparrow's Nest: the grounds, concert hall, and all the buildings, for use as the main assembly point for men of the RN Patrol Service.

Conversion of drifters and trawlers to wartime specifications was immediately put into action. Hull frames and deck beams had to be strengthened so that the vessels could be armed with guns. Minesweeping gear was installed on the *Sea Queen*, *Lively Lady* and *Silver King*, and their crews given instruction in handling this wartime equipment.

A few days later general mobilisation was announced, and Glen was even more grateful to Mr Horton for his advice, and to Mr Franklin for enabling him to become a member of the *Sea Queen*.

Throughout these days of crisis the three friends saw additional opportunities for their photographic and writing work. They sent a steady supply of material to Mr Horton who was pleased to note that they were still acting like skilled photojournalists in the midst of the momentous events taking place.

Nell and Glen were about to leave the darkroom one day when she stopped him, her hand on his arm. 'Glen, I'm so proud of you for volunteering for service with my dad. Take care of yourself, won't you?'

'I will, and thank you for your concern.' He took hold of her other arm. 'Please be there to see me come into port?'

'I will.' Nell kissed him and he held her close to him for a moment. 'You'll be in my thoughts, and I'll pray for your safety.'

'Thanks.' He kissed her back and quickly left the dark-room.

During the first two days of September their cameras were kept busy recording the evacuation of children from their area, while Jane recorded the various local opinions on paper. On Sunday the third Nell had her camera ready to record the family's expressions during the Prime Minister's scheduled radio broadcast at 11.15 a.m.

' ... *This morning, the British Ambassador in Berlin handed the German government a final note, stating that unless the British government heard from them by 11 o'clock that they were prepared to withdraw their troops from Poland, a state of war would exist between us. I have to tell you now that no such under-taking has been received, and that consequently this country is at war with Germany* ...'

When his announcement finished Flo said, 'He sounds so tired, poor man.' She stood up and, glancing at them all, added, 'God take care of us.' Then she went into the kitchen and started to mix the Yorkshire puddings.

Sunday dinner was a subdued affair. No one really wanted to talk about the future until, as they finished their rice pudding, Nell ventured to ask, 'When will you have to go, Dad?'

'Whenever I'm called, lass, but they'll have to finish converting the *Sea Queen* first. I'll just have to hold myself in readiness, as will all the crew. I'll be reporting to Sparrow's Nest in the morning. We'll have to take life as it comes now and deal with all the upheaval and disruption ahead. We've seen a lot already: kids evacuated, schools closed, holiday facilities closing down. Boats and trawlers have to be got ready so there's going to be a bigger workforce needed to do that. The organisation of Sparrow's Nest must proceed rapidly if it is to fulfil its role, and that means expansion of the facilities there.

'I think the powers that be have realised that Lowestoft and its port is no more vulnerable to air attack than anywhere else in the country, even though it is on the east coast. Any vacant buildings, such as the schools that have closed, can be used for the war effort, but extra offices and stores will have to be built too, while open spaces can be used for training purposes. Accommodation for the expected influx of servicemen can be found in the hotels and boarding houses. Everyone will just have to cope, no matter how long this war lasts.'

'Not long, I hope,' put in Flo, rising from the table and starting to clear it.

Nell and Jane helped her, and also with the washing up. Normally they would have sent her to sit down but they could tell she wanted to keep busy today.

When the final plate had been dried and put away, Nell said to Jane, 'Let's take a walk.'

They wandered out, going nowhere in particular. There weren't many people about, an air of shock seemed to have enveloped the town, but gradually there was more movement and noise. Life had to go on even though it now held a different purpose.

'From what Dad said, there are going to be many opportunities to expand *Preparations for War*,' pointed out Nell.

'We've covered a lot of it already,' Jane replied. 'I hope Mr Horton will use some of our submissions soon.'

'We must keep sending him material. Glen won't be able to now he's a member of the *Sea Queen*.'

'I think he'll still be using his camera, but now his subject will be *War*, as indeed will ours.'

'Mr Horton will sort all that out.'

'I suppose so, and I expect he'll let us know if there is anything special he wants us to tackle. Our identification as employees of *World Scene* will be of greater importance now as I expect photography will be restricted in many areas.'

'We must have a word with Glen about that. Maybe we should go to Yarmouth tomorrow.'

'Were you surprised when he asked your father to sign him on, especially as he has never been to sea except for that one day?' Jane asked.

'I was. He'd never mentioned it, but if that's what he wants, he was right to take Mr Horton's advice.'

'Are we going to?'

Nell shrugged her shoulders. 'Not sure. If women are going to be called up then I'd rather volunteer but I'm reluctant to do so yet. I think I should be around for Mum when Dad goes away. Well, for a while, until she gets used to it. But you volunteer now if you wish to.'

Jane grasped Nell's arm. 'I'd hoped that if war came we could volunteer together and stay together. I'd hoped your attitude about Ewan wouldn't get in the way of that.'

Nell stiffened and her eyes went cold. 'It's *your* attitude that is the problem.'

'Mine?' Jane frowned with surprise.

'I've seen the way he eyes you, and your response.'

'What's wrong with a bit of flirting? Any girl would be flattered to have Ewan look at her.'

'I've told you before, he's mine. Stand back.'

'Oh, come on, Nell. I've told *you*, there's nothing in it. There never was that day he returned early. If you want to believe tittle-tattle from the likes of a barmaid, then I'm sorry – you've chosen her word over mine.' Jane started to walk away then.

Nell hesitated a moment before she ran after her. 'Jane, I'm sorry . . .'

'So you should be.'

'Let's forget it. There's a war on. Life's going to be difficult enough as it is and I would like it if we stayed together.'

*

218

All thoughts of visiting Glen were banished when they reached home. He was there waiting.

'Came to report to the skipper,' he said with a grin.

'And?' prompted Nell.

'I've told him to come and see me at three o'clock tomorrow. I hope I'll be able to tell him more then,' said George.

'We were going to come and see you tomorrow, Glen, to talk about the business,' said Nell.

'Well, here I am now.'

'Use the other room,' Flo suggested.

Once they were seated, Glen said, 'We've got to keep it going. That is, if you want to?'

'I certainly do,' replied Nell.

'Me too,' agreed Jane.

'Good, but it's not going to be easy. I'll take my camera with me and do whatever I can, sending the film to Mr Horton whenever possible. You two may have better opportunities to keep the business ticking over, maybe even prospering. Have you decided what to do about volunteering?'

Nell explained their decisions.

'In the meantime, we'll look at all the options and see which form of work offers us the most chance of staying together.'

'A good idea. Now you've explained the situation, you might make some trips to London with material for Mr Horton. Anticipating this, I had a word with my father. He says that if ever you are there you must feel free to use the hotel we stayed at.'

'But that will be too ...'

'I know what you are going to say but the question of payment need not arise. You will be there on business so the charges will be met from my father's account. I have a letter for each of you in which he authorises the hotel to charge your expenses to him. Our own business will settle with him at a future date.'

219

'That is extremely generous,' said Nell. 'Are you sure?'

Glen waved his hand dismissively. 'Of course. It was Father's suggestion when he asked what was going to happen to the business now that I'll be on the high seas. I'll be easier in my mind, as will he and your parents, knowing that you have somewhere to stay in London if necessary.'

'This is wonderful,' said Jane. 'It means we will be able to keep in touch with Mr Horton personally. That will be so much better than having to rely on the post which will be chaotic now we are at war.'

'Well, I must away home,' said Glen. 'I'll probably see you tomorrow.'

After they had seen him out their excitement spilled over and they enthusiastically apprised Nell's parents of the situation. Their approval was a little more muted but eventually they were persuaded to agree to Mr Aveburn's arrangements.

'I know you are both sensible enough not to take advantage of his generosity,' Flo finally said, 'and promise me that if ever you go to London, you will go together?'

A few minutes later there was a knock on the door and they heard it open.

'Ewan,' said Nell.

A moment later he walked in, making light of the situation by saying, 'Well, we're at it.'

'Yes, looks like it,' returned George. 'Hello, Simon.'

His greeting embraced everyone, then he added, 'Mr Franklin, Dad said he would like you to go round. I've told Ewan's dad also.'

'Right,' George replied, pushing himself up from his chair. 'Flo, are you coming for a natter to Sarah?'

'May as well. These four won't want me playing gooseberry.'

When she and George reached the Evans' house, Percy Steel was already there. After greetings were exchanged, Mrs Evans suggested that she and Flo went to see Liz Steel. Liz always had the kettle on the boil and the three friends

220

were soon enjoying a good cup of tea, made to the strength she knew they all liked and accompanied by her special scones.

'I expect you were all round your wireless this morning. Not a good thing to listen to, but we'll just have to get on with it.' From Liz's tone Flo and Sarah knew she had something more on her mind.

'Well, Liz, what is it?' asked Sarah, taking a bite of her scone as Liz went on.

'I hear there's going to be a problem with cooks on the drifters and trawlers being taken over by the Admiralty. Most of the cooks already serving are over-age for call-up, and the rate of pay from the Admiralty is too low to attract capable men to volunteer for the job, especially if they're married with a family. The only solution is to fill the posts with young conscripts.'

'What? How many of them will have had cooking experience?' said Sarah.

'Exactly. If crews can't eat, the boats can't sail. It's arisen on the *Lively Lady* already. Ben Campbell's too old and Percy can't find anyone else.'

'Good grief, I hadn't thought about it, and George has never said but the *Sea Queen* won't have a cook either. Abe Naylor will be too old,' said Flo.

'Is the Admiralty doing anything about it?' asked Sarah.

'Well, there's talk that they're sending conscripts to some of the naval depots to learn, but there are objections to that. The cooks there won't have the time to devote to training them, and the conditions will be entirely different from what they are in cramped galleys on drifters and trawlers. I think the Admiralty were stumped at first but I hear the head of Lowestoft Technical College suggested a cookery school for the conscripts be established there, and conditions on board the drifters and trawlers replicated. The head of Sparrow's Nest jumped at the chance and took it upon himself to try the idea. The first experiment proved successful and the idea is to be expanded as quickly as possible.

221

'They want domestic science teachers to be instructors. Sarah, you and I have our certificates, and I don't think they'd turn Flo down. She's a better cook than either of us, we can vouch for that. What do you say to us volunteering?'

Flo and Sarah were speechless for a moment.

Liz took their silence the wrong way and pressed her suggestion by pointing out, 'We're completely free and our menfolk are likely to be away for longer periods and the kids will be evacuated. We would be doing something worthwhile and contributing to the war effort.'

'We weren't objecting,' Flo hastened to reassure her. 'Were we, Sarah?'

'No, we certainly weren't, just taken aback by something we never expected. I'm all for it.'

'So am I,' said Flo emphatically. 'And even though it's Sunday, I suggest we go and offer our services right now. I know where this good lady lives.'

They were welcomed with open arms and left for home at a brisk pace, delighted they were going to be useful.

It meant a change in the routine of their households but everyone supported their decision and was prepared to accept the new regime. Nell also saw it as a way of easing the situation when she and Jane decided the time was right for them to volunteer their service in a wartime capacity. If her mother could take on war work, so could she.

For three weeks the crews of the *Sea Queen*, *Lively Lady* and *Silver King* had to curb their impatience while they watched other boats leave before them. There was so much work involved in converting all the boats and trawlers that, even with the increased workforce, the conversions were not all completed as speedily as the Admiralty and the waiting crews would have liked.

However, the time ashore was not wasted. The skippers of the three boats saw that their crews trained every day in the use of the new equipment that had been installed, so that when they eventually came on board their transformed vessels, they were adept at handling it. The nets and winding gear essential for fishing were removed and replaced with instruments of war: minesweeping equipment was installed, a twelve-pounder gun mounted on the forecastle, a Bofors aft of the funnel, and two machine-guns in the bridge wings. What had been the fish-hold was converted to the crew's mess deck, and quarters for all hands were rearranged, though endeavours to make these less cramped were met by only partial success. The coal-fired galley in the after-deck house was still small but it would be manned by a cook trained in what had now been named the RN Patrol Service Cookery School.

The new dangers they would face at sea were never mentioned. They were accepted as part of the job they had to do, and the crews were anxious to get on with it. Reports were coming in that German aircraft were operating nightly along the east coast, and as no bombing attacks were reported it could only mean that they were dropping mines in the shipping lanes. It was known that German submarines were laying mines too.

Eventually, on a day when low cloud scudded across a grey sky, three anxious families watched the drifters, dressed for war, sail from Lowestoft harbour at dawn to meet a cold sea and head north to the Humber.

Chapter Thirteen

Reaching the Humber, where it was known that German bombers had already laid a considerable number of mines and were continuing to do so, the three drifters began their sweep.

George Franklin watched his crew perform efficiently and was pleased that the extra training ashore was paying off even though they now had to cope with a pitching boat. All was going well but he knew that at any moment the seemingly tranquil scene could erupt into nightmare; he must himself guard against complacency, and keep his crew alert at all times. Only darkness might give them some ease. The three skippers had devised their own communications signals from their days at the herring fishing and he knew all was going well. Three days into their sweep, however, visibility shortened and visual contact was lost. This did not worry the skippers; they knew the exact course the others would be taking. The sweep went on blind.

The roar of aero-engines suddenly broke over the monotonous sound of the drifter's engines. It startled the crews. Men rushed on deck in time to see a Heinkel 111 tear out of the low cloud and mist, almost at mast height, and hurtle towards the boat.

The *Sea Queen*'s crew sprang into action, taking up the positions they had practised so diligently on land. George's orders were instantly obeyed; he had trained his crew well.

The twelve-pounder came into action, and the two machine-guns were already spitting lead at the enemy. The Bofors gun was ready to play its part, too, when they could catch sight of the aircraft.

The Heinkel came at them again with guns blazing. Bullets shattered woodwork, and the glass of the wheel-house broke into a thousand pieces, narrowly missing George. Two bombs dropped from the Heinkel's belly and hurtled towards the steaming drifter. They missed, but only just, and a wash was hurled high across the boat, drenching the crew as it fell. Determined to hit back, they stuck to their posts. The Heinkel banked, ready to make another attack. In the few moments of respite, nerves held steady in a grip of steel after his near brush with death, George assessed the damage quickly from his position in the wheel-house. He saw that the machine-gunner on the starboard gun was lying prone at the foot of it and that Glen had taken over as he had been trained to do.

The German swept in again. Bullets sprayed the drifter, which was now swerving to make herself less of a target, but she could not escape completely. Bullets tore into her. The wheelhouse was riddled again and the man at the wheel crumpled with bullets in both legs. George grabbed the wheel from him. With all guns blazing, the *Sea Queen* hit back. Though the Heinkel was seen to be hit several times, the damage was still not sufficient to deter it. The aircraft gained height and headed for the drifter again. Two more bombs were hurled at the boat. George gave the wheel a vicious swing; the *Sea Queen* responded. The bombs hit the water but were too close. As the heaving sea subsided, damage to the hull near water-level was visible. Everyone was ready for another attack but the aircraft climbed away and disappeared into the cloud. The crew sensed they had gained a victory. Nevertheless, they remained alert while George, handing the wheel over, left the wheelhouse to take stock. With one member of the crew dead, three others wounded, the hull ripped open in parts, one hole dangerously near the waterline and the deck littered with spent bullets and shrapnel, he considered it wisest to head for Lowestoft.

He was making ready to do so when the *Lively Lady* and *Silver King* loomed out of the mist. Though they had escaped detection they had heard the action and now hove to, offering help. With George assuring his friends that he could manage, they left to resume their duties while he headed for home port at all possible speed.

Word that the *Sea Queen* had been sighted ran like fire through Lowestoft. Concern that she was back early brought people hastening down to the harbour, among them Nell and Jane. Flo joined them after word had reached the Cookery School.

'What do you think is wrong, Mum?' asked Nell, frowning with concern.

'No idea, love,' replied Flo, trying to sound confident though her mind was dwelling on the worst scenario. That was heightened when the *Sea Queen* drew near enough for them to see her war wounds.

'Oh, Mum, look at her! What's happened?' cried Nell, grasping her mother's hand.

'Must have been attacked.' Flo bit her lip, trying to identify the seamen she could see. Where was George? Her heart raced. No, it couldn't be! Her hand tightened on Nell's.

'There's Glen,' cried Jane with some relief, but she too was anxious about Mr Franklin.

The few moments that passed before George appeared on deck seemed like a lifetime.

'Oh, he's there.' The words came with a sigh of heartfelt relief from Flo.

'Thank God,' said Nell, in a voice scarcely above a whisper. She felt her mother's grip slacken and Jane's arm come round her shoulders to give her a reassuring hug. Nell smiled her thanks.

As soon as the boat had docked, George was ashore to

reassure his wife that he was all right. It was a brief reassurance for he had much to do.

'I'll be home as soon as I can, love. Charlie Cook was killed. Must go to see his mother.'

Flo nodded her understanding and offered a silent prayer of thanks to God for bringing her husband safely through this first encounter with the enemy. She too would go to see Mrs Cook, but later.

'I'll see you two at home,' she said. 'Must get back to the school.'

'Hello again,' said a familiar voice.

'Glen! Are you all right?' asked Nell anxiously.

'Yes, I'm OK. '

'Was it bad?'

'Pretty rough. Aircraft attacked us. Your father told you Charlie Cook ...'

'Yes. Was he the only one?'

'Yes. Several wounded but fortunately nothing too serious.'

'What about the *Lively Lady* and the *Silver King*?' asked Jane, fearing they might have endured the same fate as the *Sea Queen* and still be limping home.

'Neither was attacked,' replied Glen. Both girls felt relief surge through them at this. 'I think the mist hid them. We were unlucky that the bomber came on us first, but we fought him off. Sorry, can't say any more. Must get back on board and help.' He handed Nell a packet. 'Get those off by today's post to Mr Horton.'

'You managed some photographs?' The girls' eyes filled with amazement.

'Yes. They're so topical I'm sure he'll make use of them. I'll ring him myself when I get ashore, but get them off today!' He turned, ran back to the boat and jumped on board.

'We'd better get this package off,' said Nell.

'You go and see to that. I'll stay and take a few notes. Mr Horton may want some copy as well.'

Nell agreed and hurried away to deal with the packet, seeing that it was despatched by the quickest possible means to London.

The ambulance had arrived by now and the wounded would soon be on their way to hospital. Admiralty officials were going on board the *Sea Queen* to assess the damage and receive a first-hand account from her skipper. Jane was careful not to get in the way but moved freely among those of the crew who had come ashore, quizzing them. Because of her association with the Franklins, they all knew her and talked freely. By the time she was leaving the harbour she had a very good picture of what had happened and what these men had been through. She only hoped she could do justice to their stories and vividly portray what war at sea meant to them.

Satisfied with the information and stories she had obtained, she was just leaving the harbour when she heard footsteps behind her and turned to see Glen running after her.

'Heading for home?' he asked as he fell into step beside her.

'Yes.'

'Mind if I come with you?'

'Of course not.'

Reaching the Franklins' house, his first query to Nell was, 'Did you get the film in the post?'

'I did,' she replied, '*and* I've rung Mr Horton warning him that it should be with him in the morning. I couldn't tell him what it contained but said you had just docked after an engagement with the enemy and would ring him as soon as possible. He said he wouldn't leave the office until he had heard from you.'

'Good. I'll ring him right away.' Glen headed for the door.

'Ring from here,' said Nell. 'No need to use a phone box.'

'Thanks.' He was grateful that George Franklin had been

far-sighted enough to have a telephone installed in his home. Soon Glen was in contact with Mr Horton and could explain exactly what was on the film.

'You managed to take photographs of the action?' Mr Horton showed his surprise. 'If these reproduce well, we'll really have something that'll bring the war home to the people of this country. There's a general air of complacency here because there is no land action as yet, and the term "Phoney War" is being bandied about pretty freely. These pictures will prove we really *are* at war. Because of that, I'm sure I'll get clearance to use them.'

'Jane interviewed the crew and has made a lot of notes.'

'First class,' Horton enthused. 'Tell her to get something down on paper and phone it into me as soon as possible.'

Glen passed that on to Jane, who gave him the thumbs up sign. 'She's already on to that, Mr Horton.' Jane mouthed another message for him to pass on. 'In fact, she says she'll bring it in person tomorrow.' Glen nodded. 'Yes, very well.' And after that, 'Goodbye.' Then he put the phone down and beamed at Jane. 'He's delighted and looks forward to seeing you tomorrow, Jane.'

'You'll come with me, Nell?' she asked.

'Of course! I want to see these famous photographs. Are you coming too, Glen?'

He shook his head. 'Can't. There's a lot to sort out on the *Sea Queen*. Your father wants all the crew on board first thing tomorrow morning.'

Jane set to work immediately and worked late into the night. Nevertheless she was up early enough to catch the first train to London. She and Nell were gripped by excitement when they were shown directly into Mr Horton's office.

He rose from his chair to greet them. 'Over here,' he said eagerly. He led the way to a table on which photographs were spread out. 'These came back from our processing department just half an hour ago. I'm glad you got them into the post yesterday.' He said no more, leaving the girls to make their own judgement.

They were speechless to witness so clearly what had happened in one solitary engagement in the mist and cold of the grey North Sea. The sense of isolation was there, the valiant effort to sweep clear the shipping lanes. Here were men going about a death-defying task to make the area safe for other shipping. Then they sailed straight into a vicious airborne attack. Sweeping forgotten, they vigorously defended themselves in a running battle with a German bomber. The aircraft was shown head-on; banking away; at sea level; climbing. Bombs dropped, water spouted high. Men were shown manning guns; firing back; hit; collapsing on deck. Then there was a gap in the sequence. 'That must be where Glen had to man the gun after the first gunner was hit,' said Jane, recalling the information she had obtained about that particular incident. The pictures then showed the German plane breaking off the engagement, the crew cheering their victory, and finally the devastation that the *Sea Queen* had endured.

Nell and Jane looked at Mr Horton. 'Are they all right?'

'All right? They're wonderful and verify everything I said on the phone – they'll prove to the public there is no such thing as a "Phoney War".' He turned to Jane then. 'You've got some copy for me?'

'Yes.' She fished the paper from her briefcase as he waved them to some chairs. Horton took the typescript to his place behind the desk and the girls waited anxiously as he read.

'Yes, you've caught the atmosphere and the action wonderfully well. You take me there, right into it. Coupled with the photographs, the whole feature should make a tremendous impact.' He paused for a moment and then added, 'What else can I say, but go on providing me with material on any aspects of war that come your way?'

'Thank you,' said Nell. 'We'll do our best.'

'I'm sure you will. There are going to be a lot of new topics to interest our readers who'll naturally want to know what is happening and how it is affecting their lives. By the way, the photographs I have left over from your contribution to *Preparations for War* I can link in with an article on the "Phoney War" ...'

The girls were in high spirits on the train back to Lowestoft and on reaching home were pleased to find Glen there awaiting their arrival. Their excitement infected him, too, when they described the photographs, Mr Horton's reaction, and his request for more.

'I'll see if I can get any shots of the repairs being carried out, concentrating on the workmen,' he said. 'Jane, you can write a piece but you'll have to be careful not to mention where exactly the repairs are taking place or the extent of the damage. The Germans could seize on that and blow it up out of all proportion.'

'I'll start on that tomorrow.'

'Nell, how about you taking some photographs of the Cookery School in action?'

'A good idea,' she enthused. 'It will be a side of the war that not many people know about.'

The three of them became engrossed in these new subjects while continuously looking out for more. Glen combined his with his work on the *Sea Queen*, and things were immediately made easier for him when he was allocated a billet with a landlady who had put her bed and breakfast accommodation at the disposal of the Admiralty. Nell and Jane were glad of the work which kept their minds occupied and not dwelling too much on what had happened to the *Sea Queen*, and could be happening presently to the *Lively Lady* and the *Silver King*. Ewan and Simon could be in danger at any minute. They were relieved when the two men arrived back on schedule and unscathed, but the next day they had to watch the *Sea Queen* sail again.

The weeks rolled on. Many in Britain were made uneasy by this so-called 'Phoney War'. They carried on their normal lives feeling as if they were sitting on the edge of a volcano, but with the passage of time that unease faded.

Armies in Europe faced each other in a standoff; the expected bombing attacks on Britain and France did not materialise; the U-boat threat to shipping was there but seemed remote from everyday experience. Apart from visual reminders of the preparation for war, life seemed to carry on as normal. But a reminder of the threat posed by the German Navy, particularly their U-boats, came on the eighth of January when food rationing was introduced in Britain. The war at sea escalated and continued to be the focus of attention until April when the Germans invaded Norway.

The volcano finally erupted on May the ninth when Hitler ordered the invasion of Belgium, Luxembourg and Holland.

The *Sea Queen*, *Lively Lady* and *Silver King* were working together off the Yorkshire coast when word came through that the German Army was pouring through the Low Countries. The skippers knew that their activity would become even more intense as a result. Though the *Sea Queen* had been the only vessel of those skippered by the three friends to suffer an attack, several enemy aircraft had been sighted since but were clearly bent on other missions, returning home, or else were driven off by RAF fighters. Several other boats and trawlers reported attacks, some ports suffering more losses than others, but the fishermen, now part of the Royal Navy, stuck to their task with great courage.

It soon became obvious that on land the Allied Armies were no match for the formidable German force and before long disaster faced the British Expeditionary Force, which was heading for Dunkirk as an escape route. The order for evacuation of the troops came on the evening of the twenty-sixth of May.

The three Lowestoft trawlers were steaming for home at the time, to refuel and resume their duties, but events in France were to change that, change all their lives.

On reaching their home port they received orders to head

straight for Ramsgate immediately they had refuelled.

'Aveburn!' George Franklin's command brought Glen running.

'Sir?'

'Away with you to my home. Tell my family it's a quick turnround. Be sharp, we're off as soon as we're ready.'

'Sir!' Glen was already down the gangway and racing from the harbour.

Breathless, he burst into the Franklins' house.

Nell and Jane spun round from the kitchen sink, startled. From the look on his face they knew something serious was coming. 'Glen!'

Breathing deeply, he leaned forward with his hands resting on the table. 'Can't stop ... Captain Franklin told me to let you and Mrs Franklin know that we're away again as soon as the boat is refuelled and ready. Ordered to Ramsgate.'

'What?' The girls exchanged glances of alarm.

'Must be something to do with what is happening in France ...'

'Ewan?' asked Nell.

'Simon?' Jane queried.

Glen straightened up. 'They'll be coming in soon. We got the news first, they were still sweeping when we left, but we did see them taking their gear on board. They'll no doubt be under the same orders as us. Look, must be off. Let Mrs Franklin know.' He headed for the door.

'Take care!' both girls called at the same moment.

He raised a hand in acknowledgement and was gone.

The front door banged behind him and a strange silence descended on the house. Jane and Nell stared at each other as if what had happened had been unreal. They knew the situation in France was bad, but did this redeployment of minesweepers mean the news was worsening?

'Come on, let's tell your mum,' cried Jane.

As they left the house Nell grabbed her camera.

When they reached the Cookery School Mrs Franklin

accepted the news in her usual unflappable way but deep down there was real concern for her husband and the crew of the *Sea Queen*, sailing into the unknown.

'There's nothing I can do,' Flo commented. 'I'm better keeping occupied here.'

The two girls left and sought a vantage point from which they could see the drifters leave. Three were already clear of the harbour and heading south.

'Things must be bad in France,' observed Jane, noting the number of boats heading for Lowestoft, 'or so many would not be recalled.'

'The *Sea Queen*'s leaving now,' Nell pointed out half an hour later. 'It's been a very quick turnround.'

'Got all the photographs you want?' asked Jane as she slipped her notebook back into her pocket.

'Yes. I wish I could have been nearer but these general shots might be useful for links with what happens in the next few days.' They watched the *Sea Queen* for a few more minutes, wishing her a successful and safe voyage wherever it took her. 'Let's go home and see if there's any news on the wireless.'

It was not long before they learned that a severe rearguard action was being fought to enable the British Expeditionary Force to be evacuated from Dunkirk.

'If this succeeds and troops are brought across the Channel, there are going to be a lot of stories,' Jane pointed out thoughtfully. 'I'm going to the South Coast.'

'Where will you go?'

'Glen mentioned Ramsgate. I'll go there, see what the situation is and then move on accordingly.'

'Where will you stay?'

'I'll find somewhere. There must be plenty of bed and breakfast places with vacancies in the present circumstances.'

'Then I'm coming with you. The photographic opportunities could be tremendous. A good job we managed to build up our stock of film. Right, let's get ready.'

'What about your mum?'

Nell quickly considered the options and grimaced. 'I should tell her but she'll only try and persuade us not to go. We could just leave ... but I don't like doing that.'

'What about writing her a note?'

Twenty minutes later, each carrying a small bag with a change of clothing and some photographic items, they walked from the house, leaving behind a letter for Nell's mother prominently positioned so she would see it immediately she came into the kitchen.

When Flo opened that letter she sank on to a chair beside the table and re-read it more slowly. She sighed. There was nothing she could do. The girls had gone. She knew they were quite capable of looking after themselves and that at some time Nell would endeavour to fulfil the P.S. at the bottom of the letter: 'Will phone'. Flo offered up a silent prayer for their safety and that of her husband wherever he may be. Then she pushed herself up from the table, put the kettle on to make a cup of tea, and turned on the wireless to await the latest news.

'Good grief, what's happening over there?' George Franklin gasped when he saw the huge palls of black smoke spiralling skywards over Dunkirk.

The *Sea Queen* had made the fastest possible run to the Channel. Now she was heading for Ramsgate under George's expert guidance, bringing into play his knowledge of the channels from negotiating these waters during the herring fishing.

The crew were staring at the scene in disbelief, hoping that they were not too late to help in the evacuation.

Glen came to stand quietly beside him. 'Sir, may I get my camera?'

George glanced sideways at him. 'Yes, son. You could be recording momentous events. But don't neglect your duties or the poor devils trapped on those Godforsaken beaches.'

'I won't, sir.'

When Glen returned on deck the *Sea Queen* was nearing the entrance to Ramsgate harbour, but she was not destined to pass through it on this visit. A naval cutter was coming alongside fast and an officer was calling out for the *Sea Queen* to heave to. He climbed quickly on board and George was at the rail to meet him as he stepped on to the deck.

'Lieutenant Commander Brown,' he introduced himself and gave George a hearty shake of the hand. 'Good to see you.'

'George Franklin,' he returned. 'What's the situation here?' His glance encompassed four ships heading for Ramsgate from France.

'We got some soldiers out late yesterday and have been hard at it all morning.'

'What about this motley Armada?' George indicated the small vessels pouring out of the harbour and heading towards the Continent.

'General call went out for small boats. We've had a magnificent response. We need them to ferry men off the beaches to boats like yours that can't get in close enough.' George nodded. 'Now, just sign this paper – it registers you with Operation Dynamo, that's the name we've been given.'

George signed.

'If any of your men don't want to make this trip, get them on to my launch. No one will think any less of them. I might as well tell you, it's hell over there.'

'We're going over to get our lads out,' George called to his crew. 'Anyone not wanting to go, step forward now.'

No one moved.

'Good,' said the officer. 'Off you go then. There's a long beach over there, pick your spot. Channels have been marked but you still have to watch out for mines. Best of luck!' Then he was over the side, into his launch and heading for the next boat approaching Ramsgate.

George's orders were rasped out loud and clear. The

236

crew responded rapidly as the *Sea Queen* set off for France on its rescue mission. Not one crew member gave a thought to the dangers they would have to face there or the possible consequences for themselves. There was a job to be done and they would do it to the best of their ability.

The crew were struck dumb by the sight ahead. Smoke rose from the shattered town; fires devoured buildings unchecked; German artillery shells rained down; the beaches were packed with huddled soldiers. The *Sea Queen* was sailing into hell. Then her crew forced down any emotion. There were men here depending on them for rescue and a passage home. The men from Lowestoft had experienced attacks from enemy aircraft while minesweeping but their hearts beat faster when they saw a flight of Stukas heading for the beaches. The aircraft peeled into screaming dives that sent a chill through the heart of the helpless men below. Two destroyers standing off-shore realigned their anti-aircraft guns which were already pumping out shells at the marauding planes.

Trying to blot out what was happening around him, George concentrated on the charts he had been given so that he could issue orders to the man at the wheel, but when he heard a great cheer from the deck he looked up to see one of the Stukas plunge in to the sea. The loud explosion drowned out all other sound for a brief moment. Seawater was thrown high into the air. When the crew saw the remaining Stukas release their bombs and climb away, they realised the target had been the vessels making the rescue attempt and not the troops on the beach. They watched helplessly as two medium-sized motor cruisers, one in the act of taking troops on board, disintegrated before their eyes. Their own fate could easily be the same. George took a grip on his feelings and shouted orders loud and clear; his men's minds must be concentrated.

Carefully judging the distance from the beach, he brought the *Sea Queen* so that she was still in deep water.

Now it was up to the small boats to get men off the beaches and ferry them here. Already there were two on the way.

As far as the eye could see there were men waiting to be picked up: on the beach; queuing in the water, some of them up to their armpits; on the harbour mole. Some seemed to be wandering aimlessly; others making their own search for a means of escape.

The first of the two small leisure craft drew alongside the *Sea Queen*. Men grasped eagerly at the rope ladders the crew had lowered over the side. Now they lined the rails with hands extended, eager to help these battered soldiers who saw rescue within their grasp. George had already briefed his crew as to what should happen when they took men on board. They were ready to implement his orders. Soldiers were taken or directed to their places for the homeward journey. Tea and food were ready and immediately distributed to men who had not eaten for several days, or else had made do with what they could forage during their flight to Dunkirk. They were all so grateful, every man eager for news of what it was like 'back home'.

Glen had been able to photograph the attack by the Stukas and had taken shots of the first evacuees. Now his camera was stored safely away and he was in the thick of organising the rescued men so that the *Sea Queen* could take as many on board as possible. He was amazed by how cheerful they remained, in spite of all they had suffered. Emotions could have been running high but that applied to a very few. He heard only one grumble, one constant note of criticism: 'Where were the bloody RAF? We should have had air cover.'

'You had.' Glen was quick to come to the flyers' defence. 'As we crossed the Channel I saw three Spitfires chase a flight of five Germans and down three, but they were in the distance, obviously wanting to prevent the bombers from getting to you. They'll be trying to do that all the time, you won't even know. Better to get them there before they reach the beaches.'

The man who'd spoken grunted and said no more.

The little ships were plying their weary course to and from the beach. The crew of the *Sea Queen* marvelled at the orderly manner and patience of the troops there. Where there could have been panic and attempts to 'jump the queue' in the understandable desire to escape, very few broke rank even when the cry of 'Jerry!' rang out at the sound of aircraft. They held their positions, not wanting to lose their place in the queues for the rescue vessels. But Glen saw men on the beach dive for the foxholes they had made for cover as two low-flying aircraft appeared, spraying the area with their machine-guns. Two destroyers fired back and the guns on the *Sea Queen* were brought into action too. Though they saw several hits they were not effective. The two planes headed for another part of the beach, leaving the wounded calling out for attention.

George blessed their good fortune that a bombing raid still had not been made by the time he judged he could take no more men on board. Reluctantly he had to steam away, shouting, 'We'll be back! We'll be back!' As he set course for Ramsgate he saw the *Lively Lady* taking up position and the *Silver King* heading for a location against the harbour wall on which troops stood lined up. He called for 'Full steam ahead', to which the engineer responded with every ounce of power he could coax from his engine.

Three of the crew had taken up their allotted positions as lookouts for the crossing and the rest were ministering to the troops. They were halfway across the Channel when a cry went up: 'Aircraft!' Immediately he felt tension grip the boat. Rescued ... but are we safe? He had no need to give orders; his crew had been briefed and the guns were manned. His men knew from the attitude of the plane that they were to be on the end of a bombing run.

George watched the plane carefully, judging the closing distance. 'Hard port!' he yelled. The man in the wheelhouse responded immediately. For one heart-stopping moment the *Sea Queen* seemed reluctant to respond to the sudden change but then she did, ploughing into the sea, scooping it back to allow her passage. Two black objects were released from the plane and dropped into the water close to the boat, sending a wave cascading over her, drenching all those on deck. Woodwork split but fortunately the *Sea Queen*'s evasive action had taken her clear of the worst disaster. Her wounds were only superficial and she responded with all guns blazing. The retaliatory blast must have made the pilot think again because he turned away and climbed rapidly. A cheer of relief swept through the boat but George cautiously kept an eye on the plane as the helmsman brought the boat back on to her course for Ramsgate. He only realised the reason for the German's quick getaway when two Spitfires flashed by overhead.

They were welcomed into Ramsgate by the sound of cheering. Once they were tied up, disembarkation was begun immediately, with eager civilian helpers ready to lend a hand apart from the military officials directing the operations. Food, tea and cigarettes were passed out by women of the WVS and local organisations. Those requiring clothing were kitted out and postcards and pencils distributed so families could be contacted. A brief few words, an address, and the cards were handed back to be stamped and posted by the local organiser of this service while the men were ushered on to trains, to be transported to various marshalling depots throughout the country.

Meanwhile the *Sea Queen* refuelled, replenished supplies, and headed back for the stricken beaches of Dunkirk.

Chapter Fourteen

Bound for Ramsgate, Nell and Jane tried to obtain news about the state of the war across the Channel but heard nothing that sounded reliable. They managed to get window seats in the train from London, hoping there would be no delay, but at Gillingham it stopped and remained there for longer than expected. After twenty minutes they were becoming concerned when a train thundered by on the track alongside. A few moments later a second train followed and slowed down next to theirs.

'Must have been waiting for those two,' commented Nell. 'Look at that!' she gasped, drawing Jane's attention to the train that had stopped.

Weary, dishevelled soldiers were visible aboard it, eagerly taking sandwiches, biscuits and pies handed out by civilian women of all ages.

'They must be from France,' said Jane. She glanced at a middle-aged man and his wife sitting in the opposite corners of their carriage whose attention was also fixed on the troop train. 'Do you know anything?' she asked.

'Last we heard was that some of our neighbours who have boats on the Thames have taken them to Ramsgate in answer to an appeal. Though what good they'll be in an evacuation, I don't know. Not built for anything more than river journeys.'

'Then it's true ... the Army is being evacuated?'

'Yes. Let's hope we can get them out or it'll be our turn next to be overrun.'

The girls did not like this pessimistic tone of voice and let the conversation drop.

'Can you tell us the way to the harbour, please? We're looking for a bed and breakfast nearby,' they enquired of the ticket collector at Ramsgate station.

'There's plenty of them empty now we're at war,' he replied and gave them directions. 'You'll find some facing the harbour and the sea. Go to Culver View first – a double-fronted house, light green door and white-painted windows, at the harbour end of St Augustine's Road, almost opposite the West Pier. My wife and daughter run it but we've no one in – we would still have had holiday-makers but the war's killed that trade off. Tell them I sent you.'

'Thank you,' said the girls, pleased at their luck.

'Oh,' he called after them, 'Downing's the name.'

They waved their acknowledgement. 'Thanks.'

They were astonished by their first glimpse of the harbour which was divided into two parts. The inner harbour was full of small boats of every description: plea-sure craft that usually plied their trade from seaside towns giving holidaymakers a trip on the sea, private motor cruis-ers, two-man fishing boats ... in fact, it appeared any small craft that floated was represented. The place buzzed with activity. Several craft had been fastened end to end, with the front vessel now being attached to a tug. Queries were shouted and answered and when all was ready the tug started towards the inner harbour entrance carefully manoeuvring its tow to the outer harbour and finally the open sea. A question from Jane received the answer that the tow was bound for France and this method saved the small boats fuel so they could operate at the beaches.

'This is going to make excellent material for *World Scene*,' exclaimed Nell, bringing her camera to her eye. Satisfied with the shots of the tug, she pointed out the hospital ship tied up at the West Pier. 'It must have arrived shortly before us. The ambulances are just arriving. Come on, there'll be stories there.'

Jane nodded. This was an opportunity not to be missed. The digs could wait. They'd still be there when they had finished at the West Pier. Stretcher cases were being brought from the ship to the ambulances while the walking wounded, assisted by nurses where necessary, filed their way on to a fleet of buses.

Nell quickly took some photographs. Part of her wanted to take more but: 'We can't just stand here and watch,' she said. 'People seem to have too much to do. Let's see if we can help.'

They approached a nurse standing at the foot of the gangway down which the walking wounded were disembarking.

'Excuse me,' said Jane, 'can we be of any help?'

'Yes, thanks,' came the relieved reply. 'Help any of these men to the buses. That will let me deal with more serious cases where we're short-handed. Fill one bus first, there can't be any picking and choosing. Get that one away so it can start the shuttle service. The men will be taken to a big hotel that has been temporarily requisitioned for this purpose. All right?'

'Yes,' they chorused.

The nurse hurried away and did not return until evening was setting in. She looked exhausted but managed to ask them brightly, 'Everything go OK?'

'Yes,' replied Jane. 'Had a couple of blokes who insisted on being with a mate but we got them to see that would present a problem and slow disembarking.'

'Good. You've been a tremendous help. The ship is clear now so that will be all. Are you local?'

'No,' replied Nell. 'We're from Lowestoft, just arrived today, thought we might be of help somewhere.'

'Well, you certainly have been. I won't tie you down to helping again because I don't know when or if the ship will be here again. No doubt there'll be other ways you can help.' She gave a tired smile. 'Thank you once again.'

'Now we'd better see to our digs,' said Jane, 'and then contact Mr Horton.'

'Did you get plenty of stories?'

'I certainly did.'

'I thought you would, chatting away while you were helping the wounded to the buses.'

They found Culver View without difficulty and were welcomed by the Downing family.

'I wondered what had happened to you two,' said Mr Downing. 'I thought you might have gone elsewhere.'

'Oh, no,' said Nell and went on to explain why they were delayed.

'There's going to be plenty happening in Ramsgate while this evacuation is going on.'

'That sounds good for us,' said Jane, and explained their work for *World Scene*.

'I've got some earlier issues here,' said eighteen-year-old Susan Downing, excited to have contributors to this prestigious magazine under their roof. 'Show us your work.'

The excitement over, Jane asked, 'Can you direct us to the nearest telephone? We must ring our stories in, and I should let my mother know where we are.'

'Use ours then you've no need to go out again,' Mrs Downing offered.

'That's very kind of you. It would be much more convenient. We'll ask the operator what the charge will be.'

'There's no need for that,' put in Mr Downing.

'We must pay you,' insisted Jane. 'We get it back from *World Scene*.'

'You make your calls,' said Mrs Downing, 'while I get a meal ready. Give your mother our phone number in case she wants to contact you.' She showed them the phone in the hall.

'Do you think Mr Horton will be there?' Nell asked Jane as she picked up the phone.

'I'm sure someone will be at times like this.'

In a matter of minutes Nell was speaking to Horton himself and explaining where they were and what they had for him.

'This is wonderful! Let Jane work something out, then ring me first thing in the morning. She can dictate her copy over the phone. I'll send a motorcyclist now to pick up your films. Give me the address.' Nell told him where they were staying. 'Good. Remain there until the evacuation is over, get more pictures and stories, and we'll follow this procedure each day. *World Scene* will meet all your expenses.'

Nell's eyes were bright when she put the phone down and informed Jane of Mr Horton's requirements. 'We've certainly done right by coming here.'

After an enjoyable meal, during which the two girls were made to feel at home, Jane started writing her stories.

'I'll leave you to it,' said Nell. 'I'll go and see what's happening now down at the harbour.'

'I'll come with you,' offered Susan. 'If that's all right?'

'Of course it is.'

'I'll come too,' said Mr Downing. 'If there are more boats coming, I might be able to help.'

They had not reached the door when a loud knocking startled them.

Mr Downing opened it to find a young man in railway uniform gasping for breath and supporting himself with one hand on the door-jamb. 'Thank goodness you're here, Mr Downing.'

'What is it, Sid?' he pressed.

'You're wanted at the station – quick. Trains are queuing up. More and more ships are coming in.'

Mr Downing hurried after Sid, knowing that in the preceding days Southern Rail had drawn up contingency plans after Vice-Admiral Ramsey had taken charge at Dover and instituted a full evacuation of the British Expeditionary Force. It looked as if the number of men

245

they'd anticipated was correct.

Nell grabbed her camera and called over her shoulder, 'I reckon you'd better come, Jane. I'll help you with that later. Mrs Downing, a despatch rider should be coming from *World Scene*. Please give him this package.' She handed over a large envelope in which she had put the films she had taken since arriving in Ramsgate.

'I will. Get off with you. Stay close, Susan.'

Jane joined them and the three girls ran to the harbour.

They slowed at the scene before them. Streams of grime-covered soldiers, clothes tattered, some still gripping their rifles as if they were their most treasured possessions. Some had bandages round their heads; congealed blood streaked faces; gashes stood out on swollen hands. But what captured Nell's mind, and what she hoped her shots would portray, was not the battle scars, though these were not neglected, but the relief in the faces of these men rescued from the jaws of death or at best captivity. And behind that relief was a cheery smile, a pleasant grin; down-heartedness was nowhere visible. These pictures would help a nation look back on what had happened with pride, turn defeat into victory.

There was no panic, no rush; the soldiers walked to the station in an orderly manner. The three girls helped where necessary, and were pleased that their femininity clearly struck a chord with men pleased to hear a female voice again. They helped three men determined to leave the stretchers for worse cases and remain 'walking wounded'. After seeing them into a carriage with the WVS plying them with food and drink, the three girls left the station and hurried to the harbour.

Boats were everywhere but what appeared to be total confusion was in fact ordered chaos. Boats were arriving; their crews, two, three or four men, were receiving instructions; five or six small boats were tying up in orderly fashion behind tugs that would tow them across the Channel to save fuel and guide them into unknown waters under cover of darkness. Two drifters and a destroyer on the return trip were tied up and troops were pouring off them.

'I'll get some stories and then I'll have to get back to the digs and write them up or I'll not be ready for Mr Horton in the morning,' warned Jane.

'Right, I'll get some more pictures of the bigger ships and then come with you,' said Nell.

'And I'll get some more stories for you,' offered Susan.

An hour later they were heading for Culver View. Later that night they sank into bed feeling exhausted, both physically and mentally.

The next morning Mr Horton rang at exactly the time he had stated. Jane answered the phone and the first words he said were that Nell's photographs, printed during the night, were very good. Jane went on to dictate her copy to a typist, and when she had finished Mr Horton came back on the line.

'I've been reading as Gloria typed. This is just the thing and will link nicely with many of Nell's pictures. Keep it up, both of you! Our despatch rider will be with you at the same time this evening for the films, and Gloria will ring you same time in the morning. Don't let me down.'

'I'm going to concentrate around the harbour and pier,' said Nell when they left the house later that morning.

'Suits me,' replied Jane. 'Stories are everywhere.'

'Anything you'd like me to do?' asked Susan.

'Same as yesterday,' said Jane. 'You helped to fill in some valuable details in my reports.'

Nell stopped in mid-stride when they reached the harbour. 'That's the *Sea Queen*!' she cried, and started to run.

Jane and Susan ran after her, Jane explaining to Susan their connection with the vessel. Columns of weary soldiers were being helped ashore from it when the girls reached the quay.

'Dad! Dad!' yelled Nell, excitedly waving her arms.

Recognising the unexpected voice, George turned from

the head of the gangway where he was supervising the disembarkation. His face expressed his astonishment and he immediately handed over his position to a naval officer standing by. The skipper came down the gangway between two battle-stained soldiers. Nell flung herself into his arms and hugged him tight.

'Dad, are you all right?'

George laughed. 'I'm as right as can be! But what are you doing here?'

Nell explained quickly. He accepted her reason, knowing his daughter was sensible and could look after herself, but gave silent thanks that she and Jane had found digs with a decent family.

'What's happened to the *Sea Queen*?' she asked with concern.

'We had a rough christening. Our first visit was scary and the poor old boat took some wounds, but we survived. We went back last night and this is our first trip today. We're off again as soon as we have this lot ashore and have replenished fuel and stocks of food.' George glanced back to the deck then and said, 'I'll have to go.'

She hugged him and he received hugs from Jane and Susan too as they both wished him well. 'Take care, Dad. I'll let Mum know I've seen you.'

He winked at her and smiled. 'Thank you. I'll send Glen ashore for a few minutes if you wait there.'

They watched him squeeze past some soldiers who, relieved to be safely back in Britain, thanked him fulsomely as he strode on deck.

A few minutes later a grinning Glen was hugging them both. 'This is an unexpected pleasure,' he cried joyfully.

They quickly told him what was happening.

'When your father told me you were here, I ran straight to my bunk and grabbed these.' He thrust a package into Nell's hands. 'Films taken at Dunkirk! How lucky you're here.'

'They'll be in London and printed tonight,' she said.

'And we'll try and be around when you get in again.'

'I'll have to be off any minute ...'

'Know anything about Ewan?'

'No, I've not seen him or Simon since we left Lowestoft.'

'Will they come here?'

'I don't know. They may have orders to go to another reception centre.'

Nell nodded then grabbed Glen and hugged him to her. 'You take care, Glen Aveburn.' She held him a moment longer and looked hard into his eyes.

'I'll be all right,' he murmured.

'You make sure you are.'

Jane was aware of the current of affection that flowed between him and Nell then. Where did that leave Ewan? She watched Glen hurry away to the centre gangway, now free from soldiers. When he reached the deck he helped haul the gangway back on board. Some soldiers were still disembarking at the bow while supplies were still being taken on board via the stern gangway.

The girls watched carefully. Jane made notes while Susan made observations and Nell took some photographs, particularly pleased with the composition of two of her father and two of Glen that she hoped would print well. To these she added pictures of the battle-scarred *Sea Queen* as she sailed back to enter the maelstrom of Dunkirk and attempt to retrieve as many more men as possible from the hell on the beaches. Silently she offered a prayer for the safety of her crew, and for those of the *Silver King* and *Lively Lady*.

George kept the *Sea Queen* as close to maximum speed as possible. He blessed the hand of God for calming the sea and keeping a clear sky, though he knew that made the task of the Luftwaffe easier also. He set two hands to concentrate on keeping a lookout for any enemy aircraft, though all the crew knew they should keep their eyes open for any

249

activity in the air while going about their other respective jobs. The nearer they came to Dunkirk, the louder the sound of shelling became. Smoke from the burning buildings was worse than yesterday. They had to watch, helpless to give any assistance, as German fighters strafed the beaches. The fighters eventually turned away and concentrated on a trawler that had just filled up with troops, eager to be away from the exposed beaches, only to find themselves helpless to escape the attacks that swept from the sky. The fighters came in on the ship time and time again. When they finally broke away it was ablaze and men were jumping into the sea. Then the ship blew up, sending debris and bodies high into the air to crash back among the flaming oil spreading across the sea.

Shock rippled through the *Sea Queen* and it took George all his will power to keep heading for Dunkirk and ignore the chance of finding any survivors from the trawler. There were men waiting on the beach for them.

Nearing it, he drew heart from seeing the *Silver King* and *Lively Lady* in position, lifting men on board from several small ships. He positioned the *Sea Queen* beside them and saw his crew hurry to their places. George exchanged acknowledgements with his two friends. Eager to get as many men as possible on their way to England and home, everyone concentrated on their task then.

Jake Evans on the *Silver King* signalled that his drifter was full and set the boat on course for Ramsgate. A few minutes later Percy Steel was calling a halt to boarding procedures and signalled his intention to follow the *Silver King*. George signalled back his good wishes.

Then, above the noise all around them, came the roar of low-flying aircraft. Five Messerschmitts in V-formation raked the drifters with their machine-guns and swept on over the beach, sending troops there diving for what protection they could find.

Ewan on the *Lively Lady* had some protection in the form of the wheelhouse but his horrified gaze was fixed on the

250

Sea Queen. He saw the neighbouring drifter take the full force of the bullets. Woodwork splintered, glass shattered, and men spun to the deck never to rise again. Ewan's whole body stiffened and his mind screamed when he saw George Franklin lifted off his feet and sent crashing to the deck. 'Dad, hold on!' he yelled.

Percy Steel, himself covered in glass, scrambled to his feet in the wheelhouse, thankful he was still alive, but the tone of his son's voice alarmed him. He pulled himself upright in time to see Ewan leap from the boat and power his way through the water towards a rope ladder hanging from the *Sea Queen*.

Ewan's heart sank and a deathly chill gripped his body when he saw that there was nothing he could do for George Franklin.

'How bad is he?' Ewan looked up to see Glen standing over him, blood oozing from cuts on his face and hands.

Ewan shook his head. Despair gripped him. Tears streamed down his cheeks. 'I'll take him home,' he whispered hoarsely. He started to put his arms around George's body.

Glen saw the futility of his intention. 'Ewan! The *Lively Lady* is full. You can't hold her back. Your father needs you. Leave Mr Franklin. We'll bring him home.' He saw Ewan about to protest. 'Go!'

'Now!' The command came sharply from Terry who was taking command of the *Sea Queen*. 'He's right. Off with you.'

Ewan's shoulders slumped but he obeyed. He went over the side and swam strongly to the *Lively Lady* where his father was already getting her underway. Ewan grasped the rope ladder that had been left over the side for him and hauled himself from the water. He climbed until eager hands dragged him on board.

Percy looked questioningly at his son. Ewan's shake of his head was not necessary; Percy had read the truth in Ewan's expression. Saddened and shocked by the loss of

251

his friend he returned to the wheelhouse. There was an army to get home.

Percy manoeuvred the *Lively Lady* to a vacant berth beside a Ramsgate quay where naval personnel immediately took over the disembarkation while he made a report to a lieutenant.

'Is your boat fit to go again?' asked the officer.

'Aye, she's a strong lass,' replied Percy with affection.

'You'll take her?'

'Couldn't keep me away,' he said, determination in his voice. 'Those lads over there need us.'

'Good man.' The officer turned and signalled to someone on the quay. 'Refuelling will begin at once and supplies be replenished.'

The personal loss hit home. 'What am I going to do?' Percy whispered, half to himself. 'I've got to get those boys out but I should be with Flo ...' He knew there was only one course to take, though, and that lay across the Channel.

'Oh, my God!'

His son's exclamation startled him. Percy followed Ewan's gaze along the harbour. 'Cor blast! Why are they here?' His question was tinged with despair; he would have to break the tragic news to the girls who had seen them and were now laughing and waving with gusto.

'Dad, leave this to me. I'll tell them,' said Ewan. He hurried over to the gangway, squeezed past the disembarking troops and strode towards the girls.

'Surprise, surprise!' they shouted.

'What are you doing here?' he asked grimly.

'Pictures and stories for *World Scene*,' said Nell, gesticulating with her camera. Her voice faltered. 'You're looking very sour. Aren't you glad to see us?'

'Of course I am, but, Nell ... I've something dreadful to tell you.' He paused as if seeking words.

'What's happened?' Nell asked, her tone anticipating bad

news.

'Your father ...'

The laughter immediately faded from Nell's eyes. She stared at Ewan unbelievingly. 'Dad hurt?'

'Worse, I'm afraid.'

'Oh, no!' The words were drawn out in disbelief. This couldn't be true? Her father? Not her father. Nell felt her legs weaken; all energy drain from her body. She was only dimly aware of Jane's arm coming protectively round her waist. She stared at Ewan imploringly, willing him to say this was untrue. He reached out to her. Nell collapsed into his arms and wept. He stood perfectly still and let her cry until the sobs died away and he was able to make soothing sounds while Jane rested her hand on Nell's shoulder.

Finally she straightened up and looked at Ewan. 'What happened?'

He told her briefly, without any detail.

'What do I do now?' she whispered.

'We'll go home,' said Jane firmly. 'We should be with your mother. She'll need to be told ... Goodness knows when that will be officially, with all that's going on. Better we do it as soon as possible.'

'But what about the photographs and stories?' said Nell weakly.

Jane knew it was an automatic reaction and that her friend was not putting them before seeing her mother.

'Was Glen all right?' asked Jane.

'As far as I know,' replied Ewan.

'Will he be coming here before you leave again?'

'Possibly.'

'Nell, take the film out of your camera.'

Still dazed, she did as Jane requested.

'Have you any more?'

'Two,' answered Nell, as she took them from her pocket and handed them to Jane.

She handed them to Ewan. 'If you can contact Glen, give him these and tell him to take them here.' She wrote the

Downings' address on a piece of paper. 'We'll tell Mrs Downing, she knows what to do.'

'I'll try my best.'

'Thanks. What happened to Simon's boat?'

'The *Silver King* left just before the attack. I thought he might be here. He isn't, so they may have received orders to proceed to Dover or somewhere else. Sorry, but I must go.'

Nell nodded, tears welling in her eyes again. 'Take care, Ewan.'

'I will, don't worry.' He hugged and kissed her then turned to Jane. 'You two take care of each other, won't you?' He kissed her on the cheek but their hands touched too and in that moment Jane's desire to hold him back from danger was intense.

'We will,' was all she said.

They watched him go on board. He turned, waved, and was gone.

Nell's steps faltered as they left the station in Lowestoft. 'I don't know whether I can do this ...'

'It has to be faced some time, and the sooner the better. Wait, and the agony will only be worse. And I'll be with you.'

Nell gave her a wan smile. 'Thanks.'

They had left Ramsgate after telephoning Mr Horton, telling him what had happened and that they were returning immediately to Lowestoft. They had informed him about the arrangements for the films and expected Glen would be in touch via Mrs Downing. He had formally extended his sympathy, and said to Jane that he hoped they would continue with their stories as soon as decently possible.

Now they faced a situation they dreaded.

Nell tried the front door. It was unlocked as it always was when someone was at home. She took a deep breath and led the way into the kitchen. Her mother was sitting at the table facing the door, her hands clasped in front of her.

'Hello, love.' Her voice was expressionless, her eyes dull.

Nell held her gaze, not knowing what to say.

'It's your dad, isn't it?'

Nell nodded mutely and flung herself on her knees beside her mother. Tears flowed down her cheeks. Flo looked at Jane and held out one arm. Jane knelt down beside her friend and she too felt comfort in the embrace.

How long they remained like that Nell did not know, but when she looked up she was shocked and had to put the question: 'No tears, Mum?'

Flo gave a wan smile. 'They're all inside.'

'You knew, Mrs Franklin?' asked Jane.

'Yes, I sensed it. Yesterday I knew I would not see my husband again.' She stiffened as she asked, 'Do you know what happened?'

They told her all they knew.

Chapter Fifteen

'It's over. I've just heard it on the wireless, the last ship has left Dunkirk,' Flo Franklin announced when Nell and Jane came in from their walk.

'Thank goodness,' said Nell with relief. 'I hope our drifters soon return.'

'I expect they will, then they'll be re-equipped and back to the job they were doing before they went to Dunkirk. It's been a miracle, getting so many of our boys back.'

'A miracle too that the weather was so good,' said Jane. 'Imagine what it would have been like if it had been worse.'

'Doesn't bear thinking about,' said Flo.

'Nor does the threat of an imminent German invasion,' Nell said with a shudder.

But that did not materialise and in the succeeding days, with its resolve stiffened by the Prime Minister's rallying speeches, Britain prepared.

The battle-scarred Lowestoft drifters returned to their home port to be refurbished and re-equipped for their mine-sweeping duties.

It was a sad day for Flo when she watched the *Sea Queen* return without her husband. She took the first opportunity to meet Terry and, with the future in mind, offer him the position of Captain, even though the vessel was still formally under the jurisdiction of the Admiralty.

'I'm grateful for the opportunity, Mrs Franklin,' he said,

'but I don't want that responsibility. I'm content to go on serving as a crew member.'

Though disappointed, she respected his wishes and went to see Jake Evans.

'I'm going to need a skipper for the *Sea Queen*, Jake. Naturally I offered the job to Terry but he doesn't want the responsibility. With your permission, I would like to offer it to Simon. He has all the necessary certificates and I suppose would have taken over from you in due course. But you have his brother Neil, so I'd like to offer the position to Simon. When peace comes he can take possession of the *Sea Queen*.'

Taken by surprise, Jake looked thoughtful for a few moments. 'Flo, this is more than generous of you, but let me buy the boat when that time comes?'

She gave a little shake of her head. 'That was never my intention. I'll let Simon take it over, lock, stock and barrel. It's what George would have wanted. We weren't lucky enough to have a son. All I ask is that we arrange for a small percentage of the profits to be paid to us, but that's a matter to be discussed when we're able to sleep easy in our beds again. All I want now is your permission to approach Simon?'

'You have it. I won't mention it to him because I don't want to influence his decision. You had better see him soon, Flo. The Admiralty is keen to get all the drifters back to minesweeping.'

'Thanks, Jake, you're a very understanding man. I'll see Simon tomorrow.'

As she walked home, Flo spoke to George in her mind: I hope that is what you want. I know you thought of Simon as the son we never had, and had hopes that he and Nell ... She let that part of her speech drift away. I know you thought him more dependable than Ewan, but I'm afraid it's Ewan who's tugging at her heart-strings. Maybe giving Simon charge of the *Sea Queen* will bring them together.

*

The four friends visited the cinema that evening and each pair took their own long way home. Ewan and Nell found a seat in one of the shelters along the front where she snuggled close to him.

'Nell, I'm leaving the *Lively Lady*.'

'What?' She sat up straight at this unexpected announcement and stared at him in disbelief.

He took her hands in his. 'You know I've only stayed at sea because of Dad. Now I have the opportunity to break away.'

'But . . .' She got no further with her protest.

'I've volunteered for the RAF.'

'What?' she gasped again.

'I did it as soon as we got back. I said nothing until I heard I would be accepted. I've got what I want . . . flying duties.'

'Flying? Ewan!'

'Love, it's what I want to do. After what I saw the Luftwaffe do to our troops, helpless at Dunkirk, I want to hit back at them that way.'

'But aren't you tackling the Germans by keeping the seas clear of mines?' She had to raise some opposition to his decision even though she knew it was too late. Ewan would not change his mind on her account.

'Not in the same way. I would never feel I had hit back for those poor blighters caught on the beaches. Please understand.' He kissed her on the cheek.

'Do your parents know?'

'No. I wanted you to be the first. I'll tell them when I hear when to report which I'm told will be soon. Don't say anything to anyone else yet.'

'I won't, but I don't envy you telling your parents. I know your father sees you taking over from him.'

'Walter can do that. I'm not interested.'

'Then there's nothing more to say,' said Nell, resigned to what would be.

'Say you approve? Give me your blessing?'

'If that's what you want, then I do.'

He kissed her then and enfolded her in his arms.

Two days later a letter arrived for Ewan, telling him where to report. Now he had it in black-and-white he would be able to present his father with a *fait accompli* when he returned from the harbour.

'We'll be ready to sail the day after tomorrow,' Percy announced then like a man keen to be in action again.

'I shan't be coming.' Ewan announced firmly, though his heart was beating a little faster.

His father and mother looked at him as if they had not heard right.

'What do you mean, lad?' Percy frowned in confusion.

'I'll be joining the RAF that day.'

'What on earth are you talking about?' demanded Percy.

'When we got back from Dunkirk I enquired about leaving the Navy to join the RAF. I want to train as a pilot. The RAF badly need them.'

'I tell you what, you aren't going!' Percy thundered.

'You can't stop me, Dad.' Ewan held up the piece of paper. 'This came this morning telling me to report in two days' time. You can't defy that.'

Percy's lips tightened. He knew he was cornered. 'You damned fool! Your life's at sea, you've known nothing else . . .'

'. . . and never liked it.'

'What?' There was disbelief in his father's voice.

'I only stayed because I knew you would never release me. Well, now war has brought me the opportunity. If one good thing comes out of it, it's that.'

'What about the business afterwards?' put in his mother, distress in her eyes.

Ewan saw it, and knew she really feared the dangers he would be meeting as a pilot.

'Ma, I'll be all right. Ewan Steel is a survivor.' He went to her and hugged her. 'Don't worry. Just give me your

259

blessing. This is what I want to do.'

She gave a wan smile and touched his cheek. 'I do, and you'll have my prayers too.'

'Thanks, Ma.' He kissed her then turned to his father. 'Dad?'

His father eyed him. 'So the business will pass to Walter.'

It was his father's way of saying there'd be no going back to the family business when things returned to normal. 'So be it,' Ewan replied. 'Walter loves it, let him have it. He'll do well by you.'

'I'll not disguise the fact that I'm disappointed, angry even, but to make an issue of it will get us nowhere, and I don't want my son to leave in an atmosphere of bitterness.' Percy held out his hand. 'Good luck, lad. I know you'll make a fine pilot. Be true to yourself.'

Ewan took it and their handshake was firm. There would be no acrimony in this parting that would take them both into unknown dangers, and maybe even part them forever.

Ewan left the house with a brisk step. That had gone better than he had anticipated. He entered the Franklins' in his usual breezy style. 'Hello, Mrs F, you are looking at the saviour of this country. Mark him well.'

'Stop talking squit, Ewan Steel,' she replied. 'What do you mean?'

'I join the RAF for pilot training, the day after tomorrow.'

'What?' Flo looked at him aghast.

The door into the kitchen opened then and Nell came in.

'Thought I heard your voice, Ewan. You look as if you've had the cream.'

'I go to basic training the day after tomorrow.'

Nell didn't know whether to cry with disappointment for herself or joy for him. So all she said was, 'Oh.'

'What's this all about?' asked Mrs Franklin.

Ewan told her quickly, and reported the reactions of his mother and father when she asked him what they thought.

'Well, Ewan Steel, I never thought I'd see the day you'd leave the fishing.'

'My heart's never been in it, Mrs F. Now the world is before me.'

'Mind you survive to make it so,' said Flo. She was secretly glad of his admission; it would make things easier when she told Nell about her arrangements for Simon, but first she had to see him.

'Nothing more certain,' he replied. 'Jane not in?'

'I got some photos of the damaged drifters,' said Nell. 'She's gone to get some information about the repairs.'

He nodded. 'Fancy a walk?'

'I thought you'd never ask.' She grabbed a cardigan and they left the house.

'This is going to be a surprise for Jane and Simon,' Nell commented.

'Don't say anything to either of them. We'll all go out this evening and I'll tell them then.'

The two girls were primped and ready when Ewan and Simon called for them that evening.

'Well, what are the plans?' asked Nell as they emerged from the house.

'The Prince's,' replied Ewan.

'That's a bit superior, isn't it?' said Simon, surprised by the suggestion.

'Something to celebrate,' he replied. 'I've booked for us to have a meal there.'

'What's the celebration?' asked Jane.

'Tell you when we get there,' replied Ewan teasingly.

The hotel still managed a reasonable menu in spite of rationing and shortages. They made their choices and as the waitress moved away to the kitchen, Jane said, 'Well, Ewan, don't keep us in suspense any longer?' Her heart was beating a little faster because she'd got it into her mind, as soon as Ewan had mentioned a celebration, that he was going to announce that he and Nell were engaged.

261

She had begun to wonder how she would react if that were the case. Now she was on tenterhooks.

'I'm joining the RAF tomorrow!'

A hush fell over the table for a moment as Jane and Simon stared at him in disbelief.

Jane felt shocked for a moment but then relieved that the announcement was not what she had expected it to be.

'Giving up the drifters?'

'Aye,' replied Ewan. 'You've known how I really felt about fishing and that I only stayed because of Dad. Well, this is my opportunity so I've taken it.'

'RAF!' said Jane. 'What capacity?'

'I've been accepted for pilot training.'

'Ewan!' Simon sensed the concern in Jane's exclamation.

'You've never been off the ground,' was the only comment he found to make.

'There's always a first time so why not now? They're wanting pilots and after what we saw at Dunkirk I think they will want as many as possible. They definitely want me so I'm going.' He smiled at them all. 'Now let's enjoy ourselves!'

Flo Franklin, on her way to the Cookery School, called in at the Evans' house.

Sarah Evans opened the door. 'Flo! Come on in. The kettle's on the boil. We have time for one before we go to the school.'

'I've come a bit early because I want to have a word with Simon.'

'I'll give him a shout,' she said, indicating that he was upstairs. 'Jake told me about your offer. This is extremely good of you, Flo. Nothing has been said to Simon,' she added to reassure her that her plans were still only known to the three of them. Sarah shouted for her son and then led the way into the kitchen where she was busy getting the tea when he came in.

'Hello, Mrs Franklin. You wanted me, Ma?'

'Not me. Mrs Franklin does. Sit down, son.'

He drew a chair from under the table and sat down opposite Flo. She told him quickly of what she wished to do, if he was willing. Simon stared in amazement for a few seconds, hardly able to believe the opportunity that had just been presented to him.

'Mrs Franklin, it is an unbelievable honour to skipper the *Sea Queen*. I accept, and am extremely grateful for your generosity in offering her to me after the war also. I suppose Nell approves?'

'I haven't told her yet. I didn't want her to let the cat out of the bag. I'm sure she will, though. All I ask is that she receives some income from the enterprise.'

'You both will, you can be sure of that.'

Flo smiled. 'Then I am delighted to do this. See that you bring the *Sea Queen* back safely.'

'I will, Mrs Franklin, I will. Now I'll go and get everything arranged with the Admiralty. I expect they'll want us to sail soon.'

The authorities were pleased a new skipper for the *Sea Queen* had been found so easily, and Simon was delighted to hear the repairs were ahead of schedule and she would be ready to sail the day after tomorrow. He immediately informed his crew and found willing replacements for those lost in the evacuation. His final act was to telephone Glen who said he would be back in Lowestoft soon, ready to sail.

The four friends met on the evening before the departures, determined to make it one to remember, for who knew when they would meet again?

Afterwards, outside the Franklins' house Ewan drew Nell into the shadows and held her close.

'You will take care and come back to me?' she asked quietly.

'Of course I will, love. I tell you what, Ewan Steel is the right name for me – I'm indestructible.'

'Don't get over-confident,' she warned him seriously.

'I won't,' he replied. 'I'll have my memories of you to remind me what I could lose.'

'And see you keep them always before you.'

'I will.'

'And here's something else to remember me by.' She bent down, edging her skirt up sufficiently to unfasten one of the suspenders holding up her precious silk stockings that she had managed to buy just before they disappeared from the market. She slipped her foot from her right shoe and peeled the stocking from her leg. 'Wear that, Ewan Steel, whenever you fly.'

'As a reminder of the sweetest girl in the world? I promise that I will.' He bent and kissed her then with a passion that expressed all his love and the need to be fulfilled in the future.

Not far away Simon was putting a question to Jane. 'Is there no hope then?'

'Simon,' she reached up and touched his cheek, 'you are a very, very dear friend. I like being with you, but I cannot let our relationship be any deeper than that. Please try and understand.'

'Is there something else you aren't telling me? Something I should know?'

'Please, Simon, don't press me ...'

'Is your past maybe getting in the way?'

'Simon!' There was a touch of rebuke then but Jane admitted, 'Past *and* present.'

'I think the past has been on your mind ever since we met. You've kept it bottled up.'

'And that's how it should be.'

'You should free yourself, Jane, put this behind you for good.'

'Or maybe free demons that could destroy everything.'

'I'd risk it.'

'I don't want to hurt you ...'

'And others too? If what I surmise is right.'

Jane eyed him warily. 'What's that then?'

264

Simon hesitated then shook his head. 'Let sleeping dogs lie. Who knows who they may bite if I disturb them? And I don't want to upset you, Jane, I don't want to spoil our friendship. I want it to go on, no matter where life takes us.'

'It will always be there, Simon, I promise you that.'

'And I will remember that kiss every day I am away. Will you be there to see me sail?'

'I wouldn't miss seeing you take your first command to sea. You'll be in my thoughts and prayers every day while you're away. God bring you safely home again.'

When she lay down that night Jane wondered how much he had guessed about her true feelings for Ewan, feelings she had hoped she had kept hidden but which had almost surfaced several times recently.

When she found out Ewan would be leaving at the same time as the *Sea Queen*, Nell was torn between the two departures, but only for a moment. She had to see Ewan off. Though his mother and father were there, their parting was tender and full of promises. Nell watched the train until it had disappeared from sight then walked slowly home from the station, lost in her thoughts. Somehow she managed to keep up a desultory conversation with Mr and Mrs Steel. In two days' time Percy would find it strange to sail without his son.

Glen was disappointed when he saw only Jane come to the quay. 'Is Nell all right?' he asked anxiously.

'Perfectly,' Jane replied. 'She's seeing Ewan off.' Noting the query come into his eyes, she added, 'Of course, you won't know, having been at home. Ewan has joined the RAF. Left just now.'

After expressing his surprise and getting to know more about Ewan's decision, Glen changed the subject. 'I've been in contact with Mr Horton,' he told Jane. 'He was delighted with all the Dunkirk material. Hopes we will continue sending him other subjects. I'm going to be a bit restricted on the *Sea Queen*, but you and Nell should try to keep covering stories. There'll be plenty about as the war progresses. Horton is a contact we don't want to lose.'

'We won't,' Jane reassured him.

'Nell has a key to the studio. She can get more film from there, though the supply will dwindle, and I'm sure Horton will let her have what he can.'

'I'll tell her. Look, I must have a word with Simon.' She had noticed him come out of the wheelhouse and gave them a wave. 'Have a safe voyage, Glen. Take care.'

'And you.' He kissed her on the cheek. 'Give my love to Nell too.' Jane sensed he meant this as more of a pleasantry.

'I will,' she replied, and went to meet Simon as Glen hurried on board past his new skipper. She took the hands held out to her.

'Take care, Simon. You'll be in my thoughts.'

'Thanks. That's important to me. Look after yourself, Jane.'

'I will. You know, I think I might volunteer for some service. I feel I should.'

'Any particular fancy?'

'Not yet.'

'What about Nell?'

'Don't know. I'll have to see if she's given it some thought.'

That evening, when they were on their own, she raised the subject with Nell. Flo had gone to visit Sarah Evans, knowing she would be feeling lonely as her husband and two sons had sailed that day.

'It has crossed my mind,' said Nell, 'particularly when I recall what Mr Horton said about volunteering, but I don't want to do it just yet. Leaving Ma on her own so soon after Dad's death . . .' Her voice faltered.

'I understand,' Jane hastened to reassure her.

'You volunteer if you want to.'

'No, I'd rather we did it together.'

'We may not be able to stay together.'

'We'll cross that bridge when we come to it,' said Jane. 'In the meantime, we must do as Glen wants and keep in contact with Mr Horton. I'm sure there'll be plenty for us to cover.'

In the 1930s, in the expectation that an attack on England would come if ever war broke out, the RAF authorities under the instigation of Sir Hugh Dowding, Commander-in-Chief of Fighter Command, persuaded the Air Ministry to take a greater interest in air defence with the result that the strength of Fighter Command was radically increased.

Ewan and his peers were pushed through training quickly, but without compromising RAF thoroughness. It became obvious to his instructors that he was a keen, fit young man with a natural ability. Though he had never been in the air before, he took to it like a natural. His innate flair, the easy way he handled the elementary planes, coupled with his alert mind and exceptional eyesight, which he put down to his years of service at sea, marked him out as a fighter pilot in the making. Informed that was the course he would follow, Ewan was delighted. He champed at the bit to get on with it but was advised by his instructors to be patient and thorough in his basic training. Like him, they were frustrated when the Germans attacked English airfields on the thirteenth of August and they could do nothing to hit back through shortage of men and machines.

When Nell and Jane heard over the wireless that air attacks had begun and were concentrated on the south-east of England, they realised there would be many stories unfolding there. They wanted to grab this opportunity. Nell was nervous about putting the proposal to her mother, but had reckoned without her parent's understanding. With Flo's blessing and their promise to ring home every day,

Nell and Jane headed for London and the *World Scene* offices.

There Mr Horton gave them a warm welcome. 'I believe we are at the start of a campaign of air battles,' he said. 'The Germans will need to gain air superiority to pave the way for invasion. There are going to be many stories from the fighter stations. I have all our spare staff photographers and journalists deployed on this story, but I can always do with two more. Can you be away from home for any length of time?'

'We come with my mother's blessing,' said Nell.

'Good. I had a photographer and journalist covering the fighter station at Biggin Hill until I had to recall them a couple of days ago. If you could take over there? This sort of assignment is going to be new to you, I know. You'll be in a danger zone, covering flying activity and personnel, so you will have to be discreet about it and extremely careful not to breach security. You'll also need a telephoto lens so you can operate on the airfield's perimeter – I'll provide that. You already have your identification cards but I will give you both a personal letter explaining who you are. I will also ring the White Hart in Brasted, the pub the Biggin Hill pilots regard as their local, and book you in with the landlords, Mr and Mrs Jackson. As I know them personally, they will look after you and be able to vouch for you as well if ever the necessity should arise.' He eyed both girls seriously. 'Think you can handle this?'

'Of course,' they replied confidently.

'Now, I think it best if I get a taxi to take you to Brasted. We have an understanding with one of the fleets even though petrol rationing has restricted things somewhat.' He picked up the phone and five minutes later was waving them off.

The White Hart was pleasantly situated in the village of Brasted, in the Weald of Kent. Nell eyed the building curiously. 'Has an old world charm,' she commented. 'Hope it's as nice inside.'

'Can't be bad if the fighter boys use it,' said Jane, hitching her bag over her shoulder. 'Come on, let's find out.'

They were not disappointed when they stepped inside. They passed through a small vestibule into a half-panelled hall with an old oak staircase leading to the next floor.

'Which door?' Nell whispered. There were three before them.

'There sounds to be someone in there,' replied Jane in a equally hushed tones, pointing to a door on the right.

They pushed it open tentatively to find themselves in a long bar room. All the tables were highly polished, and the heavy flowered cretonne curtains gave it a cosy atmosphere.

On hearing the door open, the man behind the bar turned round to see who had come in. He gave them both a broad welcoming smile. 'You must be Miss Franklin and Miss Harvey, sent by Mr Horton?'

'We are,' they chorused.

'Then you are most welcome.' He put down the cloth with which he had been polishing a glass and held out his hand.

Nell stepped forward and took it. 'Nell Franklin, and this is Jane Harvey.'

'Pleased to meet you, Mr Jackson,' Jane said, judging him to be in his early-sixties. He was slim still yet giving off an air of strength derived from hard physical work, something that was confirmed by his broad hands. His eyes were bright and full of laughter, and the colour of his cheeks indicated he had not always spent his time inside establishments such as this.

'Bill, please, everyone calls me that.' He half turned to the open door behind him and shouted, 'Helen, the two young ladies are here.'

A few moments later a slender woman appeared, wiping her hands on the patterned apron tied at her waist. She wore a flowered blouse with its sleeves rolled up to her elbows, a smart navy-blue skirt and high heels.

269

'My wife, Helen. Meet Jane and Nell,' Bill made the introductions.

Helen's greeting to them was warm, and both girls knew immediately that they were going to like it here. In fact, they felt it was a home from home, a feeling that was borne out by the cosy, friendly bedrooms to which Helen took them.

'When you have settled in, come down. I'll have a cup of tea ready. Ten minutes?'

They came into the bar to find Helen and Bill sitting at one of the tables which was laid out for tea. Bill shot into the kitchen to re-emerge with a teapot and a jug of hot water. As he placed them on the table Helen removed a cover from a plate to reveal some golden-brown rock cakes.

Judging that the newcomers were marvelling at the peaceful atmosphere, Bill offered them an explanation. 'Calm before the storm. The young men will hit us with everything they've got tonight. It's only natural to let rip, seeing the tremendous strain they are under.'

'Don't get him wrong – they know exactly how far their high spirits can go, and where we call a halt to over-exuberance. They respect us for the rules we impose on them, and because of that they enjoy coming here.'

'And, Helen, they'll certainly play up to two such attractive young ladies,' Bill added with a wink at the girls. 'Got any boy friends?' He added quickly, 'I suppose I shouldn't ask that, but one way or the other, you'll soon have dashing young men all around you.'

Jane returned his wink. 'No doubt we'll enjoy their company. By the way, we don't hear any aircraft?'

'They were scrambled about fifteen minutes before you arrived. You'll hear them starting to return, and if you're outside you'll see them coming in. You'll feel something too – everyone willing them to return safely.'

'So you'll know many of the pilots personally?'

'Yes. They become "our boys", and it's hard when a

familiar face no longer appears at the bar.'

'Doesn't that affect the others?' queried Jane.

'It must, but they only show it briefly. They have their own special way of dealing with it, as you will no doubt see.'

'Mr Horton said he did not know how long you would be here so I suggest you two regard yourselves as one of the family. Treat the White Hart as home,' Helen offered.

'That is exceedingly kind,' said Jane. Then asked, 'Have you anyone else staying here?'

'At present, no. We only have eight guest rooms. In peacetime they were regularly in use, but the war has put paid to that. However, being so near the airfield, we do get pilots' wives and girl friends staying from time to time. We only allow serious relationships, and the boys know that and don't abuse it.'

They heard a car roar up and stop outside.

'That'll be Soapy,' commented Bill. 'Can't have been flying. Stood down, in their parlance,' he explained.

'Soapy? Why Soapy?' queried Nell.

'You'll see when he comes in, but don't be fooled – he's as sharp as a razor and a survivor, too. Been shot down twice. Once, over the other side of the Channel, he baled out and escaped through Dunkirk. The second time he crash-landed a couple of miles from here, trying to get his plane back in one piece. He was lucky to get out without a scratch, could have been killed. C.O. tore him off a strip for not baling out.'

At that moment the door opened slowly and a young man with dishevelled blond hair peeped round the door as he threw his hat inside. 'May I enter, Mr J?'

'You may, Soapy. But behave yourself, we have company.'

'Company? Is it interesting company or should I disappear?'

'You'll have to see for yourself.'

271

Helen, who was gathering the pots on to a tray, laughed and winked at the girls.

They saw a figure in blue officer's uniform slide languidly round the door. He stopped and stared and his drooping attitude changed in a flash. He straightened up; his whole body became taut and his eyes alert. 'Ah, company, I see, and the fair sex at that. Why were you holding out on me, Bill?'

'Thought you'd find out soon enough. I was about to explain why your nickname is Soapy.'

He let himself slouch again, allowed his eyes to take on a dreamy look, and started slowly and casually across the floor towards their table. 'Because off duty this is how you generally see me,' he said, eyeing the girls meaningfully. Suddenly he shot forward, whole body tensed, arms extended. 'Hold on, Mrs J! Your delicious rock cakes are a must.' He grabbed two from the plate as she turned for the kitchen. 'They knock our Mess food into a cocked hat.'

She laughed. 'You flatterer, Geoff Dean-Pattrington. You forget, I know the cooks up there.'

He looked pained. 'Oh, Mrs J, you've given my secret away.' He slumped down on a chair as if he had been dealt a body blow, then straightened up and looked straight at the girls. 'You may call me Soapy, but if you must call me anything else it has to be Geoff ... or Geoff Dean ... or any rude names you like to call me, but never – NEVER – Pattrington.'

'Why not?' asked Jane.

Soapy put on a stern face and a voice to accompany it. 'My dear young lady, you may learn that some day but definitely not now. I don't want the rest of my evening spoiled.' He called to the landlord who had returned behind the bar, 'Drinks, Bill, drinks! You know mine. Young ladies?'

'We've just had some tea, Soapy, but thanks,' said Nell.

He did not press her but accepted the decision with a

272

nod. His languid pose dropped, he asked, 'What are you two doing here anyway?'

He listened intently as they explained. 'Ah, so we are going to get our pictures in *World Scene*? Have you done anything for them before?'

They told him and saw a new regard for them come into his eyes. 'I remember those, especially Dunkirk and the related pieces. I was impressed so I remembered the by-lines: "Photographs by Glen Avemore and Nell Franklin".'

'I'm Nell,' she said, 'Glen's our partner. He's on the drifters currently but he took a lot of those Dunkirk pictures.'

'Sound man.' Soapy turned to Jane. 'And you must be Jane Harvey, the writer?'

She smiled and nodded.

'You took me right there. A wonderfully economical use of words. So, now you're here to cover Biggin Hill and its flyers?'

'Yes.'

'Is it official?'

'No. Mr Horton wanted nothing laying on 'specially.'

'Then you'll have to be careful. Don't let the C.O. catch a glimpse of your camera or he'll be down on you like a ton of bricks. We'll give you plenty of stories, Jane, but I advise you to use "an airfield somewhere in England" or similar terminology, and never mention a pilot by name, otherwise he'll be in trouble.'

'I'll be careful.'

Any further advice was not forthcoming as the first sound of an aircraft engine heralded the return of the fighters.

'They're on their way! Come on, want to see them?'

The girls were out of their chairs at once, marvelling at Soapy's athletic movement when he chose to stir himself.

'Can I get my camera?' yelled Nell.

'Hurry!'

She raced to her room, grabbed the bag with her photographic gear in it and ran back down again. Outside she

273

saw Soapy already behind the wheel of an open-topped sports car with the engine running. Jane was sitting in the back, leaving the front passenger seat for her. Nell barely had time to close the door before Soapy was roaring away.

'I can't take you too near the 'drome but there's a place I know that will give you a good view.'

'Splendid,' said Nell as he pulled into the gateway to a field on a slight knoll from where they had a good view across the airfield. Three aircraft were circling ready to make their landing. Nell worked her camera over the next fifteen minutes and Jane made mental notes, all the time aware of Soapy keenly counting the returning aircraft. Finally she felt the tension leave him.

'All back.' He sighed with relief and started for the car.

They followed, respecting his silence as he drove them back to the pub. He left them there to return to the airfield, saying he would see them again later.

Jane and Nell were just finishing an early-evening meal, which Helen had served in a small room next to the kitchen, when they heard loud exchanges between several men entering the bar.

'Here they come,' said the landlady with a smile. There was no resentment in her comment; rather it was touched with affection. 'Come through and meet them when you're ready.'

Ten minutes later Nell stood up and said with a wry smile, 'Let's face them.'

'Here are my two girl friends!' shouted Soapy when he saw them.

Silence immediately descended on the room and the girls felt six pairs of eyes focus keenly on them. They tried to hide their sense of shock. These flyers, on whom the fate of the whole country could depend, looked like boys.

'Jane Harvey and Nell Franklin,' Soapy called out by way of introduction.

'Hello, everyone,' said Jane.

The ice was broken; every one of them at once started to

speak. Introducing themselves, the young pilots crowded round the girls and pressed them to have a drink. Throughout the evening several more young men arrived and before long a party was in full swing. It never went beyond the bounds of propriety but these were people living on the verge of death. They needed to forget that aspect of their daily existence – it was a case of live for today, tomorrow may never come.

When the evening ended, they all said good night and kissed each of the girls. Nell and Jane did not abhor this familiarity; in fact it seemed perfectly natural. Maybe the remembrance of it would serve as an incentive for them to return safely from the next battlefield in the sky – knowing that a girl and a kiss would be waiting for them.

Over the succeeding two weeks Jane and Nell found themselves swept into the pilots' unreal world. Apart from recording the facts of battle as they affected 'a fighter station somewhere in England', Jane wrote about the incongruity of war – the peaceful countryside where life appeared to be going on as it always had, could suddenly be shattered by the roar of aero-engines, the staccato sound of machine-guns, and outbursts of bombing when the airfield came under German attack.

Letters from Ewan, still under training, were forwarded to Nell from home and always brought the reminder that he, too, would soon face these dangers. He'd become one of the young men she saw come and go without a single public expression of fear, though she knew it was there, unseen and unspoken.

She frequently used the site shown to them by Soapy and took shots of planes returning, some so badly shot up that they had to make crash landings. Though she was never able to get as close as she or Mr Horton would have liked, he was nevertheless pleased with her efforts, even though the Air Ministry would only allow him to publish those they thought suitable for maintaining the morale of the country. He liked Jane's submissions, too, and delighted in

275

the way she brought this aspect of the war to life. She and Nell, through different media, built up credible portraits of the young men, fiercely taking to the skies to confront the superior power of the would-be invader. They laughed and flirted with these men, too, knowing they enjoyed the company of the opposite sex as a relief from the horrors of air warfare. They both realised they could easily become attached to almost any one of the boys here, but knew it was probably best for all of them that they did not become too emotionally involved.

But one day Jane was alone in the bar, an hour before opening time, writing up the previous day's observations, when she heard the door open. She looked up and her heart skipped a beat. A pair of brilliant blue eyes smiled at her and shyly demanded her attention.

'Oh, hello.' His soft voice expressed surprise at seeing her.

'Hello,' she replied, and returned his smile. 'Do you want Mr Jackson?'

He swept his hat from his head and said, 'Why should I want him when I have found such an attractive girl as you?'

Jane felt her heart beat faster. Oh, he did remind her of Ewan! She blushed.

The man's smile broadened and he stepped over to her table and held out his hand. 'Flight Lieutenant Alan Sanders, otherwise known as Sandy.'

Jane noticed the DFC ribbon on his tunic. 'Jane Harvey,' she replied, taking his hand. She felt his firm grip. Coupled with that ribbon, she knew this young man must be full of a confidence beyond his years, like so many of the fighter pilots, boys turned into men before their natural time. She thought the man before her could be no more than twenty-two, and yet he was already a Flight Lieutenant.

'I'm pleased to meet you, Jane. And what a pleasant sight to greet my return to Biggin Hill! Mind if I sit down?'

'Of course not. You've been stationed here before then?'

'Oh, yes. Did my stint and then was posted to

276

Acklington, Northumberland. Supposed to be a bit of a rest, away from the fighting. It was in a way but we were patrolling the North Sea shipping lanes almost every day. Then I pulled a few strings and got myself posted back here to take over "B" Flight.'

'From Johnny Carruthers?'

'Yes. Too bad about Johnny! You knew him?'

She nodded. 'He came in here.'

He noted the touch of sadness that had come into her voice and changed the subject. 'What are you doing here?'

She told him, finding him easy to talk to. She had just finished when Helen appeared.

'Alan!' she gasped in surprise. He was on his feet immediately and when she came round the bar he hugged her to him and swept her off her feet.

'Mrs J! Great to see you.'

'And you. So you're back?'

'Yes. And don't keep this young lady locked away from me!' He got to his feet. 'Must get going and report in. Say hello to Bill for me, won't you? See you both later, probably tomorrow. I reckon the Squadron Commander will want my attention this evening.' He turned to Jane. 'And don't you be absent without leave tomorrow evening, young lady.' His broad smile and the hint that he wanted to see her again set Jane's heart racing. She was only really aware of it when the door closed behind him. She felt immediately bereft. What had happened to her in these few short minutes? She was no starry-eyed schoolgirl, to swoon at the sight of a handsome young officer with a medal.

'Dashing, isn't he?' said Helen, sensing Jane was smitten.

'Isn't he?' she sighed with a lift of her eyebrows.

'Popular member of the squadron when he was here before. We've had many a WAAF officer in here, drooling over him.'

'Anyone special?' Jane was surprised by her own question and inwardly chiding herself for asking it.

Helen smiled. 'No, not really, though there was one with whom he seemed to be getting serious. It was shortly after he arrived at the station . . .'

Jane noted the catch in Helen's voice then. Her hesitation seemed to imply something. 'And?'

'She was killed in one of the early raids on the airfield.' A momentary silence hung between them. 'Alan was very cut up and confided in me that he would never get closely attached to anyone again in wartime. I don't believe he was thinking of himself, not wanting to go through that experience again. I think he was thinking of the traumas a girl would go through if he was killed or went missing.'

'But if you're both in love, isn't it better to share that love rather than keep it at a distance?'

'That's what I told him.'

'And surely the girl should have a say in the matter?'

'Right again, Jane. And I told him that loving in wartime has a different intensity and a different meaning. Death's so close at hand. I say, grab happiness while you can.'

When Jane lay down that night, Helen's words were ringing in her mind.

Chapter Sixteen

'Hi, Jane,' Alan cried, on entering the bar the next evening, accompanied by Soapy. 'Oh, and another one,' he added, seeing Nell seated beside her. 'You kept *her* a secret.'

'Obviously you've met,' said Nell. 'She kept *you* a secret too.' And shot a reproving glance at Jane.

'The usual?' Soapy enquired of the two girls.

'Thanks,' they replied.

'Sandy?'

'I'll give you a hand,' he replied and accompanied Soapy to the bar.

'Well, you certainly kept *him* under wraps,' said Nell quietly. 'Very dishy.'

'Only met him yesterday, while you were out.'

'And kept very quiet about him! Think I could win him from you?'

'Hands off! You've got Ewan.'

'What about you and Simon?'

'Just friends.'

'I think he views you as more than that.'

'He understands.'

'So you say. But if you want to play Sandy off against Simon, that's your lookout.'

'Like you play Glen off against Ewan?'

'Are you still hoping Glen wins so you can have Ewan?

Well, forget it!'

'That doesn't matter now there's Sandy.'

'You *are* working fast.'

Jane had surprised herself with her remark. Could Sandy break down her customary reserve? But she had only just met him; didn't really know anything about him except that he was a handsome officer with the DFC. And she recalled Helen's warning about Sandy's attitude to relationships with the opposite sex.

The girls' banter stopped when the two officers returned with the drinks. Before long the bar was filled with fighter pilots, some accompanied by servicewomen girl friends who had shed their uniforms for the evening, finding pleasure in dressing as civilians again. Soon there was a general call for Soapy to get to the piano. The notes were played almost lazily with an evident skill that brought real feeling from them. The beer began to flow more freely but without getting out of hand; these men might need all their wits about them tomorrow if they faced Heinkels and Messerschmitts. The tune merged into a well-known one and soon the bar was rocking to the sound of unabashed singing that included RAF versions of the usual words.

Jane was swaying to the music beside Sandy when he suddenly stopped his lusty singing to whisper in her ear, 'I'd like some fresh air.' His arm tightened round her waist.

'So would I,' she replied quietly.

They slipped away without anyone commenting. As they stepped outside he took her hand and together they walked slowly through the village, not speaking, just enjoying being together. Jane did not want to spoil these moments for him; she knew they were precious to a man who tomorrow might be facing death.

He stopped at the edge of the village under a large oak tree that threw its canopy against the fading light of the night sky. The hush that had settled over the countryside enveloped the airfield and the silhouettes of battle-ready

Hurricanes. Sandy drew her to him. Jane did not resist. It seemed right to give him something he could remember in the midst of battle. She kissed him. He responded, but cautiously.

She stepped back. 'I'm sorry,' she apologised. 'I thought . . .'

Anticipating what she was about to say, he interrupted. 'I wanted you to do that. But I don't want you to get hurt.'

'I won't.'

'My life is very high-risk.'

'I know.'

'Then you'll know why I don't want you to get hurt?'

'Sandy, we hardly know each other, but under these circumstances does that matter? I think I'm going to like being with you.'

'And I certainly like being with you. But there's one thing I want you to understand at the start. This will go no further than companionship. A hug and a kiss, nothing more. If anything happened to me, I wouldn't want you to regret we had gone too far.'

'You are a sweet man.' She kissed him again and this time he returned her kiss fervently.

When they returned to the White Hart the party was breaking up, the pilots returning to their billets to face an unknown tomorrow.

Upstairs, Nell wanted to know what had happened between Jane and Sandy.

'Are you happy with that' she asked eventually.

'Companionship? Yes. That's what these boys really want.'

'True, but they can fall in love.'

'And you?' queried Jane.

'All I'll say is, Soapy isn't so soapy when it comes to kissing!'

'And?'

'Nothing else. I warned him at the start.' Nell gave a little chuckle. 'They'll think we're a bit strait-laced.'

Jane gave a little shrug. 'No. I think they'll respect us, and enjoy being with us all the more.'

The following day Nell received a letter from Ewan dated the thirtieth of August 1940. After reassuring her that all was well with him, he told her the course had been intensified and the authorities were looking to have some of the better trainees pass out sooner than expected as demand for pilots was growing severe. He was one of the chosen ones. Nell's heart skipped a beat and a cold chill ran down her spine.

Jane sensed that the letter had upset her friend. 'What's wrong, Nell?'

'Ewan's being pushed forward to finish the course earlier than usual. And you know what that means.'

'He could soon be facing what Sandy and Soapy are right now?'

'Oh, Jane, I daren't think of it.' Tears had started to well in Nell's eyes.

'Come here.' Jane took her into her arms, offering comfort, but also drawing comfort herself. Ewan could ... She dare not contemplate the possibilities.

Nell cheered up a little that evening. This could soon be Ewan's life, too: happy-go-lucky one moment; the next dicing with death.

Nell took photographs whenever she could but was severely restricted in what she could achieve as most photographs had to be taken from afar. Nevertheless she saw some of her work appear from time to time in *World Scene*, the photographs obviously blown up during the printing stage and therefore often appearing grainy or out of focus. At least something had been used. Jane's reports, on the other hand, were full of close observation and feeling, presenting a vivid picture of what the fighter pilots had daily to endure: combat, injury, seeing their fellow pilots plunge to their deaths, living on their nerves, exhaustion. Many of them seemed to be in a daze even when they came to the White Hart, though for an hour or two there they tried to throw that aside. She detected, though they never showed it or talked about it, the constant fear lurking beneath the surface, particularly the terror of being trapped alive in a burning aircraft.

So that the public could empathise with them, she described with vivid clarity a day in the life of the pilots: being woken at four in the morning and driven out to their various dispersals to wait interminably. They'd lounge there in Lloyd Loom chairs, reading magazines, or doze in deckchairs or on the grass, waiting uneasily for the telephone to ring, heralding the message that would send them running to their Spitfires to be airborne as quickly as possible. Assembling as they flew towards the hordes of German aircraft, moving relentlessly in formation towards their targets. Then the attack: aircraft everywhere, the Spitfires and Hurricanes attempting to divert the Heinkels that had slipped through the first attempts to stop them. Screaming engines, chattering machine-guns, the whine of falling bombs, explosions tearing the air apart, the craters, and spiralling clouds of smoke below marking the final destination of an aircraft and its pilot.

And then the nagging question: One of ours? A Biggin Hill boy missing from the White Hart tonight? Would the gathering in the bar turn gloomy, as it did every time the squadron lost a pilot?

Then the usual ritual would be enacted after pints had been drawn and distributed in silence. The senior officer, more often than not Alan, would intone solemnly as he raised his glass:

'Here's a toast to the dead already
Three cheers for the next man to go.'

Everyone repeated this with each word growing louder until the last of all ended in a roar, followed by the draining of every glass. The words always sent a shiver down Jane's spine, and Nell never failed to shudder. Glasses emptied, the evening was back to normal. Each man would cope with his feelings as best he could. Mourn they would, but each in his own way and never show it.

The first time they witnessed this ritual, Jane and Nell thought it barbaric and ill-advised, until they realised the pilots meant no disrespect to their dead comrade. It was merely their way of honouring him.

Nevertheless the loss of pilots began to affect them, especially as every time Sandy and Soapy were airborne they realised a ceremony for one of them might take place in the White Hart that same night. The fact that a similar ceremony might one day take place for Ewan began to prey on the girls' minds, too, but each of them kept her concern to herself. They both breathed sighs of relief every time they saw two particular Hurricanes land. Neither pilot ever spoke of the horrors of fighting in the air nor did Jane question them about their experiences for her regular submissions to Mr Horton; she found her subjects elsewhere.

Jane enjoyed her time alone with Alan. They derived great pleasure from just walking together in the twilight, when a mysterious atmosphere was cast over the country-side and the war seemed far away. They occasionally snatched a visit to the cinema or shared a quiet meal in a different inn whenever they could. Jane thought, This is what it could be like with Ewan, but knew she shouldn't entertain such dreams.

One day when Alan's plane did not land she experienced a sudden tightness in her chest that spread through her whole body. Her mind screamed that this could not be true. He could have landed away, baled out, crash-landed and survived ... The waiting to know was unbearable. Nell, too, felt numb but sensed Jane's feeling was the more intense. Had she been drawn to Sandy even more than she had let on? She had always denied she was falling in love with him but ... Nell tried to reassure her that the fact he had not returned did not mean the worst. Nevertheless, the atmosphere in the White Hart was almost too much to bear.

A car engine ... Soapy's! Only his sports car sounded like that. They heard the crunch of its wheels on the gravel, a car door slammed, footsteps. The tension was unbearable. The door to the bar opened and Soapy dragged himself in. He stopped just inside the bar, saw Helen and Bill standing behind it, tense with expectation. Then his eyes drifted to Nell and finally settled on Jane. He swallowed hard. Tears started to run down his cheeks. He shook his head and the girls knew the worst.

Jane's willpower deserted her then. Her stomach churned; her face went ashen as she stared unbelievingly at Soapy, accusing him in her mind of telling lies. She was unaware of Nell's hand resting on her arm in an attempt at comfort. Her mind screamed. Nell brought her arm round Jane's shoulders and eased her close. She collapsed against her friend with a cry of, 'No!' Sobs raked her body. Then she said, 'Ewan.'

The word came so softly that Nell thought she was mistaken. She couldn't have heard it right. But if she had, what did it mean? Had Jane been using her association with Alan as a sort of substitute for sharing a life with Ewan? Surely not? It had to be her own ears playing tricks on her.

How long they remained locked in each other's arms they were not aware but suddenly Jane straightened herself and swiped away the tears in a gesture of annoyance. 'I'm sorry,' she said, in a voice scarcely above a whisper.

'There's nothing to feel sorry about,' replied Nell. 'If you felt strongly about Sandy, it was natural to give way. Letting your feelings out is best for you.'

'But ...'

'Here, lass, drink this.' Bill placed a glass of brandy in front of Jane. He slid another in front of Nell, adding, 'You too.'

'Thanks, Bill.' Nell spoke for them both.

Jane took a sip of the brandy and felt it scorch through her as if determined to restore her to life. She looked across at the bar where Soapy was staring morosely into his glass of beer. 'Soapy,' she called gently, knowing what he must be going through; he had lost not only his flight commander but also a close personal friend. He turned and she beckoned him over. He brought his glass and sat down.

'I take it there's no chance that . . .' Her voice faltered.

He gave a little shake of his head and met her eyes without flinching. 'None. I saw it all.'

'Can you bear to tell me what happened?'

'Do you really want to know?'

She swallowed hard and gave a little nod. 'Please.' She placed her hand on his arm.

'He got jumped by two Messerschmitts as he was attacking a Heinkel. Though seriously damaged, he persisted with his attack and got the bomber. He peeled away, did a sharp turn, got behind one of the German fighters and shot him down. But then his plane couldn't take the strain of any more violent manoeuvres and Sandy became a sitting duck. I got the fighter that was attacking him, but it was too late. Alan was going down. I was yelling at him to bale out but it was obvious his canopy was jammed . . .' His voice choked and he could say no more. After a few minutes he got up and walked out of the bar.

'I don't think I could survive being here tonight,' whispered Jane then.

'I know, you don't want to witness the usual farewell,' said Nell. 'Nor do I. Let's go home.'

Nell was subdued in the train as it chugged its way to Lowestoft. Jane respected her silence for a while but then, sensing her friend was brooding, broke into her thoughts.

'Are you worried about Ewan after what we have seen and experienced?' she asked.

Nell nodded. 'Aren't you?'

'Yes,' replied Jane, then added quickly, 'it's only natural to feel that way about a friend.'

Nell picked up on that and wondered again what really lay behind that whispered word in the White Hart.

'You mustn't dwell on what might happen. Be positive that it isn't going to. You've seen other men survive. I'm sure Ewan will.'

Nell tightened her lips in an apprehensive expression, but suddenly cast doubt aside. 'You're right. I must be strong for him.'

'That's better.'

They lapsed into silence, each lost in her own thoughts, until Jane remarked, 'We will have to let Mr Horton know.'

'I'll tell him tomorrow.'

It only took a few moments for Flo to realise that this unexpected return was linked with the unease she'd sensed in both girls' letters home.

She sent them off to their rooms to tidy up after the journey, telling them to be quick because the kettle was on the boil. Sitting round the kitchen table later, the cup of tea working wonders as it always did, she broached the subject of what was troubling them.

'It all became too much for us, seeing young men with whom we had friendly relationships, there one day and missing the next.' Jane's voice faltered as she spoke.

'That's what happened today, Mum,' Nell took up the story. 'We heard the planes take off early, and by lunchtime we learned that Sandy, a particular friend, had been killed.'

'But there's always a chance ...' Flo started.

'Not in this case. His good pal Soapy saw it all. Sandy didn't get out of his plane.'

'Oh, I'm so sorry.'

'We'd had enough so we came home.'

'You did right.'

Nell looked distressed as she said, 'The same thing could happen to Ewan.' Tears brimmed in her eyes then.

'You mustn't think like that,' said her mother. 'The possibility is always there and we can't escape it, but our menfolk must never know how we feel. It could weaken their morale if they had to worry about us, and that would never do. Your dad made me promise that I wouldn't brood about the dangers he might face. Oh, I did, but he never knew. So don't you go thinking the worst, because it might never happen. Many people do survive wars. Why not Ewan?' She had made her point firmly and, wanting to take the girls' minds away from it, quickly changed tack. 'What about your work for *World Scene*?'

'We'll ring the magazine in the morning.'

Flo nodded. 'It will all look better after a good night's sleep, and you'll have that. I have some sleeping pills left from those the doctor gave me when your father was killed. There'd be no harm in having one each tonight.'

So it proved. The next morning they both felt more able to face life and put their time at Brasted behind them, though they would never forget the experience nor the dangers the brave fighter pilots faced.

Mr Horton was very understanding. 'I should have realised the strain I would be putting you under,' he said regretfully. 'It was very remiss of me.'

'You weren't to know how the situation would develop or that we would grow attached to the pilots,' Nell insisted. 'What would you like us to do now?'

'I would like you to stay at home and recuperate. I'm sure you will get the best of attention from your mother. Just wait there, we'll see what happens. There'll be plenty of stories coming up. By the way, have you thought any more about volunteering so you can make your choice of war work? A lot of young women are doing so, and I believe the government will bring in compulsory call-up for young women between certain ages before too long.'

288

That gave them food for thought as they kept track of the battle being fought in English skies, and their admiration for the brave fighter pilots mounted by the day. The Luftwaffe switched the bombing raids from the airfields to concentrate on London. Nell put a proposition to Jane. 'Do you think we should offer to cover stories in London?'

'We could, but what would your mother think to us going there when it is constantly under attack?'

Nell shrugged her shoulders. 'I don't think she'd be too happy, but let's see what Mr Horton says.'

When her mother had gone to the Cookery School, Nell rang the *World Scene* offices and was thankful to hear his voice.

But her suggestion met with an immediate refusal. 'I would not want you to come to London. The risks here are too great. There will be lots of stories but I will cover them with staff already living here. I don't think your mother would approve if I brought you into such danger. I appreciate your offer and this refusal does not make any difference to our working relationship. I'm sure you'll find other stories away from London.'

'Well, that saves worrying your mum,' said Jane when told Mr Horton's opinion.

Nell pursed her lips thoughtfully. 'I don't think I can sit around here doing nothing, not after what we have seen and been through so far in this war.' She gave a thoughtful little pause then added, 'Let's volunteer for something.'

Jane had been feeling the same but had not ventured the suggestion so far as it would take Nell away from home, and she was not sure if her friend was ready for that. Jane herself had no such ties. She wrote regularly to her aunt and uncle who always knew what she was doing. They offered neither advice nor criticism, only concern for her welfare, telling her they and their home were there if ever she needed them. She appreciated this freedom offered her but knew it was different for Nell.

'What about your mum?'

289

'We won't say anything to her yet. Let's just make some enquiries.'

'All right. Had you one of the Services in mind?'

'No, I'm open-minded. Let's see what's on offer, but I would like us to stay together if possible.'

'So would I.'

'Right, let's go.'

They left the house at a brisk pace, pleased that once again they had a purpose.

The clerk at the Employment Exchange welcomed them amiably and laid various options before them. Factory work, munitions, making weapons or assembling aircraft did not attract them. Though it did offer the possibility of their staying together, the thought of being cooped up in a factory day after day did not appeal in the slightest. They looked at the merits of the WRNS, the ATS and the WAAF but the chances of staying together there were slimmer. The clerk pointed out that they would be deployed according to their capabilities, and it was most likely Nell would end up in a photographic section whereas Jane was more likely to finish up in an administrative post, quite possibly not at the same base. Almost as an afterthought the clerk said, 'What about the Land Army?'

'Heard of it but don't know much about it.'

'I can't tell you a great deal either except that you'd be working on farms on all manner of jobs but not under any direct military command as you would be in the Services. There is less discipline and more freedom, though of course there are certain rules to which you must conform. If you want to know more, I'd suggest you contact the WLA office for East Suffolk.'

The girls thanked her and left.

'What do you fancy?' asked Jane then.

'I'm attracted to the Women's Land Army,' Nell instantly replied. 'Outdoor life, less discipline.'

'So am I, but I know nothing about farming.'

'Nor do I.'

'Which might go against us.'

'Well, we can only make enquiries.'

'True.'

The next day, after Flo had left the house, the two girls set out on their new quest. They were received warmly and, after giving some elementary particulars, were told to attend for interview in four days' time, bringing a medical certificate from their doctor as the WLA did not run a medical service of its own, unlike the military services.

'I suppose now would be best to tell Mum what we're doing?' Nell suggested.

'I think you're right.'

Over tea that evening Flo was made aware that they did not want to wait to be called up but wished to have a choice in the role they would play in the war effort.

'I think you've already decided on that,' she said, giving them a shrewd look. After hearing what they had done, she added, 'If that's what you want, you have my blessing. But are you aware of the life you will have to lead? You've had no experience of farm work. Up early, out in all weathers . . .'

'But we won't have the same military discipline,' pointed out Nell, who then added quickly, 'and we'll not be far from home, so you'll see more of us than you would if we were in the Forces.'

'Don't count on that, lass, I don't, but it's good of you both to think of it.'

Four days later they left for the interview, neatly dressed in calf-length plain skirts, Jane's navy blue, Nell's light grey, and short-sleeved blouses to match, over which were loose waist-length jackets. They decided, on Flo's advice, to wear simple hats and chose berets to reflect a military style.

When they reported, a typist took some details then directed them to a room where she handed over her notes to a secretary, who indicated that Nell and Jane should take a seat alongside three other girls. Everyone looked uneasily

291

at one another with no one venturing to make conversation while the secretary continued with her work. A few minutes later a door opened and a young woman came out, called a name and escorted one of the girls into the inner room. The time seemed to tick by so slowly and still no one wanted to speak. Then it was Nell's turn.

As the door clicked to behind her she felt so alone; this was the first interview she had ever had.

'Do sit down, Miss Franklin,' the young woman said, indicating a chair that faced a table behind which sat two men whose hair was greying, and a middle-aged woman who looked a little formidable but whose smile was friendly enough. The young woman joined them after she had presented each of them with a sheet of information about Nell. She grew even more nervous as they perused this.

One of the men cleared his throat then and said, 'This is an informal interview, Miss Franklin, so that we can learn something of your background, what you have done before, assess your capabilities and judge your suitability for the Women's Land Army.'

She nodded.

'I see you have lived all your life in Lowestoft and come from a fishing family,' said the young woman. 'Have you had any experience of farm work?'

Nell's heart sank.

'No, ma'am.'

'Ah, well, never mind. That doesn't mean you won't be suitable.' Nell felt relieved and her hopes rose again. She heard the young woman continuing, 'I'll tell you a little about what you might have to do if accepted. You could be billeted with several other girls in a hostel from where you would go out to work daily. Where a farmer was seeking regular help, you might be placed on his farm for a set time. The work could be milking, mucking out, looking after the animals, hedging, ditching, ploughing, threshing, hoeing, and so on. The work is heavy, make no mistake. You will be out of doors most of the time, no matter what the weather. But it can be a rewarding occupation, and you will be helping to feed the country at a time when we are not able to import foodstuffs to the extent we did in peacetime. Now, let us learn something about you.' She glanced at the other interviewers. For about ten minutes they questioned Nell, who answered them briskly.

'That's good, Miss Franklin,' said the middle-aged lady eventually. 'You sound to be a very capable young woman. Have you any questions to ask us?'

'Yes, ma'am. From the little I have learned about the Women's Land Army, it is not run like any of the other Services?'

'That is so.'

'Do we have freedom of choice as to where we work?'

'Up to a point. If you did not get on with a particular farmer, you could request a transfer and more than likely it would be granted. The farmers who employ you have to maintain a standard of behaviour specified by us, and we would listen to you if you had any complaints about your treatment. But you must be prepared to move around the county, or even the country, if a situation demanded it – such as a shortage of workers in another locality.'

'Yes, ma'am. I have one other question. You are about to interview my friend. If we are accepted, we would like to stay together if possible.'

'That is not always so, but we do try to manage it so that friends stay together. It may be that you will live in the same hostel, or there is always the possibility that a farmer may want two girls or more who will either live in together or be found digs nearby. More than that we cannot say.'

'Thank you, ma'am.'

'Our recommendations are dealt with in the County Office. You will hear from them in due course whether you are accepted or not.'

'Yes, ma'am.'

The young woman rose from her chair and Nell followed

suit. Outside she saw apprehension on Jane's face as she flashed an enquiring look at her. Nell gave a little smile and a reassuring wink as Jane was escorted into the interview room.

She felt she had done reasonably well, but wondered if her lack of experience of country life would tell against her. She hoped Jane was giving all the right answers.

When her friend reappeared she looked glum and said nothing to Nell as they walked to the front door of the building. Nell was bursting to ask what had happened but waited until they were outside.

'Well?' she demanded. 'That glum look doesn't augur well.'

Jane pouted and bit her lip and looked downcast. 'Terrible,' she replied, then added quickly, 'Terrible..ly easy,' and burst out laughing. 'Fooled you!'

Nell punched her on the shoulder. 'You had me worried there. But you really did think it went OK?'

'Yes. I thought they were all very approachable.'

'Did you say we'd like to be together?'

'Yes.'

'Good, let's hope it strengthens our case if we're accepted.'

'Wonder when we'll get to know?'

'They didn't say but we'll be notified by the County Secretary, apparently.'

They spent four anxious days before two official-looking envelopes dropped through the letterbox. Flo, who was near the front door, gathered them up and hurried through to the kitchen where Nell and Jane were having their breakfast.

They hesitated a moment, staring anxiously at the envelopes.

'Together,' said Jane.

'Right,' answered Nell. 'One, two, three, GO!'

They ripped open the envelopes and simultaneously let out loud whoops and flung their arms round each other: 'We're in! We're in!'

Flo, with an amused twitch of her lips, said, 'I suppose that means you've been accepted for the Women's Land Army?'

'Yes!' they both cried.

Nell held out the letter to her mother.

Dear Miss Franklin,

Your enrolment in the WLA has now been registered with the Ministry of Agriculture and your WLA number is . . .

Her eyes skipped over the rest but she noted that the letter had been signed by the County Secretary.

'Well, congratulations, you two! I'm proud that you're both prepared to tackle something you know nothing about. Your dad would have been too.' A catch came into Flo's voice then.

Nell went over to her and hugged her. 'Thanks, Mum.'

Jane watched, wishing her own mother and father would acknowledge her in the same way. She wondered what her aunt and uncle would say, but felt sure they would approve when they received the letter she was about to write.

At that moment there was a knock on the front door. Jane went to answer it.

'Hello, Mrs Campbell,' she greeted their next-door neighbour. 'Are you coming in?'

'Can't, m'dear, I have an appointment in town, but I thought Nell had better have this. It was stuck behind one of our letters the postman just delivered.'

'Thanks, Mrs Campbell,' said Jane, taking the envelope.

As Jane closed the door she glanced at the envelope and recognised Ewan's writing. Her lips tightened. She wished he would write to *her*. Oh, he always put in a message for her when he wrote to Nell, which had been once a week since he'd left for the RAF, but they were simple words, ending with no more than, 'Best Wishes'.

She went to the kitchen. 'A letter for you.' She held it

out to Nell. 'Went next door by mistake.'

'It's from Ewan,' she cried excitedly. 'On top of our acceptance! What a day.'

Jane said nothing but left the kitchen to go to her room. She flopped down on the bed and let all manner of thoughts run through her head. Ewan, Simon, Alan, Glen ... they all haunted her, and she wondered what her life would have been if things had turned out differently in Middlesbrough.

'Jane! Jane!' Her thoughts were interrupted by Nell who was shouting from the bottom of the stairs. She pushed herself up from the bed and brushed away a tear. 'Coming!' she called.

She felt a charge of excitement in the room as she entered the kitchen.

'Ewan's got his wings! He's coming on leave on Friday the fourteenth, a week today.'

Outwardly Jane showed enthusiasm but inwardly she felt nothing but a dull ache.

Chapter Seventeen

Five days later, on the twelfth, two identical envelopes dropped on to the mat at the Franklin house, one for Nell, the other for Jane.

'Looks official,' commented Jane.

Nell did not respond but frowned as she tore open the envelope and pulled out a letter.

> Dear Miss Franklin,
>
> As a member of the WLA you are to report to the WLA hostel at Rendham on Monday the seventeenth of November before 2 p.m. : . .

The rest of the instructions became a blur. 'Blast!' she exclaimed. Her mother looked at her enquiringly. 'Ewan comes for a week's leave on Friday and the following Monday I have to report to a hostel,' Nell complained. 'I'm going to miss most of his leave!'

'Well, love, that's war,' replied Flo. 'Worse things can happen.'

This hidden reference to her father stung Nell who regretted her own petulance. 'I know, Mum. I'm sorry.'

Flo gave her a comforting pat on the shoulder. 'It's all right, love.'

'What about you, Jane?' asked Nell anxiously as the thought crossed her mind that if Jane hadn't to go, she could be left alone with Ewan again. Relief swept through her when Jane answered, 'Same for me.'

'I'm pleased about that,' said Flo. 'I hoped you could stick together.'

Nell found a map of Suffolk. 'We'll not be too far from Saxmundham. We'll be able to get a train there.'

'I think we should ring Mr Horton, tell him what we have done,' said Jane.

'Good idea,' Nell agreed. 'He could be interested in features about the WLA.'

When they managed to contact him later in the day, Mr Horton was delighted at their decision and immediately warmed to their idea of providing material about their work.

'It's a service that hasn't been brought to the public's notice as much as the women's military Services. Features in *World Scene* could do it some good. Keep providing me with material on different aspects of the organisation: how it works, what type of girl it attracts, what the work entails, and what it is like for girls who have never been involved in country life before. There should be plenty of stories for you there. Get permission from your local authority and then provide me with the material. I'll see to getting clearance for it.'

'Anybody home?' Ewan's familiar voice rang through the house as he flung open the front door.

'Ewan!' His mother's voice was filled with joy as she burst from the kitchen. Liz Steel flung herself into his open arms and they hugged each other, bracing themselves against the impact of his sisters, Sylvia and Amy, who came rushing down the stairs shouting his name excitedly.

'I thought you two were evacuated, but good to see you,' he said.

'Home for the weekend,' replied Sylvia.

'Look at you,' said Liz as she stepped back and proudly surveyed her son in his pristine officer's uniform. 'What do you think of your brother, girls?'

'Pilot Officer now,' said Ewan, winking at them.

'Yes, sir!' Both girls straightened and gave him a mock salute.

'Off with you.' Ewan grinned and waved them away.

'When did this happen?' asked Liz as they walked through to the kitchen.

'When I finished basic training last week.'

'You didn't tell us.' She lent a little touch of admonishment to her voice.

'Wanted to surprise you.'

'Your dad will be proud, and so will Walter.'

Sylvia was putting the kettle on. 'Cuppa, brother?'

'Please, and a good one! Amy, how about a slice of that chocolate cake I know Ma will have tucked away somewhere?'

As they sat round the table enjoying the tea and cake, Ewan answered all the questions that were flung at him about his life in the RAF until finally Liz put the inevitable one: 'When do you go back?'

'A week today.'

'What happens now?'

'I join 616 Squadron, flying Spitfires.'

'Where?'

'Kirton-in-Lindsey in North Lincolnshire. The squadron is reforming there after their involvement in the Luftwaffe attacks in the south.'

'And then what happens?'

'I don't know until I join the squadron.'

She tightened her lips as if to hold words back but they had to be said. 'Wherever and whatever it is, Ewan, take care. Our prayers will be with you.'

'Thanks, Ma.' He pressed her hand, his touch warm with a son's love. Then he pushed himself away from the table. 'Now I must go round and see Nell.'

Nell was alone in the kitchen. Her mother was at the

Cookery School and Jane was in her room working on her first impressions of the Land Army. The front door opened abruptly. She heard footsteps briskly approaching the kitchen door and swung round to face it. 'Anyone at home?' called a familiar voice.

'Ewan!' Nell was across the kitchen and into his arms almost before he had stepped into the kitchen.

Their lips met in a wild kiss. Then he put her away from him to arm's length, still holding her. 'Let me look at you.' His eyes devoured her as he said, 'It's good to see you, Nell Franklin.'

'And you,' she cried, her eyes alight. She glanced at his sleeve and added a little more seriously, 'Pilot Officer Steel.'

'Ah, so you've noticed?' he said with a touch of swagger.

'You, an officer? Who'd ever have thought it?' she said with a hint of mockery.

'Ewan Steel did.' His reply came quickly and with an edge to the words.

'And I'm glad you did. I'm so proud of you,' Nell added. She flung her arms round his neck again and said, 'Kiss me.'

'I won't turn down such an invitation.' He swept her close.

The kitchen door opened then. 'Nell, what . . .' Jane began. Then: 'Ewan!' she gasped. Her heart lurched from the surprise, the sight of Ewan with his arms wrapped round Nell, the kiss she had interrupted. She fiercely wanted that experience. 'Oh!' she spluttered. 'I didn't know . . .' Her words faded away in his laughter.

'Hi, Jane, you caught us at just the wrong moment.' He released his hold on Nell and came over to Jane, eyes twinkling mischievously as he kissed her on the cheek. 'Good to see you again.'

'And you.' She met the look in his eyes with one that masked her real feelings.

'What do you think to that uniform?' Nell broke in.

'Wonderful! Congratulations, Ewan.'

'Thanks. We'll all have to celebrate this evening. A meal at the Prince's?'

'You don't want me along. There's no Simon to escort me.'

'Of course we do,' he said. 'Don't we, Nell?'

'It wouldn't be the same without you,' she replied.

Though she outwardly approved, Jane detected an undercurrent there.

'I'm not going to play gooseberry.' She had been on the point of agreeing to make a threesome but pulled back, knowing Nell would not want her style cramped. Jane went on quickly, to change the subject before Ewan tried to be more persuasive, 'Have you told him about us?'

'No.'

'What's this?' he asked when both girls paused, each waiting for the other to tell him their news.

'We've joined the Women's Land Army.'

'You've what?' he gasped in disbelief.

Jane repeated the information.

'But you know nothing about farming or even country life. You're both town-bred. You don't know what you're letting yourselves in for.'

'Doesn't matter! Land Girls don't have to have any experience, they learn as they go along, though there may be some elementary training.'

He shrugged his shoulders. 'On your heads be it. You should have joined the WAAF. Nice uniform. All the girls look very trim in it.'

'Hey, Ewan Steel, keep your eyes fixed on a couple of Land Girls,' Nell reproved him.

'What? All wellies, pullovers and thick trousers when I could see skirts and stockings, showing off shapely legs?'

Nell aimed a playful punch at him. 'You concentrate on your flying, P.O. Steel, and come back safe and sound.'

'Nothing more certain,' he replied. 'So finally we're all

301

going to be doing our bit. Good luck to us all, say I.'

'I'm afraid our news isn't all good,' said Nell, screwing up her face.

'What's this?' he asked as she paused.

'We have to report on Monday.'

'Oh, no!' He grimaced.

'Afraid so,' Jane confirmed.

Ewan shrugged his shoulders, 'Ah, well, we can't go against the needs of the nation. Where are you going to milk your cows and plough the land?'

'We have to report to a hostel at Rendham.'

'Not too far! I have to report to Kirton-in-Lindsey where my squadron is reforming, and then we'll move, hopefully to the south. Well, I must be off now. See you at six, Nell. Try and persuade her to come.' He nodded his head in the direction of Jane.

Nell made no reply as she watched him leave.

'I don't suppose you'll be trying to persuade me very hard?' said Jane icily, and without waiting for a reply, left the kitchen for her own room upstairs.

She flopped into a chair in front of the typewriter and stared morosely at the sheet of paper in the machine, not seeing the words. She did not feel like writing any more now. If only Simon had been at home, then at least they could have gone out as a foursome and she would have been near Ewan. She cursed herself for allowing her deep feelings to surface again and denounced the jealousy she was experiencing towards Nell. Nevertheless she felt loneliness closing in each night she was on her own, knowing Nell and Ewan were together. She knew she should put him from her mind but that was difficult. Why hadn't she allowed Simon to win her over? She liked him. Why had she allowed this barrier to get in the way?

On Monday morning, Ewan arrived to escort them to the station.

'Well, Ewan, what do you think of them?' asked Flo with a smile touching her lips.

He pursed his lips thoughtfully as he eyed the two girls up and down, assessing their appearance. A green pullover covered a white shirt and was tucked into the top of brown corduroy breeches which ended as they met fawn knee-length woollen socks. They wore highly polished brown leather shoes and both had left the neck of the lawn shirt open where, instead of a tie, they wore a thin cravat, the only hint of civilian status. Their hair had been arranged so that a brown felt slouch hat fitted comfortably over it, and they had set this at a slight angle to try to make it look more attractive.

'Oh, very fetching,' said Ewan hollowly.

'The truth?' said Jane.

'I'll tell you what, I've seen smarter uniforms ... After having WAAFs around, I can't really say yours is glamorous.'

'Will you forget those WAAFs?' Nell said sharply.

'I suppose yours has to be more practical than smart,' he conceded.

'Too true it has,' said Nell. 'Can't see those WAAFs you talk about mucking out.'

'Getting into country talk already, are we?'

Flo glanced at the clock. 'Enough of this banter! I don't want to see you go but you'd better be off.'

They donned the greatcoats they had been sent.

'You coming, Mum?' asked Nell.

'Rather say goodbye here, love.'

Nell understood and hugged her tight.

'Look after each other,' said Flo. 'And let me know how you get on.'

'We will, Mrs Franklin,' Jane reassured her as she too gave Flo a loving hug.

'We're on our way,' said Ewan brightly, picking up two kitbags that contained the rest of their WLA gear while they each took a small suitcase containing their personal items.

Ewan saw them safely installed in a carriage and then made his goodbyes.

'Take care of yourself, Jane,' he said as he kissed her.

'You too, Ewan.' She realised he had read what lay behind the catch in her voice when she saw that special twinkle in his eyes as they met hers. As she turned away she wondered if he really had any special feeling for her or was she wilfully reading things into that look? She climbed into the carriage and heard him making his goodbyes to Nell. When Jane sat down and glanced out of the window she saw an exchange of kisses that made her think her impression of a moment ago was entirely the work of her own imagination.

At the guard's shout, Nell got into the carriage. Ewan opened the window and slammed the door closed. Nell leaned out and he reached up and kissed her for the last few remaining seconds. At the first movement of the train he stood back. She reached out for his hand and gave his fingers a last squeeze. As their hands parted he glanced up at the window and his eyes met Jane's. She gave a weak smile and raised her hand in goodbye. Seeing Nell glance briefly in the direction of the engine, he winked at Jane then and pursed his lips in a kiss. The train picked up speed. Nell called out, 'Take care, love.'

'I will, don't worry. Ewan Steel's a survivor. You concentrate on your cows!'

His last remark brought a smile to Nell's face. She watched him out of sight. Finally she closed the window and sat down with a sigh.

'Well, here we go,' said Jane. 'I wonder what awaits us next.' They lapsed into the silence that comes with a departure into the unknown.

Reaching their destination, they were greeted by a member of the WVS who escorted them to a small covered truck fitted with two benches where four other girls were waiting, having arrived half an hour earlier on a train from the south. No one spoke but everyone knew they were being scrutinised by everyone else.

Twenty minutes later they were pulling up in front of a large brick building that seemed to be in the middle of nowhere, the last sign of habitation having been Rendham a mile back. The engine stopped and a few moments later the driver came to the back of the truck and let down the tail-board, saying, 'Here we are, girls.'

Three of them jumped to the ground and the other three handed out the luggage. The driver had disappeared and they stood waiting, surrounded by their baggage. A few minutes later she reappeared accompanied by a woman Jane judged to be about forty. She held herself erect, her commanding figure neatly attired in black skirt and white blouse over which she had donned what Jane thought to be an expensive raincoat.

The driver spoke, 'Girls, this is Miss Harriet Hardcastle. You are on the Hardcastle Estate and her father had this building converted to a hostel for Land Army girls. She volunteered to be the warden here so you will be in her hands from now on.'

'I'm pleased to see all of you,' said Miss Hardcastle. 'Let's get inside out of this November chill.'

Jane was struck by the gentle timbre of her voice. She seemed to be an approachable, caring person but best to make no further judgement until they had seen more of her.

She led the girls inside.

'Just leave your luggage here for the time being while I show you round.' She took them into the next room in which a fire burned brightly before several easy chairs. 'This is your common room, to use as you wish. The next room is the dormitory.' It was fitted out with bunk beds, sufficient for twenty girls. 'The Ministry of Works supplies all the furnishings. They're basic but adequate. Two girls share each wardrobe and chest of drawers. As you see, there is room for twenty of you. You are the first to use this hostel, which was only completed two weeks ago.'

She led the way into a passage next. 'My room is on the left. Cook's on the right. Yes, we have a resident cook. We

305

also have two kitchen maids and two domestics, but that does not mean you can leave your quarters in a poor state. I ask you all to be as neat and clean as possible. If you are, you will find that the domestics will do a good job. Now we come to the dining room and beyond that the kitchen. The passage alongside leads to the bathrooms, of which there are five, plus ten washbasins and lavatories. There is also a laundry that you can use at will. My father had electricity brought in and a special boiler installed so that there is plenty of hot water. You will need it, coming in from the farms.

'Now I suggest you bring in your luggage, choose your bunks and get settled in. I heard crockery rattling as we passed the kitchen. No doubt Mrs Featherstone, the cook, is getting you all a cup of tea. We have our evening meal at six. Off you go!'

As they hurried back to the entrance, Jane said, 'I think we've struck lucky here. It's a new place, and Miss Hardcastle is very nice.'

'We certainly have,' agreed Nell with enthusiasm. The disappointment of parting from Ewan in the middle of his leave had dispersed under the excitement of these new surroundings. 'Same bunk?' she asked as they retrieved their luggage.

'Yes. Corner one, if possible.'

They got what they wanted at the end of the dormitory, next to what had been pointed out as Miss Hardcastle's room.

'Top or bottom?' asked Nell.

'I don't mind.'

'I'd prefer the top,' said Nell.

A few minutes later Miss Hardcastle called from the doorway, 'Tea's ready.'

When they trooped into the room they received a pleasant surprise; the table was laid out with sandwiches, scones and a large chocolate cake. All the girls made appreciative comments.

'I decided this should be a special occasion as you are the first girls to be billeted here. Don't know how Cook does it on the rations. I have asked her to have tea with us and then she too can get to know you.'

The cook greeted them affably and poured out the tea. Once that was served and the first sandwiches taken, Miss Hardcastle said, 'I have a list of your names here but I don't propose to use it like a school register. I would prefer each of you to introduce yourself and say a little about your life. Who'll start?'

There was silence for a moment as everyone waited for someone to accept, then a short, tubby girl with jet-black hair framing a round rosy face spoke up.

'I'm Caroline Beecham – Carrie for short. I come from a village just south of Lowestoft where my parents had the village shop and post office. I worked as a typist in Lowestoft, cycling there every day. I'm twenty.'

'So, no farm work?' said Miss Hardcastle.

'No, but I love the country. That's why I joined the Land Army.'

'Might be different working in it.' Miss Hardcastle smiled at her. 'But I'm sure you'll do well. Who's next?'

'Jane Harvey, ma'am. Twenty-two. I was born in Middlesbrough but lived with my aunt and uncle in Scarborough for three years before I met my friend here,' she indicated Nell, 'and moved with her to her family's home in Lowestoft. I had taken up writing and worked with her and another friend on several projects for *World Scene*.' Little murmurs of admiration sounded around the table.

Nell spoke up quickly next. 'I suppose it would be best if I followed Jane, ma'am, it will broaden both our explanations. I am Nell Franklin, also twenty-two. I come from a fishing family in Lowestoft where my father owned a drifter. He was killed at Dunkirk.' Her voice faltered momentarily. 'I met Jane in Scarborough and she encouraged my interest in photography so we started working together. We met a photographer in Yarmouth and worked with him for a time. He is serving on what was my father's drifter now, minesweeping.'

'I'm Gloria Ainslie. Twenty-two. I was born in Manchester, brought up in an orphanage after my father walked out and Mother couldn't cope with four kids. I was kicked out of the orphanage when I was sixteen. Since then I've moved from job to job, the last being as a barmaid in King's Lynn. Two weeks ago I decided to come south, saw this poster encouraging girls to join the Land Army, and thought, Why not? Better help put that silly old bastard Hitler where he belongs.'

Miss Hardcastle smiled but made no comment. She was sure no farm task would be too much for Gloria who would no doubt before long be trying to glamorise her uniform.

'I'm Madge Kitson. Nineteen. There's not much I can tell you except that I worked in a cake shop in Norwich and joined the Land Army to get away from my parents.'

'I'm Karen Gatenby, a little older than the others – twenty-five. Left my job as a buyer for a ladies' fashion shop in Great Yarmouth. I was stifled there and wanted a complete change, to get outside. Besides, I could see the job folding. There's a war on. So, what better time to do something out in the open and help our boys in the Forces?'

'Well, that was very good. We all know something about each other now, except you still don't know about me.'

Mrs Featherstone rose from her chair. 'I'll go now, ma'am, if that's all right, and get on with the evening meal.'

'Of course, Mrs Featherstone, you know my story.' Harriet glanced at the girls. 'Mrs Featherstone was our cook but my father released her to do this job. Said it was far more important to feed the Land Army well than bother about him.' She smiled. 'But he does all right, has a dear friend who looks in on him and he likes her company. Now for me! Well, I'm your warden. Sort of come with this place, though the WLA were only too pleased to have me.

I did some training, which fitted in with my existing abilities. Like you, I'll come under the scrutiny of the County Representatives who make regular visits.'

She paused briefly. 'You may be wondering why I never married. The truth is I was once engaged but two weeks before the wedding my fiancé and my only brother were killed in a motorcycle accident. It was a tremendous shock from which it took me a long time to recover. Since my father was left without a son to help run the place, I stepped in.'

She stood up, receiving their murmur of condolence with a little smile, and said, 'Let's all move into the common room now then the maids can clear these things away. There are one or two more things I want to say to you.'

Once they were all seated comfortably, Miss Hardcastle addressed them again. 'I am the warden here and therefore responsible for your welfare, so if you have any problems, no matter what they are, come to me first. If I cannot handle them I can call in the County Representative. You are not here to slave for the local farmers as some of them would have you believe. You must not let them put on you. Be guided by War Ag rules and regulations and by the pay structure that body lays down. But if any farmer does try to exploit you, don't retaliate in any way – come to me. Remember, too, that by signing on to join the WLA you promised to hold yourselves available for service on the land, wherever you may be needed. However, whenever farmers make a request for help, I do take into account your individual preferences and abilities.'

Jane took the opportunity to ask a question here. 'Ma'am, do we receive any training?'

Miss Hardcastle smiled. 'I'm afraid not. There are no training centres as such, you learn as you go along. If you are going in for milking we do have some mock-ups on which you can practise, but we'll go into that later. At the moment you will work from this hostel. There may come a time when it would be more convenient for you to live near

309

the farmer you are working for, if the position has become more or less a fixture. In that case the WLA will find you accommodation. Or it may be the farmer wants you to move into his farmhouse. Again, the WLA will vet the position. Such a situation may arise if you are wanted as dairymaids, and that means because of the working hours, peculiar to dairy work, two of you would go together. Cows need milking every day but you all are entitled to time off – annual leave of one week, and public holidays and Sundays are supposed to be free. Also half a day a week and one completely free weekend in four. In the case of dairy work, this may not always be possible to fix but most farmers will try to fit it all in.

'Now, I think I have said enough. The next couple of days will be left free for you to settle in and get to know each other. I'm sure we will all get on very well together.' Miss Hardcastle rose from her chair and the girls did like-wise. After she had left the room they flopped down again with deep sighs and all started to talk at once.

By the time of the evening meal they had got to know each other better and had settled their individual territories in the dormitory. At the end of the meal Miss Hardcastle asked if they could all ride a bicycle. Only Madge said she couldn't. 'My parents said it wasn't lady-like.'

'You'll all need a bike to get to the farms. There are several in the shed at the back of this building. Make your choices tomorrow. Madge, I'm sure the other girls will teach you. You'll soon learn, it's only a matter of balance.'

Teaching Madge the next morning after choosing their machines was a hilarious affair that drew the girls into closer unity, and also brought out tales from their previous lives in which boy friends and experiences with them predominated. Gloria, with her barmaid's background, regaled them with many stories and drew them all into talking about their experiences with the opposite sex.

During the morning of their second day together, and with Madge now able to ride a bike as well as any of them, they cycled into the village. Their arrival brought curious glances from the people there who had heard of the Women's Land Army but never seen any of the recruits. Now six of them, strangely clad, were in their midst. The girls could sense public doubt that these 'slips of lasses' could do what had, up to now, been men's work.

Gloria remarked on this as they propped their bicycles outside the village shop, and concluded, 'We'll show this lot what we're made of. They'll wonder why they never had us before now.'

So it proved over the following weeks. They all approached their tasks with some trepidation, but in spite of the mud, rain, and frost, they coped and were quick learners. The end of each day brought aching backs and the realisation that they had muscles they had never thought of until they experienced the outdoor life. They shared their new skills of ditching, mucking out, tractor driving, brushing, repairing fences, checking on sheep, and all the other tasks that kept farms running. They became a close companionable group who freely passed on their opinions of the farmers they worked for. Faced with early rising, Karen's daily comment was, 'I'd rather have started in July than November' until everyone else grew to anticipate it and chorus it back to her. Eventually the weather began to change, the snow melted, and 1941 moved into better weather. Honed by the winter work, they moved happily into the spring tasks.

One day in March, when Gloria came into the common room after returning from helping a farmer with his sheep, she found Jane looking through the mail that had arrived that morning. Jane turned away from the table with a sigh.

'Nothing for you again?' queried Gloria.

'No.'

'You don't get much, do you?'

'Once a month from my aunt and uncle. Apart from that, I have only had one other.'

'Boy friend?'

'Not really, just a good friend.'

'Where's he?'

'Minesweeping, not regularly in port.'

'Nell gets a lot more than you, and I can tell they are from a boy friend the way her face lights up every time she sees the envelope.'

Jane unconsciously pulled a face. 'He's a fighter pilot.'

'And you're jealous?'

'No, I'm not!'

Gloria smiled. 'You are. I've watched your reaction when Nell receives his letters, and just now you protested far too quickly. Believe Gloria's crystal ball, based on long experience: you have a close friendship with Nell but you need to sort something out there or there could be trouble.' She left a small pause then added, 'But maybe it will all be sorted out for you ...'

Chapter Eighteen

Ewan stepped off the train in Lincoln to be met by a WAAF who gave him a smart salute as she approached.

'Pilot Officer Steel, sir?' she asked.

He returned her salute, answered her query, and followed her to the car parked at the front of the station.

'Have we far to go?' he asked as she guided the car out of the city and took the arrow-straight road north, leaving behind the Cathedral on its hill, a landmark for returning aircraft.

'About ten miles, sir.'

'Have you been at Kirton long?'

'Three months.'

'What's it like?'

'You don't know it, sir?'

'No. I've just passed out. First posting to a squadron.'

'It's a bit bleak and rather windswept, positioned as it is on the edge of the Wolds, but there's a good atmosphere about the station.'

Ewan found it a true assessment, due to the likeable Commanding Officer and the way veteran and new pilots mixed in together.

Once he had booked in at the Officers' Mess he reported to the Adjutant, an older man with a Flight Lieutenant's ribbons round the sleeves of his tunic, who gave him a friendly welcome and then took him to the Squadron's

Commanding Officer, Squadron Leader Charles Cawthorne, who wore the DFC ribbon with bar beneath the wings on his tunic. When he'd heard he was coming to this squadron, Ewan had genned up on the C.O. and learned he was a leader of skill and panache.

Cawthorne appeared to leap up from his chair when Ewan came in. He stepped out from behind his desk and, ignoring Ewan's smart salute except for a nod of his head, shook hands with him warmly. Ewan knew this man had been given the position of C.O., even though he was only twenty-two, because he had all the traits of a natural-born leader.

'Glad to have you, Steel. Just been looking at your records.' He indicated a folder on his desk. 'Very good, don't you think, Toby?' He shot a questioning glance at the Adjutant.

'They are, sir.'

'Toby, I've told you before, no formalities between you and me unless occasion demands it.' He looked at Ewan then. 'Toby should by rights be wearing a DSO and DFC below those wings – First World War. He disobeyed my orders about wearing them. Says he doesn't want to embarrass the young pilots who join us.'

Ewan was taken by the fact that these two men, who could have been father and son, were serving together.

'I'll be leaving you then,' said Toby, making for the door, 'before you embarrass me further.'

When the door closed, the Squadron Leader smiled. 'Great man, Toby. Volunteered at the start of the war, wanted to fly but was too old for that. He insisted on joining up and pulled a few strings to become the squadron's adjutant. We are fortunate to have him. Any queries about anything, go to him.

'Now, as I said, your record is good. No doubt you know that, but don't get the idea you know it all. I've seen young pilots who believed that and didn't last long as a result. You've still a lot to learn, especially about combat

314

flying. As well as new bods, we've veterans here: learn from them. They're survivors and only too willing to pass on their knowledge – I've insisted on that. I run an easy-going squadron, but I do insist on certain rules. Respect for all ranks must be observed within the rules of discipline. As for flying ... I expect you are anxious to get into the air?'

'Yes, sir.'

Cawthorne nodded. 'I've decided to attach you to "A" Flight, led by Flight Lieutenant "Bunny" Rogers. Handles a Spitfire like he would a willing blonde on a first date! You and I will fly with him at ten in the morning. I'll take you to "A" Flight now and introduce you. Before we go, any questions?'

'Yes, sir. Are we likely to see action from here? Bit remote, aren't we?'

'It may seem like that but we're on stand-by and could be called on at any time, even though we're not yet up to full complement. Patience!' He glanced at the records in front of him and added, 'Ewan, get in as much flying time as you can while we're here. It will be for real soon enough.'

'Yes, sir.'

'Right, let's away.'

The Squadron Leader walked at a brisk pace and before long they reached 'A' Flight pilots' hut close by a line of Spitfires. Pilots lounging in an array of armchairs, reading, chatting, snoozing, or playing darts, immediately sprang to attention. Their C.O. acknowledged that and with a wave of his hand signalled them to relax. 'I've brought you a new bod – Ewan Steel.'

They acknowledged him with nods, a raised hand or a smile but Ewan knew he was coming under close scrutiny as they made their first assessments. One pilot laid down his darts and came towards them; the others resumed what they had been doing. Ewan saw the stripes of a Flight Lieutenant on the shoulders of the darts player's battle-dress. He held

315

out his hand. 'Colin Rogers.' Ewan felt his tight grip and saw a pair of steel-blue eyes assessing his reaction.

'Pleased to be with you, sir.' He matched the firmness of the handshake.

'Right, Ewan, first thing: I'm not "sir" unless circumstances demand it. And I'm not Colin, either. For some reason, I'm Bunny. You'll hear all sorts of reasons why, but don't believe any of them. You'll find ranks from Sergeant upwards here, but they mean nothing in this hut or in the air. We are all pilots, doing the same job to the best of our ability. Any man here will help you in any way he can. With that philosophy in mind, we aim to be the best flying unit in the RAF. Fit in and you'll be all right. If not, you'll be posted elsewhere. As you'll have guessed, I'm a plain speaker and pull no punches, but from your reports and what I've seen in these few minutes, I reckon we'll get on. Welcome to "A" Flight.'

'Thank you, sir.'

Rogers nodded. 'Bunny, remember?'

'Yes, Bunny.'

A broad smile broke across the Flight Lieutenant's face. 'Sound like one of us already.'

'Bunny, I've told Ewan that you and I will fly with him tomorrow at ten.'

'Very good.'

'See you then.' The Squadron Leader gave Ewan a friendly tap on the shoulder. 'Welcome.'

'Thank you, sir.'

The pilots sprang to their feet until the C.O. had left the hut.

'I'll introduce you around,' said Bunny then.

Introductions were made, during which Ewan realised he was being tested on many levels, but nothing was done to make him feel uncomfortable. When he walked back to the Mess with two brother officers he felt he had been accepted for himself. There only remained their judgement of his flying ability.

At precisely ten o'clock the next morning three Spitfires took to the air. Ewan was aware that all the pilots of 'A' Flight were outside their hut and knew his take-off was the one being watched. They took off in formation, with Ewan on the port side of the C.O. They circled the airfield once and then started to climb. Reaching nine thousand feet, they broke formation to fly line astern with Ewan taking up the rear. The C.O. took them through a demanding series of manoeuvres, and Ewan had to keep all his wits about him to hold his position and keep close to Bunny, immediately in front. His tension began to ease away and had completely disappeared when the C.O. called him on the R/T (radio telephone) to tell him he was on his own for half an hour. He saw the C.O. slip away to starboard and Bunny follow. Ewan put his Spitfire into a climb and, after gaining another two thousand feet, levelled out at the base of towering white cumulus cloud. He felt free and became absorbed in the sheer joy of flying. He banked and rolled, looped and climbed, through the canyons of cloud, plunged into their depths, twisted and turned through the chasms, until finally he burst free from them to head reluctantly for base.

He almost jumped out of his seat with surprise when a voice over the intercom startled him. 'I'm right on your tail, Ewan.' He recognised Bunny's voice and cursed himself for not following the elementary rule of keeping a sharp lookout at all times. He would be in for a rollicking for that when they landed.

He felt an ass as he climbed out of his Spitfire and saw Bunny waiting for him. He was shamefaced, an apology on his lips, but Bunny spoke first. 'Better for that to happen with a friendly plane stalking you rather than a Messerschmitt.' The words were spoken quietly, with no direct criticism. Bunny knew Ewan had learned his lesson.

During the next fortnight Ewan flew eight more times

and regretted that the other six days were marred by bad weather. He got to know the pilots of 'A' Flight intimately and became part of their friendly rivalry with 'B' Flight. The Station Commander had seen the pilots in both Flights were evenly balanced so one could not claim to be best. Although the veteran pilots were in some way pleased to be relieved of battle duties, they chafed to be in action again and envied the squadrons in the south who were still engaging the enemy.

When Bunny walked into the pilots' hut mid-morning of the ninth day, all the pilots sensed the atmosphere change.

'Take-off one o'clock,' he announced. 'Shipping patrol, Bridlington to Skegness.' The atmosphere deflated a little. 'I know you expected more action, but who knows what we might meet? It's an important convoy coming south from the Tyne and we've been called in to help out. The whole squadron will be involved. We'll form up ten thousand feet over Grimsby. Normal procedure, four sections of three aircraft.' Ewan found himself allocated to Bunny's section and knew that if they went into action, the 'Vic' formation they would be flying would change to line astern and he would be the last man in his section, responsible for keeping a lookout to the rear.

The roar of twelve Merlin engines as the Spitfires were started up sent a shiver of excitement through Ewan, but at the same time he felt queasy in his stomach. This could be his first taste of real action, when his life and those of his fellow pilots might depend on his vigilance and skill.

The weather was clear with only some very high wisps of cloud marring a blue sky. The engines seemed to love the sharp air as they took the sleek fighters swiftly to the designated height. Ewan spotted Bunny's aircraft ahead and formed up on his port side. Bunny raised his hand in acknowledgement and then did the same to the pilot coming up on his starboard side. By the time they were over Grimsby, the squadron was in position. They flew north towards Bridlington with the unmistakable Flamborough

Head rock spit as their guide. Sighting the convoy of twelve ships, they took up their positions of lookouts and protectors.

They were off the Humber when the R/T crackled and a voice reported, 'Customers approaching from the south-east.'

'OK. Sharp eyes, everyone.' Bunny's voice was calm, generating confidence.

Ewan tensed. In a few minutes he saw ten Heinkel bombers escorted by an equal number of Messerschmitts, and his immediate thought was that the convoy must be carrying vital supplies to command such attention. He had no time to think any more about it. Suddenly the air seemed full of aircraft. As planned, Bunny led his section, followed by section two, to meet the approaching planes, leaving the remaining two sections as defence for the convoy should any German aircraft slip through.

Ewan followed Bunny closely, eager to protect his leader. A Spitfire slipped past him following a Messerschmitt he hadn't even noticed. In a sudden explosion the German disintegrated and shrapnel seemed to fly everywhere. Ewan automatically ducked. When he looked up, Bunny was nowhere to be seen. Ewan looked round desperately, banked and turned, saw a Heinkel pass across his sights, pressed the firing button but saw no hits. He glimpsed his leader again and felt a surge of relief. He immediately swept in that direction – an automatic reaction that saved him from the fighter pulling round on to his tail.

A bomber peeled away into a dive then towards two vessels in the Humber. Ewan saw his intention. While action proliferated around the convoy, there were two ships left without cover. He pushed the nose of his Spitfire down and went in pursuit. The Heinkel kept a steady course. Ewan knew he hadn't been seen as yet, and he had the advantage of height. Down, down ... He did not seem to be getting any closer but the altimeter needle was moving round rapidly. He eyed the two vessels. Drifters ... must be minesweeping.

The bomber began to level out. Ewan saw the bomb doors open. He banked, bringing himself into a better position. Nearer . . . he needed to be nearer . . . but the danger was imminent, it had to be stopped. He pressed his firing button. He did not see any hits but the bomber's nose came up as if the pilot had reacted to receiving a shock. He saw the bombs leave the Heinkel, but with the sudden evasive action the aiming point had been lost and they fell into the sea, sending sheets of water cascading over the nearest drifter.

Ewan banked sharply, searching the sky for the bomber, but it was nowhere to be seen. He looked down. Streaking away close to the water, the bomber sought his escape. Ewan's immediate reaction was to follow but he realised he would be far more useful back at the main job of protecting the convoy. As he banked he looked down at the drifters for a last time. The men on deck were waving their thanks. Ewan started. The *Sea Queen*! Simon and Glen wouldn't know who had waggled his wings before setting course to join the main combat. Well, not until he had written to Nell.

Dear Nell,

I saw my first action today when we were on convoy protection off the East Coast. Sent a gaggle of bombers and its fighter escort packing. I spotted a bomber heading for a couple of drifters in the Humber. Drove him off before he could do any harm. Believe it or not one of them was the *Sea Queen*!

As soon as she had finished reading that paragraph, Nell read it aloud to Jane.

'Does he say any more?' she asked excitedly.

After a moment's hesitation, Nell scanned the rest of the letter. 'No, the rest is personal.'

'Aren't you going to read that to me?' Jane teased her.

'What do you think? But I'll give you the P.S. Ewan says he might be moving soon.'

320

That day came a week after the Station Commander had informed 12 Group that the squadron was ready to resume an active role in operations against the enemy. It came in a way Ewan and the other pilots had not expected. They were sent to join the 12 Group Wing, but not on a permanent basis. Their support there would be valuable but they would return to Kirton each evening. Whenever required they flew with the Group, patrolling the London area, until finally they settled back at Kirton to await further developments which they all sensed were pending.

On the Monday morning of the last week in February, Miss Hardcastle came into the dining room when the girls were at breakfast.

'Just a reminder, Nell, Jane. This coming weekend of the first and second of March will be your weekend off. Kate, Madge, you are free the following weekend.'

'You two going home?' asked Kate once Miss Hardcastle had left.

'Expect so,' replied Nell, glancing at Jane for her agreement.

'Pity your flying boy friend isn't going to be on leave too,' said Kate.

'He's never had leave since he joined a squadron. He thinks they're likely to move and he won't get leave until that happens,' replied Nell. 'Are you heading home too?'

'Yes, bit of mother-spoiling will be nice.'

'Wish I could say the same,' said Madge, screwing up her face at the prospect of having to survive a weekend with her domineering parents.

'Why not come home with me?' offered Kate.

'Oh, I couldn't impose on your mother.'

'She'd love it!' cried Kate. 'Two of us to mollycoddle, she'd lap up every minute. You're coming. No point in having a miserable time, and you certainly don't want to spend it here when everyone else will be working.'

321

'I was pleased for Madge,' said Nell. She and Jane had managed to leave work half an hour early on Friday afternoon so they had time to cycle to the nearest station to catch a train.

'So was I. She doesn't seem to have had the brightest of lives and Kate will be good for her.'

By arrangement they left their bicycles with the station master who had voluntarily come out of retirement to keep the small country halt open when his staff of four had volunteered for armed service at the outbreak of war. Once they reached Lowestoft they made straight for home and surprised Nell's mother.

'Didn't expect you until later,' Flo exclaimed when hugs and kisses had been exchanged.

'Wangled an extra half-hour so we got the earlier train. Makes three hours' difference and saves hanging about.'

'It's so nice to have you both, but don't feel obliged to come because of me if there are other things you want to do. I'm OK now. Life is assuming a new pattern.'

Nell hugged her mother. 'We want some of your spoiling, Mum.'

And spoiling they got. Flo left them to sleep late, but once she heard them stirring she quickly took them breakfast in bed, a luxury she knew farm work precluded.

After a leisurely morning and a light lunch, Nell and Jane decided they would take a walk as the day was fair. Pleased to be out of their working garb, they dressed in plain skirts that came to just below the knee and over white jumpers wore fitted waist-length jackets. Nell's was a dark pink, buttoned below a plunging collar, while Jane's light blue jacket was belted at the waist. Flo watched them as they left the house, a tear coming to her eyes as she wished that George could have seen them. He would have been so proud of his daughter.

They went to look at the shops that endeavoured to do their best to be attractive in spite of the shortage of goods and the utility restrictions. They found much to chatter

322

about and became so absorbed they were unaware of where they were going until a gust of wind made them realise they were overlooking the harbour. Beyond it the sea was running fast and they saw a vessel beating through the waves, heading for the shelter of the harbour. Water sprayed over its bow. As it plunged to meet the next wave, Nell gasped, 'It's the *Sea Queen!*'

Jane grabbed her arm. 'Are you sure?'

'I'd know her anywhere.'

'Simon and Glen will get a big surprise to find us here!'

'And that we know about the attack on her.'

'And that Ewan was involved.'

Their excitement mounted with the progress of the *Sea Queen*. As she watched the manoeuvre to bring the drifter safely into harbour, Jane felt a flush of pride at Simon's ability. It made her wonder about her true feelings towards him.

'There's Glen!' cried Nell. 'He's seen us!' They waved back. They saw him turn towards the bridge, signal and point in their direction. Another figure on the bridge gave them an enthusiastic wave.

'Simon!' gasped Jane. 'Thank God they're both all right.'

The girls hurried to the harbourside, watching the drifter being brought skilfully to its berth. As soon as the gangway was run out, Simon and Glen were ashore to greet the girls with hugs and kisses.

Their excitement was overwhelming. 'What are you doing here?' 'Didn't expect to see you.' 'What a coincidence.' 'Are you all right?' 'The *Sea Queen* has some damage.' 'Yes, but she's a stout-hearted old lady.' 'We know someone who saved you from something far worse ...' Simon and Glen looked puzzled. 'What?' 'Ewan wrote and told me that he had scared a German bomber away from the *Sea Queen!*' Simon and Glen were astounded to hear it.

'You'll have to tell us later ... We have to go now,' said

Simon. 'A lot to see to.'

'Come to the house when you're free,' Nell told them.

'We're here to refit. Glen will be staying with me. See you later.' And the two men hurried back to their ship.

The Saturday night dance was in full swing when the four of them arrived at the dance hall, but first they needed to catch up with each other's news so found a table at the adjoining bar.

Nell related Ewan's information quickly, and both men remembered the incident vividly and said how grateful they were to the then unknown pilot.

'Judging by the scars on the *Sea Queen*, that wasn't the only time you were attacked?' said Jane.

The two men played this down.

'You're here for a refit then?'

'Natural course of events.'

'Then back to the Humber?'

Nell caught the momentary glance that passed between the two men. 'You've something else to say?'

'Well,' said Simon quietly, leaning forward on the table and cradling his glass in his hands, 'we have orders to proceed to the south coast. Can't say any more than that.'

Jane looked at him with concern. 'That could be more dangerous.'

He gave a shrug of his shoulders as if to dismiss the possibility.

'Hey, snap out of it,' exclaimed Glen. 'We're lonely sailors home from the sea, here to enjoy ourselves. We only have you for tonight as you're back to the cows and pigs tomorrow. Come on, Nell, dance with me.'

She smiled. 'I guess we should live for today.'

Simon held out his hand to Jane and they left the table. Soon all four of them were enjoying themselves on a crowded dance floor, with no thought for what might lie ahead.

*

'Your parting kiss with Glen was a bit passionate,' commented Jane with a wry twitch of her lips as the girls settled into the train the next afternoon.

Glen and Simon had made the most of this unexpected meeting by spending the morning with them before enjoying a midday meal at Mrs Franklin's and escorting the girls to the station.

'No more than yours with Simon,' replied Nell tartly, annoyed that Jane had noted her reaction to Glen's. 'He'll remember that wherever he goes. He's sweet on you, Jane, don't break his heart. I'm fond of Simon, I'd hate him to be hurt.'

'*You* warning me off?' scoffed Jane. 'Ewan, Glen, Simon ... just how many do you want? Or is it that you don't want me to have any of them?'

'Don't be so soft! Glen likes me, but no more than that. Simon loves you – don't egg him on and then drop him. Ewan you can't have, he's mine!'

'You assume too much,' retorted Jane. 'Simon knows where he stands with me, whereas you could have a problem with Glen, he has expectations, and Ewan isn't exclusively yours.'

Nell's lips tightened. 'Don't you harbour any desires in that direction,' she warned, and a silence fraught with subdued hostility reigned for the rest of the journey. It was only cast aside when, as they were cycling back to the hostel, Nell had to swerve on a corner to avoid the wagon collecting milk from the farms and ended up in the ditch, rising from it a mud-spattered figure, that brought laughter from Jane. The sound was so infectious that Nell, having got over her initial shock and realised she was not hurt, saw the funny side of the incident too. Reassured, the driver went on his way after straightening the wheel of her bike.

'Thank goodness we haven't far to go, you need to get out of those wet clothes,' said Jane, her concern re-establishing the friendship between them.

*

325

In late-March excitement gripped the squadron when orders came through for it to move to Tangmere at the foot of the South Downs near Chichester.

'Front line at last,' commented Ewan to Hugh Douglas who had joined the same day as him and with whom he had quickly struck up a close friendship.

The move went well and the squadron soon settled down in its new home, hoping it would live up to the traditions of this airfield which had played a prominent part in the Battle of Britain and which bore the scars of the severe bombing it had endured when the Germans tried to eliminate Fighter Command in 1940. It still suffered occasionally from night forays by the enemy, but they did little to upset the efficiency of the station or the morale of its personnel.

The squadron still found itself engaged in convoy patrols, but these were now over the Channel rather than the North Sea. Diversions came whenever the moon was bright and they patrolled the night skies against enemy bombers that still made incursions over England. Then came plans from Fighter Command Headquarters for its squadrons to go on the offensive and bring the Luftwaffe fighters to battle over occupied territory. The organisation for this was put into operation and eventually plans of battle were made. Once the first sortie had been made, the squadrons were continually engaged in the fighting whenever the weather was right, as well as still being delegated convoy patrols. Success followed success during the rest of 1941, but it did not always go in the RAF's favour and there were occasions when the squadrons suffered losses, sometimes heavy. Ewan's did not escape unscathed and before the summer was out, with the loss of Bunny, Ewan was promoted to take charge of 'A' Flight, a move that was popular on the station. His calculated daring was inspirational, and his charm and good looks only added to his reputation and aura. He was aware of the adulation which mounted among his fellow pilots every time he downed

326

another plane, but kept it under control; to get carried away with it might erode his vigilance and lead to disaster. He and Hugh developed a keen understanding, supporting each other in combat, and Ewan was not slow to recognise the part his friend played in his success.

'There's going to be a change today for two of you,' Miss Hardcastle announced during the second week of July. 'Mr Symonds of Cedar Farm has come round to realising that Land Girls can be of tremendous help. As two of his dairymen have decided to volunteer for the Army, he needs two of you to replace them. It will mean living in at the farm. I know the man and his wife and they are good, honest working people. A bit set in their ways, not much in favour of change, which is why they've resisted employing Land Girls to date, but now the situation is being forced on them.'

'Jane and I will do it, Miss Hardcastle.' Nell spoke up quickly without even consulting Jane.

'Good of you to volunteer but you may think otherwise when I tell you what dairying consists of. It's not an easy life. You'll be getting up at half-past five no matter how cold and wet it is; your bed will pull you back. But the cows need relieving of their milk and it has to be ready in the churns for the early lorry to collect. Then the cows have to be washed down and their stalls mucked out. Cows must be milked every day but you are entitled to your time off. I got Mr Symonds to see this and persuaded him to take two of you so you would not miss your rest time. Of course, for the Saturday afternoon and Sunday work, you will be paid overtime. As you will see, dairy work is tying but no doubt you will find it has its compensations. Are you sure you still want it?'

'We certainly do,' answered Nell quickly.

'Very good then. I will take you to Cedar Farm later this morning, so get your things ready.'

When they left the dining room Jane said sharply, 'You

327

were a bit quick volunteering. Didn't even consult me.'

'Didn't want anyone else to get it.'

'You've let us in for hard work, long days and early starts!'

'We aren't afraid of that, are we?'

'No ...'

'We'll be more on our own, and can arrange time off to please ourselves. And the extra cash will come in handy.'

'Well, I hope it works out and the accommodation is OK, to say nothing of Mr and Mrs Symonds.'

'We can always ask to leave if we don't like it.'

'I suppose so,' said Jane, still a little grumpy at not being consulted. 'Talking of leave, I'm surprised Ewan hasn't had any since joining the squadron.'

'So am I. His weekly letter has never even hinted at it, but he has said they're putting in a lot of flying time. I suppose that's only to be expected.'

They were packing when Miss Hardcastle came to tell them, 'We'll have lunch here and then I'll take you to Cedar Farm.'

On their way to eat they saw the mail had arrived and was in its usual place on the table in the common room.

'One for you, Jane, Simon's writing.' Nell passed the envelope to her. 'Ah, and one from Glen. The *Sea Queen* must have put in somewhere.'

'Anything from Ewan?'

'No.' Jane sensed regret in Nell's voice even as she tried to hide her disappointment by saying, 'He makes no set day for writing.'

They tore open their envelopes and each devoured their letters.

'The *Sea Queen*'s been attacked from the air three times. Does Simon say anything about that?'

'Not really, just that they happened and one sounds to have been rather bad but no one was hurt.'

'Glen says they were all scary but Simon's skill got them through.'

Jane felt a flush of pride at that.

'How's Glen?' she asked.

'He's fine. Enjoying the work he's doing, feels it's all worthwhile.' Nell gave a little laugh. 'I don't know whether he's trying to impress me but he says he still carries a torch for me even though he's come to see there's something in the saying, "a sailor has a girl in every port".'

Miss Hardcastle drove them the four miles to Cedar Farm where the sound of the car pulling up at the back of the farmhouse brought a man hurrying out of the cow-shed at the other side of the big square yard. He paused and looked suspiciously at them.

Miss Hardcastle wound down the window quickly and called out, 'Good afternoon, Mr Symonds, I've brought you your helpers.'

He made an inaudible grunt and started towards them. They saw a man in his sixties, shoulders beginning to stoop, grey hair peeping from below his flat cap, his jacket worn from constant use and his grey trousers tucked into the top of mud-splashed Wellingtons. His features were thin and lined by a life spent in the open in all weathers.

'Good day, Miss Hardcastle, and not a day too soon. It's a rum ole dew. My two men leave the day after tomorrow.'

'Jane Harvey and Nell Franklin,' Miss Hardcastle made the introduction.

He shook hands with them both; a welcoming warm grip but they could sense him making an assessment of them. They could almost hear him thinking, Slips of lasses, they'll never cope.

'Been around cows before?' he asked in a way that told them he knew the answer but had to ask.

'No, Mr Symonds,' they chorused.

'But we can learn,' added Jane with enthusiasm.

'I suppose so, but cows can be contrary creatures. A bit like women.'

'But you men love them – couldn't live without them.'

329

A voice from behind them ordered, 'John, bring them in, don't stand there nattering.'

They saw a small tubby woman with a round rosy face smiling at them. She was clad in a plain brown dress with a flowered bib apron over it, haltered over the neck and tied at her waist.

Mrs Symonds gave the girls a motherly hug and said she was pleased to see them.

'It's nice to meet you too, Mrs Symonds,' said Nell, speaking for them both.

'Mrs Symonds? That's a bit formal for me. Why not call me Betty? But if you think that's too informal, call me Aunty Betty.'

This suggestion made the girls feel at home and they settled for Aunty Betty.

'Now, Miss Hardcastle, a cup of tea before you go? The kettle's on the boil.'

'That would be nice, thank you.'

'John, you help the girls with their luggage while I make the tea.'

Within a few minutes they were sitting round a large oak table that occupied the centre of the big kitchen. A highly polished black kitchen range was centred on one wall while the opposite one held a long stone sink beneath a window that overlooked the yard.

Jane and Nell imparted something about themselves as they enjoyed tea and a slice of home-made cake, miraculously conjured up from meagre rations.

Mr Symonds eventually drained his cup and said, 'Well, girls, you'll have to learn fast. I'll take you and introduce to you Harold and Sid. You'll work with them tomorrow, and after that you'll be on your own.'

'Hold you hard, John. Miss Hardcastle will want to be away and she'd better see the accommodation I've readied for Jane and Nell first.'

He gave a little nod of tight-lipped dissatisfaction at being held up but knew he would have to comply. 'Come over to the cow-shed when you're ready,' he told the girls.

'Yes, Mr Symonds, we shan't be long.'

He nodded and walked out.

'I'll show you your room,' said Betty Symonds, making for one of the doors. 'You'll live as one of the family. Well, there's only John and me now. Our two sons volunteered the day war was declared, both joined the Navy. Never been to sea but that's what they wanted, so we gave them our blessing and off they went.'

'I hope you have good news of them?' said Miss Hardcastle.

'One is on a destroyer – convoy escort. The other is on anti-submarine patrols somewhere.' She was leading them down a passage and indicated a door to the left. 'That has been used as a dining room but we generally eat in the kitchen, it's handier. The next room along is a sitting room. You can use it as you wish.' She turned on to a staircase that led to a passage on the next floor. 'Here directly in front of us is the bathroom. Thank goodness we took advantage of having water piped into the house when the system between the two villages was put in early in 1939. Mr Symonds and I are at that end.' She pointed to the left. 'Thankfully, this is a big old type of farmhouse and there are four more rooms this way. The two on the left are yours. They're identical so you can't fall out deciding who has which. The two on the right are kept ready for my sons should they manage a home leave.' She opened a door to the left and the girls gasped when they went in.

'This is for us?'

'Yes. I hope you will be happy here.'

'It's wonderful,' they told her as they admired the chintz curtains, which matched the bedspread. There was a wardrobe, a chest of drawers, two chairs and a washstand from the days when washing facilities were rudimentary.

When they went outside to say goodbye to Miss Hardcastle, she said, 'I thought you would like it, I did when I first came to vet the place, and I'm sure you will get on well with the Symonds. But if you have any complaints or criticism, come to me first.'

'I doubt that will be necessary so long as we can cope with the work and satisfy Mr Symonds.'

'I think you'll find him all right, once you get to know him.'

'The sooner the better,' said Nell. 'We'd best be getting to the cow-shed. We said we wouldn't be long.'

They watched Miss Hardcastle drive away and then hurried back into the house to collect their Wellingtons which they put on in the scullery, a medium-sized room off the kitchen with an outside door.

'We've struck lucky here,' commented Jane as they hurried across the yard. 'You must have had an intuition when you volunteered.'

Nell grinned. 'Trust your Aunty Nell!'

'I fear this job might be exacting, though, and if Harold and Sid have only one more day, we're going to have to learn fast.'

'We'll cope,' replied Nell.

'Ah, here you are,' said Mr Symonds when they entered the large cow-shed, as if to say 'About time too', but they could not deny that his voice was friendly and seemed to say he was going to make the best of what at the moment he regarded as poor replacements for his men. He made the introductions and the two young men seemed friendly enough.

'We've just finished the second milking of the day. There's one early-morning and one late-afternoon,' Mr Symonds explained. 'As you can see, I've a herd of thirty cows, all Jerseys.' A note of pride came into his voice as he surveyed the cows in their stalls, fifteen to either side of the shed.

'Aren't they beautiful?' said Jane, eyeing the glistening coats of the brown and white cows. 'They're smaller than I expected.'

'They are small compared to some breeds, but they give

332

the richest milk.'

'And so placid,' commented Nell, admiring the way the cows were standing.

Harold overheard the remark and chuckled. 'Maybe they are now but they can give you a nasty ding. Treat 'em gently and let them get to know you. They all have names.'

'How on earth do you tell the difference?' asked Jane.

'You'll soon recognise each one, and they'll recognise your voice.'

'Harold, you may as well start instructing right away. I'll go and help Sid.' Mr Symonds added for the girls' benefit, 'He went to see to the cooling process.'

By the time Harold had explained the day's work, their heads were reeling with information. He smiled at the expressions of doubt clouding their faces when he had finished. 'Wishing you'd never come?'

'No, no,' they replied quickly. 'There's just a lot to take in.'

'It'll come naturally once you've done it a few times. Sid and I will see you all right tomorrow, and after that you'll have Mr Symonds. He's OK, good to work with, though at times a bit exacting, especially when it comes to cleanliness. But I suppose he's right, you can't be too careful in that respect. And he has a lot of money tied up in this herd, aside from the fact that he loves every single cow and would be devastated if anything happened to even one of them.'

'Oh, that's putting a lot of responsibility on us,' groaned Nell.

'Just follow routine meticulously and you'll be all right. I take it you have never been around cows before, let alone milked one?'

They nodded.

'It's the actual milking that bothers me,' said Jane.

'There's nothing to it.'

'All right for you to say ...'

'Just be gentle, but firm enough to draw the milk and let

the cow get to know you. I thought you might be novices so I've rigged up a frame. There's a piece of rubber in the shape of an udder so you can have a practice before touching a real cow. Tell you what, after we've finished, Mrs Symonds always feeds us – we give her some of our coupons. I'll stay behind and watch you have a go with it before I go home.'

Sid stayed back, too, and the four of them spent the evening crying with laughter before the two men cycled off home two hours later.

Jane came out of a luscious dream in which she had been flying through the clouds with Ewan. She stirred; this bed was unfamiliar. She was wondering where she was when she realised someone was knocking at a door and heard a voice saying, 'Time for up.' She groaned, and heard the words repeated. 'Yes,' she called and listened to the footsteps receding along the passage and turning on to some stairs. Then she realised where she was – Cedar Farm, and that was Mr Symonds. Milking! Nell! Was she even awake? Jane swung out of bed and, still bleary-eyed, was at the door when Nell staggered into the passage.

'Oh, you're up,' she muttered sleepily.

'I wondered if you were.' Then Jane moaned, 'What an unearthly hour.'

'We'll have to get used to it,' commented Nell. 'Bags I the bathroom!' She skipped round Jane and was in before her friend could object.

'Me tomorrow,' Jane called at the closed door.

Twenty minutes later they walked into the kitchen and the tempting smell of frying bacon put a different gloss on the start of their day.

By the end that gloss had gone. Apart from a break for a midday meal, and a brief one for a cup of tea in the middle of the afternoon, they were working continuously while trying to learn. Weary and exhausted, they staggered to the farmhouse for their evening meal. Dirty Wellingtons were washed down and left in the scullery along with their used dungarees; there would be clean ones the next day and the dirty ones were put into the copper in the corner of the scullery, to be boiled and washed.

Tired, and with aching fingers and backs, they said an early goodnight to Mr and Mrs Symonds. As they reached the door of the kitchen he called out, 'You did well today. Much more to learn and then it will become easier. But,' he gave a little pause as if he was weighing up his words, 'you'll do.' There was no mistaking his approval was sincere.

'Thank you,' they both said.

As tired as they were, they felt a wave of euphoria and a sense of achievement. The two girls snuggled into their beds and were soon asleep.

Chapter Nineteen

'Letter for you, love,' said Mrs Symonds when the girls came into the farmhouse after the first milking. She held out an envelope to Jane.

'Nothing for me, Aunty Betty?' asked Nell.

'Sorry, love.'

'What's got into Ewan?' she muttered to herself.

'It's from my aunt,' Jane said, recognising the writing as she sat down at the kitchen table and tore the envelope open. 'Oh, my God!' The words came out in an incredulous whisper but caught the attention of both Nell and Mrs Symonds, who turned to Jane and saw that her face was ashen.

'What is it, love?' asked Mrs Symonds with deep concern.

'Jane?' said Nell, unease in her voice.

'My parents.' Her voice faltered. 'They've been ... killed in an air raid.'

There was a moment of silent disbelief before Mrs Symonds automatically said, 'Where?' and Nell dropped to her knees beside Jane. The shock had drained her of all strength. She held out the letter limply for Nell to take.

'You want me to read it?'

Jane nodded.

Nell read it quickly. 'It happened in Middlesbrough on Bank Holiday Monday.'

'A week ago,' commented Mrs Symonds quietly.

'A lone raider bombed the railway station,' went on Nell. 'Severe destruction and several people killed.'

'Why so long in letting Jane know?'

'Identification problems and then tracing next-of-kin. Your aunt and uncle don't know why they were at the station and can only conclude that as it was Bank Holiday Monday, they had decided to take a trip somewhere.'

'You'll have to go, Jane,' said Mrs Symonds. 'John will help Nell.'

Jane gave a little shake of her head that Mrs Symonds interpreted as a sign of despair until she said, 'No. I haven't seen them for over four years, but it's still a shock.'

'Your aunt says she sees no point in your going,' Nell continued reading. 'From your uncle's enquiries, the funerals have all been dealt with. She adds that if you want to go to them you would be welcome.'

'I expected that of them, but I'll stay here. There's no need to upset our routine and I'd be better working.' The words caught in Jane's throat as memories of what had happened to drive her away from Middlesbrough, and how the love she had for her parents had been destroyed, tormented her. Nevertheless this tragic news had jolted her. She jumped from her chair and ran upstairs.

'Go after her,' Mrs Symonds urged. 'She's in shock.'

'Best leave her,' decided Nell. 'This bolt from the blue has grieved her but there's a history between her and her parents. I don't know what it is, she's never confided in me. It might have been better if she had. Maybe this will allow her to release what she has kept bottled up.'

But as the weeks slipped by that did not happen. The secret remained locked in Jane's mind, and she continued with life as if nothing had happened.

The Spitfires came into Tangmere watched and counted by all on the station, who admired these wonderful aircraft but

337

more so the men who occupied the cockpits. They, who risked their lives every time they took to the air, were the heart of the squadron, and no one begrudged them their privileges and high spirits.

Flight Lieutenant Ewan Steel banked his aircraft and looked down on the aerodrome. He made a perfect landing and taxied to the ribbon of tarmac used by 'A' Flight's aircraft. His ground crew were there as he shut the engine off, ready to help him out of the cockpit and receive his report.

'As good as usual, Tubby,' he said to the Flight Sergeant. 'Thanks to you and your crew.' His comments were always appreciative, even when he had a little niggle to report, and that attitude was appreciated by all.

Another Spitfire was coming in beside his. Ewan waited and stretched as he watched Flying Officer Hugh Douglas climb out of his cockpit and jump down off the wing.

'Good shooting today, Hughie,' commented Ewan with a congratulatory wink. 'Thanks for spotting that Messerschmitt on my tail.'

'Had to save all the girls from weeping over the loss of their favourite pilot.'

'You won't have to do it again this next week,' said Ewan as they headed for their flight hut.

'You off on leave?'

'Yessssss!' He gave Hugh a playful dig. 'Look after Susie,' he said, glancing back at his Spitfire with affection. 'I want her here when I return.'

'Sure will. Are you taking Legs to London again?'

Ewan shook his head. 'No. I figured I'd better show myself at home or else they'll be thinking I don't get any time off.'

'So Legs will be available?' Hughie grinned lasciviously.

'No, she won't. The best-looking WAAF on the station is only for the handsomest pilot – unwritten law.'

'Laws are made to be broken!'

'You know what happens to those who break them.'

338

They reached the hut and their banter stopped to be replaced by official exchanges with the rest of the Flight about the sweep they had just completed without loss.

At the evening informal meal in the Mess, Ewan sat next to Section Officer Annabelle Murdoch-Crafell who had come to Tangmere as an Intelligence Officer six months ago.

On that occasion conversation in the ante-room in the Mess had ceased, even that of five WAAF officers, when she walked in with the Station Commander. Her presence was immediately felt and every eye turned to this imposing newcomer whose shapely figure made her uniform look glamorous. Her dark hair held a natural wave and was cut short, curling into her neck. It framed a face that attracted attention; her mouth seemed to suggest kissing and her eyes were unconsciously inviting. There was about her an air of confidence coupled with a hint of sophistication. The Station Commander had introduced her to everyone and then reluctantly followed procedure by handing her over to her section commander, who immediately introduced her to the other WAAF officers. There she remained, knowing that every male eye kept drifting in her direction, not only to her face but also to her long shapely legs which had given her her nickname.

When people began to drift to the dining room, Ewan managed to slip in a whispered request to Squadron Officer Alvina Martin. 'Introduce me?'

'She'll be too hot for you to handle,' she replied, a teasing twinkle in her eyes.

'Try me.'

She did not respond and Ewan was on tenterhooks for a few moments, but as they moved nearer a table Alvina said, 'Annabelle, may I introduce you to Flight Lieutenant Ewan Steel?'

She turned a radiant smile on him. 'Very pleased to meet the officer whose reputation as the handsomest pilot in

339

Fighter Command precedes him. Along with his growing reputation as a pilot, of course.'

Ewan reddened. 'I'll try and keep it that way for you,' he replied as he pulled out a chair for her.

By the time the meal was over she had learned all about him – except that there'd been no mention of any special girl friend. He'd learned that she was an only child whose mother and father had died young early in 1939. Annabelle had inherited a small estate near Richmond in North Yorkshire but had decided to sell it and eliminate all the worry of keeping it viable. A year ago she had joined the WAAFs in order to do her bit for the war effort.

During the last six months several officers had dated Annabelle but her close friendship with Ewan became the talk of the station and everyone agreed they made a fine-looking couple. Only Hugh, who suspected that Ewan had a serious girl friend back home, judging by the number of letters he received, saw trouble ahead and warned him not to play fast and loose and hurt Annabelle.

When she and Ewan settled with their drinks in the ante-room that night, he said, 'I'm really sorry about this leave but I should show myself at home. Mother's beginning to wonder why I haven't been for a while. I can't tell her again that I can't get leave.'

'As it happens, I wouldn't have been able to have a week in London again,' replied Annabelle. 'Two girls in the section have reported sick. I couldn't leave Avril to cope on her own. We'll manage another weekend soon.'

'Sure we will,' he replied. 'Those last two visits to London are full of fond memories.' He gave her a look that left her in no doubt as to what he was referring.

'Repeat performance?' she whispered, seeing Hugh approaching.

'Without a doubt.'

Though they had found the last six months hard, Nell and Jane had gradually fitted into the routine of working with the cows and all it meant in the way of milking, cleaning the animals, mucking out, and having everything done on time. Once they settled in, rising early and coping no matter what the weather, they were pleased they had taken on this job. They knew they were lucky in finding a farmer who appreciated their efforts and was patient with their mistakes in the early days. They were more than pleased by the tolerance and kindness shown by both Mr and Mrs Symonds. They liked the freedom of being away from the hostel and, though they had little free time together because of the milking schedule, took up their own interests, exploring the surrounding countryside. Sometimes they met up with girls from the hostel, and they took part in functions in the local village too. Nor did they neglect their writing and photographic work, sending material dealing with life in the Land Army to Mr Horton who was pleased to bring that little-known side of the war effort to his readers' notice.

Jane was humming happily to herself as she propped her bicycle against the wall of the village post office on the Saturday of her weekend off. The weather was pleasantly warm and she had enjoyed the ride. She was only vaguely aware of a car slowing down and coming to a halt. And then she heard the driver call: 'Jane Harvey, fancy seeing you here!'

She spun round, her face lit with amazement. 'Ewan!'

'The one and only!' he grinned as he came towards her with arms held out.

They hugged each other and he kissed her full on the lips. Jane did not draw back then but revelled in his touch.

Realising that this greeting from a handsome RAF pilot was drawing attention, she drew back.

'How come you're here?' she asked, pleased that she had discarded her uniform for an attractive blue dress and matching cardigan, and had let her hair down.

'On leave. I went home. You remember old Sam Craven's garage in Lowestoft? Well, I persuaded him to lend me his car and put a drop of his business petrol ration in it.'

'So you could come to see Nell?'

'No, both of you,' came the quick reply accompanied by a teasing twinkle in his eye.

It was on the tip of her tongue then to say she would return to the farm and take over from Nell, so he could have some time with her, but Jane suppressed that idea and instead said, 'I'm afraid she's working, she'll only be able to see you for a few minutes. It's my weekend off. A pity you didn't let her know, we could have swapped.'

'I didn't know until the last minute that I would be on leave. It depends on how we move up the roster. Besides, I'd hoped to give Nell a surprise.'

'Like you did me?'

He smiled. 'I'll always remember that look on your face.'

'Was it as bad as that?'

'No. It was delightful. Hey, look, we can't just stand here talking. What's the food like at the Spotted Cow?' He glanced in the direction of the pub.

'It will be good plain fare, but it's cosy and the land-lord's an amiable man. He's looking after it for his son who's in the Army.'

'Suppose I go to Cedar Farm, have a word with Nell and meet you here outside the post office. When?'

'Half an hour. Go straight along this road out of the village. After a mile you'll see a gateway on the right with the name Cedar Farm on it. Follow the track and you'll come to the farm in a hollow.'

'Good. Half an hour it is. Then we'll go to the Spotted Cow and natter over something to eat.'

'That would be lovely.'

'Good.'

Jane watched him drive away and then turned thoughtfully into the post office, a sense of guilt nagging at her.

*

342

Ewan stopped the car close to the farmhouse. He surveyed it and guessed that the door most often used was that at the side of the building facing the yard. He headed straight for it but it opened before he drew any closer.

'Mrs Symonds?' he enquired tentatively.

Betty smiled warmly at the handsome RAF officer who confronted her. 'I am indeed, young man, but I don't think it's me you want to see. Nell is in the cow-shed.' She nodded in the direction of the building across the yard.

'Thanks. Will it be all right if I go in and see her?'

'Of course.'

With another word of thanks Ewan turned away. He paused when he entered the cow-shed to get his bearings and become used to the dim light after the brightness of the day. He heard a sound to his right and went in that direction. Then he heard a familiar voice.

'Come on, old girl, out of the way.' Nell appeared, pushing past a cow and giving it a gentle slap.

'Need any help?' he said quietly.

She started and looked round. 'Ewan!' she gasped, hardly able to believe her eyes. Then she rushed into his arms and hugged him. She looked up and met his kiss with equal fervour. 'What are you doing here?'

'Couldn't be on leave in Lowestoft and not come to see my girl. You are still my girl, even with the county swarming with Yanks?' he queried.

'Of course! Plenty of invitations come our way through the hostel. Jane and I went with the rest of the girls to a dance at one of the bases, but she and I weren't too struck. The Yanks were nice enough but not really our types.'

'Just as well! I wouldn't want to lose my two favourite girls to that lot.'

She smiled at the flattery. 'How long are you here for?'

'Just a flying visit to see you. I return to base tomorrow.'

Nell showed her disappointment.

'Can you get off for an hour or two?' He felt he had to

343

put the question but wondered what he would have done if she'd said yes. Jane was waiting for him.

Nell pulled a face. 'I can't, I'm on my own. Mr Symonds had a call from a neighbouring farmer three miles away. There's trouble and he needed help.'

'Ah, well, can't be helped.' Ewan felt some relief that his dilemma had been solved. 'Jane not around?'

'No, it's her day off and she's gone out, I don't know where. Next time let me know and I'll fix it with her so I'm free.'

'I will, but I don't always know until the last minute . . .'

'Do your best.'

'I will.'

She glanced round the shed. 'Ewan, I'm sorry but I'll have to get on. I've more cows to clean down.'

'OK, love.' He put his hands on her waist and drew her to him. They let the kiss linger to express their regret at having to part so soon.

Nell walked with him to the car. 'I see Sam Craven obliged?'

'Yes. I was lucky he could spare the petrol.'

'You always could charm him!'

'Good job I got him to teach me to drive when I was a lad, too, or I wouldn't be standing here now.' Ewan gave a little laugh. 'That would be strange. I wouldn't have been able to drive a car but I could fly a Spitfire.'

Her face became serious then. 'You be careful, don't do anything stupid.'

'I won't.'

'I'll tell Jane you were here. She'll be sorry she missed you.'

He kissed her again, jumped in the car and drove away.

Jane felt so proud to be walking beside this handsome man in his RAF uniform, showing everyone he was an officer who had won the DFC. She knew there were many glances cast in their direction, young female ones envious of her, older ones wishing they were younger and attractive enough to hold this young hero's attention.

'Did Nell get a surprise?' she asked.

'Just like you. She regretted having to work but was philosophical about it. She remarked you'd get a surprise when she told you I had been at the farm ...'

'So you didn't tell her you'd seen me?'

'No.'

Ewan gave no reason for that and she didn't ask for one.

They entered the low-beamed pub where highly polished brasses gleamed from regular attention.

'Good day, miss,' a bulky man behind the bar greeted Jane. His eyes were friendly, his smile one of pleasure at seeing a pretty young lady who had become a regular weekly customer.

'Good morning, Mr Garner.'

He raised his eyebrows. 'Haven't I told you before, it's Arthur?' he said in mild admonishment.

Her eyes twinkled at receiving the usual answer. 'Meet my friend, Flight Lieutenant Ewan Steel.'

'Pleased to meet you, young man.'

'And you, Mr Garner,' returned Ewan, eyes twinkling as he took up Jane's teasing.

'Arthur, please.'

'Very well! Now, Arthur, a pint of your best and whatever Jane drinks. I presume you will know what that is?'

'Indeed I do, sir.' He opened a bottle of gin and poured a measure into a glass. 'Wouldn't have got any young women in here before the war. It's made a difference to a lot of things. They're enjoying their newfound freedom and I reckon we're all better off for that.'

'I couldn't agree with you more, sir,' said Ewan. 'Are you going to be able to provide us with some food?'

'Certainly. It'll be nothing fancy but it will be good home cooking on the rations we're allowed plus what we get on the side.' He gave a knowing wink as he lowered his voice. 'I'll call my wife.'

345

Half an hour later they were tucking in to rabbit pie, potatoes, carrots and cabbage, followed by stewed apple and custard. They never stopped talking, bringing each other up to date with all that had happened and how they were coping with lives that, not so long ago, neither would have contemplated.

As Ewan paid for the meal, Arthur asked, 'Do you leave this afternoon?'

'Sometime, depends on Jane. Probably about six. I have to be back in Lowestoft tonight.' He glanced over his shoulder. 'What are we doing now?'

'I thought, as it's such a nice day we'd walk across the fields to the river. There's a nice walk by the water.'

'Leave your car where it is, it will be all right there. Call in when you come back and have some tea,' Arthur suggested.

'Thanks, we'll do that.'

While she was waiting Jane recalled their conversation and became aware that Ewan had never talked specifically of Nell after his first enquiries about her. Maybe he'd gleaned sufficient about her life from the quick visit. Or were his feelings for her cooling with his wider experiences since leaving Lowestoft?

Jane thrust all these queries aside when, as they walked across the fields, he slipped his hand in hers and she felt a tingle run through her. Another question raised itself then. Is there a chance for me?

Their conversation drifted into lengthening silence with which they were both comfortable, each in their own way haunted by thoughts of other people in their lives. But those thoughts and those people were thrust sharply from their minds when, sitting watching the river slip silently past, they felt the atmosphere between them become highly charged. Fingers entwined, eyes met, and both knew where this situation would have led had they had privacy. Instead their faces drew close until their lips gently met before the kiss deepened into a passionate one.

346

'Ewan!' gasped Jane as their lips finally parted. Her eyes were fixed on his but she could not read them.

She heard him say, 'Maybe we shouldn't have . . .'

'Why not?' she protested.

'There's you and Simon, me and Nell. I think we should treat these as wartime kisses, people drawn to moments of intimacy because of the circumstances.'

'But I . . .'

He stopped her. 'Don't say any more. Don't commit us. Don't cause any regrets or spoil the moments we have shared today. They could be precious in times ahead. Who knows where this war is going to take us?'

She nodded and gave a little smile. 'You always struck me as one who didn't care, who'd take life as it comes and the devil take care of himself. This war has changed you Ewan, given you a different view on things.'

'Maybe, but I think I still have something of my old self.'

'I am sure you have, and long may it last. I am attracted to both sides of you.'

'Hush, let's leave things as they are. Maybe the war will sort things out for us.'

She kissed him. 'You are a dear man. May God go with you and keep you safe. Remember me?'

'How could I forget?' And he kissed her again.

The time she had spent with Ewan was vivid in her mind as Jane cycled back to Cedar Farm. Should she tell Nell they had met? But that would throw her in a bad light; she could have taken Ewan back to the farm then and taken over from Nell. Who would know they had been together? She felt sure Ewan would not mention it. Mr and Mrs Garner might let it slip, but that was a risk worth taking. She decided to say nothing but had not calculated on what would come out when she and Nell attended a concert at the hostel the following evening.

They arrived ten minutes early and went to have a word

with Kate, Madge and Gloria while waiting to be seated.

Greetings were exchanged and then Madge spoke up with a touch of excitement in her voice. 'You were doing well for yourself yesterday, Jane.'

Her mind spun but all she could say was, 'What do you mean?'

'That handsome RAF officer with a DFC ribbon I saw you with in the village. You were coming out of the Spotted Cow about half-past two looking very pleased with yourself and with eyes only for him.'

Jane sensed shock waves from Nell whose gaze became cold with hostility as it fixed on her. 'Ewan?' she demanded. Jane was at a loss for what to say. 'Was it?' Nell pressed furiously.

Madge looked bewildered. What had she innocently unleashed?

'Yes,' replied Jane lamely.

'You saw him in the village? And you didn't say? You bitch!' Nell turned away and stormed from the building just as Miss Hardcastle called everyone to take their seats.

'What's the matter with Nell?' she asked.

'She remembered something she'd forgotten to do after we finished milking.'

'How conscientious.'

As much as Jane wanted to rush after Nell, there was nothing she could do as Miss Hardcastle said, 'Come and sit next to me, Jane, I would like a word sometime about Cedar Farm. I would have liked Nell to hear it too ...'

'I'll pass any message on, Miss Hardcastle.'

As she brushed by Gloria on her way to her seat, the other girl whispered, 'I told you to sort it out or there'd be trouble.'

And trouble faced Jane when she got back to Cedar Farm.

She went straight to Nell's room, knocked and walked in, saying, 'Don't say a word until you hear me out.'

'You ...' There was fury in that one word but Jane cut it short.

348

'Yes, I did run into Ewan in the village. We had lunch together. After all, the man was hungry and I couldn't let him eat alone. If we had known he was coming, I would have swapped my time off with you. Now, if you are having a go at anybody, have a go at Ewan. But bear in mind, he talked about you all the time,' she lied.

'If it was that innocent, why did Madge think otherwise?'

'You know what she's like – a gossip who'll make two and two into five every time. Look, Nell, I'll apply for a transfer if you want me to, but I don't want a man to come between us. We've got on well so far, we should stick together. We're OK here. Besides, I think the Symonds would be hurt if one of us left.'

Nell looked thoughtful for a moment then said, 'OK, I'll work with you, but that doesn't mean I trust you. How can I after this deceit and your reluctance to confide in me about your past?'

Jane's eyes turned cold as she said, 'My past is my business. That's all you ever need to know.'

Chapter Twenty

'John, I'm worried about those two girls,' Betty Symonds said, watching Nell and Jane from the kitchen window as they crossed the yard to the cow-shed.

'Why? What's wrong?' he said, rising from the table and bringing his cup of tea over as he stood beside her.

'Don't know,' she replied, giving a little shake of her head. 'They aren't as light-hearted with each other as they were when they first came to us seven months ago.'

'They're all right in the cow-shed,' he said.

'You're all concentrating on your work then. Besides, you wouldn't notice if it hit you in the face.'

'You're imagining it,' he replied with a dismissive shrug of his shoulders, swilling his cup under the tap. 'You read too many books.'

She took no notice of his observation but said with a worried frown, 'It all started a month ago when that RAF officer came to see Nell. I wonder if there's a bit of jealousy? Maybe I'll have a word . . .'

'Hold you hard! You'll do nothing of the kind! That could easily upset them if you're right, and maybe even if you aren't. They're hard workers and good with the herd, I don't want to lose either of them. They're old enough to sort their own problems out, if indeed they have any.' He started for the door but stopped as he lifted the sneck and looked back at her. Betty was still staring thoughtfully out of the window, though the girls had disappeared into the cow-shed. 'Heed what I say, Betty.'

She watched him cross the yard, knowing that she would not go against his wishes in spite of her desire to be of help in a relationship that she could see was under strain. She hoped that whatever had come between the two girls would soon be sorted out.

In fact there was little improvement as 1942 moved towards its end, though outwardly they were putting on an amiable front for her and John. Betty knew that when the girls were free at the same time they spent it with the other girls at the hostel instead of alone together, as they used to do. She attempted to close the distance between them by trying to make Christmas that little bit special. They appreciated what she did and relaxed in the festive atmosphere, but came no closer than politeness with each other. The fact that both of them received Christmas greetings from Ewan, Simon and Glen did nothing to ease the tension.

They watched the unfolding of the war, depressed by setbacks, heartened by victories, and all the time there was the underlying anxiety that personal tragedy could hit them as it had once before.

'You ready, Sarah?' called Liz Steel, opening the front door of the Evans' house.

'A few minutes, Liz,' she answered. 'Come in.'

When Liz went into the kitchen she found Sarah still tidying after her midday meal.

'Not a bad day for March,' Liz commented, 'but it could rain before we come home so I'd advise a mac.'

'Heard from Ewan?' Sarah asked her.

Liz gave a little laugh. 'Ewan, write? I don't think he knows what a pen is for, at least not so far as we're concerned. But I don't chide him for it, he's got a lot on his plate. And Percy? Well, it's the same for you with Jake, Neil and Simon, isn't it? It's a matter of when they get to

351

port. I suppose the three drifters are still somewhere in the Channel?'

'Expect so,' replied Sarah. She put the last plate away, looked around the kitchen and, satisfied, said, 'That's that. Now for my coat, then off to Flo's.' She went into the hall and returned a moment later, shrugging herself into her waterproof coat, having taken Liz's advice. She'd fastened it and was just picking up her handbag when there was a knock at the front door.

'Who can this be?' she muttered. 'Just when we're ready for off.'

A few moments later, when she came back into the kitchen, her face was ashen and her look of disbelief alarmed Liz. As Sarah sank on to a chair, she held out a sheet of paper. Liz took it and Sarah's arm fell limply to her side. Liz silently read the chilling words that informed Sarah her son Simon had lost his life when his ship the *Sea Queen* had been sunk by enemy action.

'Oh, my God!' The words came out in a whisper from Liz. 'Sarah!' She sank on to her knees beside her friend and took her hands in hers, desperate to give comfort though she knew she could not.

Sarah stared at her unseeingly. She should be crying but she couldn't; the shock had dried her tears.

The two friends fell silent then Sarah looked up and saw the sympathy and concern in Liz's eyes. 'I wonder if anyone survived?' she whispered.

'Lowestoft men,' muttered Liz.

'Their families ...'

'Flo!' gasped Liz. 'She's lost George, now the *Sea Queen* ... We'd best go to her. She may not know.' She looked at her friend in concern. 'You up to it, or would you rather I went alone?'

'No, don't leave me. I'll come.'

A few minutes later when they walked into Flo Franklin's unheralded, she said, 'I was wondering what had happened to you two. I ...' The words faded away when she saw their serious expressions and sensed something was wrong. She looked at them askance. Liz held out the telegram. Flo took it and one quick glance told her the worst.

'Oh, Sarah!' She hugged her friend.

'And you've lost the *Sea Queen*,' said her friend miserably.

'What's a ship compared to Simon and the others?' said Flo. 'Oh, if only I hadn't offered him the *Sea Queen* he might not have ...' Her words faltered to a halt when Sarah, drawing new strength from realising that Flo might blame herself for what had happened, broke in.

'You can't think like that! Don't ever consider it. You cannot take the blame, it could have happened whatever ship he had been on.'

Flo gave her a wan smile of thanks and hugged her again.

'I wonder if we can find out any more?' said Liz.

'The crew were all from Lowestoft so there could be other telegrams,' said Flo, 'and maybe the harbour or Naval authorities in the town will know.'

Within the hour they had gained the information. The *Sea Queen* had been torpedoed by a U-boat which was thought to have been returning from Atlantic patrol. There had been only two survivors who had been blown clear in the explosion and survived two hours, clinging to debris, before being picked up and taken to Falmouth.

'Names?' pressed Flo.

The official consulted his notes. 'Terry Winspear and Glen Aveburn.'

'I must go and see Nell and Jane,' said Flo. 'Will you be all right, Sarah?'

'I'll stay with her,' said Liz. 'Will you be able to get to Rendham now?'

'I think so if I get off right away.'

'Good grief!' At the sight of her mother Nell gasped and stopped still in her tracks as she came out of the cow-shed.

Jane, close behind, almost collided with her. 'What the

353

...?' Her words died away when she saw Flo.

'Must be something wrong,' said Nell. 'Or why come at this time?' She started to run towards her mother, splashing through the puddles left by an early-afternoon shower. 'Mum!' she called.

'Thank goodness I've found you,' said Flo, embracing her daughter. As she eased away she still clutched Nell's hand and held out her other to Jane.

'Mum, what is it?' asked Nell gently.

'I've terrible news.' She bit her lip and gave an irritated shake of her head. 'I didn't mean it to come out like that.' Her eyes started to fill with tears as she looked helplessly from one to the other of them. 'It's the *Sea Queen*.' Her voice faltered.

'What's happened?' said Nell.

'Sunk.'

'Oh, no!' both girls cried at once.

'Mrs Evans had a telegram saying Simon had been killed.'

'Oh, my God!' Nell's moan was drawn out.

'Simon!' Jane cried.

'I'm afraid it's true.' Flo's grip tightened on Jane's hand. 'Only two survivors, Terry and Glen.'

Nell felt a measure of relief surge through her at this mention of Glen even though she was torn apart by the loss of her life-long friend. Jane noticed the minute change in Nell's expression, something she would have missed if she had not been looking at her at that precise moment. Her own heart cried out. Simon ... he had loved her. Why hadn't she responded in the same way? At this moment, how she wished she had.

'Are they in Lowestoft?' Nell's query focused all their minds on the present.

'No. We made enquiries but the authorities could tell us no more than I've told you. I came to tell you straight away. Liz is with Sarah.'

'You'd better come in and meet Mrs Symonds.' They started for the farmhouse. 'How are you going to get back,

Mum?' Nell asked her.

Flo gave a grunt. 'I never thought of that. I just wanted to get here to you.'

As they entered the scullery Nell shouted, 'Aunty Betty!'

A few moments later Mrs Symonds came bustling into the scullery where Nell and Jane were discarding their Wellingtons. Introductions were quickly made and Mrs Symonds was soon in possession of the facts behind Flo's presence. She immediately offered her sympathy and bustled them into the kitchen where, with the kettle already boiling on the reckon, she had a pot of tea made in no time. She had just got it poured out when her husband came in from repairing a gate in one of the fields. He learned of the reason for Flo's visit and immediately said he would manage if the girls wanted time off. 'I can always request someone else from the hostel on a temporary basis.' But Nell and Jane would not hear of it. 'There is nothing we can do if we go to Lowestoft, Mr Symonds. Besides, Daisy and the rest are used to us now, no point in upsetting them. The milk yield might suffer.'

Flo raised an eyebrow. 'Never thought my daughter would become so considerate for cows.'

'There's something else we should consider,' put in Betty. 'How are you going to get back to Lowestoft this evening?' She went on to answer her own question. 'Difficult, if not impossible. So, Mrs Franklin, you had better stay here tonight.'

'I couldn't put you to that trouble. I'll see if they have a room at the pub in the village.'

'You'll do no such thing! It will be no trouble. My sons' rooms are always made up in case they turn up unexpectedly.'

'But, Mrs Symonds . . .'

'No buts. And it's Betty and John, please.'

'Many thanks. I'm so grateful to you.'

'Mum's Flo,' said Nell with a small smile.

'Of course,' she said.

'Then it's settled.'

355

'I'm going up to get changed,' said Jane, making for the stairs.

'So am I,' said Nell. 'Won't be long, Mum.'

'All right, love.'

'I'll just put these potatoes on and then I'll show you your room, Flo,' offered Betty.

Jane was just closing her door when Nell reached the top of the stairs. She hesitated a moment and then went after her. Again she hesitated thoughtfully but then, thinking this might be the time to offer an olive branch and heal the rift between them, she knocked. She heard a quiet, 'Come in,' and tentatively opened the door.

'Jane?'

'Yes.'

Nell stepped into the room and saw Jane sitting on the edge of the bed, her face pale and tears in her eyes.

'Oh, Nell, what a stupid war this is. Why did it have to be Simon?'

She sat on the bed and took Jane's hand in hers. 'We can never answer that. Why did it have to be my father? How often have I asked myself that and found no answer. All we can do is accept it as we have to and carry on with what we are doing, remembering that is what they would want us to do.'

'I've lost a very dear friend and a relationship that might . . .' The words choked in Jane's throat.

'Why didn't you let it?' asked Nell, guessing what Jane had been going to say. 'Was that because of something in your past?'

She stiffened, turned her head and glared at Nell. 'Fishing again!' she snapped. 'I've told you before, it has nothing to do with you.'

'I only thought it might help to talk about it . . .'

'Well, it won't. And it won't bring Simon back either!'

Nell jumped to her feet, glared at Jane and headed for the door, calling over her shoulder as she did so, 'Don't you think I'm shattered by what has happened to him too?'

*

356

When she saw her room, Flo could do no other than thank Betty again profusely, saying how pleasant it was and adding how lucky Nell and Jane were to have been directed to work at Cedar Farm. 'Thank you for being a mum to them, Betty,' she concluded.

'They're so charming and helpful,' the other woman returned. 'It is nice for John and me to have them now our sons are in the Navy.' It was on the tip of her tongue then to air her slight concern about the relationship between the two girls, but recalling John's words, she held her tongue.

In Lowestoft Liz Steel, after seeing that Sarah was settled, put in a phone call to the RAF station at Tangmere. When she said that she was Flight Lieutenant Steel's mother, wanting an important word with him, she was put straight through to the Officers' Mess. The Mess Steward could not locate Ewan but said that he would leave a note for him on the notice board.

He got the message when he went in for tea and knew there must be something wrong as he had given his mother this number only in case of emergency. He instantly rang her and, on hearing the news, immediately thought of Nell. She must be devastated; the close friendship the three of them had shared since schooldays had been broken. He should go to her. First he must find the Adjutant and the C.O. He hurried into the ante-room where tea was always served on a help-yourself basis and was relieved to see the two men he wanted sitting together in a corner. Ewan informed them of the situation and, having gained the C.O.'s permission to be absent from the station for forty-eight hours, the Adjutant said he would be in his office in five minutes to authorise the pass.

As Ewan left the Mess, he met Legs coming in for tea.

'I'm away home on a forty-eight hour,' he informed her, and went on to explain the circumstances without mentioning Nell.

Legs expressed her regret at the loss of his close friend

357

and added, 'Have a safe journey. I'll miss you.' She planted a quick kiss on Ewan's cheek.

Within twenty minutes he was leaving the Adjutant's office for the M.T. Section where his charm worked wonders as usual. Ten minutes later he was in a car driven by a WAAF who took him to the station, cheerfully waiting there an extra hour for the pilot she had to pick up later. Anything to oblige Flight Lieutenant Steel.

'Ewan!' His mother swung round from the small suitcase she was packing when he walked in.

'Ma.' He hugged her. 'I came as soon as I could.'

'I'm glad. I thought maybe you wouldn't be able to. After all, Simon was no relation.'

'We have a very understanding C.O. I got a forty-eight. How's Mrs Evans?'

'Shattered, but taking it bravely. She's on her own. With Mr Evans and Neil at sea and Marcia evacuated, I'm going to stay with her tonight. But now you're here . . .'

'You go, don't worry about me. I'll be all right. I'll come with you to see Mrs Evans, and tomorrow I'll go and see Nell. Does she know?'

'Yes. We all thought she and Jane should know as soon as possible so Mrs Franklin went to break the news. How will you get to Rendham tomorrow?'

'Use my persuasive powers on Sam Craven again.'

Liz gave a little laugh. 'He won't be able to resist those wings! Whenever I see him he asks after you, and he always mentions your flying.'

As Ewan journeyed to Cedar Farm early the next morning, he was thankful that he would not be the first to break the news to Nell and Jane.

When he turned into Cedar Farm he saw a small group gathered by the front door. It appeared that Flo Franklin was saying goodbye to Nell, Jane and Mr and Mrs Symonds.

Nell immediately recognised the car. 'Ewan!' she exclaimed without disguising the joy she felt. He must have learned the terrible news and thought of her. She started running towards him.

Jane held back, filled with a jealousy she found difficult to subdue. Nell had Ewan; she had lost Simon.

Ewan hugged Nell, expressing his sorrow at the loss of their friend. Then, as they turned to the watching group, he called out, 'I can give you a ride back to Lowestoft, Mrs F.'

'That'll save me a tedious journey. Thanks.'

Mrs Symonds immediately took charge of the changed situation. 'We'll all eat at half-past twelve.'

'But I can't impose on you,' protested Ewan.

'Nor I,' added Flo. 'You've done enough for me already.'

'Nonsense!' said Betty, with an authority that indicated she would not brook further protests. 'I can stretch what we were going to have.' She bustled back into the house.

'You girls had just about finished in the shed. I'll see to the rest,' said Mr Symonds. 'You both make the most of your visitors while you have them here.'

'Thanks,' called Nell as he turned away.

'You young ones won't want me tagging along. I'll see if I can give Mrs Symonds a hand,' said Flo, unwittingly leaving the three of them in an uneasy situation.

'Let's walk,' Ewan suggested. 'I'd offer to take you for a ride but I don't want to use more of Sam's petrol than I need.' He took hold of Nell's hand and they started off. Jane hesitated. 'You coming?' he called over his shoulder.

'You don't want me along.' Before she could receive an answer she was into the house. Her emotions choking her, Jane ran straight upstairs to her bedroom, flung herself down on the bed and cried. She felt wretched. She had no one. She was alone in a world that offered nothing. Only heartache lay ahead for her.

The minutes ticked away. How long? She never really

knew but she became aware that the sobs were less frequent now, and as they subsided further she slowly calmed down. Finally she rolled over on to her back and stared at the ceiling, her mind a blank. Eventually she went to the mirror on her dressing table and stared at herself. Her eyes were red and puffed but that would disappear when she had a wash. She met her own gaze and admonished herself.

You cried. Why? For Simon? He doesn't need your tears. Do we weep *for* the dead or are we weeping for ourselves, because of the hurt we're feeling? If so it is selfish. The past is the past. It is gone and we cannot change it. We cannot go back as if recent events never happened. There is a future ahead of us. I must face mine without bemoaning what has happened to me.

'When this is all over and we get back to Lowestoft, life is never going to be the same,' Ewan pointed out as he and Nell walked the lane away from Cedar Farm.

'You mean, there'll be no Simon?' His name caught in her throat.

'That, and the world will have changed. *We* will have changed. I won't go back to being a fisherman. I burned my boats.' He gave a little grin at the pun.

'I've known for a long time you wanted to escape that life, and as you pointed out, the war and the RAF gave you your chance. But what will you do instead?'

He shrugged his shoulders. 'I don't know. Wait and see what turns up. Maybe stay in the RAF, or go into civil flying, or . . . oh, I don't know. I won't mind as long as I have you.'

Nell stopped walking. 'You'll always have me,' she said huskily, and slid her arms up round his neck to kiss him with a passion that sealed her love for him. When their lips finally parted she added, 'Ewan, you take care. I want you back safe and sound with me.'

When Ewan arrived at Tangmere it was early evening and

he went straight to the ante-room in the Mess where he knew he would find Hugh. As his friend bustled him through to the bar, Ewan asked what had been happening while he had been away.

'Couple of sweeps. One escorting Yank bombers, on a daylight raid in northern France, and the other strafing any transport targets in the Low Countries. "B" Flight lost one on escort duty; we came through unscathed.'

'Good,' replied Ewan, and accepted a whisky from his friend.

'What about you? Sorry I didn't see you before you left. Legs told me what had happened before I heard from anyone else. You lost a very close friend, I understand?'

'Yes. Known him since before school. His minesweeper got torpedoed.'

'Any survivors?'

'Two.'

Hugh pulled a face. 'Grim. See your girl friend while you were there?' He dropped the question in so casually that Ewan responded automatically.

'Yes.' As soon as he replied, he realised there was now no point in disguising the fact that Nell was part of his life.

'Figured there was someone.'

Ewan shrugged his shoulders and went on to tell him about Nell, the threesome that became a foursome, and how the war had affected all their lives.

'So Nell's THE one? What about Jane? I detect in the way you brought her into your story that there was, and maybe still is, something special between you?' Hugh saw that Ewan was reluctant to go into that so went on quickly, 'And now there's Legs as well. Oh, my, Ewan Steel, you are making life complicated for yourself! If you want any advice, I'd say sort it out quickly or somebody's going to get badly hurt.'

Chapter Twenty-one

Life at Cedar Farm settled down but though the loss of Simon restored something of the closeness between Nell and Jane, suspicion and jealousy still lurked beneath the surface.

'A letter for you, Nell,' Betty called from the kitchen when she heard the girls come into the scullery three weeks after Ewan's visit.

'Can't be from him again,' she commented, 'I heard from him only yesterday.'

Jane said nothing, but wished she had someone to write to her.

Collecting the envelope, Nell slit it open and pulled out the folded letter. 'It's from Glen,' she said, glancing at the signature first and then reading it quickly.

'Where is he?' Jane asked. It had been on their minds ever since they had heard of the loss of the *Sea Queen*. They knew Glen had survived, but beyond that there had been silence.

'Apparently he was taken to hospital in Portsmouth, seriously wounded and suffering from exposure. As next-of-kin his mother and father were told.'

'They could have let us know,' commented Jane.

'No reason why they should.'

'They knew we worked with him.'

'True, but that was before the war. I suppose they knew

'no more than that and so had no reason to contact us.'

'I expect you are right. What else does he say?'

'He is being released on April the fifth.'

'Tomorrow.'

'He says he will be going home and will contact me from there.' Nell added quickly when she saw Jane pout, 'He asks about you and adds that he looks forward to seeing both of us. Oh, there's a P.S. He has persuaded the authorities to allow him to join the crew of the *Silver King* when it returns to Lowestoft later in the month.'

'So he could be around for a week or two. Nice for you,' said Jane, her mind fogged by jealousy.

Nell ignored the barb but fuelled Jane's attitude when she said, 'I'm due for my week's leave. I'll see if it's OK with Mr Symonds to have it while Glen's at home ...' She had seen Mr Symonds crossing the yard towards the house and went to the door to meet him and make her wishes known. She did not want Jane spiking her intentions.

Jane heard her make the request. With Mr Symonds' agreeable response ringing in her mind, she fled upstairs before they both reached the kitchen. Tight-lipped, she stormed into her bedroom, slamming the door behind her.

A few moments later the door opened, Nell poked her head round, announced that Mr Symonds had agreed and immediately withdrew.

'Why should *you* have two strings to your bow?' Jane flung after her, but Nell did not hear.

In the next fortnight Jane knew that Nell received two letters from Glen but was never made privy to their contents.

Nell did not disguise her pleasure at the thought of seeing him again as she left Cedar Farm early on Monday morning. She cycled vigorously to the nearest station, impatient for the train to speed her on her way to Lowestoft. Arriving there, she lost no time in reaching home where her mother, expecting her arrival, had the kettle on the boil.

'I hope my arrangements were all right, Mum?' she asked as she savoured the cup of tea. 'Glen coming on Wednesday and staying until he sails on Saturday?'

'Of course, love. I've made a bed up for him. I was a little surprised he didn't want to spend all his time with his mother and father, though.'

'He'll have had ten days with them before he comes here, and we will go to see them the day before he sails.'

Mrs Franklin nodded but made no comment. She was pleased to have her daughter home, and pleased that she was still in touch with Glen who had been influential in focusing Nell's mind on a career. That would be more important now that the *Sea Queen* had gone. But she did wonder how deep the relationship was and if Nell's feelings for Ewan had cooled? She hoped her daughter had taken everything into consideration and would do nothing stupid. Whenever such thoughts came to her, however, Flo thrust them from her mind – Nell was a sensible girl and her mother trusted her.

During the rest of that day and all day Tuesday Nell had a wonderfully relaxing time with her mother. Visiting Liz Steel, she learned that Ewan had been awarded a bar to his DFC and was now regarded as one of the foremost pilots in his squadron.

'I'm surprised he didn't write you about it, Nell,' Liz concluded.

'He may well have done but he'd send the letter to the farm so it will probably be awaiting me there.'

Nell knew what time Glen would be arriving and was at the station to meet him. As she waited on the platform, wondering how he would look after his ordeal, her mind turned back to days they had spent together: moments in the darkroom, his love for her, and his continued understanding and respect. The sound of the train approaching drove these idle thoughts from her mind and replaced them with a touch of anxiety over meeting him again.

The train stopped, carriage doors swung open, passengers

364

alighted and headed towards the exit. She strained to catch a glimpse of Glen. There he was, striding towards her! Her heart fluttered. He looked smart in his uniform, a duffel bag slung over his left shoulder. He saw her, quickened his step, and his ready smile expressed joy at seeing her, but Nell saw also that it hid the pale drawn face she had first glimpsed.

They came close. Glen stopped, dropped his bag and held out his arms. She stepped into them and felt them close around her. 'It's so good to see you, Nell.'

She looked up and met his kiss with her own. 'And you, Glen,' she whispered. Her heart was pounding for she could see in his eyes that the love he had once expressed for her was still there. 'How are you?'

He picked up his bag and linked arms with her. She did not draw away, realising that it would be cruel to do so to a dear friend who had nearly lost his life for his country.

'I'm fine,' he replied. 'Fit to go to sea again.'

'Still the *Silver King*?'

'Yes. She should be in tomorrow, quick refit and off again on Saturday.'

'Where to?'

'Don't know until we sail, and if I did I couldn't tell you.'

They left the station and he was soon being greeted warmly by Mrs Franklin.

'I was sorry about the *Sea Queen*,' he said to her.

Flo nodded with a wan smile. 'The loss of life was worse. Simon's mother has coped very well. I think she would like a word with you, if you are up to talking about it? It would stop her wondering.'

'Yes, sure, but there's not much to tell. It all happened so quickly. We were sailing along peacefully, doing our job, when suddenly there was mayhem. Almost certainly a torpedo. The *Sea Queen* went down fast. Terry and I were the only two on the opposite side from where the torpedo struck and so were flung clear. The rest of the crew had no chance.'

Flo nodded. 'That will be sufficient for Sarah, I'm sure.

I think we'll go and get it over with as soon as you've had that cup of tea. Then no more about it, the subject is banned.'

Nell suggested they should go to the pictures that evening. They took the long way home, neither objecting when they realised where their footsteps were automatically taking them. They found a seat, and when they sat down Glen's arm slid round her shoulders. Nell snuggled closer. They shared a silence which drew them into the same world. Finally he turned to her and drew one finger gently down her cheek.

'I still love you, Nell Franklin,' he whispered. His lips met hers then before she could answer. She felt a tremor run through her and held his kiss until it began to intensify.

The way she broke it off made him say, 'Is it still Ewan?' Nell hesitated. 'Does that hesitation mean you aren't sure?'

She gave a slight shake of her head. 'No, but I don't want you to be hurt. You are very special to me.' She kissed him lightly. 'Glen, we don't know what will happen or where this war will lead us. Let's enjoy our time together, without any real commitments.'

'As you wish.' He gave a little smile and said, 'Like the *Sea Queen*, the subject is banned. For now.'

'I hope Nell is enjoying her leave,' commented Betty as she, John and Jane settled down to their Friday evening meal.

'I'm sure Glen will see to that.' Jane went on to explain how she and Nell had met him, and how it had led them to work together.

'Wouldn't you have liked to see him too?' said John, looking up from his plate of stew.

Jane gave a little smile. 'Yes, I would, considering what he has been through, but Nell got in her request for leave first.'

Betty saw her husband look thoughtful and sensed he was

366

conjuring up something in his mind.

'I tell you what, get off early in the morning, catch the milk train, and maybe you'll be in Lowestoft before he sails.'

Jane stared at him in astonishment. 'But what about the milking, Mr Symonds?'

'I'll manage for once. Well, Mrs Symonds will give me a hand.'

Betty beamed. 'Of course I will. You must see your friend.'

Jane could not resist. She jumped up from her chair and kissed Mr and Mrs Symonds, who both displayed embarrassment and pleasure.

Though the milk train was slow because of stopping at each station, Jane curbed her impatience, knowing it provided the earliest means of reaching Lowestoft. All she hoped was that she would be soon enough. She ran from the station and Flo looked up in astonishment when she burst into the house.

'Jane!'

'Has he gone?' she gasped.

Flo glanced at the clock. 'Sails in half an hour.'

'Thanks.' With that Jane was off again.

Nearing the dock, she slowed her pace and stopped when she saw Nell and Glen standing on the quay beside the *Silver King*. They were locked in an embrace. Jane's lips tightened. This was no ordinary goodbye embrace. They were very close and looking at each other in a special way, a lover's way. Or at least that was how Jane saw it. She walked slowly forward, eyes riveted on them. She saw urgency and commitment in their conversation and then she saw the kiss that was exchanged become prolonged. Jealousy reared in her. Ewan *and* Glen! How many men did Nell want? She quickened her steps, the sound reverberating on the quay. Nell and Glen both looked in her direction.

367

Nell's eyes widened in irritation and surprise. 'Jane, how come you're here?'

She ignored that and said instead to an astonished Glen, 'Hello. Glad to see you. How are you?'

'I'm well and it's marvellous to see you too. How did you manage it?'

Jane included Nell in her answer as well. 'Mr Symonds suggested that I come early in the hope of seeing you before you sail.'

'That was kind of him.'

'Who's doing the milking?' asked Nell testily.

'Mr Symonds said he would see to it, with Aunty Betty's help.'

Nell merely nodded. She turned back to Glen. 'Take care. Look after yourself.'

'Thanks, Nell. I have lots of memories to take back with me. Keep the camera clicking whenever you can.' He spoke to Jane then. 'And you continue writing. We rang Mr Horton and he wants you to keep sending pieces about the Land Army. When he heard what had happened to me, he asked for a piece about my experiences. As you know, I'm no writer but I have jotted some aspects down for you. I left them with Nell. Maybe you can fill them out by having a word with Terry? He was in a bad way but I think he'll be home in the next two weeks and won't be allowed back to sea.'

'That bad?' asked Jane.

'I'm afraid so.'

'I'll contact him and arrange to see him.'

'Good. Keep in touch with Horton. I must get on board,' Glen added, observing that the activity there had intensified. ''Bye, Jane.' He kissed her on the cheek, looking at Nell then with longing in his eyes. 'Take care of yourself. Think of me.'

'Of course I will.' She kissed him and, knowing Jane was watching, let it linger.

Glen tore himself away and ran up the gangway to the

Silver King. A charged silence fell between the two girls as they watched the boat sail.

'What I saw there was more than just a friendly goodbye,' commented Jane sarcastically as they walked away from the quay. 'I wonder what Ewan would think if he knew about it? "I'm glad you were able to stay,"' she added, mimicking Nell. 'What would he say to *that*?'

'Don't you dare tell him!' snapped Nell.

'I wonder ...' Jane put a world of meaning into her answer. She met Nell's glare then and added, 'How many do you want? You profess to love Ewan, you're alarmed in case I tell him, and now you've got Glen too. That goodbye kiss made me wonder whether he's really in your heart or if you're just playing it safe, in case something happens to either of them. Or maybe you think I may take one of them? There's no reason why you should have two men. Which shall I go for? Ewan ... Glen? Which shall it be?'

Nell's lips tightened at this taunting.

Jane gave a little nod. 'Yes, I think I'll have Ewan.'

Nell's eyes narrowed. 'He's mine!'

'I wonder who he'd actually choose if I played rivals?'

'You know you wouldn't stand a chance. Don't you realise, you'd blow it like you did with Simon? Something hangs over you that you will not ... or is it, dare not? ... reveal. Until you get rid of that, you'll have no future with anyone.' Having pronounced her opinion, and not wanting Jane to have a chance to confound her, Nell said quickly, 'Are you going back today?' And then answered her own question. 'I expect so, you have milking to see to. You can't leave it all to Mr and Mrs Symonds. Well, I won't be back until Monday.'

Jane knew this was her dismissal. 'I'll go to the station now then. Tell your mother I'm sorry not to have seen more of her. I'll visit her when I come to interview Terry. And don't forget to bring Glen's notes back. Or are you going to hold them over me as payment for my silence?'

'Now that's an idea worth considering.'

369

'Well, when you stop considering it, turn your mind to which man you really want. Choose Glen. I'll have Ewan.'

Jane turned away then into a street leading to the station, leaving Nell to wonder if she'd really meant that.

Section Officer Annabelle Murdoch-Crafell heard the sound of returning Spitfires from her office. She looked up from the maps of northern France that she had been studying, laid down her pencil, picked up her uniform cap and went outside. There was anxiety in her heart and fear in her mind; there always was from the moment she knew Ewan was taking off until she recognised his returning Spitfire, on which he had had a special sign painted so she could instantly recognise it from the rest.

The cloud had lowered since the squadron had taken off for a morning sweep over the near Continent, but the deterioration in the weather did not present a problem for the returning pilots. The first two Spitfires broke cloud. Annabelle searched them. No painted sign. She shivered and her lips silently said, Please bring him back safely. She thanked the war, a funny thing to thank, for bringing her a love that sang in her heart every moment of every day. If it hadn't been for this war she would never have joined the WAAF and then she would never have met Ewan Steel, the man who had stolen her heart.

Two more Spitfires. One of them banked to get into position for landing. Her heartbeat skipped with joy and the dread that had dwelt in her mind was driven away. He was back! Safe! She went into the hut and resumed her work, knowing that she would see him at lunch in the Mess, and then with their forty-eight-hour passes they would be off to London to the small secluded hotel they had come to regard as their own.

With his Spitfire parked, Ewan closed the engine, pulled his helmet from his head and ran his hand through his hair. He did not move but sat staring, seeing nothing, his mind still whirling through the fight he had had with two

Messerschmitts. He had nearly been surprised by them when the flight he was leading had been split by a force of German fighters, while they were shooting up a supply train. He shuddered and that reaction focused his mind on the present. Thank goodness he had arranged a forty-eight and could forget the war in Annabelle's arms. He climbed out of his plane to his waiting ground crew and presented his usual buoyant exterior to them. As he turned away from them he saw Hugh waiting for him.

They went to the flight hut, put their flying gear into their lockers and were halfway to the Mess before either of them spoke. Hugh finally broke the silence. 'I reckon you ought to be stood down for a rest.'

'What?' Ewan stopped and with some hostility in his eyes stared at Hugh.

'You heard.' His friend's expression became deadly serious as he went on, 'You've done a hell of a lot of flying without a long break. You've constantly engaged the enemy in some way or another, you're living under a terrible strain – as we all are – but you bring more to it than others because you feel responsible for the new pilots. You were looking out for young James Griffin today and nearly got yourself jumped.'

'I've been jumped before.'

'But not as easily as today and your reaction to it wasn't as sharp as it once was.'

'Just your imagination.' Ewan dismissed this as he started towards the Mess again.

'It's not and you know it. You need a prolonged stand-down.'

'My forty-eights with Legs are good enough.'

'Well ... if you say so.'

'I do say so. Now let's drop the subject.' Ewan lapsed into a charged silence that Hugh knew he did not want broken.

As he followed his friend into the Mess, Hugh gave a regretful shake of his head. He hoped he was wrong but he suspected Ewan was beginning to live on his nerves, and that was not good. Maybe his coming brief leave would steady him.

Ewan lay on his back with Annabelle cradled in his arms, her head on his shoulder, and sighed. 'Contentment,' he whispered, savouring the moments that had just passed.

'If that's what it takes, I'm here for you whenever you like.' She twisted round and propped herself on one elbow so she could look down on him. Gently, she ran her finger across the furrows on his brow. 'I'm here to wipe those away,' she whispered, and slowly, teasingly, brought her lips to his. They remained there, letting passion build again and reassert itself.

Later as they dressed she recalled an observation Hugh had made to her just before she and Ewan left for London. 'Ewan, have you ever thought that you have been with the squadron long enough to apply for a posting to a . . .'

'Don't!' The word came out like a whiplash. This unexpected vehemence made her start and look at him with alarm.

'I'm only thinking of you.'

'Think of me by all means but not in that way,' he said, easing his voice into a gentler tone, realising his reaction had startled her. He came to her and spanned her waist with his hands. 'Sorry I snapped.'

'I forgive you, and I won't mention it again,' she said, sealing the promise with a kiss. As he turned away she caught hold of his hand and met the query in his eyes with longing. 'Don't let's go out this evening. There are much better things to do.'

'Hello, Annabelle.'

She looked up from her desk the day after they had returned from London and saw Hugh coming in tentatively, as if hoping to catch her on her own. 'Hello, Hugh. I'm holding the fort for a quarter of an hour.'

He sat down in the chair opposite her. 'How was he?'

'OK. Snapped my head off when I broached the subject so I dropped it immediately.'

'You didn't mention that I had been talking to you about him?'

'No.'

Hugh breathed a sigh of relief.

'And he showed no signs of nervous or physical exhaustion?'

She smiled and raised her eyebrows. 'None whatsoever.'

'Maybe I was reading too much into his reactions in combat. Maybe it's me who's getting jittery.'

'Hugh, please tell me if you do see any other disturbing signs in him?'

'I will, but I don't want to worry you.'

'I worry every time Ewan takes to the air.'

Chapter Twenty-two

When Jane came in from the evening milking, Mrs Symonds, who was busy at the sink, called over her shoulder, 'Nell's back.'

'Thanks,' replied Jane, and continued to her own room to get changed. As she climbed the stairs she recalled their acrimonious parting in Lowestoft and wondered if Nell would be in a better mood now. She hesitated at the door to her room but decided she should change first before confronting Nell. When she entered the room her eyes immediately caught sight of a large envelope propped up on her dressing table. She opened it and when she withdrew the sheaf of papers inside, immediately recognised Glen's writing. A quick glance told her it was the account of his experiences he had promised her. Nell was not withholding it as a price for her silence as far as Ewan was concerned. Jane immediately went to Nell's room, knocked on the door and opened it.

'Thanks for these,' she said, holding up the papers but going no further than the open doorway.

Nell, who was unpacking the suitcase she had put on the bed, turned and shrugged her shoulders as if it had been no big deal to bring them.

'I'll work on these and fill the article out with what Terry can tell me.' When Nell still said nothing, Jane started to leave then stopped and said, 'I thought we might consider a piece with photographs about the impact of the Americans on local communities.' Again Jane was disappointed when Nell did not respond to what she had hoped would be an olive branch. 'I'll let you get on with your unpacking.' Her hand was on the doorknob when Nell finally spoke.

'Jane, harsh words were spoken on both sides in Lowestoft. Let's call a truce.' She immediately drew heart, sensing the relief in Jane. 'We're too close to allow friction between us. We need each other's support, not hostility.'

Jane smiled for answer and as she stepped towards Nell, opened her arms in welcome. They hugged each other and Nell whispered, 'What you saw in Lowestoft was only an expression of the deep friendship between Glen and me. Remember, Ewan is mine.'

Jane gave no reaction to that but merely said, 'And my past is my own.'

'Whatever it's been, John, it has been cleared up,' observed Betty two days later when she watched the girls laughing together as they crossed the yard to the shed for the early-morning milking.

'I told you they would work it out,' he replied, a touch of satisfaction in his voice.

An hour later, with the boom of aero-engines growing louder and louder as more and more aircraft from the neighbouring American airfields took to the East Anglian sky bound for Germany, Nell and Jane came out to watch for a few moments. As they always did, they linked hands and said a silent prayer for these airmen who risked their lives in the German skies. Their thoughts touched on Ewan then, not knowing that a WAAF officer did the same whenever she watched the Spitfires take off from Tangmere.

But Annabelle had the additional burden of seeing Ewan living more and more on his nerves, though from all those in authority he hid his state of mind. He was viewed as an exceptional leader of 'A' Flight, respected by all his pilots who would fly to hell and back for him. To raise the matter with him again would only make the situation worse. Hugh discreetly gave his friend as much support, in the air and on the ground, as he could. Annabelle assuaged Ewan's nerves, allowing him to take her to London whenever they could escape or to grab a night in a local pub with the collusion of an understanding landlord.

Ewan's letters to Nell were spasmodic, always offering the excuse of pressure of work. Whenever he put pen to paper, he always felt guilty. In his mind Nell and Annabelle battled for his affections and Hugh's warning that he should get his love life sorted out remained to taunt him.

By November 1943 the course of the war seemed to be favouring the Allies, with all Services contributing to what people were beginning to see as eventual victory, even though they knew there was still a long road to travel.

With the sound of Merlin engines starting up, Annabelle came from her office to watch the squadron become airborne, but though she wished all the pilots well her eyes were for one plane only. She saw it take off and turned back into her office to resume her work, knowing she would remain on tenterhooks until she saw a Spitfire with special markings land once again at Tangmere.

Time seemed to stand still until the distant sound heralded the returning flight. She grabbed her greatcoat and hat and hurried from her office but did not stop in her usual place to watch. She was halfway to the 'A' Flight dispersal before she realised where she was heading. Her steps faltered. What was she doing? She had never done this before. She stopped, started to turn back, then resumed her way forward. She felt tense all through. Aircraft landed but not the one she wanted to see. Reaching the dispersal she saw pilots climbing from their cockpits and, after words with their ground crews, hurrying to the pilots' hut to shed their flying gear. So far no Ewan; no Hugh. The sound of returning aircraft faded away until there was only silence. She bit her lip, trying to quell the dampness in her eyes and the churning in her stomach.

Then – an aero-engine. Her hopes rose. Ewan! It had to be. The Spitfire came straight in without any preliminaries. No special markings. It came to 'A' Flight. Disbelief struck her then. There were great holes in its starboard wing and in its fuselage. How on earth had it managed to get back? Hugh heaved himself from the cockpit and dropped leadenly to the ground. He saw her and made his report to the ground crew brief.

'Hugh!' There was no need to say any more, the question was clear in her eyes.

He took her into his arms and hugged her. 'I'm sorry, Legs.'

'Oh, no!' The anguished cry escaped her lips and she cried then, her sobs shaking him even though he held her tight. He let her cry until she said in a tremulous voice, 'I'm sorry, I shouldn't ...'

'Of course you should. There's no disgrace in it.' He eased her gently away, fished in his pocket for a handkerchief and gently wiped her eyes.

Annabelle swallowed hard and stiffened herself, trying to bring her feelings and demeanour under control. 'Thanks.' She glanced round, taking in the ground crews already at work on the aircraft. 'What will these men think of me?' she said, a touch of self-disgust in her voice.

'They'll understand. Let me get rid of my gear and I'll walk you back to the Mess. I'll only be a minute.'

In the moments she waited for him she tried to get a grip on her emotions, wondering what a future would be like without Ewan.

When Hugh joined her and they'd started for the Mess, Annabelle said, 'Tell me what happened? Is there any hope?'

'Are you sure you want to know?'

She nodded. 'Yes.'

'Twelve Messerschmitts swarmed at us. "A" Flight was split up. I managed to keep tight on Ewan then I was jumped. In the mêlée I lost him. I managed to outfly my attackers in spite of heavy damage, which you saw. The sky seemed suddenly to be empty and then I saw a lone Spitfire with two Messerschmitts on its tail. I went to help, saw it was Ewan, but before I could get any closer they got him. He spiralled down, smoke trailing from him. I was jumped again and lost sight of him except for one glimpse when his plane had gone into a steep dive.'

'No parachute?'

'No, but as I say, I had lost eye contact. There's a slim chance, but I don't want to raise your hopes too high.'

'Thanks, Hugh.'

'I'm sorry, Legs. I wish I could be more hopeful.'

She swallowed hard. 'I have my memories,' she said quietly.

'Cherish them. He was a good man. Now look to the future. Ewan would want you to.'

A chill struck at Liz Steel's heart when she opened the front door and was handed a telegram. Alone she walked slowly into the kitchen, staring all the while at the brown envelope. She slumped on to a chair and laid the envelope down in front of her. Fear was mounting in her heart which began to beat more quickly. She stared at the envelope that seemed to be challenging her to open it. Percy? Ewan? Walter? They were the only ones who had placed her as their 'next-of-kin' on official forms. Slowly she reached out and picked up the envelope. Her hands were shaking, fingers clumsy, as she tore it open. She unfolded the paper and her eyes skimmed the cold, official words. 'Ewan!' Tears flooded her eyes and blurred the words 'missing, believed killed'.

How long she sat there in a state of shock with tears streaming down her cheeks she did not know, but the loud rap on the front door brought her back to reality. She pushed herself from her chair, wishing there was no caller yet welcoming the chance to rejoin the world around her.

378

She wiped her eyes dry as she walked to the door and hoped the evidence of her tears would not be obvious.

But it was. The first words Flo Franklin said when she saw her friend were, 'Liz! What's wrong?'

She turned away, leaving Flo to close the door and follow her into the kitchen where, slumped on the chair again, she pointed to the piece of paper on the table. Flo knew immediately that it was a dreaded telegram. She picked it up and read it.

'Oh, no!' Her words were full of despair. She hugged her friend and they wept together until Flo straightened up and said, 'I'll make us a cup of tea.'

Within ten minutes both women had taken the situation in hand. Liz wished Percy were here but knew she would have to cope without him. She thought of bringing home her two daughters, who had been evacuated with their school, but after talking it over with Flo deemed it better to leave them where they were and visit them personally to break the news. 'I'll stay with you tonight or as long as you want me to. I'll have to go to Cedar Farm to tell Nell, this is going to be hard on her,' Flo announced. 'Thank goodness she will have Jane for support.' She snapped her fingers then as a sudden thought struck her. 'You can drive, Liz?'

'Yes, my father taught me, and though we haven't a car I kept in practice by hiring a car from Sam Craven now and again.'

'Good. We'll go right away and see him. Get your things on.'

'Why? What?' spluttered Liz.

'We'll hire a car from Sam. You can drive me to Cedar Farm. It will give you something to occupy your mind.' Flo would brook no objections.

They broke the news to Sarah who knew only too well the anguish of losing a son. When they told her they planned to go visit Nell she told them to come to her on their return; she would have a meal ready. Within half an hour Liz and Flo were leaving Lowestoft.

The Symonds and the two girls were having a cup of tea before second milking when they were attracted by the sound of a car coming into the yard. Betty was on her feet immediately to look out of the window.

'It's the same car as that young officer was in.'

'Ewan!' Nell leaped to her feet and was at the window in a couple of strides but all her excitement vanished when she saw her mother and Mrs Steel. An icy sensation coursed through her. 'Oh, no!' The distress in her voice brought Jane quickly to her side. Seeing who the visitors were, she guessed what Nell was thinking and automatically grasped her hand while her own mind cried out with the horror of what she expected to hear.

In few moments any remaining hope was shattered and a broken-hearted Nell fell into her mother's arms. She felt comfort there and drew strength from her mother's presence, but there were no tears as yet.

Jane, her eyes filled with tears, turned to Liz who held out her arms. She felt comfort in the older woman even though she too wept, thankful that Jane was there for her.

Concern enveloped Flo because Nell remained still and silent, yet Jane wept.

'Nell, you ...'

Flo's words were cut off as her daughter stepped away from her and stared at her with the light of challenge in her eyes. 'No. He's not dead! He's not.'

'But, love, the telegram ...'

'I don't believe it!' she cried.

'Missing, believed killed,' said Liz quietly, still holding Jane.

'And you believe that?' cried Nell angrily. 'How can you?'

'We're at war,' replied Liz. 'It happens.'

'Not to Ewan! He told me he was a survivor.'

'He hoped he would be,' said her mother gently.

'No, not hoped! *Knew* he would be. Ewan loves me.

He's alive . . . alive! He's got to be.'

'Come back with us, love,' her mother suggested.

'Jane can go too,' said John. 'I'll get someone else from the hostel.'

But Nell shook her head vigorously. 'There's no point unless Ewan is going to be there.'

'He can't be,' said Liz, the words catching in her throat.

'You know that,' added Flo, thinking her daughter was hysterical.

'That's right, Mum, because he's been shot down, not because he's dead!'

Throughout these exchanges Jane had been silently weeping, lost in the abyss that had swallowed her with this shattering news about Ewan, the man for whom she had felt a deep affection in spite of Nell's prior claim on him. Her heart and mind were chilled. The words on that telegram were not final but they were ominous; such words were more often than not followed by a more unambiguous message of dreaded finality. She had always hoped that Nell might ultimately turn to Glen and then she could have Ewan. Now that chance was gone; she had no one. The realisation tore her. She wanted to scream at Nell to be quiet, to stop deluding herself, to accept the fact that Ewan was dead. Why could she not see it? Nell's last statement was too much for her. She tore herself from Liz's arms and hurried away and wept in her own room.

Five minutes later there was a tap on the door.

'May I come in?'

Recognising the voice, Jane twisted round and saw Flo come tentatively into the room. Jane nodded and wiped her eyes. Flo closed the door and came to sit beside her.

'I know it's hard on you too, Jane, losing a close friend, and it's not going to be easy for you with Nell adopting the attitude she has, but please . . . try and help her?'

Jane nodded and said, 'I'll do my best,' even though her heart cried out to be comforted.

When Flo came downstairs, Betty signalled to her to

381

follow her outside. 'If Nell believes Ewan is alive, then let her. And let her stay here. She has plenty to occupy her mind, she has Jane and John, and I will see she is all right. I know that telegram holds out a little bit of hope but generally "believed killed" is borne out later. She will eventually come to terms with the loss and be able to face life again.'

An hour later Flo and Liz bade them all a quiet goodbye. Nell told her mother not to worry about her, but Flo did, concerned by this unexpected reaction from her daughter. She hoped it was not going to affect her for the rest of her life.

Two weeks later, when Annabelle came into the Mess for the evening meal, she sought out Hugh. She saw him talking to three other pilots. Catching his eye, she indicated she would like to have a word with him and carried on to the bar.

In a few moments he was beside her. 'I'll get that,' he said as the steward slid a whisky towards Annabelle. Hugh signed the chit and they found a corner where they could talk privately.

'That's a bit unusual for you,' he said, indicating the glass.

'Concerned it's the effect of losing Ewan?' She gave him a wry smile.

'Well ...' He let the implication fade away.

'Don't worry, Hugh.' She patted his hand. 'It's not that. I'm just stiffening my resolve not to turn back from what is happening.'

He looked curiously at her when she hesitated to say more. 'Well, what's that?'

'I'm leaving in a couple of days.'

'You're what?' he gasped in surprise.

'I'm leaving. I applied to be posted away from here. I can't stand it any longer. Ewan haunts me here and, bearing in mind what you said about my future, I think I must find it elsewhere.'

382

'Where are you going?'

'Lossiemouth.'

'What? North of Scotland! You certainly are getting far away.'

She shrugged her shoulders. 'Maybe that's for the best.'

'I'll be sorry to see you go, but you have my blessing.'

'Thanks, Hugh. I hoped you would say that.'

Two days later, when he saw her off, he said, 'Write to me. Let me know how you get on.'

'I will,' Annabelle promised.

But two months later he had heard nothing from her, and the two letters he'd written to her remained unanswered. He could have let the matter drop, believing she wanted to cut off all connections that would remind her of Ewan, but he was curious. If he survived the next two weeks, he would be due for a week's leave ...

In due course he visited his parents in Newark and begged their forgiveness if he did not spend the whole leave with them. 'There's a personal matter I want to attend to,' he explained. 'It means I have to go to Scotland but I'll be back with you, possibly on Wednesday, and then we'll have two full days before I return to Tangmere on Saturday.'

At the guardroom at the RAF base at Lossiemouth, Hugh revealed his identity and was then directed to the Adjutant's office. A WAAF corporal in a small outer office stopped typing when he entered.

'Can I help you, sir?' she asked pleasantly.

'I would like to see the Adjutant, please.'

She nodded. 'Name, sir?'

'Flight Lieutenant Hugh Douglas.'

'Won't be a moment, sir,' she said, rising from her chair. She knocked on a door, paused and entered. A moment later she reappeared and said, 'Flight Lieutenant Mercer will see you now, sir.'

Hugh thanked her as he stepped into the Adjutant's office. A middle-aged man whose hair was beginning to

383

whiten at the temples rose from his seat behind a desk piled high with files. He extended his hand and gave Hugh a warm smile.

'Thank you for seeing me,' he said as he shook hands.

'A pleasure,' returned the Adjutant. 'What can I do for you? I have no notification of a posting here for you.'

Hugh smiled. 'No, you won't have. I'm on a week's leave from Tangmere and have come on a private matter.'

'You've come a long way. Train?'

'Yes. Going back tomorrow.'

'Anywhere to sleep the night?'

'I'll find somewhere.'

'Look no further. I'll find you a bed on the station and you must dine in the Mess tonight. I won't hear otherwise,' he added, seeing Hugh about to protest.

'That's very kind, sir, and I thank you.'

'It'll be a change to have an operational fighter pilot in the Mess, with us being a training unit for bomber crews.'

'You'll have instructors with operational experience?'

'Of course, but not with fighter squadrons. You might have to field some questions.'

'If so, I'll try and handle them. I'll probably find the different atmosphere relaxing.'

'I hope you do. Now, you said you are here on a private matter. How can I help you?'

'I am wanting to contact Section Officer Murdoch-Crafell. She came here from Tangmere.'

'Ah, I remember her well. Who wouldn't? But I'm afraid she is no longer here.'

'Not here?' Hugh looked downcast.

'Romantic attachment?' queried Mercer

Hugh shook his head. 'Nothing like that as far as I was concerned. She had a thing going with my friend but he was shot down.'

'I'm sorry,' said the Adjutant. 'You want to break the news to her?'

'Yes.' Hugh thought this lie the easiest way out.

384

'I think I had better take you to Squadron Officer Stacey Penlow.' He rose from his chair as he was speaking and led the way to another office. After introducing Hugh to the Squadron Officer he left.

Hugh found himself sitting opposite a good-looking woman in her thirties, blonde-haired and with sparkling lively eyes that took in everything. He knew he had come under her immediate assessment, and from her response knew he had passed it.

'Now, Flight Lieutenant, how may I help you?'

'I'm from Tangmere and I'm trying to contact Section Officer Murdoch-Crafell.'

'Ah, Annabelle.' The Squadron Officer smiled. 'Though no doubt you fighter boys called her Legs?'

Hugh grinned. 'That's the one.'

'May I ask why you want to see her?'

'Of course! She was very close to a dear friend of mine, Flight Lieutenant Ewan Steel. He was shot down, presumed killed, and Le—Annabelle took it so badly that she applied for a posting away from Tangmere. She promised to keep in touch but I have heard nothing since she came to Lossiemouth. It bothered me in case the loss of Ewan had had worse results.'

'You are indeed a considerate friend, Flight Lieutenant.'

'Flight Lieutenant Mercer said she was no longer here and said I should see you.'

'Indeed, what he told you is true.'

'Are you able to tell me where she is now?'

'I'm afraid not. You see, she resigned her commission.'

'She what?' Hugh was astounded.

'I'm afraid it's true. I tried to persuade her otherwise, she had great potential and much to offer the WAAF and the RAF, but she was adamant.'

'This is a surprise. Did she say why she wanted to resign her commission?'

'Just that she felt she could do more for the war effort elsewhere.'

'She didn't elaborate?'

'No.'

'Do you know where she went?'

'She left an address, but the few items of mail that we have forwarded have come back to us marked "return to sender, address unknown".'

'You have no other links?'

'Only official records that show where she was living when she joined the WAAF, but they are marked "no longer there".'

'Any next-of-kin?'

The Squadron Officer shook her head. 'No, she was an only child, and the next-of-kin on our files was recently killed in an air raid. It seems our Annabelle has completely disappeared.'

Hugh's lips tightened in exasperation.

'I'm sorry I can't help you, Flight Lieutenant. I'm afraid your long journey has been a waste of time.'

'Not entirely. You have given me some information I never expected to hear – that Annabelle had resigned her commission.'

That aspect dwelt on Hugh's mind as he travelled south the next day. He made some suppositions and wondered if they were right . . .

He was never to know. Two weeks after returning to Tangmere, Flight Lieutenant Hugh Douglas DFC was shot down over Holland and did not survive.

Chapter Twenty-three

'Aunty Betty, I'm afraid for Nell.' Jane voiced her concern for her friend when she and Mrs Symonds were alone in the kitchen one day. 'It's been six months since we learned about Ewan and she's no nearer accepting his loss. I'm frightened that there will be a catastrophic reaction when her hope is finally shattered.'

'It worries me too,' replied Betty. 'Everywhere I look for a solution, I'm thwarted. I can't find a way through to her. She's immersed in her work, seems happy enough with us, but I can detect a strange attitude of mind in her since we received the news. I can't exactly pin it down so I can't help. It's frustrating. If she were proper poorly we could do something about it.'

'I feel exactly the same. Nell's not even convinced by the few facts we have gleaned. The Squadron Adjutant was kind enough to write to Ewan's mother and tell her that, when last seen, his aircraft was in a steep dive and no parachute was seen, but Nell won't see that as the end. She never mentions the progress of the war but she must be aware of it because yesterday, out of the blue, she said, "The way things are going, Ewan will soon be coming home." That startled me, and made me even more worried about her state of mind.'

'What did you say?'

'I was so taken aback that I pandered to her.'

'Probably the most sensible thing to do. Arguing with her would not have helped. We can only be here for her, and take any chance to ease her mind towards the truth.'

So the situation remained as they all waited while the Allied invasion of the Continent on the sixth of June 1944 was successfully accomplished. They viewed this as a decisive step towards the final conclusion of this devastating war, though they knew that in all probability hard-won battles in all theatres of war still lay ahead.

'Another letter for you from Glen,' said Jane, passing the envelope to Nell one day. 'That's three this week. He must be in port.'

'He doesn't say where. Can't, I suppose. But from his underlying words I think it is possibly somewhere in the West Country.'

'And I'd say this young man fancies you,' commented a smiling Betty with a wink at Jane.

'Friendship, only friendship,' Nell briskly replied.

'That's what you say,' teased Betty, but Nell still did not rise to the bait.

'He mentions supplying material to Mr Horton again,' she said to Jane later as Betty busied herself at the sink. 'He's keen for us to keep in contact.'

'Rightly so. It's too good a chance to lose. What about another piece about the Land Girls? How the life they have been leading, which was alien to most of them, has affected their outlook now, and what they will do after the war?'

'A good idea,' agreed Nell eagerly. 'We'll show some of the rougher side of the life: early rising, mucking out, draining ditches, going out in all weathers, threshing, heaving bales, etcetera, so people realise that Land Girls haven't had an easy life safe in the idyllic country. I'm sure you can write a poignant, hard-hitting piece.'

'And you'll interpret the work without any glamour.'

Nell gave a little laugh. 'I can do that all right.'

'That will make a great juxtaposition with what the girls intend to do after they are released.'

'I haven't much film left . . .'

'We'll ring Mr Horton, see if he likes the idea and can let you have more. And I'll write to my uncle and see if he has any spare.'

The more they discussed the project and how they should tackle it, the more excited they became about it. The following day they were in a position to put the idea in reasonable detail to Mr Horton.

He expressed pleasure at hearing from Jane, asked after Nell, and when Jane discussed their proposal with him, became enthusiastic about the 'what will they do after the war?' theme, visualising it expanded to many other people on active service.

When Jane came off the telephone her eyes were bright with excitement. 'He's very keen on the idea and has commissioned us to do it. He also talked about my piece on Glen's experiences when the *Sea Queen* was sunk.'

'I remember him praising that at the time. It seems to have stuck in his mind,' observed Nell.

'He said if I could keep writing to that standard, he saw a bright future ahead for me as a writer.'

'That's good news. It's what you want, isn't it?'

'Yes. Apparently he is already formulating some ideas for the immediate post-war coverage. He hopes you and Glen will team up again when he leaves the Navy.'

'I'll have to see what Ewan thinks about that . . .'

This statement amidst so much enthusiasm for the future came as a shock to Jane who looked thunderstruck.

Nell caught the flash of anger in her eyes. 'Well, I WILL have to ask him,' she emphasised.

'Nell,' Jane snapped, 'you know as well as I do that the likelihood of Ewan's being alive is almost negligible. If he had survived the crash, we would have heard he'd been taken prisoner by now.'

Nell gave a little shake of her head. 'You're wrong. He's still alive.'

'Don't talk nonsense!' countered Jane harshly. She had

389

tolerated her friend's attitude about Ewan until this moment, but now she saw it as a dampener on the good news she had just received from Mr Horton.

'It's not nonsense!' Nell stormed, her face expressing hurt because Jane had taken this stance. 'He's alive. He said he would survive.'

'That was just talk to placate you when you heard he was going to be a pilot.'

'No!' shouted Nell. 'Why are you taking this attitude?' Her eyes widened angrily. 'Is it jealousy because he'll be coming back to me?'

Jane turned away in disgust. 'How can you still believe he'll return?' Then she snapped derisively, 'Get a grip on yourself or you'll lose your mind when you do finally realise he is never coming home!'

Nell's lips tightened. She stared at Jane aghast. 'Is that what you really believe?'

'It will, if you don't stop all this nonsense about Ewan coming back.'

'But, Jane, he will. He *will*.'

Jane grunted in disgust. 'You've ruined the good news we had from Mr Horton. Now I'm going for a walk. When I come back, if you want to keep my friendship, I don't want to hear another word about this stupid idea of yours again. I've tolerated it long enough. No more.' She swung out of the room, slamming the door behind her.

Nell stared at the door and said quietly to herself, 'He's alive.' Then she shuddered. Had she only said that all this time to counteract the suspicion in her mind that Jane might be right?

By the time she returned Nell had decided to offer an olive branch. 'I'm sorry, Jane, if I spoiled the excitement of Mr Horton's words. Let's forget what I said and put our minds to what he wants?'

Jane accepted her apology, reading more behind it. And so it proved. Nell never again mentioned her belief that Ewan was alive, though Jane suspected it still dwelled in her mind.

They took full advantage of their leisure time, enjoying sharing some of it with the girls at the hostel whenever opportunities arose, and using their new contacts to compile more photographs of Land Girls at work, depicting in particular the back-breaking labour and harsh conditions.

Sometimes they visited Lowestoft on their free days, occasionally together when Mr and Mrs Symonds kindly told them they would manage for one day.

On one such occasion, knowing that some social evenings were being arranged by Miss Hardcastle at the hostel in October, they decided to take some different clothes back with them. They were upstairs sorting through their wardrobes when they heard Liz Steel and Sarah Evans, who had been invited to share the midday meal, arrive.

'Come and see this,' called Nell from her bedroom.

Jane, who had left her bedroom door open for ease of communication, hurried across the landing and found Nell holding up a dress in front of her.

'Oh, that's a bit zazzy!' she exclaimed, coming to a stop. 'You've kept *that* one hidden. It'll be a knockout with the American airmen I suspect Miss Hardcastle will be inviting.' She admired the chiffon dress patterned with reds, yellows and browns, shading into each other. Its long sash had been twisted in front to just below the breastline.

'Mum bought it for me for my eighteenth birthday. Do you think it looks dated?'

Jane gave it a critical look. 'No. Lots of people wear pre-war clothes – have to. We don't get enough clothing coupons to keep changing fashions. It might need shortening a touch.'

'Mum will soon do that.'

'What about this one? I haven't worn it since I came here.' Jane held up a dress. 'It's plainer than yours.'

Nell stepped back to eye the white dress patterned with

small pink roses. It came tight to a broad waistband, the bodice being draped and the skirt flaring slightly from the waist. The built-up sleeves ended at the elbow and brought an approving comment from Nell, who added, 'It's just you.'

'Good. I'm glad you like it. Another one each?'

Nell agreed.

Jane was crossing the landing when Mrs Franklin called, 'Dinner's ready!' Flo was on her way back to the kitchen when there was a knock on the front door. Pleased to have the girls at home together, she shouted cheerily, 'I'll get it!' Smiling, she opened the door.

'Mrs Franklin?' A tall, well-dressed young woman put the question to her pleasantly, if tentatively.

'Yes.' She inclined her head at the stranger, her eyes filled with curiosity.

'I'm Annabelle Murdoch-Crafell. I'm looking for Mrs Steel. I called at her house and a neighbour told me I was likely to find her here.'

'That is correct.'

'May I see her, please?'

'One moment.' Flo took a couple of steps along the hall and called, 'Liz, someone to see you.'

She glanced at Flo as she bustled out. 'Yes, who is it?' She saw the stranger on the step and looked questioningly at her. 'I'm Mrs Steel.'

'I'm pleased to have found you, Mrs Steel. I'm Annabelle.' There was the slightest hesitation and then she said gently, 'I thought you might like to meet your grandson.'

Liz stared incredulously at this young woman as her announcement, which did not seem to make any sense, sank in. 'What?'

'Your grandson, Ewan.' Annabelle looked down at the child she held, wrapped in a beautiful crocheted shawl and matching bonnet, and smiled at him with what Liz recognised as boundless love. She held the baby so Liz could see

him better. Her heart lurched; that smile, and those startling blue eyes, exactly the same shade as those of a baby
she'd once held in her own arms.

'I . . . I . . .'

Flo, equally astounded, said, 'You had better come in.'
As she stepped to one side to allow Annabelle to enter the
house she became aware of Nell and Jane standing halfway
down the stairs. From their disbelieving expressions and
Nell's ashen face filled with shock, she knew they must
have heard every word. 'In here.' She hurriedly opened a
door to a room on the right.

'Thank you,' said Annabelle.

'I'll leave you alone for a few minutes,' Flo whispered
as Liz followed the new arrival into the parlour.

Anxious for her daughter, Flo turned back to the stairs
in time to see Nell shouting, 'No!' and pushing roughly
past Jane to run upstairs again.

Flo's eyes met Jane's and saw the shattering blow of
disappointment this had been to her, too. It made Flo
wonder how far her admiration of Ewan had gone, but she
drew back from raising the question. No purpose would be
served now.

'Who is she?' Jane whispered, but each word had an
edge to it.

Flo shook her head. 'I don't know, and I don't think Liz
does either. You heard her name, just as I did. Go to Nell.
I'd better warn Sarah what has happened.'

As Jane climbed the stairs her legs felt heavy, each step
an effort. Her world had caved in on her. Though
outwardly she had no claim on him, in her heart of hearts
she had always felt that the love she bore for Ewan gave
her some right to his affections. Now she felt foolish and
completely betrayed.

When she reached Nell's room she found her friend
dark-faced with anger, sitting on the side of her bed,
hammering her thighs with clenched fists and muttering
venomously between clenched teeth, 'The devil! The devil

... how *could* he? How could he?' The tears Jane had expected did not flow; in their place was hatred.

Jane sat on the bed beside Nell and put her arm round her shoulders. Before she could speak, Nell looked at her and cried out, 'How could he? It was *me* he loved!' Her eyes took on a pleading expression. 'Why didn't he tell me, Jane? Why did he let me believe I was the only one?' Her eyes dampened but still tears did not come. 'And why has *she* come here?'

Though she wanted to display her own rage and condemn Ewan, Jane knew it would not help matters, would only lead to overt hostility and further trouble between them. She steadied herself and said, 'Maybe she thought it was the best thing to do. Maybe she thought Ewan's parents should know they had a grandson. Maybe ...' Jane's speculations were cut short as the door opened slowly and Mrs Franklin came in. She glanced at Jane questioningly and Jane mouthed a silent, 'She's OK.'

As her mother sat down beside her, Nell turned baleful eyes on her. 'Who is she, Mum?'

'An ex-WAAF officer who served on the same station as Ewan. They struck up a friendship ...'

'So it seems!' put in Nell contemptuously.

'I am sure she didn't know about you.'

'You asked her?'

'Not directly, but I can tell from the way she speaks about Ewan.'

'Why has she come? Doesn't she know he's dead?'

Both Flo and Jane were taken aback by this. They exchanged sharp glances and both saw a flash of relief in the other. If anything good had come from this unexpected visit it was the acceptance by Nell of Ewan's loss.

'Yes, she accepts that there is very little hope that he survived. And, Nell, I can tell she loved him very much. Still does.'

'Were they married?'

'No. Ewan didn't even know she was pregnant. He was

shot down before she told him.'

'Oh.' Her apparent acceptance of these facts was non-committal.

Flo rose to her feet and looked down at her daughter. 'Come down when you're ready. You'll have to meet her, there's no escape. She's going to be here for quite a while. She has no one else, and though at first she resisted the offer, Liz was most insistent that she should stay. At least until something else can be sorted out.'

As the door closed Nell glared at Jane. 'See? She's sponging already, wanting to take advantage of the situation. Why the devil didn't she get the child adopted? She needn't ever have come into our lives with this permanent reminder of Ewan. Why did she?'

Jane took Nell's hands in hers and eyed her with the deepest sympathy. 'Nell,' she said gently, 'you heard your mum. This girl loved Ewan very much, so it's more than likely she loves her child in the same way, and wants always to have the reminder of Ewan close to her.'

Nell gave a low grunt of contempt. 'Looking for an easy meal ticket more like!'

'No!' replied Jane, the sharp edge to her voice startling Nell. She held her friend's hard gaze. 'Believe me, Nell, I know how she must have felt, and still does.'

'How can you?' she said scornfully.

'Oh, I certainly can.'

Nell's eyes widened with suspicion then. Was Jane finally about to confide in her?

'You see, I had a child when I was living in Middlesbrough. I wanted to keep him but my unyielding father made me have him adopted. He would hear of no other way, and also insisted I did not know where the child went. He arranged things so I could never find out. He knew people would look down on me and the family if word got out.' Jane gave a dry little laugh. 'Believe me, Nell, snobbery isn't confined to the upper classes. That was why I went to live with my uncle and aunt in Scarborough.

They were very understanding after the baby was taken away from me and helped me through a dark time. The rest you know.'

'So that's the secret you have nursed all this time?'

Jane nodded and tightened her lips.

'You feared we would look down on you?'

She nodded again.

'Oh, Jane.' Nell held out her arms to her and they hugged each other in sympathy. 'And that is why you never let yourself fall in love – for fear whoever it was would reject you when they learned the truth.'

'I could not have gone into a loving relationship without revealing it.'

'So that's why you held Simon at arm's length?' Jane nodded. 'But he loved you, Jane.'

'I know, and now I wish I had . . .' Her voice faltered.

'He would never have held anything against you. You should have trusted him.' Seeing tears of regret coming into Jane's eyes, Nell asked quickly, 'What about the father?'

'When I told him, he ran away. I never saw him again. I don't know where he went, nor where he is now.'

'Life,' said Nell hollowly.

'Yes, life,' agreed Jane.

'Well, we'll just have to make something of ours,' commented her friend.

'I suppose so. And we'd better start by going downstairs and meeting the two new people who have entered our lives.'

They reached the door but before Jane could open it, Nell stopped her. 'I don't think I can face this.'

'I don't think I can either.'

Nell swallowed. 'What are we going to do?'

Though Nell knew of Jane's affection for Ewan, and Jane was well aware of Nell's relationship with him, they now realised how much they needed each other in the face of this revelation.

Jane hesitated. 'I don't know. If we don't go down your

mum will only come looking for us, and then we'll have to go or else cause a scene, which will only make matters worse.' She gave a shake of her head and added regretfully, 'We'll have to face them.' She squeezed Nell's hand, trying to give confidence as well as draw some for herself.

Nell nodded.

Reaching the bottom of the stairs, they heard Flo's voice coming from the kitchen. When they opened the door they saw only Sarah Evans with her.

'Are they in the other room?' Nell asked tentatively.

'No, love. Liz thought it best she took Annabelle and the babe home.' The relief in the glance that passed between Nell and Jane was not lost on her. Seeing tears in her daughter's eyes, Flo held out her arms. Nell drew comfort and strength from her motherly hug and the words whispered in her ear: 'Be strong.' Flo eased her slightly away and held out one arm to Jane who came to her gratefully, finding some measure of relief and understanding in the embrace. 'Help each other,' said Flo as she released her hold.

'Mum,' said Nell quietly, 'do you mind if we go back to Cedar Farm this afternoon instead of tomorrow?'

The request caught Jane unawares but she was instantly glad that Nell had made it.

'Of course not, love,' replied Flo. 'Do what you think best.' She said no more, knowing that her daughter wanted to avoid the evidence of Ewan's betrayal. Then, as if putting the incident behind them, she said practically, 'It's no good letting the dinner go to waste so sit down. And that includes you, Sarah, you were invited.'

Though the meal was a somewhat muted affair they were all glad Sarah was there. She helped to take their minds, to some extent, off the revelation that had exploded in their midst and left so many questions unanswered.

Chapter Twenty-four

'Mrs Steel, I'm sorry to have dropped in out of the blue. Maybe I should have written first,' Annabelle apologised as they walked the short distance to the house.

'Maybe you should,' replied Liz without any animosity. 'But better this than not make contact at all.'

'You mean that?' There was a note of hope in Annabelle's voice.

'Young lady, I never say what I don't mean.'

Annabelle could see the woman beside her was a formidable lady, but one in whom she detected a heart of gold and an understanding mind, though it would not tolerate deceit or evasion.

'I wondered whether to come or not for a while because it is an unusual position.'

Though she was longing to know the full story and what lay behind these last words, Liz said, 'We're nearly there. Tell me what you mean when we get settled.'

Once inside the house Liz looked to Annabelle's needs. 'Put your coat in there,' she said, indicating a walk-in wardrobe under the stairs. 'Bring baby Ewan in here.' She led the way into the front room. 'Make him comfy in that armchair. He'll be safe enough, we'll put a cushion to stop him rolling off.' Then she added, tickling the baby under the chin, 'You'll be all right there, won't you, young man?' The child gurgled with pleasure and gave Liz such an endearing smile that her heart melted all over again.

Once everything was seen to and they saw young Ewan was falling asleep, Liz said, 'I think you and I had better have something to eat, let's go into the kitchen.' She saw Annabelle hesitate and glance at Ewan. 'He'll be all right, he's fast asleep. We'll leave the doors open so we can hear if he wakes.'

Once they were settled at the table with a makeshift but appetising meal in front of them, Liz said, 'Now, young lady, you indicated you had second thoughts about coming because you viewed your position as unusual?'

'Yes. You see, Ewan never knew I was pregnant. I wanted to be certain before I told him. I never got the chance because the day before I was to get the result, he was shot down.'

'So did anyone else know? Your family . . . people at Tangmere?'

'No. Oh, people serving at Tangmere knew Ewan and I were very close and spent a lot of time together, but no one there ever learned that I was pregnant. I went to a private doctor, not the Medical Officer at Tangmere. When I learned I was expecting I realised I would have to resign my commission and leave the WAAF. I did not want to do that at Tangmere so I applied for a posting, saying that I needed to get away from all the associations with Ewan. The authorities granted that and I moved to the north of Scotland. There I resigned my commission, saying I thought I could better serve the war effort in some other capacity. My request was granted and my real reason never came out.'

'You have been straightforward with me, I appreciate that, and I suspect you were not thinking of your reputation alone but also Ewan's. What about your own family?'

'I have none. I'm completely alone.' Annabelle went on to explain how this had come about and concluded, 'This was a strong reason for coming to you. Ewan never really mentioned his family and I did not press him. I thought he would tell me in his own good time. But I thought little Ewan should know any relations he has, and not be left like me with no one.'

Liz looked at her with sympathy. She could tell that Annabelle was sincere and deeply concerned for the baby sleeping peacefully in the next room. 'Well, you have come to a ready-made family here. There is Percy, my husband, whose herring drifter was commissioned for service at the start of the war. Our son Walter serves with him, and our two daughters, Sylvia and Amy, were evacuated with their school. They'll be leaving next July. So, you see, neither of you need ever be alone again. But if Ewan never mentioned his family, how did you find me?'

'I happened to see an address on a letter he was posting once.'

'And where are you living now?'

'I have nowhere permanent. When I decided to come here, I took rooms in Yarmouth.'

'Any plans for the future? You have a little one to look after, remember.'

'I can live anywhere, really, since I have no ties. When I lost my mother and father, I inherited a small estate. I sold that so I am comfortably off, if not rich, and can please myself, for the moment at least.'

'Then why not come to this area and be near your newfound family?'

Annabelle hesitated then said, 'I suppose I could ...'

'I'd like you to be near when Percy comes home so why not come and stay with me until then? It will give you a chance to make your own plans.'

'Oh, Mrs Steel, I couldn't. I've just walked unheralded into your life with what must have been shattering news ...'

'You could if you wanted to. I would love to have your company and to have a little one to look after again, especially as I'm likely to be on my own until this war is over. Say yes?'

Annabelle gave her a grateful smile and, jumping to her

feet, hugged Liz. 'However can I thank you for being so understanding?'

'Just say you'll stay, at least for the time being?'

'Yes, I will.'

As Annabelle sat down again a serious expression came over Liz's face. 'There is something I must ask?' She hesitated a fraction of a minute. Annabelle looked at her with query in her eyes. 'Did you love my son?'

'With all my heart.' Her tone was so genuine, filled not only with love but with unbounded admiration for him, that Liz was left in no doubt.

'And Ewan with you?'

'He said so.'

'You believed him?'

'Yes. But why do you ask this? Did he not tell you about me?' The last question came as Annabelle realised something. 'When I walked into Mrs Franklin's and met you, I thought you were surprised at seeing the baby. But really ... you were surprised at seeing BOTH of us, weren't you?'

Liz nodded. 'Ewan never mentioned you. You were a complete surprise to us all.'

'Oh ...' Annabelle's voice trailed away as she grappled with the reason for this, but in the next moment she understood when Liz went on.

'His family and all his friends expected him to marry his childhood sweetheart, Nell Franklin.'

'One of the young women I glimpsed?'

'Yes.'

'Oh, my God!' All the colour drained from Annabelle's face as she fought with this revelation.

'I saw her turn back up the stairs,' said Liz. 'Knew she must have heard every word, so I thought it best you didn't meet at that moment. That's why I suggested we leave. I take it he never mentioned her to you?'

'Never!' Through her astonishment and distress, Annabelle's eyes pleaded with Liz to believe her. She was

401

relieved when she saw sympathy, not censure. 'Maybe it would be best if I left the area altogether, went some place far away?'

'No! Not now you have found a family for young Ewan and yourself.'

'But that poor girl must be devastated ...'

'I agree, but she'll have to cope, and that will be easier done when my son no longer stands between you.'

'But the baby and I will be a constant reminder of ...'

'She'll have to deal with that,' cut in Liz firmly. Something of Ewan had come back into her life and she was not going to lose that; she knew Percy and the rest of the family would feel the same. 'You said you would stay.'

'Yes, but when I said that, I did not know about Nell. That alters things.'

'I can understand how you feel but don't take little Ewan away from us. Please stay? See how things work out?'

Annabelle could not turn away from this lady who so desperately wanted what her son had left behind to become part of her life and family. She was right. Nell Franklin would have to accept what had happened, even if she felt betrayed. She had a whole life before her and could form other relationships, whereas who would want Annabelle with another man's child? She too would have to cope, albeit with a different set of circumstances, but she knew she could. She only hoped Nell Franklin felt the same.

'I'll say it again,' said Flo, holding Nell and Jane in her arms at the railway station as they were about to leave for Cedar Farm, 'look after each other, and help each other cope with what has happened. It may seem like it's the end of the world for you, but it isn't. Don't let this ruin the rest of your life. Is it more devastating than losing Ewan? You would have dealt with that, once you accepted it. Put this out of your mind.'

'But, Mum ...'

'No buts.'

402

'I may not be able to face coming back to Lowestoft, at least while *she* is there.'

'All right! Do as you like, but don't forget me. I've already had to cope with the loss of your father.'

'Oh, Mum, I'm sorry. How could I?' There were tears in Nell's eyes as she gave her mother a special hug.

'All aboard!' The guard's shout sent them climbing into the carriage.

They squeezed together so they could both lean out of the window.

Flo reached out to take her daughter's hand in one last goodbye as the train hissed steam and slowly started to roll forward. 'I'll write and tell you what's happening ...'

'Thanks, Mum.'

'Love to Mr and Mrs Symonds!'

'How are you feeling?' Jane asked Nell as they settled in the railway carriage.

'Devastated. You?'

'Shattered.'

'How could he?'

Jane shrugged her shoulders. 'Well, we saw what it was like when we were at Biggin Hill. Those boys, flying on the edge of death one day, living or trying to live a normal life the next. Female company can help them to escape from the horrors they face in a man's world. That's the world Ewan was living in, too.'

'Well, he didn't have to go as far as he did. Soapy didn't, Sandy neither.'

'Who's to say that they wouldn't have if we had loved them and given them the chance?'

'Are you saying this ex-WAAF loved Ewan?' Nell frowned.

'Knowing him, I think it highly possible, and in an extremely volatile situation, close to death, they needed each other. Nell, we must give his memory our sympathy and understanding. You always were going to have to face life without him. I know you said differently, but deep

403

down you must have known or you wouldn't have made that remark earlier today, when we were in the bedroom with your mother. Now you have accepted his death, you must face the future with a positive attitude. It'll be hard for a while ... it will for me too, especially as I have lost Simon while you still have Glen. And remember, your mum has suffered a devastating loss of her own and coped with it.'

'Jane, you are very wise sometimes.'

She gave a little smile and then a shake of her head. 'No. I merely learned at an early age from my own mistakes in Middlesbrough, and their consequences. For a time they made me scared to face life and its problems. I found some stability with my uncle and aunt, and then in you and our friends, which made me review my life. It is only now, after what we have just learned, that I am beginning to see a way forward, hazy though it is. It will depend on circumstances when we leave the Land Army. But one thing I do know ... I think you and I should start to enjoy ourselves, not dwell on the past and what might have been. There is a future for us. Annabelle and her baby also have a future to make, but it's no concern of ours. So when we get back, we'll see what's happening at the hostel, what news the other girls have, what Miss Hardcastle has planned, and we'll give a lot more thought to Mr Horton and *World Scene*.' Jane stopped talking then and started to laugh. 'I've made quite a speech, haven't I?'

'You certainly have.' Nell grinned. The laughter was infectious and she collapsed into Jane's arms. When she straightened up she said, 'Look out, everyone, there are two determined Land Girls coming back!'

'Hello, this is a surprise, we didn't expect you back until tomorrow,' said Mrs Symonds when the two girls arrived at Cedar Farm, having completed the journey on bicycle from the local station.

'Well, here we are, and we can do the evening milking

for you,' said Nell. 'Jane, you tell Aunty Betty why we are back early while I take our bags upstairs.'

'There'll be a cup of tea ready by the time you come down,' said Betty.

Her husband, having seen the girls return, came in from the fence he had been repairing.

Jane quickly told them the bare facts and asked them not to make anything of the situation with Nell, as she felt that she had finally got her friend thinking positively. They were understanding, commiserating only briefly with her, before mentioning their own delight at having them both back.

Milking over, the girls informed Mr and Mrs Symonds that they were going to the hostel. Thankful that the October evening was mild, they changed into pretty but simple print dresses with square necklines and full-length sleeves, tight at the wrists. They put on flat shoes to cycle in, taking their high heels in carrier bags dangling from the handle-bars.

The four girls who had come to the hostel at the same time as Nell and Jane gave them an enthusiastic welcome. Other girls had come, been transferred to other areas or lodged out with farmers. Nell and Jane were quickly introduced to new faces and soon chatter flowed like a river in spate, so many tales of the local farmers and their wives, some of whom kept an eagle eye on their husbands with pretty young girls around albeit in jerseys and Wellingtons. There were stories of boy friends who were exempt from military duty, but more than anything a multitude of tales about the Americans who had flooded this area of England, which had recently become one big airfield.

'But the Americans don't interest you two, do they, unless you aren't going to remain faithful to your boy friends?' commented Gloria with a smile that said, You don't know what you're missing.

Jane saw Nell frown and moved quickly to prevent her from saying something she might regret. 'Don't ask questions, any of you, but we're back to let our hair down.' The latter part of the announcement was made with gusto, as if she and Nell were prepared for any excitement that lay ahead. Nell caught Jane's eye, gave a little smile and winked her agreement.

'Good on you!' Gloria approved. 'If it's an American you want, there's hordes of them around searching for talent. Take a few tips from one who knows!'

She was in the middle of an entertaining spiel, which had all the girls whooping and laughing, when Miss Hardcastle walked in.

'You all seem to be in a good mood,' she said as she came to join them. 'Hello, Jane, and you, Nell. Nice to see you here again.'

'They've decided to let their hair down and make up for lost time,' chuckled Gloria.

'Well, they'll have a few chances now. I'm working on a programme of entertainment, and a week on Saturday we're all invited by the Commanding Officer, Framlingham, to an All Ranks dance. I know some of you have been to functions on individual invitations but this one sounds as if it's going to be a big do. There will be two top American bands that are touring bases in this country, and of course there will be plenty to eat and drink. Transport will be laid on by the Americans and will be here at the hostel at six-thirty, to leave the airfield at twelve-thirty. I understand invitations have been sent to other groups and to girls in surrounding villages. All I say is, enjoy yourselves but behave. As I've told you before, don't let anyone think the girls of the Land Army are easy pickings.'

'You both look a real treat,' commented Betty when the girls came downstairs dressed for the dance on Saturday. 'Don't they, John?'

'They doo thaat,' he spluttered, touched by embarrassment but with admiration in his eyes.

They shrugged themselves into their outdoor coats,

406

picked up the carrier bags which held a change of shoes suitable for dancing, and bade the Symonds good night.

'Got your key?' called Betty when they reached the door.

'Yes.'

'Enjoy yourselves.'

'We will,' laughed Jane. 'And be sure you do,' she added to Nell as they got on to their bicycles. 'The past is the past, we're going to live a little.'

'So we are,' replied Nell enthusiastically, and pushed the pedals with extra vigour.

They joined the excited group of girls at the hostel and climbed aboard the vehicle, exchanging banter with the American driver and his companion. They were waved on to the base by the guards on duty at the main gate and within a few minutes were pulling up outside a Nissen hut that had been set aside with all the facilities for female guests.

'You'll see we've erected a covered walkway to the neighbouring hangar,' the driver pointed out as he and his companion helped them from the coach. 'Enjoy yourselves!'

They discarded their coats, replaced their outdoor shoes with something more appropriate for dancing, applied a little more make-up, and headed for the hangar, eager to chassé to the beat of 'In The Mood'.

They gave gasps of wonderment and delight when they entered the huge space that had been emptied of the B17 Flying Fortress now standing outside the main door. It had been replaced by a multitude of decorations hanging from the girders and walls. A band in immaculate Army uniform played from a 'specially erected dais, and along one side stood tables laden with food and drink.

'Ain't seen as much food as that ever,' commented a wide-eyed Mavis.

'Make the most of it,' replied Karen, 'we won't see the like of it again for a long time.'

'What a band,' said Gloria, swaying her hips to the rhythm.

'Here they come,' observed Caroline, noting five American airmen heading in their direction.

In less than a minute Jane found herself alone. Nell had slipped into the arms of a lithe American, whose insignia identified him as a bombardier and whose dark swarthy complexion could only mean that he was of Italian extraction. Nell glanced back at her friend and raised her eyebrows as if to say, Why you?

Jane shrugged her shoulders for reply and gave a little smile. She wouldn't have long to wait.

'It seems my crew have overlooked the most gorgeous girl.' The soft-spoken words were drawled close to her ear. Startled, she swung round and blushed when she saw a handsome fair-haired officer smiling at her with open admiration.

'Your crew?' was all she could splutter.

'Yes. They're a good bunch. The other four are on the floor already.'

More girls were coming in from the Nissen hut.

'I think we had better move out of the way,' said the officer. 'Care to dance?'

'That's what we came for.' Jane smiled and slipped into his arms. She immediately felt comfortable and it took only a few passes across the floor for her to realise that he was a very good dancer.

'Better introduce ourselves. Byron Oates ... call me By.'

'Pleased to meet you, By. Jane Harvey.'

'Jane.' He savoured it. 'I like it, it suits you.'

'I bet you say that to all the girls?'

'Only the very special ones.'

'Am I that special?'

'Maybe. I'll tell you one day.'

'Might there be another day?'

'Who knows?'

The exchange ceased when the band played the final note and everyone cheered and clapped, shouting for more.

Immediately the band struck up with 'Chattanooga Choo-choo'.

'Do you jive?' asked Byron.

'Never tried it.'

'Then it's time you learned. It's easy enough. Your friend learned quickly.' He nodded in the direction of Nell. 'She's got a good teacher, he's an expert.' He noted the concern in Jane's expression as she looked over at them. 'Don't worry, she'll be all right with Toni Pacitto. He's a bit of a loud mouth but he has the utmost respect for you English dames, as he calls you. She'll be OK with Toni. I'll get him to give you a quick lesson, too.'

Jane laughed. 'I think you'll do as my teacher.'

'Well, let's see how we progress. I'm not as good as Toni but I still think I cut a mean rug.'

It proved to be the case. By soon had Jane jiving with the rest. The dance floor became a colourful whirling scene but no one could match the intricate steps and movements of Toni and his partner. Nell had quickly struck up an understanding with him, matching him step for step at top speed. On one occasion their jiving caught the attention of the rest of the dancers who cleared the floor to watch. They were so wrapped up in the dance they did not realise they were alone on the floor until the music stopped. Nell blushed with embarrassment when the hangar resounded with claps and cheers and she realised she had been partnering the man regarded by everyone on the airfield as an expert.

'You were great,' said Toni with a broad smile. 'You deserve some chow.' He took her hand. As he led her towards the array of food, Nell felt startled momentarily to think of the changes war had brought to her life. Her father killed, a best friend gone, and Ewan, the man she'd loved, missing; yet here she was, jiving with an American she had never met before, and actually enjoying it. War did the strangest things.

'Toni, that was terrific,' said Byron as he and Jane joined them.

'Couldn't have done it without my partner. A real fast learner.' He grinned and winked at Nell. 'We'll have to try again. There are lots of dances around this area.'

'Love to,' she said enthusiastically.

'We'll make that a foursome, if Jane is willing?' said Byron, eyeing her in the clear hope she would agree.

She did not disappoint him.

They saw each other whenever time and bombing missions permitted, each of them finding that the company took their mind, if only for a brief time, off the horrors all around. Trepidation gripped Nell and Jane whenever they heard the roar of aero-engines and saw the huge bombers take to the sky, to assemble over the coast and head in formation for Germany. Anxiety would grip them until they saw the bombers return, some bearing the scars of the hostile reception they had received, and it would only be completely relieved when they received a phone call from Byron or Toni.

'Are you falling for Toni?' Jane asked one night after the two officers, who mysteriously always seemed to manage to have access to a jeep for their free nights, had dropped them off at Cedar Farm.

'No,' replied Nell with a smile. 'Oh, he's good fun and a great dancer and a continuous talker – as you are well aware – but I couldn't live with his sort all the time. Besides, he's told me about his life back in the States, and it wouldn't be for me. He knows that. We've agreed to have as much fun as we can together while he is over here, and then a goodbye kiss, happy memories, and farewell.'

'Sounds as though you have it all worked out.'

'True. What about you and Byron?'

Jane gave a little shrug of her shoulders.

'He has feelings for you,' pointed out Nell.

'You think so?'

'Yes. Has he not said anything or shown you how he feels?'

410

'No. Oh, well, a kiss and a cuddle . . .'

'A good snog?' Nell cut in sharply.

'He seems to be holding back from that.'

'It's not that your past is coming back again, and it's you who is unconsciously raising barriers?'

'Do you think it could be that?' A worried frown creased Jane's forehead.

'You like By, don't you?'

'Yes.'

'And what about his life in the States?'

'Don't really know enough to make a proper judgement. Oh, he's spoken of it in general terms – a thriving ranch in Montana that adjoins one owned by his father.'

'Sounds great. Would you be averse to that sort of life?'

'I don't think so. As you know, I'm completely free. And I know my uncle and aunt wouldn't stand in the way. They've always encouraged me to make my own life.'

'Then all I can advise is, if you think your past might cause a barrier, tell him. Don't miss out like you did with Simon.'

Nell's words gave Jane much to think about as they reached December 1944.

On the first Saturday in the month, with the squadron stood down, the four friends went to a dance in Norwich. Apart from the uniforms all around, the war seemed far away as the dance hall throbbed to the beat of the band.

Halfway through the evening, when they were sitting at the bar enjoying a drink, Byron invited both girls to a Christmas party at the base. 'It will take place two weeks today on Saturday the sixteenth. We know the whole base will be closed down for flying unless anything extraordinary happens then. At three o'clock we have a kid's tea party, with Father Christmas and presents. Then the hangar will be transformed when the kids have gone home and there'll be a Christmas dance through to next morning. Toni and I hope you'll come to both?'

'It's Jane's day off so she can give you her answer here

411

and now, but I'll have to sweetheart Mr and Mrs Symonds into letting me miss the second milking if I'm to attend both,' said Nell.

'Knowing you, baby, you'll manage,' said Toni. 'And if you don't, I'll be there with the jeep to bring you over to the dance. Can't let Cinderella miss the ball.'

Byron looked questioningly at Jane.

'Wouldn't miss either of them for the world,' she said, and saw his eyes light up with pleasure. It delighted her. Maybe the time was coming when she could be honest with him.

The tea party was a roaring success, full of excited children, especially when Father Christmas appeared with two helpers carrying sacks full of presents. The Americans revelled in the occasion, delighted to see local families happy and enjoying themselves. It took their minds off all the horrors they had faced, and would still have to face, in the fight to come. Thoughts of family life at home occupied their minds and raised hopes, too. Surely they would live to share such times with their own families again?

Byron was no exception. Thoughts of home were in his mind after the children had dispersed and Toni had gone to fetch Nell from Cedar Farm. He led Jane to a quiet corner while the hangar was being prepared for the dance.

'That was great,' he commented as they sat down.

'It certainly was,' agreed Jane. 'You Americans have brought a lot of joy to the local children. You're all heroes to them.'

'They're a great bunch of kids. We get three or four hanging around the station, but they know when to keep out of the way. Some of the guys even let them look round their ship.'

'Do you?'

'I don't encourage it, but if one of the crew wants to show them around, OK. They know I don't object if there's someone with them.'

Jane made no comment and an uneasy silence fell until they both spoke at once.

'Jane . . .'

'By . . .'

They both burst out laughing, driving the serious expressions away for a moment.

'After you,' he said.

Jane gave a little shake of her head, wondering for a few moments more whether she should tell him the truth. 'No, you first.'

He swallowed. 'All right.' He reached out and took her hand in his. 'Jane, I should have told you this before.' He hesitated. Looking her in the eye he said quietly, 'I am a happily married man with a beautiful wife and two kids at home.'

His words stunned Jane. For one moment she didn't believe them but immediately she realised that Byron was not a man to tell an untruth. 'Oh,' was all she could say. His gaze was pleading with her to understand.

'I should have told you before but I was afraid that if I did, you would abandon me and I didn't want that.' Still she did not speak so he continued, 'When I left home, my wife Linda, knowing what I was coming to, realised there would be tensions I would want to escape. She told me she would understand if I found relief in female company. All she asked was that I continue to love her and remain faithful. I can say in all sincerity that I have done. I have been out with other girls briefly, but no one as special as you, Jane. You have helped me more than you'll ever know. Just before I met you, we had had three raids that were hell; the whole crew was living on their nerves and it was up to me to hold them together. I was staring into an abyss that frightened me. I didn't know if I could shoulder the weight for them all, and it was essential that I did. Thanks to you, I managed. I didn't want to lose you so I kept quiet about my wife and family. I'm sorry, I should have told you before.'

413

She could see the guilt in his eyes and felt nothing but pity for him then. 'There's no need. You must have a wonderfully understanding wife, though.'

He nodded. 'She is, and I know I'm fortunate. But I also know I was lucky to meet a person like you. I'm sorry if I hurt you, I didn't intend to. I have told you now in case, as I suspect, your feelings for me are taking on a more serious aspect.'

'Another place, another time, yes, I think I would have fallen in love with you.'

'That means you have? Oh, Jane, I . . .'

She put her fingers to his lips to silence him. 'No, By. Leave things the way they are. Let's remain good friends.'

'Can you do that after . . .'

'Of course I can. And I'll be here for you until you go home.'

He leaned forward and kissed her. 'Thanks, Jane. What have I done to deserve loving two such wonderful people?'

'Loving . . .?' Her voice faltered.

'Yes, Jane. As you say, another place, another time.'

She reached out and pulled him gently to her. Before their lips met, her eyes never left his and in that exchange was love and understanding.

When their lips parted he said, 'Now it's your turn. What were you going to say to me?'

'It no longer matters.'

He knew from the tone of her voice that he should not press the matter.

Chapter Twenty-five

The boom of aircraft taking off reverberated across the countryside and brought Jane and Nell hurrying outside to send their prayers to the flyers passing overhead in the cold, late-January sky.

Nell sensed the tension in Jane and put her arm round her friend's shoulders. 'He'll come back. Try not to worry.'

Jane tried to find comfort in these words, though she knew that Nell too was anxious for Toni's safety. 'I hope he does, for his wife's sake.'

Nell squeezed her shoulder. 'You're a wonder, Jane Harvey. You've shown not one iota of dismay or jealousy since you told me that Byron is married and deeply in love with his wife. You could so easily have walked away from him, and had every right to do so.'

'We're good friends, Nell, and we respect each other. He needs me, and I'll be there for him until he goes home.'

'And with only three more missions to fly, that's likely to be in February.'

Jane nodded. She turned her head away but Nell had seen a tear run down her cheek. 'Do you love him, Jane?'

She bit her lip, trying to quell her thoughts and hold back the tears. Then she nodded again.

'Come here, love.' Nell enfolded her in her arms and held her tight until the droning of the planes had faded away.

They would work and await the men's return, then watch anxiously for signs of the ordeal they had been through. Aunty Betty would try to keep the conversation bright, plying them with cups of tea, until the sound of an approaching jeep dispelled the anxiety. Byron and Toni would then whisk them off for an evening together or take advantage of the Symonds' generosity in allowing them the use of their sitting room, if the airmen wanted the relaxed atmosphere of the farmhouse.

Then one evening in February, as he and Toni were about to leave Cedar Farm, Byron announced that he had checked the weather forecast for the following day. 'It promises to be clear skies and favourable conditions over Europe tomorrow. We're more than likely to chalk up our last mission, so you two get on your glad rags. The whole crew will be living it up tomorrow evening.'

Jane felt a sinking in her heart as she watched the jeep leave Cedar Farm. Sleep did not come easily to her that night. She had visions of a blazing bomber, from which no parachutes appeared, dropping from the sky. That would vanish, to leave a vision of a handsome American pilot walking into the arms of a beautiful young woman.

At ten o'clock the next morning they watched the sky fill with bombers and a cold dread filled their souls. The emotions they were feeling silenced them. When the crescendo of engine sounds faded and was completely lost, they turned to their work, but it did little to alleviate anxious minds or loosen silent tongues.

Five hours later a distant sound seeped over Cedar Farm. Jane and Nell glanced anxiously at each other. They watched the bombers return, streaming in towards the airfield, until one came in low straight over Cedar Farm.

'It must be them!' shouted both girls at once as it zoomed overhead. They saw the voluptuous blonde in a tight-fitting red dress painted towards the nose of the plane, with the words 'Lady In Red' in flowing script beneath, and after that 'By's Boys Will Be Back'. 'It *is* them!' They jumped up and down with excitement and flung their arms round each other in overwhelming joy. The plane banked and made one more run across the farm, bringing further sounds of delight from them.

'Now we can get ready for a wild night,' cried Nell. 'Let's make the best of it!'

'Where are we going?' she queried when the jeep drew up at Cedar Farm.

'Norwich!' called Toni. He saw Mrs Symonds standing at the door. 'We'll have 'em back for milking, Mrs S!'

'When we see them will do,' she called back, laughing at his exuberance.

The jeep roared away and Toni flung a couple of rugs back to the girls. 'Keep warm. We need those toes to be jiving tonight.'

'What about the rest of the crew?' queried Jane.

'They've girls to pick up from round about. We're all meeting up in Norwich. We organised some dinner for you. The hotel promised to find something special when I told them the occasion.'

'You Americans!'

Byron glanced at her. 'Ah, but you like us.'

Jane pulled a teasing face and said with a grin, 'Believe what you like.'

The evening passed off in the most joyous way. These men would no longer have to risk their lives in hostile skies – they were going home unscathed after their tour of duty. But while Nell's determination led her to make the most of what might prove to be her last jiving session with Toni, Jane was filled with regret that this could be the last time she and Byron were together.

It came as something of a surprise when he took her hand, led her away from the others and found them a quiet corner. She looked at him curiously. 'Jane, I want to thank you for what you have done for me, so I . . .'

'I've done nothing,' she replied.

417

'You will never know how much you have done, by being you and being there for me when I needed someone. So I'm taking a week's leave before I go home and I'd like you to come to London with me?' For a moment she did not speak so he took the opportunity to add, 'All above board, you know how I stand with my wife. I look for nothing in return except your friendship.'

'I promise you that friendship, By, and you will always have it. I will forever hold memories of a very dear man.' She kissed him with a tenderness that betrayed her true feelings. He was tempted to respond but knew that if he did it would ruin a relationship he too would hold forever in his heart.

'I'll come by Cedar Farm tomorrow and see when you can arrange to be away.'

Back at the farm, Jane went to Nell's room and told her of By's invitation.

'Of course you must go. I'm sure Mr Symonds will let you bring your week's leave forward when he knows the circumstances.'

The next day Jane was able to tell By that she could have her leave, it was just a matter of when. Before Byron left the farm it had been arranged that Jane would take a week's leave, starting in two days' time.

'I'll have to get started on finding a suitable hotel,' said Byron.

'Leave that to me,' Jane insisted.

'Sounds as though you have influence?'

'Let's see when we get there.'

Two days later Jane was in charge when they took a taxi from Euston. 'Strand Palace,' she informed the driver.

'Yes, ma'am.'

Jane smiled at the inference behind that 'ma'am' and winked at Byron.

He paid off the taxi and added a tip that made the driver effusive in his thanks. Following Jane, Byron admired her air of confidence as she walked into reception.

'Good day, Miss Harvey. What a pleasure to see you again.'

Surprised at being recognised, she said, 'I'm surprised you recognised me. You must have seen thousands of faces since I was here.'

'I make it my business to remember the special ones, and any friend of both Mister Aveburns is special. Now, what can I do for you?'

'Would you have two single rooms available?'

'You can have Mr Aveburn's suite. It's not in use for ten days.'

'Oh, but we couldn't impose on him without his knowledge.'

'From the instructions we have, I know it will be perfectly all right.'

Although he was at a loss to understand this exchange, Byron said, 'Whatever is decided, you must allow me to have the bill.'

'Ah, no, sir,' said Giles, raising a hand to quell any protests. 'Mr Aveburn would not hear of that. If he is not using his suite, we are instructed to allow it to be occupied by any of his friends known to us. Miss Harvey is in that category. Also, sir, the hotel has a policy that if any member of the armed services accompanies a known regular customer, there is no charge.'

'That is wonderfully generous of you.'

When they were alone, after being shown to their adjoining rooms, Byron held out his arms and said, 'Come to me, Jane Harvey, and let me express my undying admiration for you.'

She came to him, and as his arms enfolded her had to make a tremendous effort to control her own feelings.

'So, how come you have a suite at the very swell Strand Palace at your disposal?' he asked eventually.

She smiled. 'That is a long story and comes from part of my life of which you have no knowledge.'

'So you're not just a Land Girl who has ensnared the

419

affections of an American pilot? I'm intrigued.'

'You'll have to wait. I'll enlighten you over our meal this evening.'

Later he listened intently as she told him everything from the moment she met Nell on the harbourside at Scarborough.

'So you're a talented writer?'

'I like to think so.'

'You must be if this editor keeps taking your work.'

'It's what I want to do after the war.'

'Then do it!' His note of urgency was not lost on Jane. She knew By's voice and words would be with her always, stimulating her to press on when inspiration dried up, as she knew it could. 'Are you going to see Mr Horton while we're in London?' he asked.

'I don't want to walk out on you.'

He reached across the table and took her hand. 'Jane, you would never do that. Besides, it would give me another memory of you.' Their eyes held. 'There's something I would like you to do for me.' He paused, as if trying to find the right words. She looked enquiringly at him, wondering what was coming. 'Some time before too long, I'd like you to come to America and meet my wife.'

Jane was astounded by that request. 'But do you think it wise?'

'I see no problem. You're both wonderful, understanding people, and I know Linda would welcome the girl who helped me through some very trying times. Think about it. I don't want your answer now, or even before I go home, but some time, please say yes?'

At breakfast the day before they were due to leave London, they were deciding what to do when Byron said, 'These days have been wonderful, we have seen so much, enjoyed every minute together, shared moments that will live in my memory forever, but there is one part of your life I still have not seen.' He gave a little pause then added, 'Mr

420

Horton. Please let me share him too.'

Jane smiled. 'We'll remedy that today then.'

When they called at the *World Scene* office Mr Horton was out but his secretary booked Jane an appointment for two o'clock.

They returned on time and were shown immediately into the office. Mr Horton sprang from his chair and was effusive in his delight at seeing Jane as well as expressing his pleasure at meeting Byron.

'So you are the young man who has been figuring in Jane's writing about the American bomber war?' Byron's expression of surprise told its own tale. 'You didn't know?'

'No, sir, I did not.'

'Oh, dear, I hope I haven't let the cat out of the bag?' Mr Horton glanced at her.

She smiled. 'It's all right.'

'It was only a few days ago that I learned Jane was a writer,' said Byron.

'She's a very talented young lady and I see a great future for her. I was thinking about her only the other day, wondering what she would do after the war. Now that you are here it might be a good idea to explore the possibilities, give you something to think about, Jane.'

She glanced enquiringly at Byron who said, 'It's all right by me. You want to grab every opportunity you can. And from what she has told me, Mr Horton, you have been a very wise mentor.'

He waved his hand dismissively. 'I like to encourage talent when I see it, and I saw it when three young people walked into this office before the war.' He glanced at Byron. 'If you have not seen the pieces about you and your crew, no doubt you would like to?'

'I certainly would, sir.'

Mr Horton called his secretary and asked her to obtain copies of the relevant back issues.

'Before we look at the future,' he said, taking his seat behind his desk, 'tell me about Nell and Glen. I have had

421

pictures from them, as you know, but have you any idea if they have plans for after the war?'

'As far as I know they intend still to pursue their partnership. Whether they want to link it with my writing, we haven't discussed. We're awaiting Glen's return.'

'Nell wrote to me about the loss of Ewan. Has she got over it yet?'

'I think so,' was all that Jane said. She did not want to disclose any more, she did not see any need.

'Do you think she and Glen . . .?' Horton left the rest of the question implied. 'I'm not prying, but it might affect their careers.'

'It's a possibility,' replied Jane. 'They do get on so well.' After a very slight pause, and knowing another query lay behind Mr Horton's unfinished question, she added, 'I ought to tell you that Byron is a happily married man. He and I are very good friends.'

'She helped me survive my bombing tour and come out of it sane,' put in Byron, to back up Jane's statement.

Mr Horton nodded his understanding. 'Right, now I have the full picture. I would like to retain the three of you but not tie you down to *World Scene*. All three of you have talent that should take you beyond its boundaries. Yours, Jane, can take you into much wider realms. You do not want to be forever putting words to illustrations, nor do Nell and Glen want to be forever supplying illustrations to words. They have the talent to make pictures speak for themselves and therefore enter the wider world of photography. While I can see you working together on occasions, I believe you will also go in different directions and pursue your own individual goals.'

'I think all three of us will still want to continue submitting material to you,' insisted Jane.

'Of course, and that would be fine. I just don't want you to feel restricted. There will be a whole wide post-war world out there, searching for material by talented young people.'

She nodded thoughtfully. 'Thank you for being so frank.'

'You know I will be here if ever you and the others need advice. Don't be afraid to seek it.'

'You are very kind. Since you mentioned my pieces about By and his crew, I have had a thought. How would it be if I did a series of follow-ups on what the war meant to them, how they coped with returning to civilian life, and the reception they received from their communities and families back home?'

'Excellent,' said Mr Horton with enthusiasm. 'But that would mean travelling to America.'

'I'd be willing to do that. It would widen my horizons which could only help my writing.' She shot a sharp glance at Byron and saw the look of approval flash across his face.

'You could syndicate articles to papers and magazines all over America, and there could be wonderful scope there for fiction too,' approved Mr Horton.

'You make it sound so exciting,' said Jane.

'It will be, and I will revel in being able to say, "Jane Harvey? I know her well. She was a protégée of mine."'

When they reached the street, with Mr Horton's good wishes ringing in their ears, Byron grabbed Jane by the waist, swung her off her feet and whirled her round. 'America, here comes Jane! Linda will love you.' He kissed her wildly while passers-by smiled at the enthusiastic young American and the girl in his arms.

On the train back to Suffolk they managed to get a compartment to themselves.

'When will you be going home?' asked Jane, trying to hide the catch in her voice.

'I don't know, but I don't think it will be long. They won't want us hanging around. I'll come out to the farm whenever I can.'

'Please do. Knowing you has meant so much to me, and it has opened the way for my future.'

423

'You'll do well, I know you will. I'll expect to see you in Montana one day, and I'll follow the writing of Jane Harvey for the rest of my life.'

When Jane reached the farm Nell shot out to greet her, eager to know what had happened in London.

'I'll tell you when we are upstairs.'

'I'll be in soon,' said Nell. 'I've nearly finished.'

Jane was given a 'welcome back' reception from Mr and Mrs Symonds, who were pleased to hear she had had a good time in London.

She had just finished unpacking when Nell burst into the room. 'Come on, tell me everything,' she urged, plonking herself down on the bed.

Jane did not hold anything back.

'So nothing happened?'

'Lots happened, but not what you mean. If it had, we'd have lost our respect for each other and a friendship that is important to both of us. Byron wants to see me when I go to America.'

'America?' queried Nell, puzzled.

Jane told her of the visit to Mr Horton and what had come of it. 'And he has high hopes for your photography and Glen's. You ought to go to see him together.'

'Well, now there's no Ewan to hold me back ...'

'And Glen thinks a lot of you. No, loves you.'

'Ah, but who knows who he might have found while he's been away?'

'At sea?' countered Jane.

'They have to put into port sometime.'

'You know you liked him a lot, and love can grow from that, especially if you continue to work closely together. You could do worse.'

The next afternoon the sound of an approaching jeep sent a chill through Jane. Was the inevitable parting at hand? But when the two girls came out of the cow-shed they saw only

424

Toni climbing out of the jeep.

'Hi,' he greeted them, a broad smile on his face as he tipped his hat to the back of his head. 'How's my jiving chick?' He accompanied his question with a couple of quick steps and a twist.

Both girls laughed at his antics.

'Toni, why . . .' started Nell.

'Goodbye England, hello America! Toni Pacitto's on his way.'

'When?' asked Nell.

'Tomorrow morning! I've come to say goodbye.' He reached out and took her hand. 'Thanks for everything, doll. It's been swell knowing you. What a dance partner you made! Pity I can't parade our talents back home, but Ma wouldn't approve of me turning up with an English broad.'

Nell laughed. 'A nice backhanded compliment! Toni, thanks for everything, and good luck to you.' She kissed him. 'Take care of yourself.'

'I will. And you too. Get a good guy who treats you right.' He kissed her and swung round to Jane, planting a kiss on her cheek as well. ''Bye doll. Look after her.'

She looked at him with a query in her eyes. 'Byron?'

'Oh, darn, I nearly forgot. He leaves with me tomorrow. He was coming here with me but was called in by the C.O. I guess he'll commandeer this jeep when I get back.' He swung into it, called goodbye to Mr and Mrs Symonds who had come to the door of the farmhouse, started the engine and roared away with a last wave of his hand.

Jane had an uneasy time, listening for the sound of the jeep without being able to concentrate on anything else, though she tried to keep busy. Nell attempted to make conversation but gave up when her friend only made monosyllabic replies. The time ticked by and with each new second Jane became more convinced that Byron was not coming to say goodbye.

The sound reached her eventually. She ran out and was almost at the gate when she realised that she was still in her working clothes, but there was no longer time to do anything about it.

Byron pulled the jeep to a halt and was out of it and sweeping her into his arms in an instant. 'I thought I wasn't going to make it. The C.O. wanted to see me, and he wants me again later tonight. He's entrusting me with information he needs to get to higher command back home. I've just managed to slip away ...'

'You can't stay?' Regret was evident in Jane's voice.

'Sorry, I can't, as much as I want to.'

'I'll miss you.'

'Take care, Jane.'

'And you.'

Byron kissed her and she responded to the kiss fervently. Another time, another place ...

'I'll have to go.' He pulled a pilot's brevet from his pocket, pressed it into her hands and said, 'Remember me.'

'Always.'

He swung back into the jeep he had left running, glanced towards the cow-shed and saw Nell hanging back discreetly. ''Bye, Nell.' He waved to Mr and Mrs Symonds at the door, who waved back. Then he turned to Jane and their eyes met for the last time with a meaning that only they would ever know.

Chapter Twenty-six

'Letter for you, Jane.' Mrs Symonds came in from the yard as the girls were having their mid-morning break in the kitchen. 'Just seen the postman.'

'Thanks,' she said, taking the envelope. 'It's from America,' she said, excitement lifting her voice when she noted the stamp. Her fingers trembled as she slit open the envelope and drew out a sheet of paper. She immediately felt a little disappointed when she saw only a few lines.

5th March 1945

Dear Jane,

I'm safely home in Montana on two weeks' leave starting today. I was held up in the East on military matters and could not write before. I hope all is well with you?

So many memories.

By

There was another paragraph too, written in a different hand.

Jane, Thank you for looking after my husband while he was in England. He has told me how much it meant to him to have your friendship – it helped him through some terrible experiences. Love, Linda. P.S. Come and see us, I would love to meet you.

Jane stared at the words with a choking feeling in her throat. She held out the paper to Nell.

She read the letter then said, 'How nice of his wife to add a note. Better that way, love. Treasure it.'

Jane nodded. 'I will.'

'Ready?' queried Nell at the door of the cow-shed as she turned up the collar of her coat to counter the rain driven by a stiff March wind.

'Ready,' confirmed Jane, cramming her hat down more firmly on her head.

'Here we go!'

Water splashed from the puddles as they raced across the yard to the house. They shook the rain from their coats before going into the scullery where they were glad to get out of their Wellingtons and into light shoes. They ran their fingers through their hair and shook it into place.

'I'm ready for a cup of tea,' said Nell as she pushed open the door to the kitchen.

They shot a quick questioning glance at each other when they saw Mr and Mrs Symonds sitting at the table, staring glumly at a sheet of paper that lay between them.

'Something the matter?' asked Jane.

'This,' said Betty. 'You'd better read it.' She pushed the paper across the table to the two girls.

They sat down and Jane held it so that they could read it together. They looked up, curious that Mr and Mrs Symonds should look so glum.

'I'm sorry Sid has been injured and is to be invalided out of the Army, but he does say he will be perfectly able to take up his work as a dairyman again,' said Nell.

'Yes, and with the way things are going, the war will soon be over and then you'll get Harold back too,' added Jane.

428

'That won't be until after he's demobbed, and that will not be for quite a while yet. In the meantime I'm obliged to take Sid back. As you see from what he says, that's likely to be in two weeks' time.'

'So why are you both looking so glum?' asked Nell.

'Well ...' John cleared his throat. 'It means we shall have to lose one of you, and we didn't want that.'

'No, we didn't,' confirmed Betty.

'Nice of you to say so,' said Jane, taking her hand. 'But what will be, will be.'

'We might lose both of you,' said John. 'We think you'll want to stay together.'

'Well, we haven't had time to consider it but I suppose we would like to ...'

'We thought you might so John and I have decided we won't stand in your way.'

'I'm sure Miss Hardcastle will find someone else to work alongside Sid,' put in John.

'She'll be making her usual call next week, I'll ask her then.'

Miss Hardcastle proved to be very understanding and put forward a possible solution. 'I have a girl who is anxious to do dairy work but I have found nowhere to place her as yet. If you are agreeable after meeting her, she can come here to work with your dairyman, and Jane and Nell can come back into the hostel.'

A fortnight later there was a tearful farewell at Cedar Farm.

'We have enjoyed having you,' said Betty, brushing a tear from her eyes. She had sworn not to get over-emotional but when it came to it she had to let go a little. 'Please keep in touch.'

'We will,' they both reassured her as they returned her hug.

Mr Symonds was embarrassed when they turned to him. He choked out, 'Take care of yourselves. And come back and see us.'

They were both quiet as Miss Hardcastle drove them away, but by the time they'd reached the hostel she had cheered them up by pointing out that they would now be released from the demanding timetable of milking, and consequently would have more free time. 'What I would like to do is to keep you both permanently at the hostel, to work on short-term jobs as they come up. It will mean tackling a variety of work, but I think you are both capable of coping whenever a farmer puts in a special request.'

They missed the regularity of dairy work but soon slipped into the new routine. They regretted leaving Mr and Mrs Symonds and being spoiled by the elderly couple but made the best of what came their way, enjoying living with other girls again and most of all spending their free time together.

They had been at the hostel three weeks when Jane had a quiet word with her friend. 'Nell, you haven't seen your mum since Annabelle arrived on the scene. Don't you think you should visit her? This coming weekend would be a good time. We're both free.'

Nell was adamant. 'I don't want to see *that* woman.'

'There's no need for you to see Annabelle,' Jane pointed out. 'It's your mother we're talking about.' She kept thrusting Nell's objections aside until her friend agreed.

By the time the weekend came Nell had grown used to the idea and a bright morning put them both in a lively frame of mind. There was laughter in the air as they cycled to the station to catch the train to Lowestoft.

'I'm glad you talked me into coming,' said Nell when they were leaving the station and heading for home. 'I should have been more considerate of Mum's feelings.'

'Oh, love, it's good to see you!' cried Flo, flinging her arms round her daughter when she opened the door to them. Nell had not realised how much she had missed her mother's hug until now. 'And you too, Jane,' Flo added warmly.

430

They never stopped chatting, not even while Flo prepared a meal. The girls showed no desire to go out and Flo, with a mother's intuition, guessed the reason, so did not press the matter. When they were enjoying their afternoon cup of tea there was a knock at the door and Jane went to answer it.

Nell and Flo heard her exclamation of: 'Good heavens!' and a male voice respond, 'Jane!'

'It's Glen!' cried Nell, and in a moment was at the door beside her. 'Glen! How ... Why ...' And she hugged him to her when he stepped into the house.

Laughter and pleasure mingled in his eyes as he held her tight. 'I didn't expect to find you here. This is wonderful!'

They hustled him into the kitchen where the warm welcome continued after he had greeted Mrs Franklin with a kiss.

'Got in about an hour ago,' he explained. 'With the war situation as it is, a lot of boats have been sent back to their home port to continue minesweeping from there, so I'm sailing out of Lowestoft until the end of the war. Possibly until the boat is decommissioned and I'm demobbed.'

News was speedily rushed through, and then some of it exchanged again in greater depth. Glen made brief commiserations for the loss of Ewan and no one chose to reveal to him the presence of Annabelle; that could be done at a more appropriate time.

Jane told him of her visit to Mr Horton and what had been said then.

'I'm delighted you both kept in touch with him. I'm afraid I wasn't able to do very much at sea so it is good that you kept the door open after the way he took to us. And I'm delighted by what he was suggesting when you last saw him, Jane.' He glanced at Nell. 'How do you feel about it, Nell, or are you both going to stay in the Land Army forever?'

'Not likely,' they chorused.

'Don't get us wrong, we've enjoyed most of it,' put in Jane, 'but I think our futures were already mapped out before we joined up.'

'What about you, Glen?' asked Nell tentatively.

'Oh, I'm back to photography as soon as I can,' he said with such conviction there was no doubting where his future lay, 'especially after what you indicated Mr Horton said about a whole new direction for our work. What about you, Nell, will you take it up with me again?'

'Try and stop me,' she laughed. A thought flashed through her mind then. There could be a future for her without Ewan. Glen was a good man, and there was no mistaking that he was still in love with her.

'What about you, Jane?' he asked.

'I think my path will diverge from yours if I follow Mr Horton's suggestions. I hope you see it that way too after we finish the illustrated articles for him.'

'And where is that path going to take you now, Jane?' asked Glen.

'America,' she replied.

His eyes widened.

She went on to explain about the American bomber crew, holding nothing back, even her relationship with Byron, and said that she wanted to do follow-up features about them for the American market. 'But I want to go beyond that. I think there will be plenty of material there for a strong work of fiction about the difficulties of servicemen settling down again to civilian life after the wartime traumas they have been through.'

'I'm pleased you have plans but sorry it didn't work out for you and the pilot,' said Glen. 'He sounds a great guy. I hope you'll find someone else one day.'

Jane gave a slight shake of her head. 'I think I'm destined to be unlucky in love.'

When the time came for Glen to go, Jane and Flo discreetly stayed behind as Nell said she would walk with him to the harbour.

'Are you happy about this, Mrs Franklin?' asked Jane as they watched the young couple leave.

'Yes, but it has to be Nell's choice.'

'I'm so glad you are here, Glen,' said Nell, falling into step beside him.

He took her hand. 'I always will be here, waiting. I don't want to rush things. I know you need to get over the loss of Ewan. But we can have a great future together, if you will let me help you? I still love you and I always will.'

'Give me time,' she whispered.

Two weeks later Nell and Jane were in Lowestoft again but found that Glen had sailed on the *Silver King* to clear mines from the shipping channels along the Yorkshire coast.

They were about to sit down to their midday meal with Flo when they heard the front door thrown open. They stared at each other, aghast. Only one person had ever opened the door like that! But it was impossible. Who. . .?

That question was answered when the kitchen door flew open.

'Hello!'

They stared in disbelief at the smiling face of Squadron Leader Ewan Steel.

'Seen a ghost?' he asked with a laugh. 'Sorry to scare you.'

They were still speechless. Colour had drained from every face, especially Nell's.

He stepped over to her and swept her into his arms. 'I'm real,' he said, hugging her tight. 'How's my best girl?'

Disbelief still showed on her face as she pushed him gently away. Her mind was in utter confusion. 'How . . . What . . .'

Flo and Jane were shocked to silence. They sank into chairs.

'A quick explanation,' said Ewan. 'I survived the crash

433

but was badly hurt. Some French people got me away from the plane and set fire to it before Jerry arrived, so they assumed I'd perished in the flames. Didn't do much investigating, mind you. Well, the Frogs were marvellous, took grand care of me, but it was a long job. Then, when I was fit enough, they passed me on to the Resistance who were going to help me escape through Spain, but I had a relapse and needed looking after again. Well, being in their headquarters, I learned a lot, and when I was well enough they decided they could not let me go in case I was caught and spilled the beans. So I lived and worked with them, on sabotage work and gathering information that proved invaluable to the Allies on D Day.

'Eventually we linked up with an American force and the rest is history, except that with all my inside info the Americans deemed it best to hang on to me. Eventually, when I was handed over to the RAF, they wanted every little detail of what had happened too, and because I had gone missing, believed killed so long ago, would not allow me any home contact until they were completely satisfied I could tell them nothing more. Oh, and they promoted me for my pains. That's it in a nutshell, so here I am.'

Flo took charge immediately. 'Have you been home?' she asked, suspecting from the way he had behaved that she already knew the truth of that.

'No. I couldn't pass your door, Mrs F, and not enquire about my girl. And wasn't I the lucky one? Nell's here.'

'Well, don't you think it time you saw your own mother?'

Ewan held up his hands in surrender. 'Yes, I do. Come on, everyone, you've got to be there when I surprise her.'

Nell caught the glance her mother gave her and knew that she should go along with Ewan's suggestion, for he was not one to take no for an answer in a situation like this.

Flo's grip on her daughter's hand offered her strength as they entered the house. Jane hoped her presence too would help her friend in what was about to take place – she had already noticed what she took to be Annabelle's outdoor clothes on a hook in the hall.

Ewan grinned as his hand closed around the knob of the kitchen door where he had heard the unmistakable sound of something being stirred. He winked at Nell and then flung the door open. 'Surprise! Sur—' The word faded away into an astonished silence. His eyes had fixed on a second person in the room, standing beside a high chair, spoon in her hand, about to feed the child in the chair. 'Annabelle!' he gasped in complete disbelief.

She stood for a moment in total astonishment. Then the truth hit her. She dropped the spoon and flung herself into his arms as tears of joy overflowed. She whispered in his ear, 'Your son, Ewan,' and he knew the truth of it.

Nell turned and walked from the room, followed by Jane. Flo merely stopped a moment to say to Liz, 'See you later.' All she could do was nod.

It was early evening when Ewan called back at the Franklins' and asked Nell to walk with him. For one moment she was about to refuse but knew that would be no good to either of them. She slipped on her jacket and stepped out into the evening sunshine.

'What can I say?' he asked her.

'Nothing, Ewan! Don't try to excuse yourself. That would be beneath you. Answer me one thing. Did you love her when . . .?' She let the rest of the question hang in the air.

'I don't really know. She was there at a time when the pressure on me grew almost overwhelming.'

'And now?'

'I don't know. How can I? I've just returned. I didn't know if Annabelle would still be around.'

'She's very much around, and I think she loves you very much. Did you try to find her?'

'No, I came straight to you.'

Nell's heart skipped a beat. What was he going to say?

435

What if he asked her to marry him? What would her answer be then? There was Glen, and she was reminded of what had passed between them. His name rang out in her mind and she almost screamed aloud, 'God help me!'

'So, what now, Ewan?'

He stopped walking and turned her to him. He looked deep into her eyes. 'Nell Franklin, you are a wonderful person. I ...' he paused. 'I'm sorry if I'm going to hurt you, but I'm going to marry Annabelle. There's ...'

As she put her fingers to his lips to stop him from saying more, her heart lurched in disappointment and relief. 'Ewan Steel, I loved you, and I think there will always be part of you in my heart. But I know you are doing the right thing, and because you have, you will find true happiness.' She reached up and kissed him.

'I hope you find someone who will make you happy too.'

'Oh, I know I will.' The certainty in Nell's voice brought a question to his lips but he held it back, believing he already knew the answer.

'And give Jane that message too,' was all he said.

The day after their resignation from the Land Army had been accepted and the partying was over, Jane sat in her bedroom at the Franklins'. Once again my life stands at a turning point, she reflected. Middlesbrough, I had to leave. I had been in Scarborough long enough, and had to move on. Then the war – how that changed everything and brought new perspectives, new thoughts, new loves. What if Simon had survived? What if Ewan had turned to me? What if Byron hadn't been so in love with his wife? Too many 'what ifs'. Life is life, circumstances change, no one can predict what the future holds, but of one thing I am certain: I love my writing and I will make sure that it counts for something.

She opened her typewriter and started to type.

'The B17 took to the air from an airfield in Suffolk, England. Its American crew of ten were on the threshold of

436

an experience that would change their lives forever.'

Jane paused, read the words to herself and said silently, America here I come! Get ready for Jane Harvey.

Dangerous Shores

When Abigail Mitchell is a little girl her father, John, inherits a large estate in Cornwall from his uncle. He chooses to move his family from their comfortable living in Whitby to the rugged Cornish coast, in the hope of securing a more prosperous future in the South. John soon incurs the opposition and wrath of their neighbours, the Gainsfords, a powerful old Cornish family. However, as Abigail blossoms into a young lady, she finds herself mixing socially with the younger Gainsfords and attracted to the eldest son Luke Gainsford. She agrees to marry him in spite of his rakish reputation and her father's objections to the match. Abigail soon learns she should have heeded her father's warning when she uncovers Luke's secret life...

Reach For Tomorrow

The year is 1891. Marie Newton is the daughter of a famous painter, Arthur Newton, and she has inherited much of her father's skill. Luckily her father is happy to encourage his daughter's talent, agreeing that she may attend a prestigious art school in Paris. Accompanying her on her journey is her best friend, Lucy, a young widow. The girls find themselves entranced by Paris and each finds a sweetheart, though this does not bring happiness for Lucy. In order to help Lucy recover, Arthur proposes that the girls join him and his wife on a visit to America to visit relatives. But Arthur's past is about to catch up with him...